GENE RODDENBERRY'S Andromeda™

WAYSTATION

STEVEN E. McDONALD

A TOM DOHERTY ASSOCIATES BOOK
NEW YORK

This is a work of fiction. All the characters and events portrayed in this book are either products of the author's imagination or are used fictitiously.

GENE RODDENBERRY'S ANDROMEDA™: WAYSTATION

Edited by James Frenkel

A Tor Book
Published by Tom Doherty Associates, LLC
175 Fifth Avenue
New York, NY 10010

www.tor.com

Tor® is a registered trademark of Tom Doherty Associates, LLC.

ISBN 0-765-34409-2
EAN 975-0765-34409-0

First edition: May 2004
First mass market edition: December 2004

Printed in the United States of America

0 9 8 7 6 5 4 3 2 1

For Sylvia,
for loyalty and courage
rarely matched

ACKNOWLEDGMENTS

The theory is that writing keeps me sane—well, to a point. The truth is that I consequently drive everyone around me crazy.

This is by way of explaining why my editor, James Frenkel, has spent months studying certain arcana in preparation for the day when the book was set, and I could be safely—and deservedly—beset by ravening hounds of hell. Jim, I have only the best things to say about you for many reasons.

Thanks to my wife, Sylvia Lau-McDonald, for pitching in with notes, comments, and correction. Sometimes it isn't about writing, it's about rewriting—as our daughter Miriam, who just added sports writer to her accomplishments, is finding out.

Mark Cantwell, Mutt to my Jeff. I can't say enough.

For ethereal support, thanks to Ashleen, Debra, Carol, and CJ.

In the virtual world, a shout-out to folks at *Sanity Assassin* (http://forums.delphiforums.com/sanityassassin), both my co-mods and various guests—some of them can be found hidden in these pages. Steff, Paul Jack, Mario, Jens, Micah, Harris, Ian, Kady Mae,

ACKNOWLEDGMENTS

Kirk, Jard, Robert, Patty, Mary, and so on, and so on, you've been an incredible support.

Sixteen bars at 130 beats per minute to my fellow musicians in the Tapegerm Collective (http://www.tapegerm.com) for letting me take an extended leave of absence.

Thanks to Wendy Despain, manager of the official *Gene Roddenberry's Andromeda* Web site, to various fan site owners, to Seth Howard for a long discussion about Trance's true nature, and to everyone who helped me acquire episodes.

Finally, thanks to Laura Bertram, for bringing some intriguing aspects to the character of Trance Gemini, and, more generally, to the cast and crew of the show.

—Steven E. McDonald
Tucson, Arizona

OTE

This story takes place directly after episode four of season three, "Cui Bono."

There comes a time during the history
of any civilization when the art of diplomacy
as expressed in the handshake, hug, and knife
in the back gives way to the art of diplomacy
as expressed in the use of massed cannon
and smart bombs.

—GENERAL KORDOS RIEKAN,
DIPLOMACY AND WAR: A PREDICTIVE PERSPECTIVE,
CY 9263

GENE RODDENBERRY'S

Andromeda™

WAYSTATION

ONE · BROAD HINTS AND DEEP MYSTERIES

> Never shake hands with a razorpig.
>
> —INFORMAL HIGH GUARD MOTTO,
> CIRCA CY 5000

othing was clear. That scared her, as much as she could be scared.

Her name was Trance Gemini, at least for now. Her skin was gold ading to pink in some areas, and her long red hair was caught int ght braids, some of which were woven into an ornate design tha fset her sharply pointed ears. Depending upon mood or need, he ·e could seem soft and caring, or become a mask of cold determina ·n. Even her shipmates, long used to her mercurial state, had n· ·pe of predicting what she would do, say, or manifest next.

She was watching the stars, looking for the lines of force, and try ·g to divine individual characteristics. She was standing on the hug ·servation deck of the *Andromeda Ascendant*, a former System ·mmonwealth High Guard starship that was the epitome of th· ·n fist in the velvet glove—her outward beauty, composed in th· ·in of curves with only a handful of straight lines, concealed a· ·lity to destroy entire star systems. Prior to the fall of the old Com

monwealth, the 1.4-kilometer-long *Andromeda Ascendant* had carri
a complement of forty-seven hundred. Now it was occupied by o
a handful of people. Trance had left her mark on the ship, howeve
the hydroponics gardens had flourished in her hands, and she h
placed plants all over the ship. Andromeda was extremely pleased.

She was Trance Gemini. Once upon a time she had been young
purple, and equipped with a prehensile tail. All those things w
gone. Her tail, always a useful tool, had been shot away in a firefig
Her younger self had gone forward in time, and she had come ba
ward to replace her, and temporal paradoxes be damned. She h
come back from a terrible future, a time that had claimed all t
many of the people she had known, as well as an increasing chunk
the universe.

She had said, time and again, that her agenda was to create the p
fect possible future. Yet she had arrived amid chaos in a place wh
time was out of joint and almost limitless quantum possibilities ra
ated into the future. Faced with too many choices, she had narrow
them to one. In that instant she had locked down one reality, co
demned a brilliant Perseid scientist to the fate he had already s
fered, and saved a human she cared about from a horrible death.

She had made the choice out of friendship, for better or wor
She had easily admitted that later. She had also admitted that she h
no idea as to the long-term consequences of her actions. It was alm
the complete truth at the time. Within seconds she had felt her me
ory starting to blur and shift, leaving her feeling as though she w
looking at her own existence through smoked glass.

It was not the first time she had been through that particular te
poral nexus, but she was going to keep *that* piece of information to h
self, at least for now. She had caused one man to sacrifice himself
the good of billions. A fair trade, perhaps . . . no, she was certa
Gaheris Rhade had been a trusted and admired first officer, and he h
betrayed the ship and her crew when the Nietzscheans had revol
against the Commonwealth. He had murdered the captain, his frie
and been frozen in time as the *Andromeda Ascendant* moved inexora
toward the event horizon of a black hole. Three hundred years la
the ship had been pulled free. Rhade had been devastated when he

ered what had happened since the Nietzscheans—*his* people—had
ught down the Systems Commonwealth.

mposing his will on the great starship, and taking on the salvage
w that had rescued her, he had set out to repair the damage and
uild, by any means necessary, the Commonwealth.

He had failed, his efforts leading to exponentially worsening con-
ons. Trance had lived in a future of black despair and endless
ruction. When the opportunity arose, she had marshaled her
ers and ridden the probability stream until she reached the nexus
needed. Time and space were tangled in complex knots at that
t, victims of an out-of-control tesseract machine that was folding
e a bit too efficiently.

he had stepped out of her present and into her past. Her younger
had nervously changed places with her—she hadn't remembered
g quite *that* shade of purple—and she had gone to speak with
de.

he conversation had not been a long one. When it was over, she
taken him through a spatio-temporal interface, leaving him on
Andromeda Ascendant just before his betrayal. She had left, but she
w what had happened then. Gaheris Rhade had, in defiance of
poral logic, shot his younger incarnation, taken his place, and
rsed events by allowing himself to be killed by the man he had
ayed.

veryone else believed that the mysterious tesseract generator was
sole source of the space-time distortions. Trance, however, knew
truth—that the tesseract generator was only one of the reasons
e-time had suddenly begun tearing itself apart.

he universe had needed to realign itself following Rhade's final
ns. She had not helped the healing process much by looping
nd once more, coming backward from a future that was only
ginally less terrible. Her younger self was, if anything, even more
ous about changing places with her. There had been no choice
r than to take the second journey into the nexus. There was far
much at stake for her to hesitate.

here was a price for her determination, however. With each deci-
she made, each step she took to set things right, she endured

another mental upheaval as her memory realigned to each chang
the timeline. The shifts felt like tidal currents pulling at her m
and sometimes all she wanted was to be swept away. Keeping al
pieces in the proper places was no easy task, even for her.

There was so much to do, still. Sooner or later she was goin
have to let more of the truth out, and bear the consequences.

Someday she would have to tell them all what she really was.

Still, things had changed. She hesitated to trust that the cha
were all positive, but she could hope. She had put too much of he
into this to fail now.

Nothing was clear anymore. Nothing.

She bowed her head for a moment, and took a deep breath, tr
to focus. She looked up again, centering herself, and letting her
drift until the starfield was all she was aware of.

"Help me," she whispered. "Please. Help me."

Captain Dylan Hunt, the tall, towheaded commander of the Sys
Commonwealth starship *Andromeda Ascendant*, strode out ont
expansive Command Deck. There was always pleasure in the mo
of contemplation before his mind turned to command is
Andromeda was a live being, and he could feel her pulse, her heart

Come to think of it, he could *literally* feel her pulse or heartb
he wanted to—all he had to do was reach out to *Andromeda*'s an
avatar. Seamus Zelazny Harper, their sometimes-lunatic engi
had built the avatar using old High Guard manuals found on a
mer High Guard station. He had started with a standard ma
nance android as his template and by the time he was done he
created a perfect match for the idealized image that the ship
used. The avatar was slender and exotic, but the sylphlike appea
was deceptive. He had fought alongside her on several occasions
always felt slow and clumsy in comparison.

To his right, standing at one of the bridge consoles, Androme
Rommie, as she preferred to be called—turned her head to lo
him. Her face was still, and she said nothing, but it was enoug
make him take a mental step backward to see what he was doi
pique her curiosity.

e was smiling, he realized. One of those big, beaming smiles, full
nshine. Alarmed, he realized he was on the verge of becoming
y.

adiant joy and gleaming hope." Dylan turned to his left, still
ng. The words were bright, but in the dour, laconic drawl of Tyr
azi they had all the qualities of a dirge. "Have you seen the light
e Divine then, Dylan, and decided to follow the Way?"

s suggestions went, it was certainly not a bad one. Wayists were
ng the most peaceful beings in this brave new Systems Common-
th that he had kick-started into existence. He had seen for him-
that the Wayist path could tame even the ferocity of Magog.
, one Magog, the Reverend Behemiel Far Traveler. Rev Bem had
heir small company suddenly, driven by a need to find answers to
pected questions. It was the best path for Rev to take, Dylan
, but he still felt the loss on a spiritual level.

yr, of course, felt quite free to mock the Way. The religion
uraged a passivity that ran counter to everything in the Nietz-
n culture's philosophy, where survival by any means was the ulti-
goal. Bioengineered into existence by Drago Museveni, who
urned his own son into the first of the Homo sapiens invictus
s, Nietzscheans had inherited a drastic philosophy—they were to
e perfect, unconquerable people. It was the perception that their
ence was threatened by Commonwealth policies toward the feral
og that had caused the Nietzschean prides to unite in a revolu-
Ultimately, the Commonwealth had fallen. With the onset of
ong Night, the Nietzschean prides had turned on each other. In
n's time they had been warriors, poets, artisans. That was no
er the case.

yr had indeed survived, outliving the rest of his pride, but it was
exactly a worthy achievement by Nietzschean standards. It had,
ad, made his genetic line suspect—if the Kodiak Pride had fallen
re their enemies, then it indicated weakness.

e had no time to retort to the Nietzschean, however. Beka Valen-
was standing at the pilot's console, leaning slightly backward. Her
lips quirked slightly. "Tyr's got a point. A good point." She
d across Command, to where the slight and extremely rumpled

figure of Seamus Harper was standing and staring into a mug of [fee]. Inducted into the reconstituted High Guard or not, there w[as] chance that Harper was ever going to come close to any sort of [uni]form code.

Harper suddenly realized he was being looked at. "Huh?"

Oh, yes, a typical Harper moment. Normally he lived in over[drive] but there were moments when he underwent a complete discon[nect].

Harper looked at each of them in turn, his face screwing up [fur]ther and further in confusion. He finally looked back at [Beka.] "Wh*at*?"

Another Harper tic. Seamus Harper could turn any monosy[llabic] word into one containing two syllables or more. It was definitel[y] his most appreciated talent.

"You slipped something into Dylan's breakfast, didn't you?" [Beka] said. "I know you, Harper. It's that crazy engineer stuff you do.'

Tyr turned to look at Harper. The big Nietzschean had the ex[pres]sion of a man regarding a bug he was contemplating crushing. I[n the] Nietzschean's case that might be *exactly* the thing he had in mind[.]

"Hey, wait a freakin' minute!" Harper protested, his expre[ssion] shifting between astonishment, disbelief, and annoyance in rapi[d suc]cession. "Why would I do something like that?"

"Wouldn't be the first time," Beka said.

"Oh, come on, that was a freakin' *accident*!" Harper cried as [Tyr,] Rommie, and Dylan turned to look at Beka.

"Tyranian joy-juice," she said.

"So I didn't *know*, okay?" Dylan, Tyr, and Rommie looked ba[ck at] Harper. Dylan wondered if this was what life had normally bee[n like] on the *Eureka Maru*, Beka's salvage ship. More sullenly, H[arper] added, "The guy in the store said it was like orange juice for hu[mans.] I thought it would be good with breakfast."

"It took us a week to get Trance back to normal," Beka said [rue]fully, looking at Dylan.

"You mean whatever passes for normal with Trance," H[arper] added.

"I believe I understand what has been behind my good mo[od...]

," Tyr said quietly. Dylan's smile faded as he tensed. Tyr couldn't
taking this seriously, could he? Then again, Dylan couldn't
ember *any* indication of a good mood on Tyr's part lately.

Oh, no! Ohhh, no!" Harper said, holding up a hand as Tyr
ped off of the command riser and walked toward him. Dylan
ost started to smile again at the contrast. Tyr was very tall, very
, and extremely muscular. His expression was calm, but his gaze
not waver in the slightest, and the mass of long dreadlocks that
g halfway down his back only added to the image of a predator
g up a snack.

Harper, on the other hand, was a wiry, rumpled man of average
ht. While it was not a good idea to underestimate Harper's ability
fight, he was no match for Tyr.

Harper turned to Rommie. He was beginning to look desperate
. "Rom-doll, you see everything—"

Rommie's holographic avatar shimmered into view next to Harper,
ding him. "We all know how good you are with my systems,
per."

He does have a way with women, doesn't he?" the android avatar
to the holographic avatar.

creens lit up with the image of the ship's core AI. "That's one way
utting it."

So," the android Rommie said, "I can't vouch for you, can I?"

Harper had now worked all the way through to slack-jawed aston-
ent. "I don't freakin' *believe* it. Rommie, if I'd been messing
nd with your circuits—"

Perhaps you have a secret agenda," said Tyr.

Dylan could almost see Harper's brain suddenly going full blast, as
gh someone had thrown a switch. "Yeah, right, like *I* care, Tyr.
stuff's your department. Well, yours and Trance's."

I have a secret agenda?" The sound of Trance's voice made
yone turn toward the Command Deck entrance. Dylan, know-
all too well what Trance was capable of, wondered how long she
been standing there. "And why are you trying to scare Harper?"

yr raised an eyebrow. "The spirit of fun," he said.

"Oh, sure," Harper said with a sneer. "Your idea of fun is blow
stuff up. Or shooting things. Or shooting them and *then* blow
them up."

"I think we've had enough fun for now," Dylan said. "We're
in the business of making new friends, and I want everybody read
make the best possible impression when we reach Kantar. Even
Mr. Harper."

Harper looked down at his rumpled clothes, then across at B
"This is just fine, right, Boss?"

"Oh, for a lot of things," Beka said. Harper had been her engi
on the *Eureka Maru* for years before they had encountered Dylan
far as she cared, Harper could wear whatever he wanted, just as
as he got the job done and didn't scare the clients. "Just not for t
diplomatic missions Dylan likes to bore us with."

"I don't think it'll be so boring," Trance interjected. Somehow
baby-doll voice managed to fill the deck.

All levity was suddenly gone. Trance Gemini was an enigma,
every time there seemed a possibility of finding explanations for
other questions arose. She was the most disingenuous person D
had ever known. She had signed up with Beka's crew on the *Eu
Maru*, but no one had known her background—no one had aske
this day and age, even with the formation of a new Commonwe
questions could get you killed.

"Well," Dylan said with a smile, "I do like to keep my crew e
tained."

Trance did not return the smile. Her expression was deadly
ous, and Dylan realized that she was not blinking. He had a mor
tary and unnerving feeling that he was suddenly trying to stare d
a snake. He wasn't sure which bothered him more—the idea
Trance's objectives might always be obscure . . . or the idea tha
might one day suddenly make complete sense to him.

Trance Gemini without the slightest attempt at obfuscation
not cause for comfort.

The background sounds of the bridge, all the beeps, hums, hi
and the quiet pulse of the sublight engines took on an oppre
quality, everything seeming too loud.

Dylan wasn't willing to let the sounds close in on him, unnerving further. "What is it, Trance?" He kept his tone just shy of full authority, shading it with concern.

She walked up to him, still unblinking. He was more than a third meter taller than she was, but if he had ever hoped to intimidate with his stature he had failed long ago. Everyone else involved in the salvage of *Andromeda Ascendant* had become furious at Dylan's spirited defense of his ship against the trespassing salvage crew. Not Trance. Trance had teased him and led him on a merry chase.

When Trance announced that she was fed up with the attempts to take Dylan down and kill him, and that she was quitting the operation, Beka's Nightsider client, Gerentex, had cold-bloodedly shot once at point-blank range. Up until that point, Dylan had been taking the struggle almost as a game, even when dealing with Tyr's mercenary band.

Dylan had flown into a rage. While he had no intention of killing anyone, he certainly intended to deal out some pain. His mother came from a line of heavy-grav-adapted humans and as a result he was fast, light on his feet, and could punch at least twice as hard as an ordinary human. His High Guard training and Argosy Special Operations skills were a bonus. Except for Tyr, the mercenaries had not stood a chance.

Somehow, though, he had ended up with half of the trespassers as his crew. Trance should not have been among them—to all indications she was dead, and beyond any attempt to save her, even if they had known what species she was. He had been quite surprised to find her fully recovered, quite cheerful, and showing absolutely no sign that she had been shot.

"Life is filled with surprises," Trance said softly. Rommie heard, of course; the android's hearing was acute. Dylan noted Rommie's quizzical expression.

Dylan waited.

Finally, Trance said, "Lighthouse keepers."

Rommie was looking completely baffled now. "What? That wasn't exactly a complete sentence, Trance."

Trance's face screwed up as she gave all the appearance of st
gling for words.

"Here we go again," Tyr muttered. "Mystery and confusion."

"When I get my flashes . . ." Trance started. She shook her h
glanced at Rommie, then fixed her gaze back on Dylan. "It's n
precise, Dylan. Things come in jumbled and confused and . . . a
have to focus really hard to . . . to . . . I don't know!" She flapped
arms helplessly. Now she was back in little girl mode.

Dylan had grown too used to Trance's mercurial states to pay
shift any attention. "Lighthouse keepers," he prompted.

"Oh. Right." Trance squinted. "Watch out for the lighth
keepers was the first thing." She wrinkled her nose. "A plagu
lighthouse keepers was another. And cold." She shivered. D
didn't think that was an act. "Lots of cold."

"Whoah!" Harper exclaimed, his face lighting up. "If we're g
someplace with lots of snow, I'm bringing a snowboard."

"I don't think it's that kind of cold place," Trance said, turnin
look at him.

"Ooookay," Harper said, just a little too frantically. "Everyb
who's in favor of turning the ship around and going somewhere
raise your hands and say 'aye!'" He raised a hand. Everyone
ignored him. "I'm gonna say I told you so, guys, right before we
blown into itty-bitty pieces."

Tyr rolled his eyes, then glared at Harper. "Mr. Harper, I fa
find your defeatist commentary either amusing or relevant."

"Does this have anything to do with where we're going?" D
asked her. This latest performance from Trance made him wond
they were on the verge of a colossal mistake.

"I don't know." Trance looked confused, as though she had
track of an important thought. "Maybe." She frowned. "Not the
part, though."

She was silent for a few moments longer.

Finally, she said, "Something's wrong, Dylan, that's all I know.

"All this," Tyr rumbled, "to say that we must stay alert."

"It's more than that, Tyr," Trance said urgently. "It's more
that."

Or perhaps it is less than notable." Tyr shook his head and turned to his fire control console, leaning on it. "I have heard more coning mutterings from would-be fortune-tellers. At least their goal o part the gullible from their money."

ylan glanced at Beka, who was watching Trance with rapt atten"Beka?"

ka looked at him, and he could see the lines of concern in her Beka had been through too much to discount any possible warngn. She was the best Slipstream pilot he had ever known, but her ad been difficult, with everything from a family rife with crimio her own daily battle against her addiction to Flash, a powerful that could enhance a pilot's reactions tremendously—at the cost stroying them physically.

ll, he trusted her to assess the things Trance had said and give n appropriate response. Beka was his strong right hand.

Ve know Trance's flashes," Beka said, finally.

Ve know how much trouble we can get into as a result," Rommie Beka and Dylan looked around. Rommie had her arms folded s her chest, and a determined look on her face. "Although I will : that she seems to be somewhat less chaotic since her . . . ;e."

ance gave Dylan a look that said, in no uncertain terms, *I'm ated.*

esides, it isn't just the flashes," Beka continued. Directly to :e, she said, "We always could count on you for happy accidents, :e."

her I'm-so-cute voice, Trance said, "I'm your good-luck ı."

ou are also quite annoying when you do that," Tyr grumbled.

he voice of Mr. Happy," Harper said. "Keep this up, Tyr, and I onna slip something into your food."

lis nanobots would handle it," Trance said. Her face suddenly blank. It was brief, but Dylan was startled. "Dylan, remember

yr's nanobots?" Dylan said, baffled. Nietzscheans used a complex re of genetic and social engineering, along with a liberal dose of

nanotechnology. As a result they were tough, fast, and smart, an a
fied breed of humans now classified as Homo sapiens invictus.

"Just nanobots. All you have to do is remember the nanobots
right time."

"Right. The nanobots."

"And the lighthouse keepers," Beka reminded him.

"And the plague of lighthouse keepers," Tyr added. "Wh
that is."

"Well," Beka said, "we can't just dismiss it out of hand. I jus
I knew where to look for ideas."

"That's my job," Rommie said.

The holographic avatar shimmered into life and said, p
"Actually, it's mine."

The ship's interface lit up again. "I hope you two aren't go
start arguing."

"Never," said the holographic Rommie.

"Depends on the subject," the android responded.

"Just don't kill the messenger, okay?" Trance said. Eve
turned to look at her. "Figure of speech."

Tyr glowered at her. "If anyone could figure out a way to ki
Trance, I might be tempted."

Dylan sighed. He hated it when Tyr got into a grumpy
Then again, Tyr's use of emotion as a tool of manipulation was
fine-tuned as Trance's.

It was time to break the chain and get on with business. "
how long until the next Slip point?"

Beka glanced at one of her consoles. "Just under five minute

"Good enough. Harper, go do whatever it is you're doing."

Harper bounded onto the Command Deck riser. "Sure
Boss." He headed for the bridge exit, chuckling to himself. "An
was I doing? Just being Seamus Zelazny Harper, freakin' *genius*!

"And a model of modesty, too," Beka called after him.

"Trance?" Dylan said.

Trance hesitated for a moment. Then she said, "Got it." Sh
lowed Harper. Both of them had their favorite bolt holes o

—Harper's was Machine Shop 17, while Trance's was the hydro-
cs gardens.

ylan waited for a few moments, until he was certain that Trance
gone, then turned to Beka. "Transit to Slipstream as soon as you
I'll be in my quarters."

eka glanced quickly at Rommie, who responded with a shrug that
ntially said, *Hey, he's Dylan, he's designed to act weird.*

Okay," Beka said after a moment. Dylan was almost always on the
mmand Deck when the *Andromeda Ascendant* transited to Slip-
m. "I'll put it on shipwide when I'm ready to go."

Thanks," he said, and left Command. He was aware of Rommie
ing to follow him, and then changing her mind.

his was shaping up to be a hell of a day.

n was comfortably settled into his office chair, his long legs
ped up on his desk, when Rommie's holographic avatar shim-
d into existence. Even though he knew where to find the various
ectors that created the illusion of this slim young woman stand-
efore him in a formal at-ease stance, he still marveled at the
e and cleverness of Vedran technology. It still tugged at his heart
his homeworld of Tarn-Vedra seemed to be utterly gone, some-
hidden by the Vedrans as the Commonwealth collapsed follow-
he assassination of the Vedran Empress.

e and *Andromeda* had been frozen in time for more than three
lred standard years. Despite his initial bravado, he had under-
d the magnitude of his loss—*their* loss—and it had threatened to
g him to his knees. Somehow, between his motley crew and his
tion to re-create the Commonwealth he had known, he had con-
d to stay sane.

ill. . . .

'm not quite as idealistic as I used to be, am I?" he asked Rommie.
ie raised an eyebrow. "Actually, I think it's worse than that," she
He sat back, knowing he had set himself up without thinking.
r teeth have lost that Space Ranger Bob gleam. You'll have to do
thing about that."

He snorted, not quite laughing. "For a warship, you're fu
mischief."

"For the captain of a warship," she noted, "you're remar
relaxed."

He sighed. "I really wanted to hold on to the past, Romn
really tried."

"The present won't let you do that."

"It never does." He pushed away from the desk, putting hi
down on the deck. He nodded at his casual shirt. "It took me
than two years to stop clinging to the uniforms and the symbols

She smiled. "I know. I was here. Speaking as one who cares,
glad to see you finally hang up the uniform. You're still High G
whether you're in dress uniform or breeches and a sleeveless shi

"There's a picture I'm not sure I'd like to see." He sighed
and shook his head. "That really isn't the point, Rommie. I have
go of the past. If I can't do that, how can I figure out the future

"By taking it one step at a time like the rest of the universe
suggested. "I prefer to leave the long-term planning to Trance
seems to have an idea of where everything is going."

He sat upright, attentive, his musing pushed aside for the mo
"Our good-luck charm was struggling to find the right thing to

Rommie mused for a moment. Dylan wondered how many d
ent things she was doing in that span of time. "Perhaps those n
rious powers of hers are starting to fail."

"I don't know," Dylan admitted. He looked around his qua
They were sparsely decorated, with a few trophies and a handf
treasured items. This was one of the few places on the ship
Trance had not managed to make her presence known in the for
plants. "She's been subdued for a few months."

"She did derail history," Rommie said. With the exception of
and Trance, who had an unpleasant future to look forward to,
were all supposed to have gone out in a blaze of glory. Tranc
given them a painfully graphic description of the coming cat
phe . . . and Dylan had used that, and Trance herself, to chang
course of events.

Trance had seemed a lot less prone to her flashes since then.

So she could have burned herself out," Dylan said.

Or moved our track so far away from the one we were on that she
't get a grip on what comes next. All hypothesis, of course. Trance
ears to operate on some kind of multiplexed quantum level that I
't really understand. I do my best work in shooting at things, not
chsaying and reading minds." She suddenly looked toward the
ing. "Shipwide is on."

Heads up, everybody," Beka said, her voice carrying through the
re length of the ship. Dylan braced himself automatically against
chair. "Transiting to Slipstream in five . . . four . . . three . . .
. . . one . . . now!"

White light suffused the ship and Dylan felt himself being shaken
stretched as the *Andromeda Ascendant* shot through the Slipstream
al she had opened and dove into the nest of cosmic strings that
prised the Slipstream itself.

The transitional sensations continued until Beka guided the huge
's Slipstream runners into contact with the streams she needed.
lity reasserted itself.

Dylan took a deep breath, waiting for his nervous system to shake
the transitional effects. When he was ready, he said, "We need to
some answers, Rommie, and I don't think we have much time."

TWO • BY THE LIGHT OF A BURNING MOON

> We have noticed that some people do not take kindly to personal visits.
>
> —SYSTEMS COMMONWEALTH TAX INSPECTOR
> JAGO PEARCE, ON WHY HIS STAFF REQUIRED
> PERSONAL ARMOR, CY 9384

Trance's personal haven was *Andromeda*'s immense hydroponics dens. When she had come aboard, she had been delighted with wonderful variety of plant life—some of the species she had fo had supposedly been extinct for centuries.

The hydroponics gardens served the dual purpose of provi the *Andromeda Ascendant* with fresh oxygen and a broad selectio vegetables. The ship was equipped with air recycling equipr that could more than meet the needs of a full crew, but the hy ponics provided an important element—air that didn't smell or machine-cleaned.

Trance had worked her way through the gardens during her couple of months aboard the ship. During that time she had cle the cluttered areas, allowing each plant its breathing space. She pruned, transplanted, seeded, and nurtured, sometimes spen hours rooted to the spot as she contemplated a particularly diff

e. Beka had once called her a wood sprite, but that had been back
er purple pixie days, when she had been disarmingly cute.

hese days, she thought, she was probably more dryadlike.

Never mess with a dryad," she said quietly, but she had already
ed on from that thought. The vague flashes she had brought to
an were gnawing at the edge of her mind. She had hoped that
e time in her gardens would help her clarify her thoughts.

he celestial landscape had helped far less than she had hoped,
ever, and she had an uncomfortable feeling that the gardens
ld offer no help either.

he picked up her pruning shears. Frowning, she leaned over one
er tiny bonsai trees, contemplating the crooked branches. After a
moments' regard, she turned to another of the tiny trees. Not
e, either. She put the shears aside, sighing.

tepping back, she focused on the trio of bonsai.

or some reason, the pattern was not coming clear to her. She
ed to the left, and then to the right, reached out for the shears
n, and promptly changed her mind.

he picked up one of the bonsai and held it out in front of her. Clos-
her eyes, she tried to clear her mind. Slowly, she walked forward,
lenly shifted left, then right, and proceeded to weave gracefully
nd one obstacle after another without once opening her eyes.

ime to stop. She opened her eyes again, and gently placed the
sai on a stand. Surrounded by large-leaved plants, the little tree
ost vanished from sight. No matter. She knew where it was. She
ys knew where things were, particularly living things.

he stepped away from the tree, assessing the change. She was
sed to see that the balance of energy had returned to equilibrium.
smallest things could make such significant changes. Move a
t, find harmony. Throw a switch, lock down the timeline. That
of thing.

n the other hand, this more balanced garden of hers did not
ess the main issue—sorting out the muddy impressions tumbling
ugh her mind. She desperately wanted to be able to tell Dylan
ething more useful, more pertinent. Something better than
g him the equivalent of *there's trouble on the way*.

She stepped back a little, so that she could sit cross-legged on soft loam that bordered the access path. She rested her chin on hands, letting her mind drift, caught up in the delicate traceri the plant life around her. Once she placed herself in harmony the plant energies, she could extend her awareness throughou *Andromeda Ascendant*, and from there out into the celestial fiel she didn't mentally ping-pong from one probability path to ano she might pick up something useful—and there was a chance tha might be able to bring some sort of stability to her shifting mem

She cleared the wandering thoughts away, and took deep bre She really did not need to—a point that everyone on the ship pected, considering her propensity for getting over dying on a re basis—but the technique helped her to relax and focus.

She was beginning to feel sunlight warmth when somet touched her mental boundary. Annoyed, she snapped back out o meditative state and looked around.

Her eyes widened with surprise. "What?"

A few yards away, a somewhat less mature voice also said, "W

Trance stared into the shocked purple face of her younger "What are *you* doing here?" she demanded.

Wide-eyed, the younger Trance was peering at her around a she had been pruning. She was wearing a rather garish multihued shorts and halter-top outfit that left her midriff bare. Her multicol hair and accessories somehow managed to blend with the clothes.

The younger Trance's prehensile tail snapped up, flicking in a tion. "Who are—" she started, halting with a gasp. "You're *me!*" frowned. "But what are you doing here?"

"What are *you* doing here?" She almost added *we changed place* stopped herself in time. Things were starting to get confusing a She stood up, like a plant reaching for sunlight.

"I've always been here." The younger Trance's nose wri slightly as she considered that statement. "Well, not always *here* always . . . here. Oh."

Trance struggled with her memory, trying to place this mor but there was nothing there, no memory of this meeting. *I've st sideways.*

"Things are going to go badly," she said simply. She stepped
ard the purple girl, holding out her right hand. Hesitantly, the
unger Trance took it, holding on delicately. She felt a flush of solar
mth as the circuit was completed. Her skin first shaded to a bur-
ed and translucent gold, then deepened and darkened, glittering
hough thousands of tiny stars had come to life, and her eyes filled
h amber swirls.

Suddenly she was seeing not only the surface world, but the pat-
s of energy that existed both beneath and above that surface. Her
ple counterpart gasped softly, and she took that as an indication
t she was seeing much the same. Together, they turned and started
lowly follow the path through the gardens. There was no destina-
a in mind.

"How bad will it get?" the younger Trance asked. Then, before
answer could be given, the purple girl gave her older counterpart
hocked look. "Oh, no! What happened to our tail?" Her tail
ped around, close to her body, and she caught the end of it in her
: hand. The tip vibrated rapidly, a sure sign of anxiety.

"There was a battle," she said, melancholy tingeing her voice. The
nger woman responded with a sad-eyed look. "There was nothing
one could do. I had to learn new ways of moving."

"Not to mention finding a whole new wardrobe." The younger
sion nodded at her older counterpart's snug red-gold leather out-
"Not that we seem to have had *that* much of a problem."

Trance smiled. "This comes a lot later. When it starts getting to be
ctical."

"When it starts getting bad."

"When it starts getting bad." Trance shook her head. "I don't even
w when it'll start for you. I used to, but everything's changed so
ch."

The purple girl gave her another startled look. "Following the
bability tracks is becoming difficult?"

"I don't know," Trance admitted. "Everything *seems* okay . . . but
shouldn't be happening. I shouldn't be meeting you."

"I'm not the right younger you, am I?"

"I don't think so, no." Trance frowned, trying to grab hold of the

threads of several ideas. Forming something coherent out of the
and pieces she was getting was difficult. She contained the powe:
both chaos and order, but she rarely had a choice as to which
would manifest at any given time. Chaos had the upper hand a
moment, and she was starting to feel that she would have had an
ier time arguing with a battalion of lawyers. "I'm not even sure t
real."

"It seems real enough."

Trance looked down at their linked hands, seeing the swirl
energy there. "It looks real enough." She looked up. "Maybe th
just our mind trying to help me work things out."

"Our mind is like that," the other Trance said. She shrug
"Still, if it seems real to us, then it is real."

Trance chuckled. "One of these days we're going to start ge
our tenses mixed up."

"All of our grammar." The younger Trance flashed a mischie
grin. "Although it's really fun to get Tyr confused. He's so *glum*
full of himself."

In all seriousness, she said, "It's hard enough to keep the st
straight *now*. It isn't going to be easy holding everything togethe:

"We can't always warn them of what's coming," the you
woman said. "I know that. I've had that experience. Sometim
doesn't help even if you do come up with a warning in time." Th
of her tail vibrated in sympathy with her frustration. "Sometime
only thing I can give them is something they don't understand."

"It would be so much easier if Dylan or Beka . . . or even Ty
Harper . . . could see things the way we do. Maybe they could pu
pieces together for themselves." Trance pursed her lips, her exp
sion both thoughtful and regretful. "If they could . . . if they c
they wouldn't have to walk through the fire."

"It isn't for them." The younger Trance knelt and touched
leaves of a small plant. Their consciousness was drawn into the p
into the root system, and into the connective energy structure o
garden. In a flash, Trance built up a map in her mind. The cold, s
tured lines of the irrigation system snapped them both back to

sent moment. "They couldn't deal with it. Most species suffer
n single-line perception."

'I have to figure out why this is happening," Trance said.

Purple Trance crouched to inspect another plant, turning her head
way and that. After a few moments' consideration, she took out a
ll pair of clippers and made a couple of quick, judicious snips.
ere. All better." She stood up again, putting the clippers away.
mething in our future is disrupting things."

'Upsetting the probabilities?" Trance mused for a moment. "If
per's tesseract machine . . . no, I don't think it's that. This isn't
y enough."

'For want of a nail," the younger woman said. "For want of a nail,
kingdom was lost. We have to find the nail, whatever it is."

'Or a needle in a haystack," Trance said unhappily. "I hate it when
gs get complicated. At least when they don't have to. I like my
s to stay simple."

'Me too." Purple Trance smiled, and flicked her tail from side to
.

t was time. Trance saw the acknowledgment in the purple girl's
as well, a slight moue of disappointment. There never was
ugh time, even when she had all the time she could want. It was
ply a matter of what happened when. Racing the clock sometimes
her ragged and exhausted, even though many of her races were
only in her mind as she looked for the best possible solution to a
s.

Their hands slipped apart, and Trance's enhanced viewpoint
ckly faded away, leaving her feeling lost. Her purple counterpart
a blank look for a moment, then blinked twice as her reality
serted itself. "Wow."

Stay alert, and stay safe," Trance advised her younger counter-
. She wished she had some memory of this conversation, if
ed it had happened at all. "They need us. That's why we're here."

I won't forget." The purple girl tilted her head, looking momen-
y distracted. "So much to do . . ."

I have to go," Trance said. She was reluctant to break the spell—

it was rare that she enjoyed such an idyll as this, a bubble of p
free-floating in the cosmos. No decisions, no directives, no des
tions. "I'm still not completely clear, but I think I know more no

"Good luck," the younger Trance said. She smiled sweetly, a
uine expression. There really had been a touch of true innoc
before her change, she decided. "For the perfect possible future.

"Exactly." With that, Trance turned and began to walk back a
the pathway. When she glanced back, the purple girl was gone.

Dylan Hunt, bold, bright-eyed captain of the lone surviving *Gl*
Heritage–class High Guard battleship, lay on his bed, staring a
ceiling and contemplating lies and evasions—mostly his own.

The truth was, simply put, that he still mourned everything th
had lost. A Commonwealth that had been a million worlds str
not fifty, protected by a High Guard that more often acted with
passion than the swift cruelty they were capable of. His fiancée,
Riley, who had tried, and failed, to rescue him. He had even lost
azed, the world she had brokered, where the old values still stood
a traditional High Guard cadre trained and fought as they ha
thousands of years.

Sara had meant that world to be the heart of a new Comm
wealth. He had made the right moral choice in the end, as diffic
it had been. Sara's world, her hopes, had fallen to isolationist cho
He had felt the memory of her slipping through his fingers.

He had begun adapting to this dark time with frightening s
ness, learning from the all-too-severe lessons doled out to him
had begun his quest with a kind of wide-eyed eagerness to reviv
old ideals, something the old purple Trance had encouraged from
moment he had discovered her sitting up cheerfully when she
supposed to be stretched out lifeless.

"You're like the first candle of millions to come," she had said
he could have sworn that he saw bright spirals of light glittering i
eyes. He had been fascinated with her. "It isn't going to be eas
you, but you can do it. It's like learning to make plants grow, y'k
Besides, you're tall, and you're kinda cute, and we'd better get g
because I think there's going to be all kinds of pieces to pick up."

Rommie had shimmered into view, a quizzical look on her face. Do you come with any kind of guidebook? You're quite confusing."

Trance had grinned. "Just stick with me. You won't have trouble following along."

"That," Rommie said dryly, "is precisely what I'm afraid of."

Within days his idealized view of existence had come under fire in e form of a corruption of High Guard rituals and values. He had t even begun to properly process his knowledge of the state of the own Worlds before being plunged full-tilt into horror.

His own descent had begun then, slowly but steadily. The *Androm-a Ascendant* had ceased to be a tool to be used to benefit a new Commonwealth. Instead, she had become his own personal instrument of rce. No doubt Tyr liked that idea a great deal—always field a force onger than that of your opponent, and strike swiftly, preferably th a certain degree of subterfuge involved.

He sighed and sat up, rubbing at his eyes. He had hung up the igh Guard uniform alright, and had no intention of adopting that the new High Guard, but he still ached for his old idealism.

He was already sensing the corruption at the heart of the new ommonwealth. He had immediately resisted the political push to ake him First Triumvir, but sometimes he wondered if he had made e right choice then. There were periodic reminders that the Commonwealth was moving on despite him—around him, even. Having baby-sit Beka's Uncle Sid, the notorious Sid Profit, as he made a d for Triumvir had been bad enough, but it was something that uld be handled. Except, of course, that Sid wouldn't be easily han-ed. By the time the dust had settled, thousands were dead, Sid's siness rivals had been destroyed, and Sid himself was sent on his y with the blessings of the Commonwealth.

There was a bright shimmer to one side of the bed. "You're think-g about Uncle Sid again," Rommie said.

"And you're wearing your psychiatrist hat again," Dylan said umpily. "Lights."

The lights turned on, slowly increasing in intensity. Dylan blinked. ep seemed to be a difficult proposition lately.

"It's my psychotherapist's hat, actually," Rommie said primly. She

tilted her head, as though regarding him. "You should be glad, as
quite a bit cheaper. And you *were* thinking about Sid."

Dylan nodded slowly. "I was thinking about Sid." He sigh
"That bastard's the epitome of everything that went wrong with
Commonwealth, Rommie, old or new. It's people like Sid who see
first weakness and move in. After that it's a feeding frenzy."

"And never mind his effect on Beka," Rommie said.

Dylan didn't take the bait. Rommie was pushing a bit to see wh
he might be sensitive. "Beka's capable of handling his effect on l
Rommie." He pushed back the sheets and got out of bed. The art
cial gravity field on the *Andromeda Ascendant* was set to a level co
fortable for most, but for him, with a heavy-gravity genetic struct
inherited from his mother, it seemed far too weak. He sometimes
as though a careless step would send him flying into the ceiling.
admit I don't understand why she's resisted the temptation to sh
him out of an airlock."

Rommie raised an eyebrow. "Strong family ties, perhaps?"

"Of the noose around the neck variety." He shook his head.
dealing with the Magog Worldship means accepting a Comm
wealth where people like Sid are the norm . . ."

"You're afraid that we won't be able to handle the Worldship wl
it gets going again."

That was a thought he had wanted to keep buried as long as po
ble. A massive construct of huge, interlinked modules, the Mag
Worldship was big enough to carry a small sun within its confines
also had a monstrous deity—the Spirit of the Abyss. The Nova Bo
Beka had launched at the Worldship should have destroyed the cr
completely. Instead, most of the energy from the artificial nova I
been sucked away by the Spirit. The Worldship had been left deac
space, but would eventually get moving again. Time was running c

Dylan had made the Worldship a pressing issue. It had sped thi
up a little bit here and there, but for the most part nobody re
seemed to give a damn. So there were lots of Magog on the way.
you needed was bigger Gauss guns and a lot of smart bullets, that v
the reigning philosophy, especially among the Nietzscheans.

It wasn't that easy. Andromeda knew that. She had been up aga the Worldship twice. Both times she had failed. The second time she had almost been destroyed.

"It's coming," he said simply. "It's coming, and one day soon we're all going to wake up as Magog breakfast food."

"An engaging thought," Rommie said. "At least you couldn't be considered the single-serving size."

He gave her a dour look. "Thanks for the comfort. I'll sleep *so* much better now."

"You're welcome. I have some answers for you, by the way."

"The lighthouse keepers."

"Indeed." The hologram assumed a more formal position, looking at a point just over the top of his head. "Much of what I found is of a generic nature, of course—a lighthouse, essentially, is a lighthouse, intended to serve the purpose of warning sea craft away from treacherous coastal areas. These structures can be in the form of everything from the tall cylindrical buildings common to Earth and numerous other planets, with a rotating light of great intensity set on top, maintained by a lighthouse keeper, to the floating lights of Pen'hra, guided by a network of AIs, which not only provide warning of treacherous waters, but can, if needed, provide aid and rescue to water craft in difficulty."

"So that covers the lighthouses and lighthouse keepers," Dylan said.

"Not quite," Andromeda countered. "I found references also to several security organizations, as well as three vague references to a planetary defense system."

"Which planet?" Dylan was starting to get an idea of the direction Trance's flashes had taken, although he was still far from putting all the pieces of the puzzle together.

"That information seems to have gone missing," Andromeda said with a hint of annoyance in her voice. "Of the security organizations, all but one are defunct, and the lone company still operating is based in Kartob IV. That world is located in Triangulum, and is thus in the wrong galaxy to be of current concern."

"Which leaves the planetary defense system," Dylan mused.

"Or something else entirely."

"Meaning?"

"A name for an organization such as the Knights of Genetic Purity, perhaps, purpose unknown. We are entering the realm of speculation at this point, however."

Dylan padded across his quarters into his office area. He sat down in his chair and put his feet up on the desk. He regarded his toes idly, trying to keep his mind clear and open to see if anything might occur to him that had some kind of bearing on this situation.

"The phrase 'the plague of lighthouse keepers' seems somewhat easier to interpret," Andromeda said, following him into the office. "Again, there are multiple references, all with a common theme—the effect of the post of lighthouse keeper upon the individual granted that position."

"At a guess," Dylan said, leaning back and trying not to feel the weariness creeping through him, "issues of loneliness and stress."

"More than that, there are numerous recorded instances of lighthouse keepers falling prey to various forms of insanity. While some stories appear to be quite apocryphal, and ghost stories abound, other cases are quite well documented. The problem appears to have resulted from a tendency to select individuals who seemed capable of a solitary life."

"No wives, no children, no nearby towns to visit for a drunken night?" Dylan said.

"Precisely. As a result, many keepers cracked from the condition. Alternative ideas were, as a result, mandated. These included automation of lighthouse systems, as well as the requirement that those hired as keepers have at least a companion, as well as an assistant."

"Insanity," Dylan said softly. His eyes took on the half-closed look that indicated that he was busy processing an idea. "Rommie, this should be starting to make sense by now, but it isn't. It's making even less sense than it did before."

"Maybe," the hologram said with no tinge of irony in her voice, "that is the point."

Trance was on her way back to her quarters, thinking back over her earlier encounter, when the cosmos shuddered and deposited her somewhere else.

This is beginning to get weird, even for me.

She unholstered her force lance, thumbing it on and setting it to
: effectors, the tiny but highly effective smart projectiles that could
n through almost any armor. The lance made a small whine as it
ne up to full power.

She was no longer on the *Andromeda Ascendant*. She looked
und, carefully. She was standing in broken terrain of some kind,
wreckage of a city enduring a long and difficult war. She could
r the sounds of battle, well in the distance, and the sound of heavy
pons firing at steady intervals.

t was night, and the air was filled with dust. The smell of carnage
: came to her made her feel ill, and momentarily weak. So much
th, so needless. This was not the future she was seeking, so why
she here? She could feel no familiarity with this world, so it
ned unlikely that she had ever been here.

here were fires all around, lighting the destroyed buildings and
shed roads. A few of the fires threw infernal light across scatter-
of bodies, both complete and otherwise, but she could neither
nor sense anything living, no matter where she looked.

he savage nature of the destruction gave her a strong desire to
but tears would not come. By this token, she knew that she had
ething to learn here. After she had found and dealt with whatever
called her here—whether this was real, or occurring in a corner
er mind—she could mourn.

here was another source of flickering light, less easily identified
the fires that lit this dying city. Hesitantly, she looked up into
ky.

his world had a moon, and it was burning.

he had no idea what kind of weapon might have caused this par-
ar catastrophe. Nova Bombs worked specifically on suns. A point
larity bomb would either have ripped part of the moon away,
hed a hole through it, or imploded it.

ne looked away again. It didn't matter what kind of weapon had
used, at least not to her. What mattered was that someone had
ashed catastrophic destruction on a planetary scale. It might be
og at work, or Nietzscheans, but someone was responsible.

Slowly, she walked through the ruins, keeping her awareness
and trying to avoid falling into a pit of depression.

She had been walking for more than two hours, listening t
weapons fire get closer, and then recede again, when she found
or rather he saw her.

"Girl," he said, from somewhere inside a pool of shadow
voice husky and broken, "are you crazy?"

She was shocked by the sound of his voice. "Tyr?"

"It is indeed," he said, and she saw movement in the shadow
the glint of light from something metallic—no doubt one of
beloved multibarreled guns.

She moved toward him. "I don't even know where we are."

"You are in a very, very bad place, Trance Gemini," Tyr sai
she moved closer, and crouched, Trance recognized something e
his voice. Weakness. "I don't know how you are here, but if yo
something other than a figment of my imagination, you have m
terrible mistake."

She smiled. "And you always said I talked too much."

"I have too many words and too little time," he said.

Her vision adjusted to the darkness, and she gasped as she re
what he meant. Tyr was terribly changed. His leonine drea
were gone, leaving him bald. There was a long, wide scar acro
top of his head. He had an eye patch over his right eye, and more
on his cheeks. One arm and one leg had been replaced with c
netic prosthetics. Two fingers on the other hand were also prost

"Too many battles," he said after a moment. "With each one,
that much older, that much slower, and eventually I became v
am, working my old trade, and earning the retirement benefits o
trade."

"You're a mercenary again?" she asked, struck with horror.

"Oh, yes." He coughed suddenly, then drew in breath v
wheeze. "In the end, it was all I could go back to."

She found a comfortable position next to him, listening whi
looked him over.

Noticing her inspection, he said, "I am dying. I very much
that there is anything you can do."

he looked up, into his face. "Tyr . . ."

One battle too many," he said. There was no note of complaint in
voice. "Are you here, then, to carry away my spirit as it relin-
hes the body?"

he smiled. "I think that would be more Rev Bem's job."

Ah. Yes." Tyr raised his eyebrows. "How is the good Reverend
emiel Far Traveler?"

I don't know," she admitted. "Well, I hope. Tyr, what happened?"

He frowned. "You know. You were there." He paused for a moment.
nce, it is difficult to think. You were on *Andromeda*. . . ."

I need to know, Tyr," she said. She was looking him over again.
saw the problem now—he had been hit by rounds from a Gauss
and at least two had penetrated his armor. He was bleeding pro-
ly, and she could sense the internal damage the smart bullets had
ed. An ordinary human would have been dead long ago. She
ed up, into his eyes. "You're right, I can't help you here. I might
be able to help us all, but I need to *know*."

he wheezing was growing worse, and his eyes were starting to
. With an effort, he refocused. "I was a fool," he said. He was
enly wracked by a coughing spasm, and blood foamed at his lips.
ce placed her hands on his shoulders, doing what she could to
his pain. He was silent for a moment. "We were attacked. Dylan
ated to take direct action, and I grew frustrated and angry with
So I abandoned Command, and took out a Slipfighter, intending
al a few blows." He closed his eyes, his face anguished. "I was a
I did nothing but get in the way. The *Andromeda Ascendant* was
oyed. I alone survived, barely . . . and it would seem that you,
escaped."

t only seems that way," she said softly. "What happened then?"

e coughed again, then settled down. "My Slipfighter was dis-
d, and I was cast adrift. Within an hour, I was taken prisoner. I
ncarcerated and questioned, but my captors seemed little inter-
I in any knowledge I might have had. I was merely imprisoned,
ortured or subjected to drugs or surgery. One day I was released,
papers and a menial job, and left alone." He stopped talking
. His breath was beginning to come in short gasps.

"Slowly," Trance said. "Take it slowly."

"You need to know, you said." He tried to push himself into [a] ter position. Carefully, she helped him sit up. "Eventually I wa[s] to get to a ship. I had the ambition of following my schemes, yo[u] I was too late. Olma, into whose care I gave my son, Tame[s] betrayed me by handing him to the Sabra-Jaguar coalition. He [is] them now as the Nietzschean messiah, the reincarnation of [Drago] Museveni." He lifted a hand, weakly. "The reincarnation of the [pro]genitor was supposed to *reunite* the prides! Instead, this is wh[at I] have wrought."

"This is a Nietzschean world?" she said, shocked.

"One of many left in flames," he said. "The prides will be re[u]n[ited] in death. There are few of us left. Before long there will be no [more] than two lone Nietzscheans, fighting over piles of rubble."

"Was there nothing you could do?"

He looked at her, sadly. "I was a pariah from the moment my [pride] was destroyed, girl, and more so once my bone blades were tak[en by] those tunnel creatures." He held up his normal arm. Tyr had [been] abducted by a mysterious group of aliens and returned with his [bone] blades neatly removed—no evidence of surgery, even. Ther[e had] never been an explanation as to why or how it had been done. [His] fellow Nietzscheans thought me weak, and treated me as little [more] than a kludge."

"So you returned to being a mercenary," she said.

"With all else taken from me, and no will to die easily, it wa[s all I] had left." He coughed again, and more blood foamed at his lips. ["The] money is of no importance. I keep enough for food, shelte[r, and] weapons. All else I give to the Way. The Reverend would be pr[oud of] me, I am sure."

Trance heard the note of sarcasm. "Rev Bem would say som[ething] about the Divine, and you would act grouchy but secretly be ple[ased.]"

He gave her a mournful look. "I could never have bee[n that] transparent."

"Not always," she said gently, "but as you learned, your [face] changed."

"Yes, it did," he said. "But in the end, I forgot to follow it. I destroyed everything."

His eyes fluttered rapidly, and she felt him swiftly weakening. "Tyr . . ." She paused, fighting back tears. "Tyr, you were always my friend, no matter how obnoxious you could be. I won't allow this to happen."

"You cannot change what is," he said softly. "Not even you can do that."

"This hasn't happened yet," she told him. "This is not the perfect possible future that I know we can have."

"It is the one that we have," he said. "Enough debate. It seems my time is here."

"Yes," she said, "it is."

He took a breath. "I am Tyr Anasazi," he said, barely above a whisper, "out of Victoria . . ."

He fell silent, his breathing stilled, his eyes glassy. Trance felt his life flow away into the darkness. "You were Tyr Anasazi, out of Victoria by Barbarossa," she said, "and you were superior." Cannons boomed in the distance. "And I swear *this will not happen!*"

She looked up at the burning moon.

The cosmos shifted again, and she found herself on her knees in the middle of one of *Andromeda*'s corridors. She was weeping.

She looked down, and gasped.

Her hands were stained with blood.

THREE · BUILDING FOR A BETTER FUTURE

A curious revelation: as we progress through life, we make this decision and that decision. Yet the choices we might have made remain with us, silent or not.

For each of us there is a multitude of echoes and reflections, unto infinity.

— CHARMA BESENCHI,
MIRRORS AND MIRACLES,
CY 9545

Trance stood, shaking. She and Tyr had often come into conflict one thing or another, but seeing him as such a broken shell heartrending. No matter what the others on the *Andromeda Ascen* thought, she was not impervious to pain. Physical distress she c moderate to a great extent, but emotional pain was another ma entirely. She knew she was emotionally attached to these peop that had been part of the bargain from the outset.

She looked down at her bloodied hands again, trying to force experience into a more understandable shape. This had been no ter of extending her mind along lines of probability. Somehow had been there with Tyr as he died.

Doggedly, she pulled herself back to reality. She was running o time to grab hold of events so that she could turn them to advant

She lifted her hands in front of her face. What she did now w

crucial to their survival. She had to make the right choices, in the
ght sequence. Her head began to swim with a sea of probabilities.
In a fraction of a second she was focused on the present reality
ain. She knew where to go first, and what needed to be done.

Tyr, she thought, *by dying you managed to tell me how we're going to live.*
In the blood on her hands, as she looked more deeply than any
aided human could, she saw a few of Tyr's nanobots.

She began running.

mmie's holographic form materialized in the corridor that Trance
d just vacated at a run. She looked around in an all-too-human way,
hough she didn't need to.

"Trance?"

There was no answer. She frowned, something else she didn't need
lo. Had it concerned her, she might have blamed her programmers
the nonfunctional behavior. At that point one of her other selves
uld have reminded her that she had a more or less infinite capacity
learning—which, naturally, included behavioral elements.

She dematerialized again, reappearing a few meters away, past an
ersection. She tried a few other nearby spots, but there was still no
a of Trance, or of the anomaly that had caught her attention.

She returned to the original location, still frowning. Daring to
e, she sent her consciousness rippling through the length and
adth of the ship. As she had expected, she could find absolutely no
a of Trance. It was baffling—Trance seemed to have to make an
rt to make herself visible to the internal sensors, a point that
ld prove disastrous someday. Besides, that sort of ability had no
e in an orderly universe. *Her* orderly universe.

Now she was starting to look annoyed. Not only that, but knowing
looked annoyed irritated her. Her android avatar was beginning to
e a very bad influence on her.

he sighed heavily.

ealizing what she was doing at almost the same time as she was
g it, she closed her holographic eyes and put a hand over her
. While this made very little impression on her actual percep-

tions, she did manage to produce a momentary but interesting e⸱ as the holographic fields went out of phase. Vedran technology been brilliant, and often unsurpassed, but the Vedrans thems⸱ had been pragmatic, prizing life and culture above machinery.

As an artificial intelligence, growing to readiness as the wa⸱ heart of the *Andromeda Ascendant*, she had learned quickly where place was with the Vedrans, and within the Systems Commonwe⸱ Born out of technology, she had become a person, and she was that way. The dark times that she and Dylan had emerged in wer⸱ less accepting—these days many people saw her as no more tha⸱ extension of antiquated technology, something to be erased if⸱ became inconvenient. Fortunately Harper had provided a p⸱ solution to the problem by building her android avatar.

"You look like you've got a headache."

Rommie switched her attention back into the outside world. hadn't just been standing around brooding, of course, but all o⸱ other processes were running in the background, under the co⸱ of the main AI.

She realigned her holographic fields to execute an instant degree turn, causing Beka Valentine to take a step back, startle⸱ *hate* it when you do that!"

"Sorry," Rommie said.

"No you're not." Beka folded her arms across her chest, gi⸱ Rommie a challenging look.

"Because I'm a machine?" She raised an eyebrow.

"No," Beka said with a grin. "Because you enjoy scaring the out of me by doing that."

"Oh."

"You don't?" Now Beka seemed concerned.

"Well . . ."

"You do?" There was a long moment of silence as the two star⸱ each other in confusion. "Rommie, *wars* have started over less this. Yes or no?"

She frowned in a way that she knew made her look hope⸱ helpless, which made Beka grin broadly. "I really never gave i⸱ thought."

"A brain the size of a small moon, and you never gave it any ought," Beka said. "Rommie, sometimes you shock me."

Rommie smiled. "I'm not exactly one for practical jokes. I'm quite od at blowing up small moons, though."

"One of your more lovable qualities, I'd say. Some moons serve it."

"Not to mention some planets."

"Let's start small."

"Your Uncle Sid?" Rommie suggested.

Beka mock-scowled. "Hey, low blow."

"Sorry."

"No you're not." Beka grinned again. "Besides, we can't blow Sid until I've figured out where he's got all his money buried. *Then* you stuff him into a lifepod and use it for target practice."

"Why waste a lifepod?"

Beka snorted. "You're mean."

"I'm a warship," Rommie said with an elfin grin. "I'm licensed to bitchy and irritable and willing to blow things up at short ice."

"And people say *I'm* bad-tempered." Beka paused, making an obvi- s effort to drop the banter and be serious. "So what's going on, way?"

Rommie frowned again. "That's just it . . . I don't know. I picked a couple of anomalous energy readings. I also thought I had nce on visual for a moment, but she vanished."

Now Beka was starting to look worried. "Anomalous energy read- s. I really, really hate it when you say something like that."

"As in there'll be hell to pay?" Rommie said.

"Usually. There are definitely words that come right before major ible. So . . . anything more specific?"

"Nothing." Rommie frowned in thought. She shut off the self- icism in a flash. There was no point in fighting it, she supposed. was supposed to be adaptable, after all. "A double blip on my sen- s, neither one long enough to give me any concrete readings."

"And Trance in the general area." Beka's expression had become a e-eyed look of disbelief. "This can't be good."

Rommie shrugged. "I can't make a statement either way un
have more data."

Beka was looking at the deck, frowning. "Well, you *could* start
the blood. . . ."

"Blood?" Rommie echoed.

"I think that was what I said." Beka pointed and Rommie focu
There were a few tiny droplets on the deck. "I think I'm offic
worried. Unexplained blood is *never* good." Beka crouched down,
ing her head. "I wonder who it belongs to?"

"Belonged," Rommie said absently.

"Huh?"

"You used the wrong tense. Belonged, not belongs." Rommie
herself into her main systems. The most formal of her selves
over the sensors. "And the answer is . . ."

"Tyr," Andromeda said, appearing on a flatscreen as Beka loo
toward the nearby junction. "DNA match, not to mention a lo
dead nanos."

Beka looked up. "Maybe he cut himself shaving?"

"I doubt that," Rommie said.

"We could always ask him," Andromeda put in.

"Let Dylan know first," Beka said. She stood up. "I hate to say
really would like a simple, straightforward, and boring diplon
mission for a change."

Trance had made it to Machine Shop 17 in record time, managin
make a grand entrance with lots of noise as she ducked around,
sometimes banged into, the piles of parts and gadgets Harper
stacked up. The apparently random mess made no sense to any
but Harper, and he would have had a major fit if ever the place
been tidied up.

"Harper!" she called out. "Harper, I need you!"

As though by magic, Harper popped up from behind a pile of
cuit boards and cases. He was holding a tool in each hand and w
ing goggles, and she could have sworn his hair was messier t
usual—a difficult achievement for Seamus Harper.

he didn't want to even speculate on the source of the stains on the
t of his shirt.

The boy genius is called," he said cheerfully. He started to push
oggles up, then realized he was about to poke himself in the face
one of his tools. He put both of them down, then pulled off the
;les. He seemed completely oblivious when one of his tools rolled
, clattered through the pile, and vanished from sight. "You know,
ce, I've been waiting *so* long to hear those words. 'Harper, I *need*
' The part of the universe that is not male but is desired by males
lays a vast and frustrating underappreciation of my sheer bril-
:e, innate talents, and general lovableness."

Harper—"

It's freakin' *unfair*. So I'm a little messy, okay, I can understand
some people might have a problem with that. Sometimes I talk a
: too much—"

Harper—"

Iow he was pacing around, carried away on the wings of his
Is. ". . . and some chicks just want the strong silent kinda
. . ."

Harper!"

Ie swung around and stared at her, a look of shock on his face.
z, Trance, no need to yell at me. I'm givin' you my complete
ition here."

he glared at him. "Was there a point?"

Huh?"

I came in and said I needed you, and you started complaining
it women, the universe, and you."

Iis eyes seemed to lose focus for a moment. Then he was back
n. "Oh. Yeah. It was freaky hearing it come from you. You're, like,
ister. My big sister."

he smiled. "We all take care of each other." She grew completely
)us again. "I need you to do something very important for me. It's
of work, and it needs to be done really fast."

he held up her hands.

Iarper's eyes went wide. "Holy—!" He took a step back and

almost fell over one of his piles. "What the hell happened? You [ ]
der someone?"

She looked sadly down at her hands. "No." She looked up at [ ]
again. "I can't explain what happened, but I got thrown into the fu[ ]
I don't know where, I don't know when, but I found Tyr. He was dy[ ]

Silently, Harper handed her a well-handled box of wet wipes [ ]
took out a few and made an effort to clean her hands. The imag[ ]
the devastated world and its burning moon refused to go away.

"I have to stop this *now*," she said, throwing the used wipes i[ ]
nearby bin. "I have to make sure we're ready, or none of us [ ]
make it."

Harper waved his hands in the air, looking desperate. "[ ]
okay, I'm gettin' *really* confused here. Is this something to do [ ]
tesseracting?"

"I don't know," she admitted. "I don't think so, but we don't [ ]
time to figure it out right now."

"And you need me to build something?"

"A lot of somethings," she said. "Actually, it's more like *rebuil[ ]*

"Uh, Trance . . . ?" Harper said. His eyes went wide.

There was a prickly feeling at the back of Trance's head. She [ ]
what she was going to see, even before she turned around.

"Seamus?" The light girlish voice was all too familiar. "[ ]
wait. . . ."

Trance turned around. A purple version of her was hanging b[ ]
tail from a railing. There was that mutual shock again.

"He's not your Seamus, is he?" Trance said.

"No, he's"—the purple Trance's tail suddenly unwrapped, an[ ]
fell, clattering, into one of Harper's unruly piles of stuff; she s[ ]
up, looking woozy, and said, affirmatively—"not." With that, sh[ ]
down, and added, "*Ow*," in a distracted sort of way.

Harper looked from one to the other, then back again, [ ]
rubbed at his hair first with one hand, then with the other h[ ]
Finally, he said, "Oooookay." He looked at Trance as thoug[ ]
wanted to ask a question, but he didn't know what the question w[ ]

"No, he's not," Trance said in a very matter-of-fact way. [ ]
looked at Harper. "She's not *my* younger self."

"Okay," he said, wincing. "If you're going to try and explain this,
n gonna have to go get drunk, because that's the only way it'll make
nse. If it makes sense."

Purple Trance was standing up again. "He *sounds* like my Seamus."

"Just how many of you guys *are* there?" Harper asked.

"I don't know," Trance said, "and I'm not going to try figuring this
t yet, I told you that." She gave the purple girl a shrewd look. "As
ng as you're here, you can help him."

That got a big smile. "I *love* to help," the other Trance said
thusiastically.

The enthusiasm unfortunately manifested in other ways, as the
rple girl tried to escape her landing place without giving too much
ught to either the effects of gravity or the random nature of the
jects she had plummeted into. Consequently she began her effort
h a surge, found herself sliding back, tried to get her balance with
 aid of her tail, and when that failed, by windmilling her arms.

That didn't work either. She vanished once more beneath the sea
 chaos, then reappeared again. "Oops." She looked at the mess
und her. "Boy, Seamus, you sure are messy." She looked up at him.
u should tidy up in here."

He didn't answer. He was too busy staring at her, either completely
azed, or simply shocked speechless.

"Just get out of there," Trance said sternly. "We need to get to
rk."

lan arrived at a jog, his force lance in his left hand and a puzzled
k on his face. "What's going on?"

Beka pointed at the blood spots on the deck. "That's going on."

Dylan crouched to take a closer look, then looked up at Beka and
mmie. "Somebody's been bleeding without permission."

"It would appear that Tyr is the culprit, Captain," Andromeda
l. "It is certainly his blood. I have no idea how it came to be on the
k here."

Dylan stood up, frowning. "I don't recall Tyr having gotten into
 fights recently. I think I would have noticed that." He looked at
a. "You *do* think I would have noticed that, right?"

She tilted her head and gave him an oh-so-patient look that him she definitely had no patience at the moment. "Dylan, we ⟨ have time for jokes."

He sighed and nodded. "It's never easy." He pressed fingers t⟨ right side of his neck, activating his subdermal comm unit. "Tyr, is Dylan."

At the sound of Dylan's voice booming over the Command D⟨ speakers, Tyr looked up from his fire control panel. He liked to tune the system as much as he could, fitting it to his style and refl⟨ Harper was a brilliant engineer, and sometimes quite impressive scruffy kludge, but he only built and maintained these systems. was the one who had to operate them. What worked well for Ha⟨ would be disastrous for him.

Rommie's android avatar was the only other person on the C⟨ mand Deck. Dylan had gone off after Beka's mysterious call.

"Dylan," Tyr drawled. "What can I do for you?"

There was a pause. Then it sounded as though Dylan was ta⟨ a deep breath. "Uh, Tyr . . . did anything happen that might ⟨ resulted in your bleeding onto my ship?"

Tyr's eyes widened in surprise. "I . . ." He glanced at Rom⟨ who was studying him intently. Well, she would find no evidenc⟨ evasion, he could be certain of that. "My dear Captain Hunt, I ⟨ no idea what you are talking about."

The flatscreens lit up with the head and shoulders displa⟨ Andromeda. "It would appear that someone using your blood ⟨ impolite enough to spill a little of it on Deck Fourteen."

The holographic Rommie shimmered into being. "She always ⟨ a bit testy when she has to send in the maid."

"I get a bit testy when we start having mysteries," the android a⟨ said. Then she smiled brightly. "On the other hand, there's alway⟨ chance I'll get to hit something and make myself feel better."

"There are other ways of relieving tension," the hologra⟨ avatar said.

"Shooting things helps, too," the ship avatar said.

That brought a scowl from the holographic avatar. "You two are impossible."

The hologram faded away.

"Well," Tyr said, raising his eyebrows and looking at the android, "at least we appear to derive some pleasure from our hobbies."

Dylan slipped his force lance back into its holster. "I guess the solution to this is going to have to wait for a while."

"If there *is* a solution," Beka said. She shook her head. "I used to think my life was crazy before, Dylan, but now I *know* it's crazy."

"Speaking of crazy," the ship avatar said, "I have a location on Trance."

Dylan nodded. "Where is she?"

"That would be the crazy part. Which one?"

Beka and Dylan looked at each other, startled. "Which—" Dylan started.

"Coming through!"

Dylan and Beka turned together, surprised by the shout. Both immediately stepped sideways, getting out of the way of the golden figure racing toward them. Without pause she dashed between them.

Dylan and Beka turned simultaneously again. "Trance—!" Dylan shouted.

Trance turned 180 degrees without pausing, running backward. "I can't have time!" she called back, before turning back. She ran into an intersection and out of sight.

"Well," Beka said, staring at the intersection, "*that* was a White Rabbit moment." Dylan was looking puzzled. "*Alice in Wonderland.*"

It didn't help. "Somebody can explain it later," Dylan said. He nodded at the intersection. "Where's she headed?"

"I have no idea," the ship avatar said. "She disappeared as soon as she went past the intersection."

"There's nothing wrong with your sensors?" Beka asked.

"Nothing. Harper's been upgrading me consistently since the tuners attacked."

The holographic avatar said, "We've both noticed some cu[r] anomalies, however."

"Unfortunately, I have not managed to analyze them as yet," ship avatar added. "They occur without warning, and are extre[m] brief, from the picosecond to microsecond range. They might be tial anomalies of some kind."

"Could we be passing through a region where this sort of t[...] can happen?" Beka said.

"Not that I know of," the ship avatar said. "If so, it would be type we have never before encountered. Most spatial distortion gravitic phenomenon of one kind or another, such as the re[...] around a black hole."

"It's possible that some kind of temporal distortion is involv[ed] the holographic avatar said. "Dimensional distortion is also w[ithin] the realm of possibility."

"In other words," Dylan said heavily, "we don't know, we [...] know, and guessing will just drive us nuts."

"I would say that covers it," the ship avatar said.

Beka had now worked up to her I-don't-believe-this express[...] With her full mouth and big eyes, this gave her almost a chil[d] look. She pushed her hair back with a hand. "I love my job."

"Dylan," the ship avatar went on, "I didn't finish telling you a[bout] Trance's location."

"We just *saw* Trance's location," Beka said.

"One of them," Andromeda said. "I also have her on visua[l] Machine Shop Seventeen."

"For how long?" Dylan said.

"She was there before you were almost run down."

"Alright. Any sign of an anomaly there?"

"One," the holographic avatar said.

"Which might explain the *other* Trance," the ship avatar added

"Other Trance?" Dylan and Beka echoed together.

"Purple," the ship avatar added.

"I think we'd better go and look," Dylan said.

"I'd say that's the captain-y thing to do, Captain Hunt," Beka [said]

"I'd have to agree, Captain Valentine," he responded.

They started off at a quick jog. "Do you think the universe is ready
more than one Trance?"

Beka had her I-don't-believe-it face on again. "I know *I'm* not."

arper, this is Dylan. We're on our way down there."

Harper looked up from his workbench, his face twisting into an
mutation of a frown and a sneer. "Y'know, Trance, I really, really
er it when the boss stays up on his perch and leaves his favorite
genius to, well . . ." He thought for a moment, and finished with,
. genius. Geniusize?"

The two Trances exchanged a look. With a smile, the purple one
, "I love him anyway."

Harper flicked a row of switches. "Do you mind? You're freakin'
out here."

I am?" they said simultaneously.

Harper?" Dylan said over the comm. "Speak to me."

Harper punched a button, then pressed the side of his neck. "Oh,
oss. Sorry about that, just got lost in the sheer dazzling light of
own brilliance there. What's up?"

Golden Trance was rolling her eyes, while the purple one snick-
. He realized that he had really paid very little attention to the
all change in her personality since the switch. All that had really
ered was that she had been just about his best friend since she
joined the *Eureka Maru* crew.

was still freaky that this particular version of the purple Trance
rently had a slightly closer relationship with some alternate ver-
of him than plain old best friend. It rattled him even more that
lidn't seem to be bothered by the fact that *he* was the alternate
on from her viewpoint.

s Trance with you?" Dylan said.

he question made him uncomfortable and cautious. He felt as
gh he'd been caught doing something bad.

Uh, yeah," he finally said. He glanced at both of them. After a
ent, he made up his mind. It wasn't a hard decision, considering
he was feeling more and more guilty with each passing second.
're gonna ask how many, aren't you?"

The machine-shop door opened. Beka and Dylan walke glancing from side to side, and then staring straight at the Trances.

"I've got two," Harper said. "So how many do you have, boss

Dylan and Beka looked at each other, then at Harper. "(Dylan said.

"Sorta," Beka added. "She disappeared."

The holographic Rommie shimmered into life. "On the hand, it could be two, as I detected one on Deck Fourteen, just b Beka discovered the blood."

Harper and the golden Trance looked at each other. Fi Trance said, "It's still only one, then. That was me. The blo mean." She frowned. "I guess the other Trance could be me, know I was here when . . ."

She trailed off, looking completely lost.

"That was Tyr's blood," Dylan said.

"I know," Trance said. "I didn't kill him, I promise. Some else did."

Beka pushed her hair back with both hands this time. "You l Trance, sometimes listening to you is cause for a migraine."

"I can't help it!" Trance snapped. "I'm not in control of e thing. Something threw me forward in time, and then pulled me again. I guess there was something I needed to know."

"About Tyr?" Dylan asked.

"About the way things could be." To Harper it seemed tha took on a strange and desperate look. "There are so many place times that things could go bad. . . . Dylan, I just need you to trusting me, that's all."

Dylan seemed about to say something, and then stopped.

"We're still your good-luck charm," the purple Trance said.

Beka and Dylan exchanged looks.

"What *I* want to know," Harper said, looking back up fro workbench, "is whether that's double the luck, or luck squared. F way it's ultra-freakin'-cool." He hunched over his workbench a "Anyway, could you guys take it somewhere else and let the Ei of the spaceways get his work done?"

Einstein was a theoretician," the holographic Rommie said, primly.

"Theoretician, shmeoretician," Harper said with a sneer. "Okay, so what? So old Al never picked up a screwdriver or a soldering iron, he was still a pretty damn smart guy, which is the point I'm tryin' to make here, folks, because Mrs. Harper's boy Seamus is *also* real smart, as well as being a practical magician. Y'know, the difficult we do right away, the impossible takes an hour longer?"

"I love it when he babbles," Beka said with a sigh.

"You do?" Dylan answered.

She looked at him. "You sometimes have trouble with irony, don't you?"

"So what do we do about this?"

"Frankly, I don't know." She looked over at the purple version of Trance, who gave her a sunny smile in return. Harper knew neither she nor Dylan had a clue what the three of them were working on. Whether Andromeda did was another matter. "Wait and see, I guess. Always worked out pretty well when it comes to Trance."

"Okay." Dylan turned to Harper. "Well, Mr. Harper, carry on. Just not to accumulate too many Trances."

"Yeah, really," Harper muttered.

"Dylan?" Tyr's voice boomed tinnily in the scattered confines of the machine shop. "You'd better get back up here."

Dylan pressed the side of his neck. "On my way." He sighed. "It never stops."

He and Beka left.

The holographic Rommie glanced around, then looked straight at Harper. "You really ought to tidy this place up, Harper."

She faded out.

"Everyone's a critic," Harper grumbled. He swung around, tapped a keyboard for a moment, then stabbed at another button. "Showtime!" He grinned, and then grew serious again as he looked at the two Trances. "This is going to max out our supplies, you know that? Rommie's gonna have to suck down a couple of asteroids to make it up."

"As long as it works," Trance said. "I have to go."

"Where?"

"Command." She frowned. "I think. The way this day is goin
could be anywhere."

With that, she left.

"Y'know," Harper said, leaning back in his chair, "that took
less time than it could have. Which is why I'm the genius and so r
other folks aren't me." He frowned. "Okay, I think that made se

"You've always known what to do," the younger Trance said.

Suddenly she was in his lap, her arms around his neck and he
wrapped around him. "Ah, jeez!" he exclaimed, standing bolt up
and dumping Trance to the deck.

"Ow?" she said.

"Okay," he said, backing up. "Too freaky. Wayyyy too freak
me."

She got up, dusting herself off. "Okay." She smiled and
scampering off.

"Freaky," Harper repeated to himself as he sat down again.

In the *Andromeda Ascendant*'s missile construction facility busines
proceeding smoothly, but swiftly. Drones sped to and fro with r
rials while the robotic assembly arms did their work. As each
missile, its warhead firmly in place, was completed it was picked
a robot crane and deposited carefully in an eight-space rack.

The machines worked with a steady, precise rhythm, disgorg
new missile every two minutes.

Offensive missiles, Andromeda noted, not a single defensive
sile among them. That was okay; she was well stocked with those
was quite intrigued by the payloads, but had already decided n
say anything to Dylan yet.

Still, she had to wonder what Harper and Trance were up to.

"This is not the way I wanted to get my exercise," Dylan compl
as he and Beka jogged into the Command Deck. He had his
lance out again, while Beka had drawn her Gauss pistol. Arriving
pared to shoot was always a good idea these days.

Beka didn't answer. No surprise there. He was at a loss for w
himself at the moment.

Tyr was standing to his left, at the fire control station. Rommie
s standing to his right. Both of them were turning their heads
istantly.

"Too weird," Dylan finally said.

"That's what I like, Captain," the android avatar said. "A good
ective analysis."

The Command Deck was a chaos of motion and light. Versions of
ince were appearing and disappearing in ghostly, shimmering
rs, often moving around the deck as though in fast-forward. He
ild recognize Trance in some of the phantoms, but others were lit-
more than moving blurs. None of them seemed aware of the oth-
, or of those on the Command Deck who were watching them.

Dylan turned at the sound of running feet. For a moment he
in't sure if *this* Trance had any more substance than the others, but
hand on his arm confirmed her as real. Well, apparently real.

'Something, somewhere, is very broken," Beka said, wonderment
ler voice.

Trance was staring at the odd ballet. "Oh, no."

'Have you done something we should know about?" Tyr said
dly.

Trance shook her head, not saying anything.

Rommie strode toward them, ignoring the phantoms as she walked
ough them. "Is there anything you can tell us about this, Trance?
ything at all?"

Trance closed her eyes for a moment, then opened them again. "It
t happening now."

'Very odd," Tyr said, raising his eyebrows, "considering that it is
te evidently happening now. Unless we are all being deceived in
ie fashion."

'No, we're not," Rommie said firmly. "It's real."

"That isn't what I mean," Trance said. "I mean it's being triggered
iewhere in the future. I just don't know by what. Or when. Or why."

'Let me guess," Rommie said. "You don't know how, either."

Trance shook her head.

Dylan holstered his force lance again. "Whatever this is, it seems
be harmless. So far." One of the phantoms glided up to him,

paused for a moment, then moved away again. "On the other h
it's weird and creepy too."

Trance looked up at him, seemingly dismayed. "You think
weird and creepy?"

Beka holstered her Gauss pistol finally. "Trance, some days yo
weird and creepy, and I think that's exactly what you want."

"Not this time," Trance said. She reached out tentatively
another of her phantom reflections came up. The figure swirled
vanished. "I just want to know what's going on." She looked genui
lost, Dylan realized. "What it means."

"What it means," Tyr said, leaning against his console, his a
crossed over his muscular chest, "is that we have no doubt had
aboard this vessel for far too long." He turned his head to watch
ghostly figures flickering around him. "I, for one, would prefer
reality to be more stable, less mutable, and free of enigma."

"This sort of thing bothers me, too, Tyr," Rommie said. "I k
there's no supernatural aspect to this, but the lack of a concrete ex
nation is very annoying."

Dylan walked down onto the Command Deck. Rommie smoo
turned and followed him, stopping next to him as he took his c
mand station. After a brief pause, Beka followed, looking a lot
certain.

"Andromeda," Dylan said, looking around, "any idea what's g
on here?"

Andromeda's head and shoulders appeared on screens around
bridge. "None. Obviously, these manifestations are nothing like t
we saw earlier."

"No kidding," Beka said.

Trance had yet to follow Dylan and Beka. Dylan turned aroun
look at her. She was staring at the phantoms as they moved aro
seemingly hypnotized. One moved up to her, and once again
reached out. As before, the phantom wavered and vanished.

Rommie's holographic avatar shimmered into life. "I believe w
experiencing quantum mechanics in action here. What we're se
may be occurring in real time, but not in this dimension."

"Something's made the walls between probability lines t

nce said. "None of this is real, it's just possibilities leaking
ough."

"The things that could be?" Dylan said. His universe was starting
eel surreal, never a good thing.

"The things that will never be," Trance said. Hesitantly she
ked into Command. The phantoms swirled and vanished as she
ved through them. "These are the echoes left over after decisions
made."

"I think I will stick with clear decisions, then," Tyr said. He
rted derisively and turned away from her.

Beka said, "Trance, this has got to have something to do with you."

"I know," Trance said. She closed her eyes for a moment. Suddenly
phantoms started to fade away. She opened her eyes and looked at
a. "It isn't just me, though. I just can't put it all together."

"Looks like you've got it under control," Dylan said, feeling more
eful than convinced.

"Maybe," Trance said, looking at him. "I don't know if I did that,
t just happened."

Command was clear now. "Well, whoever and whatever, some-
g appears to have worked."

"Unfortunately," Andromeda said, her flatscreen image looking very
oyed, "I am still having a great deal of difficulty locating any energy
rces that might be responsible for these various phenomena."

"Does that mean you've got something?" Beka asked.

"Little more than before," Andromeda said. "Picosecond-length
e energy bursts with no immediately identifiable signature."

Dylan sighed. If it wasn't one thing, it was another. He would have
d to complain about the way the universe was treating him, but he
w all too well that a case could be made that he had set himself up
he first place.

"And there's another one," Andromeda added. "Machine Shop
enteen."

Dylan and Beka started away from their stations, giving each other
ary look.

"Hey, Boss." It was Harper. His head and shoulders appeared on a
en next to Andromeda's image.

Dylan and Beka stopped. "Mr. Harper," Dylan said.

"If you guys picked up anything up there, it's 'cause she just le

"Left?" Beka said.

"Like, *poof*, left," Harper said, looking and sounding anno "One second she's jumping in my lap and making with the con ments and . . . uh, yeah, anyway . . . then she just vanishes." D and Beka looked at Trance, who gave them an embarrassed shru return. "I gotta tell you, this whole experience just about freake out, and you know I don't freak that easily anymore."

"Jumping in your lap," Dylan echoed. The image that prese itself made it difficult for him to think.

"An exhibition of frighteningly poor taste," Tyr grumbled. " not surprised."

"She wasn't me," Trance said weakly. "That is, she was me, I different me than me."

"Trance," Rommie said, giving her an almost cross-eyed l "please don't."

"Oh. Okay."

"This is getting confusing," Beka said.

"Getting?" Dylan responded. "I'm at the point where I can't think in straight lines anymore." He turned and went back to his tion, rubbing at his forehead. "Okay, something is going on here don't know what and we don't know why, and we could waste our running around in circles trying to figure it out."

"Okay," Beka said, giving him a puzzled look. "So what are saying here, exactly?"

"We proceed as planned," Dylan said firmly.

"Into the valley of death," Tyr said darkly. He tilted his he look at Dylan. "I am overcome with joy."

"Until we get some clear answers," Dylan said, allowing a c manding edge into his voice, "we might as well go on to Kantar.'

To Dylan's surprise, he saw Tyr shiver. It was barely notice but it was there, as though he were reacting to a cold draft. "I an uncomfortable . . . with this."

"Uncomfortable or not, Tyr, it's our job," Dylan said, the ed voice growing sharper. He focused, unblinkingly, on Tyr's eyes.

til we get some answers, and figure out what we need to do about
e phenomena, we're going to do that job."

here was a long silent moment as Dylan and Tyr watched each
r. There had been a time when this kind of confrontation had
more than its share of danger. Tyr's collection of plots and plans
g with his innate sense of self-preservation had made their early
ionship an aggressive balancing act.

inally Tyr nodded. "Very well. I shall acquiesce to your intent, sir,
e hope that this course will prove fruitful rather than dangerous."

Think of it as a vacation," Dylan said.

Right," Beka said, giving him a disbelieving look. "A vacation."

tle under two hours later they were ready for the final Slip jump
antar. This had not been the simplest of journeys—most of the
a starship could get from one place to another with one or two
, with little additional transit time. This journey had taken them
Slips, with one Slipstream portal separated from the next by at
a day of normal-space travel at their highest velocity. It would
taken less time and effort to do a grand tour of the three galaxies.

ylan, Beka thought, desperately wanted to get away, even if his
of getting away meant going *somewhere*. As far as Beka had
ys been concerned, getting away meant *getting away*—no destina-
no direction, just running hell for leather away from whatever
najor problem was.

e had learned, painfully, that she couldn't outrun herself—and
was exactly what she had been trying to run from. The ever-
ing list of failures, weaknesses, and miscalculations that had
ed to plague her life was something she could never escape, no
er how hard she tried.

ars after falling in with Dylan she still had her flaws, her weak-
s. Staying emotionally and mentally afloat sometimes became a
e that left her exhausted.

ylan was under no illusions about her, she knew that. It didn't
to matter to him. He had faith in her ability to get the job done.

He had faith in all of them. Having known so many people in her
who would exploit every weakness, every flaw, she had been surpr
by Dylan Hunt. Sure, he wanted to exploit her talents as a pilot, ju
he wanted to exploit Harper's talents as an engineer, but he had d
so in a way that she had never known—bolstering her confidence
putting his trust in her. He respected her, both as a pilot and a per

She smiled as she reached up and hit the switch that brough
Slipstream console down. There was a full complement on the C
mand Deck now, Harper having emerged from his playpen—
one Trance, she was happy to see. Tyr, at his console, looke
though he was about to go to sleep but she trusted that about as m
as she expected her Uncle Sid to take up the Way.

She made some quick adjustments on her consoles, then gra
the pilot handles firmly, instantly picking up the flow of the *And*
eda Ascendant.

Still smiling, she increased their velocity by five PSL—five per
of the speed of light. She had always believed that the faster a
entered a Slipstream portal the easier it was to navigate.

That . . . and she liked to fly fast.

Time.

She let herself flow into the system as she opened the Slipstr
runners.

Automatically, she said, "Transiting to Slipstream in fiv
four . . . three . . . two . . . one. . . ."

Light, noise, everything blurring. She hardly noticed, lost ir
world. As the ship whipped and spun through the streams, she ca
reached out, making sense of the chaos. She found the thread
needed, aligned the immense craft, and caught the streams ir
runners.

Almost done.

Breathing steadily, her focus taken completely by the task at h
she guided *Andromeda* through the tangled web of Slipstream.
was something only beings with a flesh and blood component c
do; synthetic life-forms such as Rommie could not find their
through the Slipstream—*Andromeda* had once been propelled ir
after her first encounter with the Magog Worldship; with the e

w having died at the hands of the Magog she had spent a year lost,
ble to find her way out again.

assable Slipstream pilots could be found everywhere—Dylan,
per, and Tyr among them. Trance kept pretending to be a klutz,
Beka didn't believe it for a second.

Dylan had told her repeatedly how good she was, how much of a
n pilot she was. She accepted that. It helped to define her.

One day it had simply come to her. She wasn't just good. She was
best. Nobody could come close to her.

The streams snapped and whipped. Leaning into the shifts, play-
the controls by feel, she kept pace with the changes.

Time.

She played the grips, slipping *Andromeda* from one set of streams
nother, then another. A final shift and she brought the ship back
into normal space. *Andromeda* was traveling at close to maximum
city; Beka intended to trim back to something a little more con-
ative eventually, but for the moment she wanted the last leg to be
r as quickly as possible.

She released the grips, grinning. She reached up and turned the
stream hood off, stretching as it rose back to its rest position.

She turned to Dylan, who was standing at his console in parade
position, something that she always found amusing—he just
dn't shake the years of training and practice.

Mission accomplished," she said. "We're right on target."

Dylan was about to answer when Andromeda's image suddenly
aced some of the tactical displays. "Captain, we have an incoming
smission."

There was a brief hiss, then a clear metallic voice—a recording,
an guessed. ". . . territorial boundary. You are ordered to turn
k immediately. If you cross our system border we will take imme-
e action against you. Unidentified vessel: you are approaching the
tar System territorial boundary. You are ordered to turn back
hediately. . . ."

Dylan looked startled. "Not quite the reception you expected?"
a asked.

No," he said. "Kantar never used to be hostile."

"Stop here and try Plan B?" Beka said.

"What's Plan B?" Harper asked. "And why doesn't anybody
tell me about this stuff?"

"Because Plan B, Mr. Harper," Dylan said, "consists of makin
up as we go along." He turned to Beka. "Plan B it is. We'll try
contact the Kantar government, and if there's no joy there, we'll
somewhere else."

"Coming to a stop," she said, reaching for her controls.

Andromeda reappeared on the flatscreens. "Captain, the mess
just changed."

Beka started trimming *Andromeda*'s velocity, bringing the star
to a graceful halt.

"Alright," Dylan said. "Let's hear what they're saying now."

". . . repeat: bring your vessel to a stop immediately and prepar
be boarded. Follow the instructions you are given, or we will dest
you. Respond."

The tactical displays flashed up as Andromeda said, "They seen
be using an advanced stealth technique, and they are very fast. /
there's a lot of them."

Dylan stared at the tactical displays. Beka readied herself
Dylan's orders—just giving up wasn't an option.

"Let's give him a response," Dylan said finally. "This is Cap
Dylan Hunt of the *Andromeda Ascendant*. Who are you?"

The central display screen cleared. The head and shoulders of
tense-looking middle-aged man appeared. "I know you, Cap
Hunt."

Dylan raised his eyebrows. "I don't believe I've had the pleasur

The man's eyes didn't waver. "I am Colonel Willard Kaczyns
command the Fourth Battalion of the Kantaran Lighthouse Ke
ers. Stand down and prepare to be boarded. I will offer no furt
warning."

In my heart, I have never seen the point of killing when
embarrassment will do. Put aside the perfect blow and
instead seek a way to break your opponent's belt and buttons, so that he stumbles upon his fallen trousers.

—KORENDO MASTER OF MASTERS SHIAHN,
THE SUBSTANCE OF STYLE,
CY 8233 (3RD REVISION)

veryone turned to look at Trance. She, in turn, was staring at the
ntral display as the colonel's image vanished and was replaced by
e of the tactical displays.

"Oh, no," she whispered.

Before Dylan could say anything, she turned and ran from the
mmand Deck. He didn't spend any time worrying about her; this
sn't the time.

"Beka," he said, "get us out of here."

"You've got it," she said.

Andromeda appeared on several of the flatscreens. "Captain, they
 activating weapons. Firing. We have six incoming missiles."

On the tactical display half a dozen triangles had appeared, con-
ging on *Andromeda.*

"Countermeasures," he ordered. This was just what he needed to
mplete his day—a battle for absolutely no good reason. "Damn it."

Andromeda unfurled her huge electronic countermeasure fans. Glo
ing a soft violet, the ECM fans were intended to confuse and j
enemy radar and the sensors on incoming missiles. Ship-to-ship w
fare was a tricky business, made trickier yet by the certain knowle
that any given opponent might well be equipped with the mean
make any kind of countermeasures pointless.

The ECM fans were the gentler part of the equation. Even as t
were unfolding, defensive missiles shot from ten of _Andromeda_'s fo
launch tubes. A handful of drones followed them into space, ready
provide guidance and communications.

Warfare in space had come a long way from the days when suc
meant being the one who could hit hardest, fastest, and long
There was always a bigger ship with more powerful weapons. W
counted these days was strategy and sheer cleverness.

Ten defensive missiles shot toward the incoming half dozen. 7
battle should have been a foregone conclusion.

"Missed?" Dylan said.

"All ten," Rommie said.

"According to the telemetry," Andromeda said, her image appe
ing on the flatscreens, "they didn't even see the attacking missiles.'

"Oh, great," Beka muttered. "Now what?"

"Brace for impact," Andromeda said, in a very matter-of-fact w

Everyone except for Rommie grabbed a console or the near
reliable object.

The Command Deck reverberated to the explosions, one af
another in rapid succession. The ship vibrated as though she had b
picked up and shaken—one of the curses of the antigravity syst
On the one hand, the AG field effectively reduced the ship's mass
few grams, allowing for some impressive maneuvers. On the ot
hand, when she took a forceful enough hit, it could be a painful ex
rience for the crew. Dylan had once compared it to being insid
giant baby rattle with a very angry baby doing the rattling.

Rommie, staying perfectly balanced, said, "Either their armam
is very weak, or they just baby-tapped us as a warning."

"I believe it was a warning," Tyr said. "I'm not too excited by this
uation. I suggest we blow them out of the sky."

"That's an option," Dylan said. He took a deep breath, not willing
commit to acts of destruction just yet. "I'm going to hold that in
serve."

"And give them time to destroy us as they have already threat-
ed?" Tyr was definitely unhappy about this course of action, which
s too bad. Tyr wasn't the one making the decisions.

"Until I say otherwise, Tyr," Dylan said, "we'll stick with defensive
asures only. We don't know just what we're up against here, or the
erall strength we're facing. Let them play their hand."

"We're just going to sit here and see what happens?" Beka said,
ing him a concerned look.

Dylan shook his head. "Get ready to start backing up on my signal.
wly, then pick up velocity. Maybe we can get out of here without
much more insanity." He looked back at Tyr. "Tyr, ready on
es one through forty, defensive only, get ready to lock in a firing
ution as soon as they open up . . . *if* they open up. Andromeda, see
ou can get Colonel Kaczynski to talk to us."

Tyr gave Dylan a sullen look, then turned his attention to the cen-
screen. Dylan ignored Tyr's studied display of attitude.

"He's answering," Andromeda said.

The center tactical screen cleared to display Colonel Kaczynski's
d and shoulders once again. "Well?" the man said brusquely.

"I'm not too impressed by anything except your rudeness," Dylan
, half smiling. He had never been one for displays of contempt,
Tyr had, over time, taught him its value as a tool. The trick was in
ping it subdued enough that it wouldn't provoke an immediate
ressive response. "Now that you've let off some steam, would you
d telling me what the hell is on your mind here?"

Kaczynski was silent for a moment, staring. Dylan had gone from
nding relaxed to wrapping his words in ice and steel.

Finally, the colonel found his voice again. "You are trespassing on
reign territory. That's what's on my mind. I've already explained
consequences of that."

"Fine," Dylan said, his tone of voice not changing in the slightest.

He was really getting tired of idiotic behavior, whether from indiv uals or from planetary governments as a whole. "I'll take my ship of here, and let the Commonwealth know that Kantar is off-limit

"Oh, *please!*" Kaczynski said contemptuously. Dylan was caugh surprise. "I am not going to be so easily deluded, Hunt."

"What?" Dylan was at a loss now. "Our purpose here was to br the Commonwealth charter to Kantar. You don't want anything tc with the Commonwealth, fine, we just turn around and go away."

"Oh, yes," Kaczynski said. "Just like the Commonwealth has d with several other sovereign systems." Dylan started to object, t closed his mouth. Since the new Commonwealth had begun to fo there had been quite a bit in the way of underhanded dealing black ops. He had done his best to stay away from that aspect of Commonwealth, but it wasn't always possible. "These things eve ally come back to bite you on the ass, Captain."

"Alright," Dylan said. "You've no love for the new Comm wealth. But I remember Kantar being a loyal and open member of old Systems Commonwealth."

"You'll have plenty of time to read our history texts, Capta Kaczynski said. "Provided that you surrender, of course."

"I'd like to hear a summary anyway," Dylan said. "Humor an High Guard officer."

Rommie started to correct him. Dylan waved her to silence, le ing her looking baffled.

"Your precious Commonwealth abandoned us, Hunt. *That* is summary. Nothing to spare for the peripheral worlds, no supp during the conflict with the Nietzscheans." The colonel's face reddening slightly now. "And once all was in disarray, with the H Guard routed, what did our Vedran masters do?"

"Nobody knows what happened to Tarn-Vedra," Dylan said so Kaczynski snorted. "And you believe that?"

"I know that," Dylan said. "Tarn-Vedra is . . . was . . . my ho world."

Kaczynski seemed taken aback by that. "Then you have mad attempt to reach it?"

Dylan glanced at Beka. She was looking worried now. He tur

is attention back to the screen. "We made an attempt. We believe we might have made it about halfway there."

"Somehow," Kaczynski said bitterly, "they broke down the Slipstream routes to Tarn-Vedra. The last reports—"

"Are that Tarn-Vedra itself vanished completely," Dylan said. "now."

"It wasn't destroyed in the war," Kaczynski said. "We were *abandoned*. Made dependent upon your damned Systems Commonwealth, and then abandoned to bloody insanity. The Vedrans could have stopped what happened, but they chose to run away."

"Maybe," Dylan said. He wasn't going to let himself be drawn by Kaczynski's statements. Dylan had received some answers over time, enough to suggest that the Vedrans had somehow taken their entire system and moved it . . . somewhere else. Where, exactly, was the question. How they had done it was just as big a question to contemplate.

"There is no 'maybe' here, Hunt. The Vedrans ran." He paused a moment. "The Lighthouse Keepers are the direct result of that. We became a target for raiders and vandals, for Nietzschean pirates looking for easy pickings."

"So you learned to fight back," Dylan said. "And to protect your borders. Not a bad thing if you don't take it too far."

"Don't mistake us for ignorant isolationists, Captain. We maintain our sources."

Dylan signaled to Beka. "I don't mistake you for anything, Colo-"

Beka played her controls, nudging the *Andromeda* into motion. While the ship was subject to all normal laws of physics the thrust from her engines could be aimed in any direction—and given the considerable power generated by those engines and the AG field that reduced her mass, the *Andromeda Ascendant* could carry out flight maneuvers that would have left many other ships spreading parts across a cubic light-second of space.

"You will not find us unkind, Captain," Kaczynski said. He had calmed down now, apparently taking Dylan's willingness to talk as a concession of some kind.

"On the contrary, Colonel," Dylan said sternly. "So far this has

been a quite unpleasant encounter." Dylan took a deep breath, ⟨
aware that he was committing them all to a potentially disastr⟨
course of action. "I think it's time we called it a day and went our s⟨
arate ways."

Kaczynski sighed. "That will not be possible, Hunt."

"That remains to be seen."

"You are hardly the first . . ." The colonel trailed off, looking d⟨
for a moment, then back up. His face was suddenly a cold, dispassi⟨
ate mask. "I see. You're a damned fool, Captain Hunt."

The screen blanked, then returned to tactical display.

"No more need to be sneaky," Beka said.

"Best speed to the Slip point," Dylan said, "and then anywhere
here."

"The Kantaran ships are on the move, Captain," Andromeda s⟨

"Oh, this is good," Harper said. "This is *really* good. As if my
didn't already suck enough."

"You've had worse," Tyr said. He looked calmly down at his
control panel. "Shall I begin destroying them now?"

"I don't think we need to do that," Dylan said. "Which doe⟨
mean we shouldn't defend ourselves."

"I think that would be a very good idea," Rommie said. She ⟨
glancing from her console to the main screens and back. "I'm det⟨
ing multiple missile launches, as well as plasma and particle be⟨
weapons at full charge."

"This Colonel Kaczynski seems determined to piss me off," D⟨
grumbled.

"Hey," Harper said from somewhere behind him, "he already ⟨
ceeded with me. I'm all for giving him an ass-kicking."

"Mr. Harper," Dylan said mildly, "shut the hell up. Tyr, we ne⟨
firing solution that'll give us a broad spread."

Tyr's hands were already in motion, but he gave Dylan a dubi⟨
look. "Our weapons proved useless last time. Why should—"

"It's a distraction," Beka said, grinning. "We'll get some of ⟨
incoming. It's the shotgun approach."

"It's the expensive approach," Rommie said. "We'll have to s⟨

tting nasty if this keeps up—our defensive stockpile won't last
rever."

"It doesn't have to," Dylan said. He turned to Tyr. "Bring the PDL
rrets and AP cannons on-line. Split control with Rommie and
ka." He turned to Beka. "How are we doing?"

"Approaching fifty PSL," she said. "I think that's the fastest I've
er backed up."

"The Kantarans are starting to outpace us," Andromeda said. On
e screen a number of fast-moving triangles winked out. "The good
ws is that we just took out thirty percent of their missiles."

"Keep it up until we run out," Dylan said. "They're not going to
p."

"Then we should demonstrate our seriousness," Tyr said, an edge
anger in his voice. "I say to hell with this game!"

"Oh, great," Harper said. "Just what we need. A mutiny, and
ess what, it's our favorite Nietzschean. So what the hell did we
pect?"

"Harper," Beka snapped, "shut up."

Dylan didn't move. No threatening gestures, no posturing, noth-
; to worsen Tyr's attitude. "Mr. Anasazi, this is not a time for argu-
nts. Do your job."

Without answering, Tyr turned back to his console. Forty new tri-
gles sped outward from *Andromeda*'s image on the screens. Almos
mediately, another forty followed.

It wasn't going to be enough.

"Time to Slipstream?" he said.

"Thirty seconds," Beka answered.

"Another thirty percent," Andromeda said. "The last volley look
ely to account for fifteen percent of the missiles launched in th
st thirty seconds."

Tyr loaded and launched another volley.

"Captain—" Andromeda started.

He had already seen it. Five Kantaran fighters, in formation, ha
ldenly gained velocity and were outrunning their own missiles.

"Tyr, Beka, Rommie," he said quickly, "target the missiles with th

AP cannons. Get a lock on those fighters and discourage them—cl[e]
fire only, don't shoot anyone down." Not yet, anyway, he thought.

One by one the missiles were vanishing from the tactical screen[.]

The Kantaran formation, however, kept coming.

"I cannot get a lock," Tyr snapped. He slapped his console, fr[us]
trated.

"Lay down fire anyway," Dylan said. "We just need to cover—"

"Trouble," Rommie said. "There's a line of fighters in our way. [We]
won't be able to go to Slipstream."

The Kantaran formation slowly broke apart, each of the five sh[ips]
coming in on a different vector.

"Evasive," Dylan snapped.

"Too late," Andromeda said. "Hold on."

Almost immediately a series of loud thuds and bangs resona[ted]
through the ship. The deck lurched beneath their feet. Harper l[ost]
his balance, coming down heavily. More explosions followed as b[oth]
fighters and missiles chewed at *Andromeda*'s hull.

Harper ducked and rolled as sparks cascaded from nearby pan[els.]
"Jeez, Rommie, did the folks who made you stick fireworks behind
the panels, or what?"

"I'm a sensitive girl, Mr. Harper," the ship replied primly. "[We]
have another formation incoming."

On the tactical screen, another five ships had formed up and w[ere]
sweeping in. This was getting to be consistently irritating.

"Evasive!" Dylan snapped. There was no indication of cou[rse]
change. Beka should have been whipping the ship through all ki[nds]
of unlikely maneuvers by now—even if they couldn't shake th[ese]
guys, they didn't have to make their job easy. "Beka, you can start a[ny]
time now."

He turned angrily, staring at her. Didn't she get it? Her failure [to]
follow his commands endangered his ship. Endangered all of them[.]

Beka was frozen in place, lost in some kind of panic. Great, af[ter]
all this time as his XO she had to go to pieces *now*.

Explosions thundered across the hull, and the ship shook. Harp[er,]
still on his hands and knees, scuttled out of the way of more casca[d]
ing sparks. "Y'know, this stuff *really* sucks!" He pushed himself to

"So much for all that great Commonwealth engineering, huh?
t a load of junk."

will excuse your rudeness, Mr. Harper," Andromeda said. "I
you to start taking care of the more major issues occurring
n my power and engine systems."

Vhat she means, *kludge*," Tyr said in a mocking tone, "is get your
lless carcass out of here and cease being an annoying bug." He
d to Dylan. "What the hell is wrong with her?"

low the hell should I know?" Dylan snapped. "I'm a ship's cap-
not a psychologist." Dylan strode over to Beka's station. "Beka!"
urned her head to look at him, but it was the thousand-meter
of the lost. "*Captain Valentine!*"

:r mouth worked silently for a moment, then she whispered,
n . . . Dylan, I . . ."

»h, the hell with it," Dylan muttered.

: hauled off and slapped her in the face with his right hand,
ing her head back.

»oookay, that's it, I'm outta here," Harper said, and with that he
out of Command.

ka was suddenly sobbing like a little girl. "Dylan, I can't do it, I
lo it!"

: sighed. More explosions rocked them, spinning the ship.
'e getting killed here," he snarled, glaring at her, "and you're
ing yourself a goddamn pity party? *Not on my ship!*"

: hauled off again to backhand her across the other cheek, see-
:r flinch. He never completed the movement—Rommie had
d with blinding speed and grabbed his wrist. She didn't squeeze
but it still made him gasp. "Dylan, what do you think you're
?"

hat's *Captain Hunt*," Dylan growled, glaring at her. "I'm trying
p her out of whatever state she's in."

's what she needs," Tyr said, sounding almost reasonable. He
d up at the ceiling, his eyes tracking the positions of explosions
: outside of the ship.

'hat she needs," Rommie echoed, her angry look going from
» the other. "Brutalizing her is what she needs? I don't know

what's going on right now, *Dylan*, but if you ever do somethin
that again, I will immobilize you."

"Don't you threaten me," Dylan snapped. "I'll have you disa
bled!"

"We can discuss this later," Rommie said. "Right now we h
battle to fight." She released his wrist and pushed him back
"Beka, I'll take over."

Beka gave her a pathetically grateful look. "Thanks . . . I jus
just can't."

With another angry look at Dylan, Rommie slipped her hand
the controls. "Evasive maneuvers, aye . . . Captain."

"It's about time," the ship avatar said.

Dylan and Tyr both lunged for consoles to anchor themselve
Rommie, connecting with her ship-self, was too fast for them.
Andromeda Ascendant began full-power maneuvers, both Dyla
Tyr were thrown backward. Both men landed heavily. Dylan,
regret, landed on his tailbone.

"Sorry," Rommie said with deliberate insincerity. She al
Dylan a small, sarcastic smile. As he got back to his feet,
noticed that Rommie had reached out and held on to Beka, pr
ing her from taking a tumble.

"Disassembly," Dylan hissed.

Rommie's smile vanished.

The thunder of explosions diminished, but Dylan knew it wa
a matter of time before the Kantarans got a lock on them again

Tyr had gotten up as well, and he had the darkest, angriest e
sion Dylan had ever seen on him. Great. More trouble. His
went to his force lance. Tyr, seeing this, slowly folded his arm
his chest.

"I don't need the two of you growling at each other like
dogs," Rommie snapped. "If you can't do *something*, get the h
of Command!"

"I'm *in* command," Dylan growled. "Remember that."

"And I, *sir*," Tyr snarled, "have no desire to work alongsi
imbecile who cannot fight a simple battle!"

Fine!" Dylan yelled. "Fine! Run away, Tyr. You always *were* a
blem. Go solve yourself. Go save yourself. We don't need you."

Tyr seemed about to answer, then changed his mind. With a sharp,
it nod, he stalked out of Command.

Good riddance," Dylan snapped.

I don't believe what I'm hearing," Rommie said with a look at
, "from any of you."

Shut up and fly," Dylan growled. "We'll show these bastards what
ommonwealth ship and captain are made of."

Yes, sir, Captain Ahab," she said, and turned back to her work.

He started to answer, then decided against it. He pressed the side
is neck. "Harper? What are you up to?"

There was a sigh, then Harper's voice. "Listen, I know you're kind
n the stupid side here, boss, and, like, I'm the off-the-scale
us, but even an idiot like you can probably figure out that, hey,
, the wizard of engineering is probably, well, engineering. As in
g to save our asses, okay?"

Mr. Harper—" Dylan started, fuming inside at this latest insubor-
ion.

Listen, Boss, just shove it you-know-where, okay? I've got more
rtant things to do than blow steam with you. Such as, for exam-
—Harper took a deep breath and screamed—"*saving our asses!*
, that should be clear even to you. Hell, even Tyr should under-
that one. Now, don't bug me again. Oh, yeah—you can threaten
ove me out of an airlock, but it's your ass if you do. Harper out."

That little . . ." Dylan grimaced, feeling the muscles in his face
ack tighten to the point of pain. Harper had better stay out of
ach or Trance would have to glue all of his teeth back in.

really, really, wanted to hit something.

ow.

plosions rippled around the *Andromeda* then, shaking the ship
tly. Dylan fell over again, while Rommie held on to Beka.

didn't waste time getting up. "Full offensive armament, tubes
rough forty. Fire at will."

———

Tyr had stalked out of Command with a specific destinati
mind—if the great Captain Dylan Hunt could not bring hims
hit back properly at these people, then he would. He would
Slipfighter out into the midst of the battle and give the Kanta
demonstration of the way a true warrior fights.

He was the last of Kodiak Pride. He had fought for his surviv
of his life. Even stripped of his bone blades he would continu
fight until—pieces of his enemies' flesh hanging from his blo
teeth and claws—he was finally brought down like one of those
bears.

His fists clenched as he anticipated the coming struggle. H
Tyr Anasazi, out of Victoria by Barbarossa. He was superior. *Sup*

Captain Dylan Hunt, that throwback, could never understan

He started to run. Having the wind at his heels would get hir
the fight faster. Faster, better, *superior*.

Suddenly Trance was in front of him. Thrown off balanc
staggered to a halt, almost running into her.

"Trance," he said, baffled by her appearance. "I have no tim
your annoyances, child."

"I've no time for your posturing, Tyr," she said.

The sound of missiles and plasma bursts against the hull
through as dull thumps here. In his gut, he could feel the shift
turns of the continuing evasive maneuvers.

"Very well," Tyr said. "Let us both be on our way."

"This is where I was going," she said softly, her eyes not m
from his.

"Very well," Tyr said patiently, "you are where you wish to b
I am going to where I wish to be. A positive outcome for us bot

Explosions like drumbeats now.

"Tyr," Trance said, her voice still soft, "I can't let you go out
no matter how much you think you want to. It would be a mista
bad mistake."

"It will be a mistake to attempt to stop me," he said, starti
grow angry. Surely Trance wasn't so stupid as to stand in his wa

"If you go out there in a Slipfighter," Trance said, "you'll g

f us killed, and the life you have will be a misery that ends in
e. You'll lose everything you have, everything you hope to
. . even your son."

My—" He stared at her, dumbfounded. What could she know of
n?

verything," she said.

e saw that she was holding her force lance.

ou wish to preserve my life by killing me, is that it?" he said. His
dropped to his Gauss pistol, ready.

o," she said. She sighed. "I was hoping you'd be reasonable and
this easy, Tyr."

he reasonable path would not involve threatening me," he
ed, and started to draw his pistol.

e stepped forward, moving inside his guard so smoothly and
ly that he could not change defense tactics. She thumbed a
h on the force lance, and its monomolecular segments expanded
ecame rigid as magnetic fields repolarized.

he end of the two-meter lance struck him in the chest and shoved
ackward as it completed its extension. Before he could get his
ce again, Trance was whirling, bringing the lance down across
wer right arm. There was a moment of searing pain, then
ness, and he found that he could neither feel nor control his fin-
The Gauss pistol slipped from his hand, clattering to the floor.
ance turned and caught the pistol with the end of the lance,
ng it flying away.

will not yield!" he shouted.

know," she replied. "You're Tyr Anazasi, blah blah blah, supe-
lah blah blah, etcetera."

ge welled up now, unreasonable and blinding. Whatever Trance
he was going to die at his hands—however much effort it took.
not be mocked!"

h, blah blah blah," she said, sneering at him. "Blowhard."

unsheathed his knife, a finely honed piece that could easily cut
gh steel. He would see what she was made of, oh yes. This was a
at had been due for a long time.

He ran at her, yelling at the top of his lungs.

She stood her ground until the last possible moment. The[n]
was gone, springing up and over his head with catlike speed [and]
grace.

He turned to see her land on the deck behind him, the force [lance]
held in a ready position.

"You can stop at any time," she said. "I won't mind."

With another howl of rage, he ran at her again. This time he [dived]
at her, intending to tackle her about the waist and bring her d[own]
force lance and all.

It worked. Almost.

As they went down, she folded up, and he felt her feet hit h[im in]
the lower stomach. Suddenly he was flying through the air a[nd]
helpless. He hit the deck on his back, the thud of impact joinin[g the]
distant explosions. The breath went out of him for a moment.

He still had his knife, though. He could still—

Trance landed lightly at his right side. Without pause, she sta[mped]
down on his right wrist. Pain shot up his arm, and he involun[tarily]
released his grip on the hilt of his knife.

This was not going well for him, he realized. He failed to u[nder]
stand that concept. How could it not go well for him? He was st[rong,]
fast, superior. Trance was a little *slip* of a thing who liked plan[ts,]
riddles and being a good-luck charm.

"Time to stop, Tyr," she said. She lifted her foot and kicked [away]
his knife, sending it after the Gauss pistol. "I don't want to hu[rt you]
any more."

He rolled over and came to his feet. "I've wasted enough time [on]
you, girl. I have a job to do."

He turned to make a run for the Slipfighter hangar.

He was barely aware of Trance as she went past him in a flyin[g leap.]
She was suddenly in the way again.

This was getting tiring.

"I'm sorry, Tyr," she said.

He thought he was ready for her now.

She struck at him with the force lance. He ducked, lunged[...]

abbed it firmly, intending to either tear it from her hands or to yank
r toward him.

Instead, she pinned the bottom end of the lance against the deck
d used it as a pivot. She kicked off, folding up, and kicked out,
coiling with tremendous speed.

The heels of her boots smashed into his face. His vision and
areness swam. He was aware of Trance landing on the deck nearby,
t he seemed to have lost the ability to make his body do anything
t he wanted.

He tried to stay on his feet, but he couldn't. He sat down heavily
the deck.

He had to resist the darkness. He had to.

He was going to get up. He could do this.

Superior.

Trance's right boot caught him in the jaw. He felt his jaw break,
a moment of intense pain, and then nothing more.

at was interesting," Rommie said, shimmering into view and look-
down at Tyr's supine form.

That's one word for it, I suppose," Trance said. She thumbed
force lance switch again. The magnetic fields shifted and the
omolecular segments collapsed. "I had to stop him."

I'm sure you did," Rommie said, looking up. "Everyone's behav-
very oddly, to say the least."

The Lighthouse Keepers," Trance said. "They're making it hap-
"

Whatever you're planning to do, now's the time."

Good. Beka should get ready to get us out of here on no notice at
Trance started to jog down the corridor, heading for Command.

There's a problem there," Rommie said, moving her holographic
ge to keep pace with Trance. "Beka appears to have lost all self-
idence and has fallen into a state of panic."

Oh. So Dylan's flying the ship?"

Dylan's being a martinet." Rommie frowned. "He's insufferable.
violent."

"Oh, no."

"I'm flying myself at the moment," Rommie said, sounding pleased. "Or, at least, my android avatar is doing so while Androi keeps track of the tactical situation." Rommie scanned the ceiling explosions thudded once more across the hull. "We're in se trouble."

"I think I can help. You already know about the missiles Harper built."

"Yes," Rommie said. "And I have to say that nanobots are an i esting payload."

"They're the only thing that will save us," Trance said. "Ge magazines ready, and get the first forty set to launch. Wait u reach Command. I can take over from you there."

"I can fly myself," Rommie said. "It's just—"

"This isn't about you flying yourself," Trance said. "I'd lov leave you to do that, but to make this work I have to be on the controls. It's going to be instinct on my part."

"Understood." There was a pause. "Missile tubes one thr forty loaded and ready. I've locked Dylan out of fire control."

"Good idea."

Trance broke into a run.

"What strategy do you have in mind?" Rommie asked as Tranc

"Bull elephant," Trance said. "It's the only one I can see that wo

"Bull elephant?"

"It's an Earth animal," Trance said, glad to have something to her mind off of the running and the pounding of explosions. "T are analogues on other worlds, of course. The bull elephant gigantic land mammal."

"You're comparing me to a gigantic mammal?" Rommie said, ing confused even as her image, facing Trance, kept pace with he

"In this instance, yes." Trance rounded an intersection. "Eleph were hunted for their ivory tusks, and one of the methods for I ing them involved setting the hunter's subordinates to harry exhaust the creature, which the hunter would then kill."

"This sounds promising," Rommie said dryly.

"It's better than you think." She was on the last stretch now.

ll elephant would fight back, charging its attackers. Sometimes it
uld crush or gore one or more of them. Sometimes it would kill or
ure enough that it could escape."

"I think I see what you intend to do," Rommie said.

"It isn't subtle," Trance admitted, "but we have an advantage. We
t have to stay alive long enough."

"We're taking far too many hits," Rommie admitted. "I'm losing
wer, I've lost weaponry, and I can't guarantee Slipstream capability
more than ten minutes. Harper's doing what he can, but the truth
hat it may take weeks to repair the damage that the Kantarans are
icting."

Trance had reached Command now, and could barely believe her
s. Dylan was strutting about angrily, red in the face and utterly
echless with rage—that was a relief. The android avatar was at the
ht controls, doing her best to minimize the damage being inflicted
the Kantarans. Beka was huddled by her feet, miserable, tears
aming down her face.

he didn't have to see him to know that Harper had been changed
ome unpleasant way. As long as he kept holding the *Andromeda
ndant* together, it didn't matter.

I have to get us out of this," she said to the android.

You know," Dylan suddenly yelled, "I am *so* sick of treachery and
ayal! Everybody, and I mean *everybody*, has it in for me!" He strut-
toward Trance, his fists clenched. "Especially you, Trance. You've
n nothing but trouble. Trouble!"

Dylan," Trance said mildly, "shut up."

I will not shut up! *I* command this vessel, not you!"

You are no longer in command, Captain Hunt," Rommie said
nally. "Under High Guard Command Charter article 13302, sec-
two, provisions one through five, which states that in the event
a ship's AI, supported by the ship's chief medical officer, should
the commanding officer unfit for duty, said commanding officer
be immediately suspended from duty."

You just made that up!" Dylan yelled.

he did not," Andromeda said. "The High Guard Command
ter, 727th Amended Edition, can be accessed in your quarters.

The relevant section has been bookmarked for you." Androm
paused, but Dylan had nothing to say. "Let it be noted that the A
the *Andromeda Ascendant* finds her present commanding officer u
for duty. Does the chief medical officer concur with this assessme

"I am Trance Gemini, chief medical officer of the *Androm
Ascendant*," Trance said firmly, "and I concur with the assessmen
the ship's AI."

Dylan spluttered helplessly.

"Captain Hunt," Rommie said harshly, "I am requesting that
surrender your weapon, leave Command, and confine yoursel
your quarters until further notice. Fail to comply, and I will take
steps as are needed to incarcerate you for the time being."

Dylan seemed about to say something. Then he tensed, as tho
about to draw his force lance and fire.

"Don't," Rommie said. "I will inevitably break several bones w
disarming you."

Angrily Dylan reached down and pulled out his force lance, h
ing it out to Rommie. She took it. "You'll pay for this," he his
"You'll all pay for this."

He turned and stormed out of Command.

"He's going to be so mad," Beka whispered.

Trance looked at Rommie, and the android nodded. Step
away from the flight station, the android bent down and lifted I
easily to her feet. "Come on, Beka," she said gently. "I'll take ca
you. Trance is going to get us out of here."

If I can, Trance thought. She was on her own here, no help fo
coming from any corner of the universe.

Rommie set Beka down in a corner of Command, then went
to her own station. Trance grasped the flight controls, closing
eyes for a moment, shutting out the sounds of explosions.

"I estimate that we have no more than nine minutes before b
damage becomes critical," Andromeda said. "At that point our a
cial gravity field will lose coherence."

Trance was barely listening. She had found the lines of best p
ability. Her hands played the controls, putting the ship into a
spinning maneuver. The explosions ceased for a moment.

Another shift, and she was charging a group of Kantaran fighters.

"Fire one through five!" she snapped.

"One through five, aye!" Rommie responded. The missiles appeared the tactical screen, heading into the Kantaran group, but unable to ck on. That didn't matter, not with these missiles.

"Reload as we go," Trance ordered.

"Reloading, aye." Rommie looked up. "This had better work."

Trance threw the ship into another tight maneuver, rolling over, ling velocity, then applying thrust on a new heading. They were hit ain, but only twice.

"Fire six through fifteen!" she said.

"Six through fifteen, aye. Missiles away. Reloading."

Trance sent the huge ship charging toward another group of ackers.

"First salvo has detonated on time," Rommie said.

"Fire sixteen through twenty."

"Sixteen through twenty, aye, second salvo has detonated."

Trance could feel the confusion emanating from parts of the Kan- an fleet. By now they would be starting to realize what had been ie to them.

She adjusted their course. "Twenty-one through thirty."

"Twenty-one through thirty, aye, third salvo has detonated," mmie said.

'I am detecting an increase in Kantaran radio traffic," Andromeda l. "There appears to be a certain amount of agitation."

'Fourth salvo has detonated. All tubes reloaded and ready."

Trance adjusted her course again, charging another group of Kan- n fighters. This group didn't even bother with their weapons. ead, they tried to get out of her way.

'No doing," she said, her eyes narrowing. "Fire thirty-one through y."

Firing thirty-one through forty, aye. Missiles away. Reloading."

Radio traffic is continuing to increase. Warnings are being ed."

Too little, too late," Trance said. "They wouldn't let us go, I'm not ng *them* go. Alright, get ready to fire one at a time on my mark."

With that, she put the ship into a wild wobbling spin around i
own axis.

"Fire!" she snapped.

"Firing, aye!" Rommie answered.

Missiles hurtled away one after another, each on a different vecto

"Reload and continue firing at will," Trance said. "Empty t
magazine."

"I think I'm going to be sick," Beka moaned.

The number of missile traces from *Andromeda* continued
increase. By now, even though Trance had essentially made the ship
sitting target, there were almost no missile impacts and no indicati
of plasma bursts or particle beam strikes. The tactical screen was s
filled with the traces for Kantaran vessels, but now they seemed to
barely moving, all attempts at formation lost.

"The magazines are now empty," Andromeda reported. "All m
siles away, and detonating as intended. The Kantaran fleet appears
be in some disarray."

Trance gradually killed the gyroscopic spin, bringing the ship t
level plane at full stop. Her head was spinning a little, but she put tl
down to having to keep track of so much while simultaneously kee
ing the best probabilities together in her mind.

"We are holding steady," Rommie reported.

"Can we still make it out of here?"

Rommie tapped away at her consoles and frowned. "Yes, we c
but I would suggest we find a system where I can extract raw mate
als from an asteroid belt. It will take at least a week to effect e
basic repairs. Our Kantaran friends inflicted a surprising amoun
damage."

Trance closed her eyes for a moment and sighed. It wasn't just
damage to the ship, either. The psychological changes in the c
could well be permanent, or damaging in some other way.
glanced at Beka, who was still huddled miserably at the other side
Command.

"Let's see how their ships look," Trance said.

The screens cleared to show a panoramic view of a part of
Kantaran fleet. The ships appeared to be drifting aimlessly, and

ne seemed, in some way, foreshortened. To one degree or another,
ch ship had shifting patterns of black moving over it. That would
entually change. Harper had designed these nanobots in a hurry,
t he had made sure to build in a time limit as part of their instruc-
on set.

"Alright," Trance said, allowing herself a small smile. "Open a—"

"Open *nothing*!" an all-too-familiar voice grated. Trance sighed.
yr sometimes didn't have the sense to stay down when it was in his
st interests. "I am taking command! This ship is *mine*!"

Tyr was leaning heavily on the entrance to Command. The lower
lf of his face was swollen and darkening—that was going to take
r some time to fix, she thought. His voice was slurred because of
e physical damage, but the fire in his eyes was unmistakable—he
d his goal, and he was going to achieve it.

"Tyr," Trance said, "you need to get to Medical."

"You," he slurred, "are dead."

"That doesn't work very well," she said calmly.

Tyr raised his right hand, aiming his Gauss pistol at her. His hand
s shaking, but his aim remained somewhere in the vicinity of his
ent. "I am willing to repeat the attempt as many times as it will
e."

Rommie started toward him, and Tyr's aim switched. "I wouldn't
that. I can shoot you two to three times before you reach me."

"After which," Rommie said, sounding quite reasonable, "I will
you as a punching bag until you cease being so troublesome. Tyr,
aren't taking over anything today. You need to get a grip, get to
dical, and *wait*."

"This really isn't you, Tyr," Trance said.

Tyr's aim shifted back to Trance. "Who are you to say?"

He started toward Trance as Rommie said, "Considering the
avior displayed by everyone except for Trance and I, I believe
are."

"I am taking command!" he yelled. His face went gray and droplets
weat broke out on his forehead. He gritted his teeth and added,
not tolerate argument."

Oh, tolerate this!" Beka snapped from behind him.

He started to turn. There was a loud, hollow bang, and T
stopped. After a moment, the Gauss pistol slipped from his finge
and clattered to the floor.

Slowly, he tilted his head and looked at Trance for a moment,
though baffled. Then his eyes closed and he fell, crashing to the de
with a remarkable lack of grace.

Beka, a piece of broken conduit clutched in both hands, looked
from Tyr, staring at Trance and Rommie as though expecting to
punished at any second. "Did I do the right thing?"

"Yes, you did," Trance said.

"Well, you *could* have shot him," Rommie said.

"I could have . . ." Beka's eyes went wide, and she stared down
her Gauss pistol, snug in its holster, as though she had never seer
before. "Oh, no."

"Oh, yes," Rommie said. "This is better—Trance can fix blu
trauma to Tyr's thick skull quite easily." She looked at Trance, cu
ous. "Just what *did* you do to him, anyway?"

"I won the argument," Trance said softly. She turned back to
pilot console. "Open a channel."

"Opening a channel, aye," Rommie said, and the center screen
up.

Neither Colonel Kaczynski's look nor mood had improved si
the last conversation. Right now he looked quite ill, in fact.

"Colonel Kaczynski," Trance said with a smile. "I suggest takir
few deep breaths and trying to relax. Stress isn't good for you."

"Where the hell is Hunt?" he demanded.

"Captain Hunt is . . . relaxing," Trance said. Rommie turned
head and raised an eyebrow. "I've been delegated to deal with you

Kaczynski was silent for a moment, apparently fighting an an
outburst. "I see. And you are?"

"Trance Gemini, chief medical officer."

"Chief—!"

"Chief medical officer." Trance smiled again. "Please, Colo
calm yourself."

"I—" he started. He fell silent again. After a moment he saic
suppose I'm at your mercy here."

"Yes you are," she said. She had learned a lot from watching Dylan
rk through these situations. Even when his actions resulted in the
miliation of his opponents, he was somehow able to maintain a dis-
ingly cheerful air that left them without a clue as to what he had
e. He claimed he was no diplomat. She thought he was quite
ong. He just didn't *want* to be a diplomat.

"Very well," Kaczynski said. "If you must gloat, please get it over
h quickly."

"I don't intend to gloat," she said. "Actually, I intend to take us out
here as quickly as possible."

"Then why are you even bothering to talk to me?" he said, seeming
uinely puzzled. "Finish us off and be gone."

"No," Trance said. "I'm talking to you because you need to know
at I've done."

"I can guess," Kaczsynki said. "Nanobots. And how long do we
e until they finish eating our ships?"

"They're not eating your ships," Trance said. "All they've done is
nodel them a bit. All of your propulsion and Slipstream capability
one, along with your weapons. In other words, you're adrift, and
can't shoot at us anymore."

"And we make excellent targets for practice, I'm sure," he said
lly.

With a cheerful smile, Rommie said, "Well, if that's what you'd
fer, I'm sure we could oblige."

"You are attempting to confuse me," Kaczynski growled.

"Apparently, we're succeeding," Rommie said.

"Your life support," Andromeda said, picking up the conversation,
ll continue to work—in fact, you will find that its capacity has
n expanded, in case your colleagues cannot reach you quickly. In
ition, your communications are unimpaired. You will be able to
nmunicate with each other, and with your base, as well as broad-
: emergency calls."

"In fact," Rommie said, "emergency beacons should already have
n triggered."

Kaczynski's eyes flicked downward for a moment, then he looked
again. "I see." He took a deep breath, sighed, appeared to relax.

"Quite generous, I suppose. So . . . you have won the day. Now wh
Return with revenge in mind?"

"No," Trance said. "Now we leave, and we leave you alone. C
tain Hunt meant exactly what he said."

"If you need help in the future," Andromeda said, "we will be p
pared to provide it. However, you will have to make a formal reque

"We can take care of ourselves," Kaczynski said.

"Then consider the matter closed," Andromeda replied.

"Take care, Colonel," Trance said. "Good-bye."

With no further ado, she put the ship into a broad, looping turn,
the course for the Slip point, and opened the throttles to maxim
Getting out of this system at top velocity seemed like a good idea.

She reached over her head and hit the switches to bring the S
stream hood down. Concentrating, she fed power to the Slipstre
core.

"Transiting to Slipstream . . ." She opened the runners. "Now!
Existence burst into flares and streaks of white, and they were a

FIVE ▪ WHERE THE BUSES DON'T RUN

"Have you seen my force lance?"

—HIGH GUARD SPECIAL ATTACHÉ
GORUS EN'KER, THREE SECONDS
BEFORE HIS ASSASSINATION, CY 8336

This is not good," Trance said.

Plunging into the Slipstream, the *Andromeda Ascendant* was shud-
ering and shifting. It was taking everything Trance could summon
keep the Slipstream runners locked to any of the streams, and
ere was no sign of the transition effect abating.

"We have a problem," Andromeda said, her image appearing on
e flatscreens.

"No kidding," Trance said.

"Besides the obvious Slipstream issue," Andromeda said, a little
stily, "two of the Kantaran ships have either followed us into Slip-
eam, or have been drawn in behind us. Either way, we will have to
d a way to deal with them."

"Do you mind if I worry about them later?" Trance said. She was
owing afraid that the ship would shake apart if she tried to stay in
e Slipstream.

"I'm detecting multiple problems in the Slipstream core," Rommie said. "Nothing Harper can't fix, but he won't be able to do anything until we transit back to normal space."

"I don't think we can keep this up," Trance said unhappily. At leas they would be far away from Kantaran space.

"I am detecting a very minor fluctuation in the AG field," Andromeda said.

Trance's eyes went wide. "That's worse than not good," she said. "Transiting from Slipstream *now*."

The transition was the worst she had ever experienced. *Androm eda* shook wildly, and all manner of creaks and groans came from all corners. Back in normal space, the ship began rolling end-for end, barely responding to Trance's commands at the pilot station

"I'm stabilizing," Andromeda said, finally, her eyes and head mov ing as she appeared to look at readouts—an illusion of course, but provided a certain humanizing touch. "AG field fluctuations hav ceased, thanks to Mr. Harper."

"That was quick," Trance said, feeling relieved.

"Okay," Harper said, his voice booming over the comm syster "who the hell's doing the driving up there?"

"I am," Trance said. She sighed. "One of those desperate tim things."

"Huh?"

"Desperate times call for desperate measures," Trance said. "Usually committed by really desperate people."

"Yeah, well," Harper said, "desperate is the word. So where t hell is Beka, anyway?"

Trance glanced around. Tyr was still lying where he had falle Beka was sitting down again, her knees pulled up with her arr wrapped around them. Her head was down. Trance wasn't sure if sl was crying or not.

"She's . . . not feeling well," Trance said.

There was a pause. "Y'know, Trance, I'm not feeling so freak hot myself right now."

The holographic Rommie shimmered into being. "I have a pair my maintenance androids on the way to get Tyr to the Med Deck.

What was that about Tyr?" Harper said.

He isn't feeling too well either," Rommie said as the holographic
r shimmered out.

Okay," Harper said. "What the freakin' hell is going on around
 Where's Dylan?"

Relieved of his duties and confined to his quarters," Andromeda

What?"

Harper," Rommie said, "explanations are going to have to wait."

Oh, God," Harper moaned. "This is the part where you tell me
 three seconds from blowing up and I'm the only one who can
 erything in time, right?"

ou have more than three seconds, Mr. Harper," Andromeda
"However, there is considerable work to be done."

eginning with the Slipstream core," Rommie said. "It was possi-
 transit to Slipstream, but was inadvisable to remain there."

arper's head and shoulders appeared on one of the flatscreens. He
d terrible. His face was smeared with sooty residue, there was a
ing bruise on his right cheek, and he seemed to be ready to throw
 any moment. "I fixed the AG field generators already," he said.
ewalk. Everything else . . . jeez, guys, it's a freakin' mess."

ou've pulled me through before," Rommie said, smiling. "I have
 confidence you'll do it again."

eah, well, that's what this here boy genius does," he said, but
ut his usual enthusiasm. "Rommie, we're okay for a few more
tes, right? Like, we're not going to blow up or anything?"

vo maintenance androids, ungainly-looking humanoid figures
almost featureless black carapaces, entered Command. One was
ing a stretcher. They carefully loaded Tyr onto the stretcher,
d it up, and left again.

ot just yet," Rommie said.

kay," Harper said. "I gotta go get something before my head
 up. Harper out."

e image blinked off.

ance looked over at Beka. She still had her arms wrapped around
nees, but now she was looking up. The side of her face that

Dylan had slapped was livid. "I feel lousy. Damn, do I feel lousy."
head dropped to her knees again. Her voice muffled, she said, "So
one just tell me I wasn't doing Flash again."

Sadness welled up in Trance for a moment. She went over to F
and knelt by her. "You weren't doing Flash, Beka." Beka looked v
her, silent. "The Kantarans used some kind of weapon that n
everybody act weird. That's why you feel sick—we're out of ra
and your body is trying to shake it off. I don't know how long
take."

"I feel so *miserable*," Beka said. Tears welled up in her eyes
streamed down her cheeks. She reached up and touched the sid
her face.

"Dylan slapped you," Trance said. She didn't see the poir
avoiding the truth.

Beka started at her in confusion. "He . . . why? Where is he?"

"We threw him out of Command," Trance said.

Beka's eyes went wide. "You threw him out of Command? Oh
Oh, no." Suddenly Beka's mouth quirked, and she made a little sr
ing noise. "Oh, my God."

All of a sudden, Beka buried her face in her knees again, her sl
ders shaking. This time, though, she was laughing. Trance sm
Beka was going to be fine.

With a final snort, Beka's laughter stopped. She looked up at Tr
again, her eyes still wide. "This has been a crazy day, hasn't it?"

"Yes," Trance said. She stood up. "I have to go down to Medi
need to get Tyr patched up."

"What happened to Tyr?" Beka started to get up. She seemed
tle shaky.

"Well . . ." Trance tried to figure out a good way to phrase it.

Rommie saved her the trouble. "Trance beat him up when he
to take a Slipfighter out. And then you knocked him out with a
of conduit when he tried to take over the ship."

Beka looked from Trance to Rommie and back again. "T
insane."

"I agree," Trance said. "Are you up to staying in Command
Rommie? We've got a couple of crippled Kantarans to bring in

"I was wondering when we'd get to that," Rommie said.

Beka's eyes narrowed slightly, and she smiled. "Trance, the way my
d feels right now, I hope the sons of bitches don't give us any
ıble."

"Good," Trance said. "I'll deal with Dylan as well."

Beka was quiet for a moment, then she nodded. "It wasn't him,
 it?"

"No," Trance said. "But we have to deal with what the Kantarans
to all of you."

She gave Beka another smile, and started for the exit. Behind her,
 heard Beka say, "Rommie, locate our guests, target Bucky cables,
 bring 'em in. You don't need to make it a smooth ride."

is quarters Dylan was stretched out on his bed, his eyes closed
tly. He wasn't sure which was worse—the splitting headache, the
rning in his stomach, or the way the room started spinning when
pened his eyes.

Maybe all three.

Ie tried to remember what had happened. He had no recollection
etting to his quarters, and his last fully coherent memory was of
Kantarans opening fire on the *Andromeda Ascendant*. Everything
 that was just a sequence of blurs that he couldn't make sense
-each time he tried to bring them into focus his headache threat-
l to become a migraine.

Ie had never had a migraine in his life. He didn't want to start
. He just couldn't summon the strength or the willpower to call
ielp or get to Medical.

Ie had to do something.

Iis stomach churned again, and he rolled onto his side, pulling his
s up, trying to breathe steadily until the spasm passed. He was
ed in sweat, his hair matted to his scalp.

You look terrible." Rommie's words drove like spikes into his
.

Not so loud," he whispered. He relaxed a little. "What the hell
ened? I either have the worst hangover I've ever had, or I caught
thing."

"You could call it a hangover, I suppose," Rommie said. Her v
was much quieter now. He opened his eyes carefully. Rommie's h
graphic avatar was standing a couple of meters away, her arms fo
"The Kantarans apparently have a weapon that uses an electror
netic field to disrupt the normal biochemical functions of the br

"I think that would explain why my head feels like a Nova B
hit it," Dylan said. "Two questions." Tentatively, he started to
himself into a sitting position. The room started spinning again,
Rommie blurred. He felt the cold sweat break out. "How do we k
it, and how did I get here?"

"On the first question, we ran away." Rommie gave him an ur
tain look, then seemed to steel herself. That wasn't good. It m
that he wasn't going to like what she had to say. "On the second c
tion . . . you were declared incompetent under High Guard r
ejected from Command, and confined to quarters."

He had made it into a sitting position, finally. He could fee
sweat running down the middle of his back, and he shivered. "T
not good."

"No," she said, "it's not. You were quite the martinet. My phy
avatar had to step in to prevent further violence."

"*Further* violence?" Dylan said, his head coming up sharply. I
an unwise move. The pain in his head was so intense that all he sav
a few moments was a sea of white populated by a few rushing star

"You struck Beka," Rommie said. He couldn't find the wor
respond. What sort of monster had he turned into? "Beka wi
fine, fortunately."

"Was it just—" he began.

"No, it wasn't just you," she said. "Harper became more ob
ious than ever, Tyr became irrationally aggressive, and Beka
apart."

"Trance?" he muttered.

"She remained quite normal . . . or at least she didn't vary
whatever passes for normal for her. She got me into the Slipstre

"I'm going to try standing up now," Dylan said quietly. "The
room seems like a good place to be right now."

"Medical would be better."

"Probably." He reached down for his force lance and found only an
pty holster. "Damn it. High Guard protocol. You had to disarm me."
"Yes."

"I'll live with that." Slowly, he got up. At first he staggered like
runk, but with an effort he managed to get his balance. He had
ended to open his force lance to its full extent and use it to help
1 get to the bathroom, but he could manage without it.

"I will need to keep you under observation, Captain," Rommie said.
"Not—"

"For the moment," she said primly, "that means continuously."

He sighed. "Alright."

She smiled. "It isn't as though you have anything that I haven't
1 before, Captain."

There was no sense in arguing. One of her prime concerns was
safety, and there was no way he was going to be able to change
mind. She was going to monitor him whether he liked it or not.
 the bargain, she would be relaying his vital signs to Trance's
lical bay.

nstead, he concentrated on getting one foot in front of the other,
lifting his feet too much. He kept his eyes on the deck, trying to
ntain equilibrium.

You'd better fill me in on what happened," he said as he inched
g.

he did. He listened silently, hardly able to believe the report. It
ied as though the worst had come out in all of them, except for
ace—and even there they still had a mystery on their hands.

It would, incidentally," Rommie added, "explain Trance's remarks
ut 'the plague of lighthouse keepers.' In this instance, however, it
t something that affects the lighthouse keepers."

It's delivered by them," Dylan said. "Not quite the warm welcome
 expecting."

le had finally made it to the bathroom. His stomach roiled again,
 violently this time. He barely managed to reach the sink before
rew up. The spasm was over quickly, but it left him feeling weak
shaky. He quickly cleaned up the mess and rinsed his mouth out.
 seemed to take forever to get his sodden clothes off. He was

grateful for the momentary respite from the clammy feeling, b
was short-lived. He turned on the shower, set it as hot as he tho
he could stand it, and got in. The water heated quickly, cascading
his head and shoulders, and he had to make an effort to not turn
the heat. It took a couple of minutes, but he began to feel a little
ter. As the muscles loosened in his neck, shoulders, and back
remorseless headache diminished a little. The sheer act of washing
glorious. He hated the idea of turning the shower off and getting

Finally, he did. He quickly toweled himself off, glad to have
clammy sensation gone. His equilibrium seemed to be almost ba
normal, though he otherwise still felt like death warmed over.

Wrapping the towel around himself, he went to get fresh clot

While Dylan was busy pulling himself together, *Andromeda*'s and
avatar had left the Command Deck. Beka had seemed to be d
alright, although the readings from the Command biomedical se
indicated that she was in some physical distress. As long as there
no drastic changes, Rommie felt quite secure in her decision to
Beka by herself.

Her destination was one of the hangar bays. The two Kan
ships that had managed to follow them were sitting there, en
and weapons now completely dismantled by the nanobots that
coated them.

As she walked into the hangar, she issued a silent command to s
down the internal defense systems. The Kantaran pilots had alr
been warned to stay in their vessels until instructed otherwise.

The two Kantaran fighters were a dull yellow in color, with
identification markings. Matte-black splotches showed where
nanobots had clustered. As she walked toward the fighters
splotches were growing smaller—Trance and Harper had deliber
given them a fast reproductive cycle along with a truncated life
once their goal was achieved.

She smiled. It was an elegant solution. Unfortunately, it
unlikely to work twice.

She stopped in front of the two fighters, looking up at them.
craft were utilitarian, lacking any of the grace of her own de

en the Nietzscheans included a certain degree of artfulness in their
hter designs. These ships were ugly little brutes.

She unholstered her force lance and activated it. It was more of a
ecautionary measure than anything else—a gesture to keep the pi-
s in a polite and pliable mood.

Drones rolled ladders up to the side of the ships, adjusting the
ghts before locking them in place.

"Alright, gentlemen," she said, her voice echoing over the pilots'
ckpit radios, "you can come out."

With loud hisses, the cockpit canopies slid back. The pilots stood
slowly, disconnecting themselves from biosign monitors and life-
port equipment. They both wore dark gray flight suits, with
ignia at the shoulders and name patches on the right side of the
st. One was male, the other female. Both had close-cropped dark
r. The pallor of their faces suggested that they had not spent any
e away from their base or their ships recently.

At first they seemed uncertain of themselves, looking around the
e hangar, and then down at her.

"Come on down," she called. "If you're carrying any weapons, you
either leave them in your spacecraft, or surrender them to me."

The two pilots glanced at each other. "We have no personal
pons," the male said.

Carefully, the two eased out onto the ladders, climbing slowly
n. Once they reached the deck, they went to stand together
ween the two fighters. They had assumed a rigid military stance,
r eyes focused past her.

"Welcome to the *Andromeda Ascendant*." She holstered her force
e and walked up to them, looking them over. Her sensors indicated
weapons. Preliminary biosign scans had more worrying news. "Our
icial gravity level is too high for you, isn't it?" she said.

"Ma'am," the woman said, not looking at her, "we are your prison-
We expect no particular accommodation for our needs."

"Well," Rommie said, folding her arms across her chest, "I
dn't consider myself a good hostess if I let you suffer." A flash of
ulation and a silent exchange with her ship-self was all it took to
t the AG field locally. "That should be more comfortable."

"Thank you, ma'am," the male pilot said.

"You're quite welcome," she replied. "And you may call me R
mie. We generally don't stand much on formality here."

"Understood, ma . . . um." The pilot swallowed nervously.

"I assume we will be interrogated," the woman said.

"As in questions, drugs, torture, deprivation, and general sad
abuse to derive answers?" Amazingly, they both managed to g
even paler. "No. Well, we *might* ask you a few questions. The re
neither acceptable nor particularly interesting."

Her holographic avatar shimmered into being at her side. The
pilots glanced at each other again. "Any questions we ask wil
solely for the purpose of ensuring your comfort and safe return."

"You can call her Rommie, too," Rommie said. "We are
avatars of the *Andromeda Ascendant*."

"Your temporary quarters have been prepared," the hologra
Rommie said. "We will repatriate you as soon as we can."

"Please precede me, and I'll escort you there," Rommie said.
two pilots started to walk stiffly past her. "And, please, *at ease!* Yo
going to injure yourselves if you're not careful."

"Yes, ma'am!" they said in chorus. Neither one appeared to rel
any appreciable degree.

"And we thought Harper was hopeless," her holographic twin
Rommie rolled her eyes and sighed.

Dylan managed to make it to the Med Deck without losing equ
rium again, but by the time he got there he once again felt as tho
someone had driven a spike into his forehead. Even the normal
lighting was too painful—he made the last part of his slow, caut
journey with his eyes almost closed.

Trance was still working on Tyr when he walked in and sat d
heavily on the nearest chair. The Nietzschean was conscious, bu
prone on one of the beds, staring up at the ceiling.

"Hey, Boss!" Harper said cheerfully. Each of the words seeme
boom inside his skull, generating red flowers of pain. "Geez, you
lousy."

Harper was sitting up on one of the counters. "Thank you for your
essment, Mr. Harper." Dylan closed his eyes as Harper pushed
nself from the counter. It did nothing to help him when Harper's
es smacked into the deck. "I understand you were rather rude and
ubordinate."

"Yeah, well," Harper said, "it sounds to me like my usual charming
I sweet self, only more so."

'Playing the arrogant worm," Tyr said. He had trouble phrasing
words properly.

'Huh, listen to the Boy Target over there, will ya?" Harper said,
ining. "At least I didn't get myself beat to a bloody pulp."

'Harper," Trance said quietly, "that is completely inappropriate."

'What she said," Dylan muttered.

Trance walked over to Dylan, looking him over. "Tyr's going to be
fine, and Harper's over whatever this was."

I just need something for the headache," he said. There was a sud-
pressure against his left shoulder, followed by a loud hiss. "Hey!"
Trance stepped back, smiling, holding up the hypospray she had
I on him. "My special concoction," she said. "Clears headaches,
les stomachs, boosts energy, and makes you regular. Well, actually,
n't know about that last part, but the other three are true."

I hate shots," Dylan grumbled.

You're gonna love this one, Boss," Harper said, grinning. "I feel
dancing on tables. I could work for a week straight."

Rommie's holographic image shimmered into life between Harper
Trance. "Considering the damage I've sustained, Mr. Harper,
week may not be enough."

Dylan closed his eyes again, and sighed. With any luck, things
Id improve from this point onward.

Or not.

He stood up carefully. Trance's shot seemed to be working but it
Id be a while before he felt fully functional. What he really
ted to do was crawl into his bed and sleep for a couple of days.

Alright, people," he said, "we've got work to do."

———————

Harper's ebullience was gone by the following morning. Dylan
called a breakfast meeting to decide their next few moves. Non
them appeared to be too interested in food, he noticed. He, Beka,
Harper were all drinking far more coffee than was good for th
Tyr, looking more dour than usual, was sticking to fruit juice. Tr
had a glass of water in front of her, but Dylan suspected that wa
the sake of appearances.

"Repairs," Dylan said. "Main priority at this point."

"For which we're currently in a bad position," Rommie
"While Harper and Trance's idea worked very well—"

"Very well?" Harper blurted. "It worked brilliantly! Boy ge
style."

"It was Trance's idea," Dylan said.

Trance smiled.

"I made it work," Harper muttered.

"This isn't a competition, Mr. Harper," Rommie said, giving h
stern look. She looked back at Dylan. "While it took care of the N
taran fleet, the production of the missiles and their payloads
sumed my remaining onboard supplies. Had we restocked be
leaving for Kantar, this might not be so pressing a situation."

"So noted," Dylan said. "Mr. Harper?"

Harper shrugged. "We got our asses kicked badly, Boss. I'm
ning around doing patch jobs with spit and string, but I need p
and I need raw materials for the machine shop." He sat up strai
He looked worried, something Dylan rarely saw. "The AG fi
gonna hold, and I've got the Slipstream core on-line again, but I
know how long that'll hold."

"The exotic matter pulser is showing signs of potential stress
tures," Rommie said.

"Which means we'll have a rough ride," Beka said.

"Are we near any debris fields?" Dylan said.

"No," Rommie said.

"Andromeda places us about seven thousand light-years outsid
the Andromeda galaxy," Beka said.

Dylan stared at her for a moment. "Good throw," he said, fina

"This wasn't exactly where I meant to go," Trance said apologetically.

"If the Slipstream core holds up," Rommie said, "we should be able to make it back to Commonwealth space in approximately four weeks."

"Four weeks," Dylan echoed. He thought for a moment. "I could take the *Eureka Maru*—" Beka shot him a look. He had tried to apologize to her for his actions, but she had simply brushed it off. She had seemed fretful about her own behavior, however. She couldn't afford to start doubting herself again. "Or Beka could."

"A round-trip transit time of eight weeks, plus layover time, makes that highly impractical, Captain," Rommie said.

"Then what do you suggest we do?" Beka said.

"We first need to get rid of our guests," Tyr said.

"We could throw 'em out of an airlock," Harper said.

"For once," Tyr said, "we think alike."

"Hey! I was kidding."

"Oh." Tyr looked mildly disappointed. "I wasn't."

"We'll send them back where they came from," Dylan said. He sat back and rubbed at his temples. A faint residue of the previous day's headache seemed to be welling up again. He pushed his coffee mug away—all he needed now was caffeine poisoning. Harper, on the other hand, would probably go from guzzling coffee to swilling can after can of Sparky Cola. "It'll cost us a Slipfighter, but I can live with that."

"Do you want them to turn around and come after us again?" Tyr said, astonished. "Along, no doubt, with whatever is left of their immense fleet."

"First of all, Mr. Anasazi, we won't be here," Dylan said patiently. "Secondly, they'll have a difficult time backtracking without a working navigation system, a working Slip drive, or fully functional communications."

"Navigation software and hardware will self-destruct once they exit from the Slipstream," Rommie said. "The Slip drive will likely be destroyed. Initially, they will only have an emergency beacon and the ability to receive incoming transmissions. Outgoing transm[i]sion capability will be enabled after ten minutes."

"I see the potential for a disastrous outcome," Tyr said, look[ing] directly at Dylan. There was no overt challenge in the look. Tyr h[ad] an unwavering ability to see the ways in which a given course [of] action could run counter to his own survival. "If the Slipstream dr[ive] should fail, then we will be nothing more than a sitting target."

"Our guests won't be departing before we're ready to leav[e," Dylan said, sitting back. "By that time Mr. Harper will have the Sl[ip]stream drive stable. Correct, Mr. Harper?"

Harper seemed to look inward for a moment, then he shrugg[ed.] "Sure."

Tyr turned his gaze on Harper, who shifted uncomfortably. "Y[ou] seem less than certain."

"It's a Slipstream drive," Harper said, sounding a little te[nse.] "Gimme a break here. It breaks, I fix it. That's why they pay me the [big] bucks." He glanced at Dylan. "That's *if* they paid me the big buck[s."]

"Adventure is your reward, Mr. Harper," Rommie said.

"In which case," Beka said, "we're filthy rich. I'm with Harpe[r. I] like real money."

"If money talks," Trance said, "what's it saying?"

" 'Spend me, spend me,' " Beka said. She grinned. "That's usu[ally] what it says to me."

"Especially after you got away with Sid's credit card," Rommie s[aid.]

"Oh, yes," Beka said. "Sid's money has a way of being very l[oud] and insistent."

"Just like Sid himself," Dylan said. "The issue right now [is] money. We need to get to a system where Andromeda can pro[cess] raw materials. After that we head for the first system we can re[ach] that will take Commonwealth scrip, pick up whatever Androm[eda] can't manufacture, and get ourselves to a High Guard base so we [can] drydock to finish any outstanding repairs."

"I like the way you make that sound so easy," Beka said. "We [need] to make three Slips for the first part of that. Then we're in for a l[ong] haul."

"And," Rommie added, "the best-case scenario after *that* is ano[ther] en Slips, with between-Slip periods ranging from two hours to days."

"Well," Dylan said, shaking his head, "I guess we'll all have to fine-e our hobbies, won't we?"

"I'm sure Trance has her plants," Tyr said, glowering at her. She his glare with a sunny smile. Dylan had seen Andromeda's rding of the Trance-Tyr fight. While Tyr had obviously been off game, making foolish moves, Trance's abilities were frightening. a had witnessed the first appearance of this version of Trance and description she had given him of her fighting skills—dispatching a up of attacking Kalderans—had been no exaggeration. "I have ty of weapons I wish to clean, overhaul, and adjust. And test."

"Well," Dylan said, "you won't be disturbed in the combat practice e."

"Oh," Tyr said, a bit distantly. "You, sir, are quite right." He had o look away from Trance.

"Hey, Tyr," Harper said, "I can improve on those guns of yours. ow, give 'em a power-up."

yr turned to look at him. "A power-up?"

"Sure." Harper was starting to look excited. "Better batteries, e power . . . hit harder, fire faster. I've got some great ideas for big multibarreled monster of yours."

yr was looking dubious. "I've been satisfied with my weapons so

"ou can be more satisfied," Harper said.

believe he intends to add a barrel that serves soft ice cream," mie said.

oth Tyr and Harper turned to look at her. She looked steadily at them, half smiling.

"On the other hand," she added after a moment, "I wouldn't mind g some improvements and enhancements to my own weapons they're rebuilt. I'm one of those girls who likes *really* big guns."

"m not touching that with a ten-meter force lance," Beka said.

iiiight," Harper said.

lan sighed and looked at Trance. "Everybody's a comedian." ance just smiled.

SIX • ONE MORE RABBIT HOLE

We made room for the variables.
We tweaked all the settings.
We did all we possibly could have
to ensure our success.
But now, in the deepest darkness,
in the deepest darkness we float.
We are becalmed and bereft
in this place without stars.

—FROM THE FREE VERSE CYCLE
STARPILOT'S FATE, BY THAN POET
LAUREATE EXPANSE OF HEART'S-FIRE,
CY 9204

"Harper's not kidding about spit and string, is he?" Beka said.

"No, I don't think he is," Dylan admitted.

She and Dylan had spent a good part of the past three days
walking inspection of the internal damage to the *Andromeda A*
dant. It wasn't as bad as it could have been—no one had hit them
a point singularity bomb, unlike their encounter with the *M*
Worldship. There were no huge gaping holes right through the
just a lot of little holes, sections of hull blown away, and we
structures smashed. The ECM fans were a mess. Andromeda
broken down the two Kantaran ships for raw materials, but i
only been enough to patch a handful of hull breaches.

Beka and Dylan had talked seriously about cannibalizing sor

e other spacecraft kept aboard *Andromeda*—possibly even Tweedle-
e and Tweedledum, the two giant planet-combat mechs. In the end
y had decided against it. Neither of them had any intention of giv-
up anything that could be advantageous in an unexpected battle. It
s going to be quite a while before they were in anything approaching
d shape, and they could not afford to give up any of the Slipfighters.

"On the other hand," Dylan said, "I just hope Harper's got some-
g more than spit and string in mind for the Slipstream drive."

One of the small junction flatscreens lit up with Andromeda's
ge. "Judging by the amount of vulgar language Mr. Harper is
g, I would say that he is definitely not having an easy time." She
sed for a moment. "No spit or string involved, however."

"Well," Dylan said, "that's good." He glanced at Beka. "Isn't it?"

"That depends," Beka said. She had settled for a simple white shirt
black pants for the walk-through, and looked considerably more
fortable than he felt. "Harper burbling and cooing at things,
y. Harper making grandiose proclamations of his own genius,
's okay too."

Harper swearing," Dylan said, not liking the direction this was
g, "is not good."

Extremely not good," Beka said. She looked as worried as he had
seen her. "If anybody can get *Andromeda* going, it's Harper. If
swearing and tearing his hair out—"

No hair-tearing yet," Andromeda said. "Lots of foot-stamping
tantrum-throwing. I'm having a difficult time restraining myself
n spanking him."

Don't!" Beka blurted. Wide-eyed, she looked at Dylan, and then
at the screen, where Andromeda was patiently waiting. "I mean,
t spank him. Not don't stop yourself from spanking him."

She means that he might enjoy it," Dylan said with a half smile.
eka turned her head to look at him again. "Dylan . . ." She paused
moment. "*Ewwww.*"

Takes all kinds," Dylan said simply. He looked at the screen.
training yourself is probably a good idea, Andromeda. Just get
to calm down and stay on task. It's nice and quiet out here, but at
t I'm not a country boy."

"I'm not so sure about that," Beka said.

She began walking down the corridor again, her boots crunc on the scattered plastic and metal.

"This is quite depressing," Andromeda said. "I look terrible feel worse. How can I show up for a battle looking like this?"

Dylan grinned, eliciting a smile from the flatscreen image. "I worry," he said, "we'll get your gown ready in time for the ball.'

"Just get me some serious upgrades," she said. She smiled at again, suddenly all elfin innocence. "After all, it's my birthday so

"I do not consider this advisable," Tyr said as he and Dylan st into the brig and stopped. "They are enemy combatants."

Patiently, Dylan said, "Tyr, I don't see an enemy at the mon and I don't see any combatants. I *do* see altered circumstances, a plan to roll with them, not fight against them."

Tyr folded his arms across his chest, giving Dylan a skeptical l "And you somehow believe that this will give your Commonwe an edge in convincing the Kantaran government of its innate g intentions?"

"Ejecting them out of an airlock," Dylan said, "would certa make a bold statement in the opposite direction. Very Nietzsch Tyr, but not particularly Dylan Hunt."

"Granting requests such as these invites surreptitious action," grumbled. "The viper in the bosom, the dagger in the night, the son in the cup."

"These are a couple of line fighter pilots," Dylan said, irrit despite knowing that Tyr was doing the right thing by pointing the negative consequences of what he was about to do. "They're Nietzschean politicians."

"Merely alien military personnel with homeworld loyalties," said. "I believe, sir, that you are deluded, and, further, that this wi a grave mistake."

"Well, if so, it wouldn't be the first one I've made," Dylan co tered, "and it certainly isn't likely to be the last." He looked squarely in the eyes. "I recall making a decision to take on a cer Nietzschean mercenary a few years ago."

"Every decision has consequences," Tyr said.

"And as Trance said to me one day, every choice creates its own
[pat]h." The more he argued this with Tyr, the more certain he became
[of] his choice.

"And you feel secure in homilies uttered by Trance?" Tyr said
[wit]h a snort. "You would do just as well perusing the shirts and stick-
[ers] on sale in gewgaw shops on any world or drift."

"Your objections are noted, Mr. Anasazi," Dylan said.

With that, he turned around and walked to the far end of the brig.
[Ty]r followed, adjusting his Gauss pistol holster for a smoother draw.
[Dy]lan sighed. It wasn't so much Tyr watching *his* back, but Tyr
[wat]ching Tyr Anasazi's front, along with every other direction. After
[the] insanity a few days previously, it made him nervous . . . and more
[tha]n a little irritable.

The two pilots were in facing cells at the end of the brig corridor.
[Tha]t had afforded them eye contact as well as making it easy to talk
[wit]h each other despite the clear barriers that kept them penned in.
[The]y had been promised humane treatment, and that was exactly
[wha]t they had received. Trance and Rommie had both made regular,
[b]rief, visits to deliver food and observe their guests. Neither of
[the]m had shown any sign of wanting to make a break for freedom—
[if a]nything, they appeared to be utterly compliant, and willing to toe
[the] line wherever they found it drawn.

[T]yr stood next to Dylan and glanced from one captive to the
[oth]er. "I would venture to say that life aboard the *Andromeda Ascen-*
[dant] agrees with our prisoners."

[T]yr was right. Both pilots had lost their pallor and seemed to have
[deve]loped a more robust look. They also seemed to have shed some
[of th]eir rigidity.

["A]ttention!" Dylan said with quiet force. The pilots were on their
[feet] in a flash. Dylan was certain he heard their boot heels click together.

["E]xcellent discipline," Tyr said, "for kludges."

[D]ylan glared at him. Tyr held his glance, but said nothing.

[T]urning back to the pilots, Dylan lifted a hand and said, "At ease."
[The]y assumed a parade rest position that looked uncomfortable.
["Tra]nce tells me that you've decided that you don't want to go home."

"Yes, sir," the male pilot—Lieutenant Micah Wright—said. spoke in a clipped manner that made Dylan wince. He wished s of these people could leave their Academy days behind and being cadets.

Dylan turned to the woman, Lieutenant Paula Pogue. "Is this you want?"

"Sir . . . yes, sir!" She took a deep breath, looking directly at She had big brown eyes that were accented by her pale skin an cropped hair. "We've talked about this for a couple of days, an realized that it's what we both want."

"We love Kantar," Wright said softly, "but there is more to universe than our world and its isolationist policies."

"So," Tyr said quietly, "you are in rebellion against your gov ment."

"No!" Wright exclaimed, shocked. "No. We fought to protec world."

"We simply have no one to go back to," Pogue said. She lo down at the floor for a moment, then back at him again. "Neith us has any surviving family."

"You have your squadron," Tyr said.

"We wouldn't even have that," Wright said. "At least not away. If we return in one of your Slipfighters, there will be he pay."

"Even if there wasn't that," Pogue said, "we would be grou for a time, for debriefing. No matter what the truth is, we might be grounded for life. We would rather our colleagues think us de lost, at least for a while."

Dylan held her gaze, silent.

"As we told Miss Gemini, sir," Wright added, "we are forr requesting asylum."

"You can call me Trance," said a familiar voice. Dylan and turned to see Trance walking down the brig corridor. She gave a cheerful smile. "'Miss Gemini' sounds silly. It makes me sound a schoolteacher." She frowned, playing the pixie. "Not that sch teachers are silly, I mean."

Dylan turned back to the pilots. "Once we're in better shap

n have a courier take a message back to Kantar." He looked at ance, who nodded, then at Tyr, who gave him a noncommittal rug. He turned back to the pilots again. "Well, we can use a few tra hands. There are conditions, however."

"Yes, sir!" they chorused.

"First," Dylan said, "you stop doing that."

"I think it's rather charming," Tyr said.

"You would," Dylan said. "There will be restrictions. You'll carry ckers at all times. If you're found in an area of the ship where you n't belong, I'll authorize Mr. Anasazi to shoot you. You will pond immediately to all orders from the Command staff."

"Understood, sir," Wright said quietly.

"You intend to use us as crew members?" Pogue said, nonplussed.

"Absolutely," Dylan said. "You won't have any rank—which is in rt supply around here as it is—but you will be part of the crew, at st for the time being. As such, I expect you to carry out all duties igned to you, and to otherwise spend as much time as you can in cating yourselves." He took a deep breath, let it out slowly. "Once reach Systems Commonwealth space, you can decide for your-es whether you want to remain aboard or move on. A High Guard mission might not be out of the question."

"We'll take it one day at a time, sir," Wright said.

"That works for me," Dylan said. He turned to Tyr, nodding. "Mr. sazi, if you would be so kind?"

yr produced a pair of tiny tracking devices that would allow romeda to follow the two pilots anywhere in the ship. They were e for insurance than anything else—the internal surveillance sys-s could do the job just as well. While the trackers would allow romeda to follow their movements in the damaged areas of the , the real point was psychological. If Wright and Pogue were ning anything, having the trackers pinned on and being told that would deal with them if necessary would most likely undermine r self-confidence.

he same reasoning lay behind Tyr applying the tiny devices. Tyr d have the most benign and gentle expression, and he still scared le when he focused his attention on them.

Wright and Pogue seemed uncertain of their grant of free
standing just inside their cells and hesitating to step out.

Finally, Dylan said, "Out, both of you. We'll get you settle
your quarters, then draw up a list of your duties for the next few
Rommie will familiarize you with the bridge. Welcome to the
Mr. Wright, Ms. Pogue."

"Thank you, sir!" they chorused, snapping crisp salutes.

Dylan winced again. "First order of business—no salutes, o
ask Tyr to hit you. Understood?"

They looked at each other, then at Tyr, then at Dylan. "Yes,
Wright said quietly.

"Then we should get along fine," Dylan said. He turned to Tra
"Miss Gemini, if you'll show them to their quarters?"

Trance stuck her tongue out at him, then grinned. "My
sure . . . *sir*."

Dylan gave the two pilots his long-suffering look. "It's never e

Two days later, Harper lay sprawled over a much-abused conso
Engineering, trying to patch broken waveguides and reconnect f
optic lines that had come loose during the battle. Not only wa
finding the job tedious, he was finding it painful. His stor
throbbed, and he was getting a headache.

He was also beginning to feel a little irritated with Dylan. Oka
he was a miracle worker. It just seemed as though Dylan wante
miracles *now*, instead of such time as Harper could deliver tl
Sometimes Dylan could be as impatient as a Nightsider.

He shifted, trying to get more comfortable. As he did so, his
caught a bonding tool. He lunged for it, but missed. It clattered int
console. He reversed his movement instantly, just in time to av
shower of sparks as the tool shorted something out inside the cons

"Just. *Freakin'*. Great!" he howled.

Adding injury to insult, he slipped backward from the console
ended up in a rumpled pile on the floor.

The day really wasn't going well, he decided.

"That sounded pretty bad," Paula Pogue said, sitting up fron
position behind another console and giving him a concerned l

Ier movement scattered some of the flexis strewn around her, and
ne hurriedly gathered them together.

"Yeah, it was bad," Harper muttered, stomping back to the con-
ole. He lunged over it, and into the cavity he had been working in—
hy the hell any of these consoles had been built against bulkheads
as a mystery to him—and retrieved the bonder. It was blackened,
ut still working. "Ah, the hell with this crap. I'm gonna see if I can
g a bypass without blowing us to hell."

"You need a break," Pogue said.

"What I need," Harper said, "is to get this freakin' job done so we
n get the hell out of here."

"I get that point," Pogue said sharply. She stood up, wiping her
nds on her blue coverall. She walked over to him and looked him in
e eye, unwavering. "You need a break, Mr. Harper. You've pushed
urself too much."

"Says you," he muttered, uncomfortable with her steady gaze.

"Says me," she echoed. She put her hands on her hips, and suddenly
e was glaring at him. "Harper, I haven't been aboard for very long, but
doesn't take very long to get an idea of how you are. It's okay when
u're a complete nutball. Right now you just sound exhausted and
nky." She jerked a thumb back at the console he had been trying to fix.
hat means mistakes and accidents. We can't afford either of those."

"I'm fine," he insisted.

"My ass you're fine," she snapped. She stepped closer to him. "It's
eak time. You're going to take an hour off and lie the hell down, or
strap you down and have Trance dope you up."

He glared at her. "Where the hell do you get off acting like my
ther?"

"I'm your crewmate," she said, putting her left hand on his chest.
here I come from, you take care of your wingman and your wing-
n takes care of you." Before he could say anything, she put a finger
er his lips. "If we're going to survive, Seamus, we need to look out
each other. I expect you to do the same for me."

He stared at her, speechless. She had a point. He *was* exhausted, and
could make the kind of mistakes that could blow *Andromeda* to hell.
"Well?" she asked, taking her finger from his lips.

"Okay," he said. He blinked, realizing how crusty and sore his e
felt. His back and shoulders hurt, and he still had the headac
"Maybe two."

"Two it is," she said with a slight smile.

"I bet Trance can come up with something to keep me going a
that," he added.

"I'm sure she can. Stay here." Pogue walked across the deck to
cooler that Harper always brought along when he was working in
depths of Engineering. She fished out two cans of Sparky Cola
came back, opening them both. "I figure we can drink on it."

He grinned. "Letting you into my private Sparky Cola stasl
looking after my wingman, huh?"

She grinned. "You bet."

"I guess I can live with that," he said, and took a gulp of the c
She sipped at hers. Trying for a more conversational note, he s
"So, you going to let your hair grow out now?"

She smiled and ran her free hand over her cropped hair. "Absolu
Maybe not to any great length, but it'll be a relief to be done with
regulation haircut. I may even start wearing makeup and dec
clothes."

He took another gulp of cola. "Yeah, well, you're gonna have
ask Beka or Trance about that. Rommie's got a thing going with
hair, but she's kinda one-note with her outfits."

"Like someone else I know," she said. "You planning to ever co
your hair and wear decent shirts?"

"Hell, no," he said, giving her a mixture of a grin and a sneer.
a mark of genius, looking like this."

"It's a nerd beacon," she said with a laugh. He frowned at her,
she laughed again. "It's okay. I'm just teasing."

He gulped down the rest of the cola. "Yeah, well, that's what t
all say." He crumpled the can and tossed it over his shoulder. It lan
squarely in the recycling bin, making a tinny rattle as it hit the ot
cans. He regarded her sleepily. "Okay, I guess it's time to go lie d
for a couple of hours."

She smiled. "Yes, it is. Rommie, will you wake him up in a co
of hours?"

Rommie shimmered into view, looking a bit stern. "I'm a warship, not an alarm clock." Pogue frowned at the hologram. "Of course, it does mean tormenting Harper, so I'll be happy to do so. I have a wonderful recording of a full bagpipe band playing the 'March of the High Guard' that should do the trick."

"Oh, joy," Harper said.

"Well," Rommie said, "*I* think so."

"Good night, Mr. Harper," Pogue said.

"Yeah, g'night," Harper muttered, shuffling toward the exit.

Behind him, he heard Pogue quietly counting backward from five. Just as she reached zero, he felt the familiar pressure that came with drinking Sparky Cola too fast. The result was an enormous belch—he was impressed with himself; it was a real blue-ribbon effort.

Grinning hugely, he left Engineering.

Once Harper had left, Pogue and Rommie turned to look at each other. "Before you ask," Pogue said, grinning, "it's a barracks trick I learned years ago. The timing depends on whether it's beer or a soft drink. But if they gulp, they're going to belch."

Rommie stared at her, looking befuddled. "You must have been fun at parties." Pogue laughed. "On the other hand, I used to have four thousand High Guard lancers aboard."

"That's potentially a lot of noise."

"To say the least." Suddenly Rommie's face took on an expression of deep sadness. "I miss them sometimes. Losing my crew left an ache that's never quite gone away." She sighed. "Someday I'd like to have a full crew again."

Pogue regarded her seriously. "You've told Captain Hunt about this, of course?"

"Oh, yes. There's supposed to be something in the works, but the wheels of bureaucracy turn slowly. It could take a year or two before anyone is assigned to us." Rommie regarded her steadily. "In the meantime, you and your colleague are a start, at least for the moment. It's your choice in the end, of course."

"I think I'm going to stay," Pogue said with a smile. "I could get spoiled here."

"Just don't betray us," Rommie said, her expression deadly serious "I've had enough of it. We all have. Keep in mind that I'm a warship and I *will* kill you if I think it's in our best interests."

"I think that point has gotten across very well," Pogue said rue fully. "While the idea seems not to have occurred to Mr. Harper ye Mr. Anasazi made his opinion very clear without saying a word. He a beautiful man, but quite terrifying."

"Yes, he is," Rommie said, smiling again. "I'm satisfied about th intentions you and Mr. Wright have, but I'm afraid that you'll have t endure the Sword of Damocles for a little longer when it comes to m crew." Pogue frowned, missing the reference. "Large pointy obje hanging by a thread over your head. A wrong move, and it's all over."

Pogue nodded. "Understood. More mythology for me to lear I'm still in the middle of the Greeks." She made a moue. "I have say I empathize with the labors of Hercules—fixing you seems like impossible task."

Rommie smiled. "It's been done before, Ms. Pogue, and I've nev needed Hercules to help out. Literally, in fact, as *The Labors of Hera les* was a High Guard long-range cargo hauler with a lughead of AI. Great personality, mind you."

With that, Rommie shimmered out. Pogue stood in thought for moment, then went back to the console she had been working on.

A few days later, Harper's manic energy was back in full force as he ma his final round of checks and tweaks—*several* final rounds, as it turn out, because he apparently didn't want to accept that there was no mc fine-tuning to be done on those things he was able to fix right now.

His nervous energy was beginning to put everyone else on edge at least that was the assumption. Even Trance, who had managed be the model of decorum during the enforced pause in their journ was getting twitchy around Harper.

At least the job was getting done. They were finally going to able to get out of the doldrums and, albeit slowly, get somewhe Maybe then everyone would be less edgy and frustrated.

———

a couldn't seem to get comfortable at the pilot station, no matter
y she shifted or balanced herself. She felt oddly unsettled and
re than a little uncertain of what she was doing. Hardly a surprise,
ugh—after all, nobody knew if the *Andromeda Ascendant* was going
old up, even after Harper's work. They needed too much in the
of parts and supplies to be really secure.

t suddenly occurred to her that Dylan was going to be really,
ly ticked at her if things went wrong and they blew up in Slip-
am. He would probably hold a grudge against Harper as well.

he had to suppress a giggle. Rommie glanced at her, curious. Beka
ed a hand at her, unwilling to explain the goofy thought she had
had.

our weeks ahead of them, just to get back to Commonwealth-
dly space. It promised to be an exhausting journey, even with
n, Harper, and Trance taking over some of the Slipstream flying.
, Slipstream was a strange environment—just as they had been
wn this far out when things went wrong, it might be possible for
:o shorten their coming journey by playing the streams once they
e the transition to Slipstream. She had done this before, but
r on the scale that she was contemplating now. She would have to
s close to perfect as she could manage, though—one slip, and
would probably be worse off than they were now. She had no
e to explain to Dylan that she had tried for a shortcut and ended
a even deeper woods.

ae sighed, suddenly feeling weary. It would be a snap to get them
•f this if she could just mix up a batch of Flash, just enough to . . .

er head began to pound, and she felt her strength pour away like
r. She grabbed the sides of the console in front of her, feeling
erately sick and ashamed. *What the hell am I thinking?*

3eka?" She hadn't noticed Rommie coming to her side. The
oid laid a gentle hand on her arm, giving her a concerned look.
at's wrong?"

eka stared at her, unable to form words for a moment. Finally,
tumbled, "Flash. I was thinking about Flash. About it helping me
s home faster."

"Beka . . ." Rommie started.

"I'm having crazy thoughts," Beka said. She closed her eye
took a deep breath, trying to bring herself under conscious co
At this rate she wasn't going to be able to fly. "I'm scared, Ror
I'm afraid that I'm going to screw up getting us out of here."

"You won't," Rommie said. She squeezed Beka's arm slight
trust you completely. We all do."

"I don't," Beka muttered.

Rommie was silent for a moment, looking at her. Finally, she
"My guess is that there's some kind of residual effect from the
taran attack. I've noticed that everybody except Trance is exhil
unusual responses to the stress we're under. Trance is, well, Tra

"Good for her," Beka said, almost managing a smile.

"You need to go and talk to her," Rommie said firmly. "Sh
probably find something to help you."

"God, I hope so," Beka muttered. "I feel miserable right n
can't believe I was thinking about Flash."

"You thought about it, and you talked about it, and you dealt
the temptation," Rommie said, releasing her arm. "I don't see an
Now get to the medical bay. We need you ready to fly us out of l

Trance didn't seem surprised to see Beka. To Beka's surprise,
ever, Micah Wright was stretched out on a diagnostic table, lo
pale and drawn.

"Migraine," he said, when he saw Beka. He started to sit up
stopped, wincing, shutting his eyes. Droplets of sweat broke o
his forehead.

Trance, who was filling a hypospray, turned around and frow
him. Without argument he laid back down. She stepped over to
pressed the hypospray to his neck, and pulled the trigger. There
low hiss. After a moment he relaxed a little, and his face beg
regain some of its normal color—not that there was much to re
as far as Beka was concerned.

Trance turned to Beka, smiling. "All I need now is Tyr."

"You've seen everybody else?" Beka said, startled. "Today?"

Today," Trance confirmed. "Migraines, headaches, upset stom-
. . . I'm seeing all kinds of things right now."

Stress sucks," Beka said. At least she seemed to be feeling better
Micah. After a moment, she decided it was apples and
ges—while she had a physical problem, her biggest issue seemed
e psychological. "Count me in on the headache list." She hesi-
d for a moment, then added, "I'm kind of . . . weak in the knees
t now, too."

rance frowned and looked down at Beka's legs. "Did you bump
something?"

eka stared at Trance for a moment, uncertain whether this
nent of cluelessness was the real thing or not. "Let's just say that
everything that's going on, I'm having a few confidence issues."

Oh," Trance said. She put the hypospray into a holder, picked up
her, and snapped an ampule into place. "Rest and relaxation
ld probably be better, but this should help give your body and
n a boost. That should help your state of mind too. Other than
, I think we could all use a week on a nice warm beach with
lutely nothing to do but be lazy."

That sounds like a plan," Beka said. Trance pressed the hypospray
er shoulder and pulled the trigger. "I hope you've got plenty of
stuff handy. It's going to be a long trip."

ace's concoction had helped a lot. Beka's headache had vanished
in a few minutes, and she had felt a surge of energy that had
en back the shadows. She wasn't about to start doing back flips
n the corridors, but she could at least face her appointed task.

ack at the pilot station, she ran through some final checks. While
was doing so, Dylan walked into Command. His movements
ed leaden, and he looked as though he wasn't quite focusing on
urroundings.

Dylan?" she said, concerned.

lowly, he turned his head to look at her. "Yes?"

You okay?"

le seemed to think about this for a few moments. Finally, he said,

"Yes." He smiled. "Trance had to play doctor with me." He frov
and shook his head. "Wait. We weren't playing doctor."

He stopped, looking baffled.

"You were feeling lousy in some way," Beka said, trying to st
chuckle at the lost look on Dylan's face. "She had to fix you up."

"Right," he said. "I feel a hell of a lot better." He stopped to t
again. "You ever feel better in slow motion?"

Beka opened her mouth to try to answer the question, and
realized that she didn't *have* an answer. Whatever Trance had g
Dylan, it had left him amazingly mellow. It was a good thing
didn't need Dylan to be in the same time zone right now.

"I was getting cranky," Dylan said. "Sick from the stomac
down, too."

"Dylan," she said, "I think you're probably about to give m
much information."

"Probably," he said mildly. "Captain's privilege."

"That plays two ways," Beka said, smiling. "I'm exercising mi
tell you to stop right there, mister."

"Right," he said. "But it's *my* ship."

"Not if she shoots you and takes over command," Rommie
Both Dylan and Beka turned to look at her. She was giving th
half smile. "Not that I could possibly advocate mutiny, of cours
I'm an android and I'm designed to protect the interests of the C
monwealth at all times."

"There's a big fat loophole in there, isn't there?" Beka said. "
tell. I grew up around people who never said anything that didn't
a loophole built into it."

"Are you suggesting that I'm a conniving person?" Rommie s

"I've known you for several years, Rommie."

"Moving on," Rommie said, without changing expression a
avoided offering a riposte to Beka's comment, "are you ready to
us out of here?"

"Just what I was going to ask," Dylan said sleepily. "It's time to

Beka turned her head to look at him. "I think I got the idea at
point, Dylan. Next time Trance gives you a shot, make sure
doesn't overdo it. You're just too weird right now."

"She said I needed it," Dylan said. "I'll snap out of it if I need to. Trance says so."

"Trance says a lot of things," Rommie said.

"And a lot of what she says is right," Dylan responded. "Okay, so a t of what she says isn't quite right either. Plus there's all the weird uff." He frowned. "I think I need coffee."

Beka shook her head. "I think you need to hang on to something." he reached overhead and tapped the switches that activated the Slip- ream hood. She opened a shipwide commlink and said, "Heads up, lks, I'm about to take us out of here. I need everybody on station w. Mr. Harper, are we good to go?"

"We've been good to go for hours, Boss," Harper said. He unded irritable. "Just get our collective asses out of here before I go mpletely nuts, okay?"

"Spoken like a scholar and gentleman, as always," Rommie said, oking rueful.

"Yeah, right," Harper snapped. "Whatever. Harper out."

Rommie and Beka exchanged a look. "Overworked and under- id," Beka said.

"Whatever it is," Dylan said, "he sounds pissed."

Beka didn't answer. She was too busy concentrating on her work ormally she would simply have opened the throttle and made : ;h-speed run for the Slipstream portal, but caution was the watch rd for the moment. It really didn't matter how fast they were mov ; in normal-space terms when the portal was opened—an entirel ferent set of rules came into force at the moment of transition.

Carefully, she increased their forward velocity. "One more rabbi e," she muttered. Opening shipwide again, she said, "Transition to Slipstream in five . . . four . . . three . . . two . . . one . . . *now!*"

The portal burst into life ahead of them, the runners caught hol l the universe went white and shook furiously as the *Andromed endant* drove on into the Slipstream.

She keyed the shipwide again. "Ladies and gentlemen, we are o way."

SEVEN • THE PRICE OF A BROKEN HEART

> Just as you get comfortable with the universe, the bitch
> hits you smack in the teeth . . . with a hammer.
>
> —ADMIRAL KADYMAE KELLER,
> AT THE DELPHIC
> CONFLAGRATION, CY 8733

Beka's palms were sweating as she brought the *Andromeda Ascen*
back into normal space from the first Slip jump. So far so good.
quickly scanned her instruments, then reached up to shut off the S
stream hood. As it rose she clenched and unclenched her hands,
ing to get her fears under control.

She knew she could do this. She knew it.

The next jump was going to be a short one, but at least the
Slip point wasn't too far from their present position. She was be
ning to map out their Slipstream journey in her head now, which
her, was always the key to getting where she wanted to go. Some S
stream pilots, such as Dylan, were content simply to open a portal
plod along, unable to see even a couple of jumps ahead. Her ab
went far beyond that, and she was sure she would start finding sh
cuts within the next few jumps. If she could find one Slip point s
that showed even the slightest sign of regular travel, then she c

most guarantee that their travel-time estimate could be tossed out—
upstream travel had its own peculiar set of rules. The more often a
route was used, the more direct, swift, and reliable it became.

Andromeda just had to hold together long enough. They were all
hoping for a miracle at this point—a debris field would be a godsend,
even if it meant being at a standstill for a few more days while
Andromeda took care of repairs and rearming.

Beka scanned her instruments again. Nothing. They hadn't even
reached the outer edge of the galactic rim yet. It gave her the creeps
to realize there was almost nothing out here but infinitesimal
amounts of hydrogen. If something happened now, they could still
use the *Eureka Maru* to find their way back—but it would mean aban-
doning *Andromeda*, possibly forever. She didn't think she could leave
the *Andromeda Ascendant* to die alone in the deep dark.

She took a deep breath, trying to get hold of her more depressing
thoughts. They were going to be okay. Nobody was going to abandon
Andromeda. There was always a solution—Dylan and Rommie had
demonstrated that time and again, while Harper was an absolute master at pulling life-saving solutions out of nowhere in time to stave off
calamity.

The fear just wouldn't go away.

She opened a comm channel to Engineering. "Harper, how's it going
down there?" She was startled at how loud and abrupt she sounded.

"Jeez, Boss," Harper snapped. She couldn't blame him for being
annoyed with her tone. "You could at least wait until I screw up
before you bite my damn head off."

"Sorry," she said. She tried to relax, but it just wasn't happening. "I just
wanted to check, that's all. Trying to stay on top of everything here."

"You're gonna give yourself an ulcer," Harper muttered. "Hell,
you're gonna give *me* an ulcer."

"*Harper*," Beka snapped. Silence. She noticed Rommie looking at her
then. "All I wanted to do was find out if we're holding together, okay?"

"We're holding together," Harper answered petulantly. "End of
report, Harper out."

"He's a little testy, isn't he?" Rommie said.

"Probably got out of the wrong side of bed," Beka answered.

"I doubt he got in either side of his bed recently." Rommie tu
back to her instruments. "Everyone needs to be very consciou
exhaustion, Beka, with the exception of Trance."

Beka gave Rommie an unhappy glance. "Yes, Mom."

"Beka," Rommie said sharply, "understand something here. If
thing happens, *my* life is on the line. I've survived the loss of my
before, but I was pretty much whole at the time. Right now I'
very bad shape, and I'm depending completely on you and the o
to get me through this. I don't need any of your grandstanding, F
You don't need to prove anything to me."

"I can do this," Beka said stubbornly. She realized that she sou
almost childishly petulant, but she didn't know how to stop it.
increased their forward velocity slightly, alert for any warning si

"I know you can," Rommie said. "Let's just say that I'm nervo

"Understood," Beka said. "I just need to do my job. It keep
calm." Beka was silent for a moment, staring down at her con
"Hell, it keeps Dylan calm."

"Something else to keep in mind, I suppose," Rommie said,
ing back to her own console.

"I suppose," Beka said.

She closed her eyes for a moment, wishing that the wait befor
next Slip point was over. More than that: she wished this swirl of
ings would just go away.

As always, however, she was having no luck with wishing.

Trance had been relieved that their first Slip had gone well, but
was still much that was nagging at the back of her mind, includin
vision she had had of a frozen world. There was a direct path
where things were now to that place she had seen, but she had y
be able to put it all together. For all she knew they would
encounter that world years in their future.

For the moment, she was content to spend some time i
hydroponics gardens, moving through her plants, spraying
trimming there, moving around those living in pots and pla
Working with living things, nurturing and nursing them as ne
brought her great joy.

She looked up and around, suddenly aware of a new presence. Not alternate version of herself this time, though, but the android ommie, standing at the end of the main path.

Trance smiled beatifically. "Hello. Do you like plants and trees?"

Rommie raised her eyebrows, looking around at the garden as ough trying to fathom exactly what it was. "In terms of my pro-ammed aesthetics, yes." She looked directly back at Trance. "That, wever, is in terms of my programming."

"Rommie-in-the-box," Trance said.

"Rommie-in-the-box," the android agreed. She walked up to ance, then knelt down, pressing the fingers of her right hand into loam. "I can feel the electrical impulses in the soil and use my sen- s to map the things that lie beneath it."

"But then the organic response is missing," Trance said gently. mmie turned her head to look up at Trance. "The appreciation. one thing to be able to scan something, analyze the scent by lying forensic methods, and match it against a database to find out at it is. It's another thing entirely to just take in something like this hout analysis. You allow yourself to be subjective rather than ective."

Rommie looked back down at the loam, pinching a piece of it ween her fingers and holding it up to her nose. "That's one of the gs I'm working on. That's the thing about being an artificial intel- nce, Trance. We're like any other sentient—we can learn and w. I like being what I am, but I don't have to play Rommie-in-the- to do that." She dropped the crumbled loam and dusted her ds together. "You can thank Mr. Harper for some of my ability to ch myself . . . although I still haven't made up my mind whether ng me the ability to be hormonal is a good or bad thing."

rance shook her head. "I wouldn't know, but as long as you can it off . . ."

ommie grinned. "It's a function I prefer not to access." She stood suddenly serious. "I didn't come by to talk about sentience and etics."

didn't think you did," Trance said. She had a good idea of what n Rommie's mind—and why the android had come to her rather

than anyone else in the crew. "I can be fun company, but I don't t
now's the time for that."

"Now is definitely not the time for that," Rommie said. "Tr
I'm practical. I'm a warship. My philosophy centers on one thi
load up my armory and point me at a target. In the past few v
I've encountered exactly one thing I could shoot at, and that al
got me killed."

"Everything else disturbs you," Trance said.

"Putting it mildly," Rommie answered. She sounded frustr
almost angry. "We're in the middle of nowhere, trying to get
where, I look like a decade-old High Guard practice drone, I ha
supplies, no nanos, no missiles, and a total of one working cann
can be thankful, I suppose, that I have functioning Slipfighter
some ancillary ships."

"We still have Tweedledee and Tweedledum," Trance said.

"I don't know how much help they'd be in space," Ro
grumbled.

"They did a great job with the Magog swarmships that attacke

"They were sitting ducks attached to my hull," Rommie prot
"Of course they did a great job. They couldn't miss."

"So," Trance said, not looking away from Rommie, "we're v
able. One or two more Slips and you can start fixing that."

"It's still scary," Rommie said. "I'm not used to being afraid, Tr

"It's okay to be scared sometimes," Trance said sweetly. She i
diately regretted allowing herself to sound so perky. "I bet eve
sometimes gets scared. Think of it as being part of that growin
cess you were talking about. It's very healthy."

Rommie gave her a half smile. "That isn't all of it, Trance."

"I know." Trance picked up a spray bottle and handed it
android. "I've still got stuff to do, so you can help me while yo
okay?"

They started down the path. Trance suddenly turned to the
stepping onto a barely visible access path as Rommie followed.

"That's a nutrient mix," Trance said without looking back. "
ever you see a plant that looks like it needs it, just go ahead an
away."

Rommie found a candidate immediately, and gave it several precise squirts from the bottle.

Trance had stepped into a group of tall plants, and was barely visible. She turned, assessing the growths she was looking at. Taking out her shears, she made several quick cuts, pleased with the way the plants seemed to brighten. She scattered the off-cuts around so that they could decay and feed back to the plants around her. The chemistry-set method was all well and good, especially the way that the Commonwealth had implemented it, but she believed strongly in adding the natural component as well.

She looked back at Rommie, who was diligently spraying plants. Trance crossed over the path to Rommie and took the spray bottle from her, adjusting the nozzle. "This isn't a battle, Rommie. They'll take the nutrients just as well if you mist them."

Rommie took the bottle back and began carefully misting the plants. "I came down here to talk about you."

Trance smiled slightly. "Not about me," she said. "About what's been happening around me, or to me, or however you want to put it."

"Yes." Rommie looked at Trance for a moment. "I'd like to talk about you too, but that always leads nowhere."

"Rommie, it isn't about who I am or what I am," Trance said softly. "I'm just a tiny, tiny part of things."

"You have a propensity for being in the middle of things, Trance." Rommie's eyes crossed as she focused on a flying insect that was trying to land on her nose. "Right now, though, I'm a lot less concerned about you generally than the things happening around you. I've said before—I get very cranky when I can't quantify things. I haven't been able to quantify many of the events that occurred just prior to the battle with the Lighthouse Keepers. I'd like to know what's going on, Trance, and I'd like an honest answer."

Trance started back to the main path, and Rommie followed. "Rommie, I wish there were some way you could tell that I was telling the truth, but my body doesn't work the way you need."

"I know that the truth with you is fluid," Rommie said, sounding sure.

"My whole existence is fluid," Trance said. Not smiling, she

looked directly at Rommie. "It's also hard to know what to do
what not to do. Everybody has this idea that I'm cunning and dev
and somehow I secretly know all the answers. Well, I don't. There
times when I'm really, truly, terrified. I can't fail, Rommie."
closed her eyes for a moment, but all it did was allow old image
surge up. "I've seen what happens if I do."

"Which is your contention," Rommie said, "but we have no w
confirm anything, do we? What about these recent events?"

"Believe me," Trance said, "I wish I knew. Things just started
pening. I'm sure there's a reason behind it, but . . ." She shook
head. "When there's another one of me around, I usually *expect* i

"Do you mean that this happens to you a lot, Trance?"

Trance sighed. "No, that's not what I mean. What I mean is
these were all pretty rude surprises."

"Could the Kantarans' mind weapon have had any effect on y

Trance shook her head. "Even if it had, it wouldn't result in
happened. Reality was having small fits. Anyway, it seems to
stopped now."

"For the time being," Rommie said. She frowned. "I still
have answers, do I?"

"Sorry," Trance said. She turned to the right and started
another access path. "Let's get these plants down here. The
crotchety if they're left alone too long."

Tyr was standing in the darkness of the observation lounge
Dylan walked in. The tall Nietzschean was looking out at the d
points of light that were all the illumination they had this far
deep space. One more Slip, however, and they would be somew
lot less foreboding. He was grateful for that fact.

"Hello, Dylan," Tyr said. He sounded contemplative. "
myself restless. I had hoped to center myself here, but it seems
will not work."

Dylan stopped next to Tyr. "I had the same idea, Tyr. Un
nately, I don't think there's any way to not be on edge until we g
of this situation."

"If." Tyr's voice was solemn.

'When," Dylan countered firmly. "*When*. It's a matter of time, 's all."

'Ever the optimist, sir." Tyr didn't look away from the dark vista ore them.

'We always find a way," Dylan said.

'Not always." Tyr finally looked at Dylan. "Need I remind you we began this doomed voyage in the first place?"

)ylan sighed. "Would you like me to find an albatross and wear it nd my neck?"

An . . . a what?"

The Rime of the Ancient Mariner," Dylan said, smiling. "A long poem it lost seafarers in ancient times. One of them shoots an albatross— d of bird—and dooms the entire crew. His punishment is to wear lead bird around his neck. He's the one left to tell the tale."

'yr was silent for a moment, then he said, "Dylan, there are times n I truly am afraid for your sanity." He turned away from the low. "Good night."

Good night, Tyr," Dylan said affably.

 moment later he heard Tyr say, "Good night, Rommie, and no, cannot move quietly enough to evade my senses."

Good night, Tyr," Rommie said seriously. She walked up to n's side. "Sometimes he carries that superiority business a little ar."

 try to ignore it," Dylan said. "He's turned out to be worth toler- for the most part."

Ve could say the same for Trance," Rommie said.

Ve could," Dylan said. "Which leads to the next point—did ce have any answers?"

he taught me how to feed and trim plants," Rommie said, ning. "I believe she also attempted to explain aesthetics, the e of fear, and why chocolate is good. She did not, however, have xplanation for the phenomena affecting her several weeks ago."

hould we be worried?"

Jnanswered questions are always cause for worry, Captain."

 simple 'yes' would have done," Dylan said, amused.

 m more concerned about the fact that multiple types of phe-

nomena were involved, not just one. We have Trance's assertion
she traveled forward in time on what would now be an alternate
line. We have at least one alternate Trance—and Trance believe
each of the alternates actually came from different timelines. Fi
we have the ghosting on the Command Deck. The first few
seem extremely important, but they aren't as important as the la

"Why?"

Rommie had her most serious expression now. "While the imag
saw appear to have no tangible existence, that's not true—we wer
ing across the boundaries of multiple realities. At best, this is har
At worst, it would indicate that reality is somehow breaking down

"Bad," Dylan said.

"Very," Rommie added. "If those boundaries give way, we
have time to ask why."

"How likely?"

"Not very. Which, considering our past history, doesn't
much."

"It's these moments of reassurance that I treasure, Rommie.

"I do my best," she said.

Wright was in the medical bay again, with another migraine
time it was accompanied by a sudden nosebleed that had left the
of his uniform sticky with blood. At first Trance had thought
some kind of accident while working in the damaged corridors

She had quickly gotten the nosebleed under control and hi
packed with cotton. The migraine took a couple of minutes
while one of her special medical concoctions did its work.

"I hate this," Wright muttered. "Haven't had a nosebleed li
since Jenblossom broke my nose at the Academy. First it w
someone was pumping my head full of air, then out it comes, a
migraine kicks in." He carefully touched the bridge of his nos

Trace looked at her readouts. "It looks like something e
your blood pressure and did so very quickly. It's almost down
mal now, and you seem to be okay."

"I don't feel okay," he mumbled. "It's better than having a mi
though."

That's the way," she said, smiling brightly. "Focus on the positive."

He tried to smile back, but it was a weak effort. "Listen, I'd try to flirt here, Trance," he said, "but I'm having too many problems, so is Pogue."

Everybody seems to be," Trance said.

I thought we'd been hit by our own weapon," he said. He swung legs over the side of the diagnostic table and sat up. "I still think s pretty much the case, except we've been thinking of the wrong pon. I need to talk to Dylan."

nicknamed 'the mind torpedo,'" Pogue said. She, Wright, and crew were sitting in the commissary, drinking coffee.

The full-scale weapon basically unleashes a torrent of energy at its et, achieving results very quickly—you've seen this for yourselves."

ght took a sip of coffee. "The torpedo works on a much smaller . It's designed as a fallback device if a ship manages to escape."

The torpedo detonates close to the hull of the target vessel," Pogue : on, "scattering thousands of microscopic transmitters that stick ace. Each individual transmitter is essentially harmless."

t's the accumulation that does the trick," Rommie said. "Given , the effects on the crew cause a breakdown, with potentially dis- us consequences."

Like making stupid mistakes," Harper muttered.

Dr Micah's migraines," Trance said. "The physiological side effects langerous. This time he had a massive nosebleed. Next time it d be a stroke. I'm keeping him on medication that should help with nigraines and keep his blood pressure down, but I don't know how that'll last." She looked around the table, displaying her worry. "I having to give you medication, and that could be very dangerous."

've seen it cut Dylan's reaction time down," Beka said, giving n a concerned look. "You're creepy on that stuff."

Better that than having me running around ranting about who ate trawberries, or whatever," Dylan said.

arper looked confused. "Huh? Strawberries?"

ylan held up a hand. Harper sat back looking at Trance, who ed and shrugged.

"So," Dylan said, sitting up, "we find out where they hit, them off, and start having normal lives again."

"It isn't quite that easy, Captain," Pogue said. "Begging An eda's pardon, it was a bit like shooting at the broad side of More than likely you were hit by several torpedoes. By now have networked."

"Then you tell us what to do," Tyr said, glowering. Pogue ered right back, silently. The sight amused Dylan. Tyr hadn't match, but Pogue wasn't going to be intimidated.

"We'll need to disrupt them somehow," Wright said. "Or transmitters have been shut down, they can be scraped off the masse. Before that, if anything gets close enough to cause d they'll defend themselves."

"Then I suggest we make that solution the first order of b after this next Slip," Rommie said. "I'm very much looking f to this one. A prime selection of raw materials will improve greatly."

Beka stood up, smiling. "Time to *really* get this show on th folks."

Harper and Pogue headed down to Engineering—Harper wa fiably nervous about the state of the Slipstream core, never everything else. There had been some noncritical problems si first Slip, but those had represented little more than tidying Harper.

While the rest of the crew headed for Command to wait time before the next Slip, Trance headed back to the medical pick up her hypospray and a medical kit with her various conco Even Dylan was accepting the shots as routine now.

She had just reached the medical bay when the universe around her. She was caught so completely unawares that she bled and fell headlong, catching herself at the last moment.

"Welcome aboard the *Perseus Triumphant*," a woman said. Trance looked up to see a tall middle-aged woman with cropped blond hair and emerald-green eyes looking down at h was wearing what appeared to be a modified black High Gua

n, and had a Gauss pistol in her left hand, although it was no
gn that Trance had ever seen before. "I am Captain Diana Hunt,
ditary shipmaster."

Nice to meet you," Trance said. "Sorry about the undignified
val."

Captain Hunt regarded her steadily. "You may stand, slowly." She
ed to a bronze-skinned man standing next to her. "Perseus,
ve her of that . . . whatever it is."

It's a force lance," Trance said, standing up slowly. She smiled at
eus as he took it from its holster. "Be careful with it. Force lances
individually keyed, and you'll be zapped if you try to fire it or
it."

Open it?" the android said.

It opens out into a quarterstaff," Trance said. "It's a pretty useful
pon."

I imagine," Hunt said. "So."

here was a moment of silence, then Perseus said, "It's her."

hat statement startled Trance. "What?"

Trance Gemini," Captain Hunt said. She smiled slightly. "It's
a while since I saw you last, Trance, but the years haven't done
any harm."

You don't have questions about how I just appeared out of thin air
t in front of you?" Trance said, confused.

It's quite a trick," Perseus said, "although the landing needs a lit-
vork."

h, this is going to get complicated. "I'm, uh, not your Trance," she
Hunt and Perseus looked at each other. "That's why I arrived the
I did. I'm from another timeline, and I have the feeling I'm a
way from home."

You always were one for surprises," Hunt said. Smiling, she
hed out with her free hand and squeezed Trance's shoulder. "You
e a great moment to arrive, however."

I'm under attack," Perseus said. "There's a swarming pestilence
d the Doeia. Our support group got bogged down and my
nses were overwhelmed. We finally scraped them off of my hull,
there are some stragglers on board."

"Not for long, though," Hunt said.

Perseus handed Trance's force lance back. "We learned ea
not to attempt a dialogue with the Doeia. They're utterly an

"What do they—"

There was a loud chittering and scraping behind her, an
turned in one swift movement.

"Like that," Perseus said.

Facing her was a spidery creature, about her height. It was w
some kind of plastic armor that covered its thorax and its eight j
limbs; it was walking on four of the limbs, while the other four
tioned as arms. A plastic mask covered what appeared to be the
Under the mask she could see a mouth filled with rows of tiny
Sixteen unblinking eyes arranged in rows of two stared at them

The Doeia lifted a long slender weapon, but it was too slow.
and Perseus were firing to either side of her; her own shots
instinctively. The Doeia staggered backward, its armor and ma
ping apart and its weapon flying out of its thin hands. For a m
it tried to get its balance using three legs, two undamaged arm
tically snatching at other weapons. Then the barrage took its to
it fell, kicked twice, and lay still.

The three of them holstered their weapons. Perseus
momentarily lost in thought, then said, "That seems to have be
last of them, Captain."

"About time," Hunt grumbled. She turned to Trance. "W
you here?"

"I don't know," Trance said honestly. "It just happened. O
ond—"

The universe twisted again, and she was suddenly back
familiar medical bay.

She definitely needed answers, and soon, but she didn't ha
slightest clue where to look.

She had never felt so helpless.

"I wish I had a better idea," Trance said as Rommie pinned a
to her collar. She gave the android a despairing look. "At least
have an idea *when* something happens, if not what's going on."

I'm hoping for a little more data than that," Rommie said. She
ped back slightly, frowning. "Well, there you are. Or it is."

For right now," Trance said, "wherever it is, I am."

Wherever you go, there you are?" Rommie suggested, her right
row raised.

Trance grimaced. "There are times when I'd like to take a vacation
n myself. You're lucky. You can."

Only one of me," Rommie said.

The holographic Rommie shimmered into life. "Patently untrue. I
schedule rest cycles for myself, as can Andromeda."

How long do those last?" Trance said. "Microseconds?"

Picoseconds, usually," the holographic Rommie said. "Not quite
enough to get bored."

Right now," Trance said, "I wouldn't mind being a little bored.
rything's getting too exciting lately."

I'm heading back to Command," Rommie said as her holographic
nterpart faded out.

I'll be there in a minute," Trance said. "I just need to gather some
gs."

Good enough."

ommie left. Trance went to her workbench and gathered
ther the small kit she needed. For the moment Beka and Dylan
e her main concern, so she could keep the kit to a minimum.

eady, she left the medical bay. She hadn't taken more than three
s before she lost track of reality altogether and felt herself—no,
herself this time, just her perceptions—thrust into the future.
y were racing toward catastrophe, and from there forward all she
d see was an ever more tangled morass of timelines until darkness
ned them all.

uddenly shipwide was on. "Ladies and gentlemen, hang on to
hats, here we go again. Slipstream in five . . . four . . . three . . .
. . . one—"

Beka!" Trance yelled. "Don't!"

—transiting to Slipstream now," Beka concluded.

rance started running as the *Andromeda Ascendant* jumped to
tream.

EIGHT • A PAINTED SHIP UPON A PAINTED OCEA

> It isn't "ghost ship," it's "ghost ships," plural. A few go i
> every month and they never come back—bad Slips, bad
> maintenance, who knows? Sometimes they go in and a
> long, long time later they come out again. You don't wa
> to know about those. Slipstreaming is about skill . . . an
> it's about luck.
>
> —HIGH GUARD ACADEMY SLIPSTREA.
> INSTRUCTOR MARDI GIACOMO,
> CY 8823

Her sense of dread increasing with each step, Trance raced t
Command. She had been unable to open a channel to Comman
now she was convinced that their only hope was for her to get
on foot. The rapid cycle of probability lines running throug
mind didn't help—she could barely focus on the lengths of co
she was racing down.

Not far now.

The universe twisted again.

Oh, no, not now.

She almost stopped, but the corridor had remained familiar
was still the *Andromeda Ascendant*—and it was *her* version of th
All she had to do now was figure out *when* she was.

Voices in the corridor, around an intersection. She turned th
ner and saw Dylan and Beka together.

She knew the location, too. It was the point at which she had
turned from her inadvertent future jaunt to witness Tyr's death.
They had been discussing the mysterious blood drops, and . . .

Trance almost laughed.

"Coming through!" she shouted, not slowing her pace. Startled, Beka
and Dylan stepped aside, letting her through. Any moment now . . .

"Trance!" Dylan called.

She turned around, running backward. "I don't have time!"

She turned and sprinted down another corridor, wondering if she
could have used this time to try to prevent the things that were going
to happen. The possibilities played out instantly in her mind. She
found nothing but disaster if they changed course now.

No pain, no gain . . . that's stupid. The universe twisted again, as she
had hoped, and she knew immediately that she was back in the right
time and place.

Well, almost the right place. She let out an inadvertent squeak as
she stumbled and almost fell into Beka. Where she had expected to be
and where she was were quite a few meters apart.

She was in the right place, however. Frantically, she grabbed
Beka's arm. "Beka, trust me, you've got to get us out of Slipstream
now!"

Dylan, Rommie, Tyr, and Wright were gathering around them
now, staring at Trance.

"That was quite a jump," Rommie said.

"In more ways than one," Trance said. "We need to get out of
Slipstream right now, or something very bad is going to happen."

Andromeda appeared on several of the flatscreens. "As in making-
life-worse bad?"

"As in it'll-only-hurt-for-a-second bad," Trance said. "Trust me!"

Dylan nodded at Beka. "Do it."

Beka gave Dylan a helpless look. "Dylan, if we exit Slipstream
now we—"

"Where there's a portal out, there's a portal in," Trance said.

"Gotcha," Beka said. She reached for her controls.

"Hey, Boss!" Harper's voice almost boomed over the comm system—
the urgency.

"Harper," Beka said, "I'm busy."

"Gonna be a hell of a lot busier if—oh, *jeez!*"

"'Oh, jeez' is definitely not good," Dylan said.

"It's worse than not good," Beka said. She had suddenly bec[ome] very pale. "Dylan, half of my systems are down and the other hal[f] freezing."

"Harper," Dylan said, "we've got problems up here."

"There's worse freakin' problems down here, Boss," Ha[rper] responded. There was the sound of snapping and fizzing somew[here] in the background. "I dunno what we're about to lose, but it's g[oing to] really freakin' *hurt*." Somewhere in the background Pogue yelpe[d]

"I'll see if I can help," Tyr said. Dylan nodded and the N[iet]schean left Command at a sprint.

"I'm losing the core," Harper yelled. "I don't know what th[e] happened but the exotic matter lens started to fracture and [it] screwed up the pulser. I'm trying to keep everything togethe[r but] I've got other stuff going down as well. Cascade *ow goddamnit.* [fail]ures."

"We've got systems down or locking out up here," Dylan sai[d]

"I need some kind of emergency bypass," Beka said frantica[lly.] can't get us out of Slipstream otherwise."

"I'll see what I can do, Boss, but you gotta remember, I'm [a] genius, not a miracle worker."

"That wasn't what you said last week, you liar," Trance said.

"Hey, golden girl," Harper answered. He sounded a bit [more] cheerful, which was what she had wanted. "Miracles comi[ng up.] Harper out."

Dylan looked around at Beka. "Keep trying."

"What do you think I'm *doing* here, Dylan?" Beka snapped.

Dylan's expression started to darken. In a flash, Trance ha[d a] hypospray out, loaded, and against Dylan's neck. There was a [soft] hiss, and Dylan's expression relaxed.

Suddenly the ship began to shudder violently.

"Trouble," Rommie said.

"One of the runners is starting to lose cohesion with the st[ream,]" Beka said. "If the other one goes as well, we're dead."

ndromeda appeared on the flatscreens again. "I'm attempting to
on as long as I can."

he ship shuddered even more violently this time.

)f course," Andromeda added, "that may not be long enough to
us."

till nothing," Beka said. "This is goddamn frustrating!"

)w!" Andromeda said, sounding and looking piqued. Everyone
d at the main flatscreen, startled. "Mr. Harper did something
mely off-specification."

ance saw Beka's control console change.

t's gonna be tricky," Harper called over the comm, "but I can get
t of here. I think."

m ready," Beka said. "I don't have full control yet."

hat's the tricky, Boss."

ance was almost blinded by the probability lines again, but she
ged to focus on the one they needed. "Harper, let me call the
g, okay?"

here was a pause. Then he said, sounding uncertain, "For my
n goddess, sure, babe."

he ship began shuddering violently. This time the vibration
t stop.

tarboard runner is now completely disengaged," Andromeda said.

he portside runner is losing cohesion," Beka said. "Trance, we
wait. Trance?"

m completely losing the core!" Harper yelled.

ance held up her right hand and counted off three. "Now, Beka!"

ka initiated the Slipstream transition commands.

m losing the portside runner," Andromeda said.

ne shuddering increased in violence. *Andromeda* was going to
apart if this kept up. Just a little longer . . .

ow, Harper!" Trance yelled.

ortside runner is now completely disengaged," Andromeda said
y, as though she wasn't being shaken to pieces.

nere was a tremendous bang as they were hurled out of Slip-
n.

———

"This is going to *so* screw up my record," Harper was complain‍

"I doubt it," Tyr said flatly.

While Beka had set up the Slipstream exit, he had set th‍ from its control station on the catwalk that overlooked the im‍ engine. On Trance's mark, he had shut the core down—just ‍ the plug, in short. It had worked, even though it wasn't the w‍ body wanted to exit Slipstream. In the process the exotic matt‍ had shattered and the pulser had taken enough of a pounding ‍ it beyond the hope of repair.

"One thing's for sure," Harper muttered, looking down i‍ now-quiet core pit, "we aren't going anywhere for a while."

"As Dylan keeps insisting," Tyr said, "some things are only ‍ ter of time."

"Oh, surrre," Harper said, throwing his arms up—which ‍ point at which the lighting and the artificial gravity field sh‍ "Oh, freakin' great! *Now* what?"

Red emergency lighting came on, giving the cavernous ‍ hideous look. At first Harper was focused on fixing *this* probl‍ until he realized that he was floating in midair over the Slip‍ core pit, and if the artificial gravity field came back on now, h‍ long scream ahead of him.

"Don't move!" Tyr's order seemed to come from right beh‍ feet.

Naturally, Harper moved, trying to see where Tyr was. The ‍ sent him drifting farther.

"Mr. Harper," Tyr said patiently, "if you don't pay attentio‍ going shoot you, do you understand?"

"Got it," was what Harper meant to say. "*Eep!*" was the sou‍ actually came out.

He felt Tyr's hands grip his ankles. Slowly, he was drawn ba‍ until Tyr was able to grab the waistband of his pants and swi‍ around. Tyr had swung over the railings of the catwalk, lockin‍ self into place by crossing his ankles.

Tyr got Harper to the railing and let go of him as soon as th‍ neer had gotten onto the catwalk. With a single graceful mov‍ Tyr drew himself back and swung himself to the catwalk, look‍

e world as though he operated in microgravity day in and day
Harper could barely remember how to move in microgravity—
ody wanted to do all the wrong things. Feeling sick, he clung to
ailing. That was the inner ear, he remembered, trying to get him
ced. *Great, now I get to upchuck.*

e turned his head and opened his mouth, then closed it again
Tyr said, "Don't waste time with thanking me, Mr. Harper. Fix
hip."

nm system is down," Rommie said, "but there may be a
around for that. We can patch through the *Eureka Maru* and
vehicles, and both Dylan and Harper have their subcutaneous
mitters."

'or now," Dylan said, "we're not going anywhere. Which means
it the hard way, using the *Maru* there and back." Dylan started
n, as did Beka.

e lights went out.

'm not sure which circuit that was," Rommie said. "And the AG
at the same time."

know," Beka and Dylan chorused.

nergency lighting came on, bathing everything in a dull red.
n and Beka were in midair, floating slowly toward the ceiling.
, looking aggravated, muttered, "It's never *ever* easy, is it?"

ka, on the other hand, looked quite comfortable. "Hey, you
a word."

oth of you may add another at any time," Rommie said. "That
'ouch' right after your keisters hit the deck when Harper gets
G working again." Rommie turned her head to look over at
h Wright. "Mr. Wright?"

m fine," he answered. "I was holding on to my station."

Ve could leave them up there," Trance said helpfully. Both she
.ommie had managed to stay on the deck. Rommie had clutched
.dge of a console. There was no telling how Trance was manag-

Iey!" Beka said, looking startled.
Vhat she said," Dylan added.

Rommie looked at Trance. "I think they want to come dow

"I think so too," Trance said. "We could wait until they
from the ceiling."

"Might be too late," Rommie said. "Seriously. You know h
Harper works."

"*Very* fast," Beka said. She had drifted over Trance's head.
my butt the way it is, thanks."

"Are you helping?" Rommie asked Trance.

"Why not?" Trance said cheerfully.

They kicked off simultaneously, Rommie aiming for Dyl
Trance heading for Beka. They caught their respective targets
the waist, slowing from the added mass—Rommie slowed
more than Trance, thanks to Dylan's greater mass.

Both used their free arms to cushion their arrival at the
killing their momentum.

"Free ride's over," Trance said, releasing Beka.

"Thanks," Beka said, floating against the ceiling. "I thin
looked down. "You know, it doesn't look *that* far up from dow
Looks like a *long* way down from up here."

"See you down there," Trance said.

She pushed off again and went floating feetfirst toward th
Beka drifted past her. Rommie, still holding Dylan, had just
deck and was going into a crouch to kill her momentum.

Straightening up, the android looked up at them. "Eve
okay up there?"

"Perfect," Beka said.

"I think you can let Dylan go now, Rommie," Trance said.

"Oh. Of course." She released Dylan, looking at him.
Captain."

Beka and Trance touched down, and Trance had to grab
shoulder to stop her from bouncing up again. Beka looked at
started to ask a question, but Trance said, "Don't ask."

Dylan was carefully settling himself at a console. Beka c
pushed off, angling herself toward the pilot station, catching h
using it to swing herself around and into place. Her boots
clumping noise on the deck. Trance followed, a little more de

Vell," Dylan said, taking a deep breath, "that was a fun interlude
een disasters." He looked at Rommie. "Can we do something
the emergency lighting?"

ommie tapped at her console. "Blue-shifting the lighting in
mand," she said as the lighting became cooler and brighter. "I'm
tant to do that all over the ship, especially in Engineering."

Jnderstood," Dylan said.

Ve're dead in the water," Beka said. "I've got nothing here."

A painted ship on a painted ocean,'" Dylan said.

he Rime of the Ancient Mariner," Rommie said, "by Samuel Tay-
oleridge."

lbatross," Dylan said absently.

Vhat?" Wright said from behind them.

ylan carefully turned his head to look at the pilot. "Coleridge's
. tells the story of an old sailing ship that ventures out farther
any ship has ever been. When they get stuck, an albatross—a
·d—turns up to guide them. For some reason, the mariner shoots
erything goes to hell, and his shipmates make him wear the
e." Dylan paused for a moment. "Albatross. Portending winnow-
oom."

sounds . . . charming," Wright said. He didn't look too thrilled.

's quite the epic," Rommie said seriously. "One thing after—"

ommie," Trance interrupted, "what's the *positive* part of the
?"

he positive part," Tyr said from the entrance to Command, "is
e survives to tell his tale. As shall we." He glided into Com-
, grabbing his console and swinging around it to a stop. "Mr.
er believes we can route comms through the *Eureka Maru*."

Ve came to that conclusion as well," Dylan said. "How is Mr.
er doing?"

r raised an eyebrow, which gave him quite a disingenuous look.
e well, once I retrieved him from his inadvertent dive into the
it."

ka raised both eyebrows, making a moue of surprise but saying
ng.

iss Pogue," Tyr added, "is helping a great deal."

"We have a lot of microgravity and low-gravity experience," said.

"Then," Dylan said, "you'd better get down to Engineeri see what you can do to help Mr. Harper. Tyr, get him there, Mr. Harper know that we're setting up the comm solution."

"On my way," Tyr said, turning himself around and pushi Wright followed him, moving almost as easily.

"I'd better get out to the *Maru*," Beka said.

"At this rate," Rommie said, "I'm going to end up as a cra tramp steamer."

"You'll never fall that low," Dylan said. "Beka, do it as fast can." Beka kicked off and sailed out of Command. Micrograv some advantages—at least until someone turned the gravity b or a wall got in the way and provided a reminder about basic physics. "Rommie, I need some kind of status report."

Rommie was looking worried. "Bad, bad, and worse," she sa looked at Dylan. "Dylan, my core AI isn't responding. Neithe holographic avatar."

Dylan closed his eyes and gritted his teeth. "Damn it."

Trance moved up to Rommie, putting a hand on the a shoulder. "They'll be okay."

"If they're not," Dylan said, "we could be in even worse t Let's hope Harper's up to his usual standard."

Rommie stared down at her console, looking as though s about to cry.

"Harper, can you hear me?" It was Beka's voice, echoing in his

Grunting slightly as he worked his way along an access tu panel that was burned on the inside, Harper said, "Loud an Boss. Hey, Dylan, you catchin' this station too?"

"Mr. Harper," Dylan responded.

"So speaks Mr. Excitement," Harper answered. He pul panel off and shone a flashlight inside, wincing as he saw the d

"I'm not feeling particularly lighthearted at the moment," said. "We've lost both the core AI and the holographic avatar.

Yeah," Harper said, "I figured that'd happen." He realized he
nded annoyed, which annoyed him even further. He shone the
light farther down the access tube. More visible damage. Pogue
ld be able to figure out some of the problems where she was, but
Tyr and Wright were pretty useless when it came to doing
—neither one was trained for the job. "I've got redundant back-
and Rommie can help update."

t's that easy?" Beka said, sounding surprised.

Nope," he said. He hauled himself uncomfortably around to a
position. "It's all gonna depend on the hardware. I'm finding
screwed up here that I've *never* seen screwed up before, and
s saying something on this ship." He fished in his pockets, finally
ing up his wire. He snapped one connector into the jack at the
of his neck, unraveled the cord quickly, and plugged the connec-
n the other end into a nearby diagnostic socket. "Okay, boys and
, shut the hell up while I get right under the hood here and work
Seamus Harper magic."

an instant he was connected with the cybernetic landscape of
Andromeda Ascendant. Not everything in here was driven by the
there were plenty of autonomic systems for him to look at on his
to the heart of things. He passed defenses, some of which he had
d himself, scattering passwords and ciphers as he went by.
was always a rush going into the system.

ddenly he was there. The cybernetic heart of the *Andromeda*
dant rose about him like a glowing city. There were stories in
buildings and once you learned to read them you could be set
e.

looked up, scanning the sparkling and glowing images around
immediately finding some of the problems. Some he could fix in
Others needed work in the real world.

ey, Andromeda!" he called. "You awake, gorgeous?"

e was suddenly there, a sparkling, semitransparent image. "Don't
she said. She seemed unsteady. After a moment, she sat down.
er, I have a hell of a headache." She looked up at him. "AIs don't
adaches."

"I'm just glad you're pretty much okay," Harper said, relieved
turning into bypass city out there."

"Can you get me out of here? I hate being deaf and blind an
dying of boredom."

Harper scanned the cyberscape again. "It's gonna take a
babe. I think there's some reconfiguring you can do in here
help." He pointed to several different areas. "Try those to start
I've gotta get back out into the real world before Tyr decides to
something."

"Okay." Andromeda stood up, looking up and around. "Se
soon, I hope."

"Count on it," Harper said, jacking out again. It took
moment to readjust to reality. He plucked the flashlight from wl
floated and tapped the side of his neck to activate his subcuta
transmitter. "Found Andromeda, guys. She's got a headache, sh
but she seems okay otherwise."

"Any ideas on how to get her back into operation?" Dylan as

"Some," Harper said. He started inching along the acces
again. "She's gonna have to do some work herself, and onc
done I can put together a bypass that'll get her on-line. If I
that, I can get holo-Rommie out as well."

"As fast as you can," Dylan said. "What about AG and
power?"

"Working on the AG right now," Harper said. Carefully, he
off a panel. "I'm not gonna get it back all the way right no
added, "so don't go taking any big steps. Main power'll come
see which main relays and breakers got toasted." Harper sho
flashlight into the circuitry. "I'm gonna have to shut down lots
ship, Boss."

"Just as long as it's nothing critical," Dylan said.

"No problem." Something fizzed and snapped, stinging H
hand. "Jeez! Yeah, anyway, the regular drive did an emergenc
down when we kicked out of Slipstream. I haven't had time t
check it, but it looks okay, so once I get AG and main powe
we'll be able to move."

"We don't know where we are," Beka said.

"Take the *Maru* out," Harper said. "The astronav isn't as good as one *Andromeda* has, but it'll give us a rough idea of where we are."

"What about communications?" Dylan said.

Harper did a quick calculation in his head. "We're good up to a thousand meters," he said, "and you don't need to get that far out to a reading."

"Okay," Dylan said, "do it. Go out about two hundred and fifty meters."

"We could be anywhere," Beka said. "That was a hell of an exit."

"No kidding," Harper said, quickly splicing broken and burned wires. He knew he was making a mess as he went along, but he didn't have a choice. "Look on the bright side, huh? We don't have to clean up a ship full of dead Magog."

"I didn't need to remember that," Beka said. She was quickly running through the preflight checklist and feeding power to the engines. "I'm good to go."

"Captain Valentine," Dylan said formally, "permission granted to move the *Andromeda Ascendant*."

Beka grinned. "It's just a drive around the block," she said. "Hey, at least it gets me out of the house so Mom and Dad can have some fun."

Carefully, Beka engaged the thrusters, moving the *Eureka Maru* forward toward the docking bay entrance. It was a frustratingly delicate task—normally she would just activate the AG field, power up, and go, full-tilt.

Reversing thrusters, she came to a full stop just past the 250-meter mark. Looking through the freighter's front windows, she was relieved to see darkness peppered by unblinking stars.

She turned to the astronavigation computer, requesting a positional analysis, waiting impatiently as it went through its observations and calculations. The *Andromeda Ascendant* could finish this in a hundredth of the time, maybe even faster, but the big ship had far more to work with, as well as far faster systems—a dedicated neural network.

Finally, the computer produced a result. Beka stared at it for a [few?] moments, then opened a comm channel. "I've got a result."

"Where are we?" Dylan asked.

"In the middle of nowhere," Beka said heavily. She grim[aced.] "There's nothing for parsecs in any direction." She felt like cry[ing,] but pushed it aside—that was Kantaran weaponry speaking, no[t her] own emotions. "It looks like we managed to actually come out i[n] the Andromeda galaxy. I guess that's progress."

"That's progress," Dylan said firmly. "There are more compli[ca-]tions than we expected, but it's all just a matter of time."

"Right," Beka said. Suddenly she felt exhausted. More and m[ore] seemed to be going wrong, and it was just getting to be too much. [She] had never had this much trouble before Dylan came along.

Not true, a smaller inner voice insisted. She closed her eyes [and] tried to will the negative feelings away, focusing on the pos[itive.] Dylan had come along and put an end to her scrabbling for a li[ving.] Now she helped to make a difference. She still encountered low[lifes] and scum, but now they were in politics—criminals with respec[table] faces.

"On the good news side of things," Harper said, "your in-h[ouse] boy wonder and neighborhood genius has just fixed the AG a[nd is] now turning it back on."

"Still miles to go, as they say, Mr. Harper," Dylan said.

"Or parsecs," Beka added quietly. "*Lots* of parsecs."

Sighing, she activated the thrusters and turned the *Maru* arou[nd]

> Reality shifts beneath our feet on a constant basis. It's
> nothing more than the universe making little adjustments
> to keep things in line, which is why most are not aware of
> it. Those who are aware of it, however, usually go quite
> mad as a side effect. We sometimes call these people
> "prophets."
>
> —REMNIMAAT, PERSEID PHILOSOPHER,
> CY 6422

rper was flitting about the Command Deck, referring periodically
a stack of flexis clutched in one hand and punching at controls with
other. Pogue was still down in Engineering, dealing with assorted
e problems—this apparently including gathering up a collection
ools that Harper had left in his wake like a trail of bread crumbs.
There had been some desultory talk of getting the *Eureka Maru*
ly for its long haul. They were going to come back with the cargo
stuffed, supplies shoved into every spare corner, and probably
gs strapped to the exterior by the time they were done. As far as
per was concerned, however, just acquiring a replacement lens
pulser wasn't enough—the *Andromeda Ascendant* might not sur-
another jump into Slipstream. They couldn't even risk trying to
her.

ylan was unwilling to leave her right now, even with Harper and
mie still aboard. Harper had managed to fix the AG, bring back

main power, and check out the normal-space engines, which w
down to fifty percent of their capability, but getting the core AI b
was proving to be a monumental task. Harper had been jacking in
out of the ship's cybernetics system on what seemed to be a h
hourly basis for the past three days.

He sipped gingerly at the glass of cavenga juice Trance
handed him when she arrived in Command just after Harper
charged into . . . what *was* he doing, anyway? He was all over
place. Trance had sworn that the juice was just what D
needed. Maybe it was meant to help him concentrate? Give
stamina?

Maybe the idea was to burn his taste buds out—she hadn't
anything about the taste. It tasted as though someone had sta
with some kind of fruit, managed to make it bitter, and then po
in sugar to try to cover the bitterness.

He turned his head to look at Trance, who smiled back fro
console where she was entering data from a flexi Harper had sh
at her on his way past. Dylan smiled weakly back.

Beka, who was wearing one of her more impractical l
dresses, sidled over to him. Ducking her head and lowering
voice to a whisper, she said, "You don't look too happy with
stuff."

"It's . . . no." Dylan looked down at the glass. He had barely tou
it. "It's not my taste."

"Well," Beka said, "maybe it's something I'd like." She reache
the glass.

"Beka," Dylan said, alarmed, "I wouldn't—"

She had the glass, however, and there was no stopping her.
Valentine, fearless guardian of the universe, was going to chec
out. She took a sip.

Beka Valentine, fearless guardian of the universe, managed t
herself from spitting the juice onto Dylan's maroon shirt. It
close call.

"Oh, God," she spluttered, her face screwed up and redd
She put the back of her free hand to her mouth and gave D
wide-eyed helpless look. "This stuff is supposed to *help* you?"

That's what she says," Dylan replied nonchalantly. "She's my doc-
you know."

Oh, right," Beka said hoarsely. "*Always* trust doctors, sure, yep."
swung around, holding the glass away from her, frowning at
nce. "Trance, what the hell is—"

uddenly Harper darted by them. Just as suddenly he darted back,
ked the glass from Beka's hand, and said, "Thanks, Boss, cool!"

—this stuff," Beka finished weakly, turning to watch Harper with
xture of horror and fascination—exactly what Dylan was feeling
t now. He had a vision of his engineer taking up residence in a
room for the next two days.

Harper—" Dylan started.

Harper wasn't even halfway across Command before he'd tilted
his head, upended the glass, and swallowed the entire contents in
gulp.

Oh, no," Beka said.

Harper doubled back and put the glass back in Beka's hand. "That's
e great stuff, what a *rush*!" He turned around yet again and
med his original course.

eka and Dylan looked down at the empty glass, then up at each
r, then over at Trance, who grinned and gave them a little wave.
and Dylan looked back at each other. Quietly Beka said, "I hate
en she does that sort of stuff."

f it works," Dylan said, "I'm all for it. Even Harper can't keep
g forever."

Ladies and gentlemen, boys and girls," Harper suddenly
unced, whirling around and flinging the stack of flexis into the
all-around boy wonder and heroic stud of the century Seamus
zny Harper has done it again! No, not inflated my ego to mon-
us proportions, being the modest guy that I am. I've tunneled
romeda out from under the debris." He turned to the main
reen. "Babe, come on up and show your gorgeous face!"

he screen flickered to life, displaying Andromeda's head and
lders. She looked down at them, then smiled. "It's good to be
, even in this state."

And we also have—*ta-da*—holo-babe Rommie!" The hologram

flickered into life, looking very confused, glancing around
crew. "I was going to do the swimsuit edition," Harper
attempting to be nonchalant, "but I figured now wasn't the ti
that."

"Oh," said holo-Rommie. "I think I might have liked that
looked down at herself. "Some other time, I guess. I seem t
some corrupted data in here." She turned to look at Harper. "
job, Mr. Harper."

Holo-Rommie flickered out.

Andromeda squinted slightly and looked in Harper's dir
"I'm working on the corrupted data side of things. I *still*
headache."

"Probably needs a hardware fix," Harper said absently, a
focusing on something else. He tapped rapidly at some keys. "
asec. That should help."

Andromeda gave a rapid shake of her head, as though cleari
morning cobwebs. Her hair promptly turned several shades of

"Oh," Rommie said, watching this unexpected adjustment.

Holo-Rommie reappeared, looking at the screen. She als
"Oh." Then she too shook her head. Her hair turned shining g

All heads turned to Rommie, who gave them a bemused sn
think I prefer my present look," she said.

"Well," said Andromeda, "at least my headache's gone. We
the image issue later."

"If we want to," said holo-Rommie.

"I think *you* need to go and read a trashy fleximag until
gets you fixed," Andromeda said sternly. "I'm a warship, not a
model."

"Hey!" holo-Rommie said. "Anyway, how'd you know ab
fleximags?"

"Lucky guess," Rommie said, folding her arms and giving
a dirty look.

"Oh."

Holo-Rommie vanished.

"Okay," Harper said, spreading his arms and making an eff
to look horribly embarrassed, "maybe I was a little *too* quick

raw with holo-Rommie." He looked at Rommie and swallowed, ard. "Hey, I only get 'em for the articles."

"She's a total space cadet," Beka said, glaring at him, "and I don't nean that in a nice way, either."

"Oh," Harper said. "Yeah, I guess she's coming across that way. Could be worse, though."

"Could it?" Dylan asked.

Beka started to cut Harper off, but it was too late. "There was this ink-haired chick a while before we ran into you guys."

"Haruko," Beka said sourly. "We had her as a passenger. Picked er up at Mamimi Drift."

"Yeah," Harper said with a lopsided grin. "I thought she was really to me—"

"Desperation speaking of course," Beka said.

"*Anyway*, that was until she whacked me in the head with a guitar and arted yapping about robots." Harper rubbed his forehead absently. Trance patched me up."

"She paid good money," Beka said defensively. "We didn't find out til later that nobody else would take her, and for lots of good rea-ns, too."

"I'll keep this in mind if we encounter any pink-haired women rrying guitars," Dylan said patiently.

"She really was kinda cute, though," Harper said.

"Desperation," Beka said, making a face.

"Hey!" Harper objected.

"Okay, people," Dylan said, wanting to cut the exchange off and t down to business, "we need a game plan here."

"I've got an idea," Harper said.

"Mr. Harper?"

"Beka takes the *Maru* out, hits the nearest debris field, and brings ck a chunk of rock for the *Andromeda* to work on."

"I'd need to find an asteroid the *Maru* can carry," Beka said, look-; at Harper. She glanced at Dylan. "I'm not too worried about mass normal space—the AG field will handle that. It's in Slipstream that worried about."

"Break it up," Harper said. "You could load the cargo pod."

"That'll take too long," Beka said.

"Not if you give it a little bit of momentum first," Dylan sa[id]. "Objects in motion tend to stay in motion, right? Break it up on [the] right vector and the work gets done for you."

Beka shook her head. "Not a good call. First, some of that st[uff] could punch through the pod. Second, even if I made that work, [the] pod's only going to carry a couple of hundred tons of rock that wa[s]—"

"That's barely enough raw material to patch up a couple of hole[s]," Rommie said, "and that's only if I can find the right elements. [I] don't have the time for multiple trips, and the risk versus ben[efit] analysis is not good."

"So," Dylan said heavily, "we'd better figure out where Be[ka's] going and how long it's going to take—"

"I don't think she needs to go anywhere," Andromeda interrup[ted].

Everyone turned to look at the flatscreen, where Andromeda [was] looking at them. Beka blinked, obviously surprised. "I don't?"

"Dylan has to go," Andromeda said. Beka and Dylan looke[d at] each other, then back at Andromeda. "I've been searching my as[teroid] navigation databases, and I've found something interesting. It's ca[lled] Waystation and we're practically in the neighborhood."

Thirty minutes later the entire crew, including Pogue and Wri[ght,] were gathered in one of the briefing rooms. Flatscreens were a[live] with images, including Andromeda's head and shoulders.

"When Slipstream theory was first worked out," Andromeda s[aid,] "and practical experiments began, nobody had any idea how lo[ng a] Slipstream field could be maintained, or how long a ship could st[ay in] Slipstream."

"It took hundreds of years to get any sort of real understandi[ng,]" Dylan said admiringly. "Every jump was a risk."

"In the first century of Slipstream travel," Andromeda said, "[more] than two hundred vessels were lost—out of two hundred and twe[lve."]

"The point being that these people were pioneers," Dylan [said.] "Pioneers push the limits, whether it's settlers looking for new l[and,] someone trying to break a speed record, or the first-generation s[hips.] In this case they were pioneers over the speed of light."

"Is this the High Guard history lecture, then?" Tyr drawled.

"Consider it the setup, Tyr," Andromeda said.

"Basically," Beka said, "they found out they could get from point A
[to] point B faster than light."

"Wasn't that easy," Harper said.

"Harper's right," Andromeda said. She pointed toward one of the
screens and it obligingly lit up with an image of the Andromeda
[gal]axy, overlaid by a schematic. The image rotated, showing the twin
[blac]k holes at the center of the galaxy. Short lines were drawn on the
[ima]ge. "Slipstream jumps were generally very short, and exploration
[was] confined to a relatively small area."

"However," Dylan said, leaning forward and resting his elbows on
[the] table, "the itch to explore more and go farther out each time
[nev]er goes away. Someone always wants to go off the map."

[A]ndromeda gestured again. A number of bright red points appeared
[on t]he map. Lines connected to them, and new lines threaded out from
[the]m. "As exploration moved farther out, supply lines were created.
[Dep]ots were built on or in orbit around a number of planets scattered
[acro]ss the Andromeda galaxy. These stations expanded the frontier,
[allo]wing much of the galaxy to be mapped, explored, and exploited."

"And then," Dylan said, "they hit the rim. Next stop, the outer
[dark]."

"Naturally," Beka said, "they'd gotten that far, so they didn't want
[to s]top."

[T]yr was inspecting his fingernails, looking bored.

"They were about to go right off the map," Dylan said.

"Bunny-hopping to the next galaxy over," Harper said. "Except
[they] were doing bigger hops."

"The explorers didn't confine themselves to a single direction,"
[And]romeda said. She gestured and the galactic image rotated, blue
[line]s branching from it in a number of directions. "They also didn't
[mov]e without preparation."

[T]his time the scattering of dots was yellow, some on the rim, some
[tow]ard the upper and lower edges of the galactic center.

"This was the Long Jump," Dylan said, looking in turn at the
[scre]en, and then at his crew. "The only galaxies explorers ever

returned from were the Milky Way and Triangulum, which is
efforts eventually focused on them."

"The supply stations on the rim were a necessity," Andro
said. "Ships returning from missions usually returned with su
and fuel exhausted, often damaged. Reaching anywhere bey
supply station would be impossible."

"As the millennia passed," Dylan said, "life ceased to be
frontiers and exploration and started to be about the Systems (
monwealth. Slipstream travel had become an uneventful reali

"So," Andromeda said, gesturing again, "the supply stations
taken over by the High Guard and converted into High (
bases." Images flashed onto the screens now, both still and m
showing a series of High Guard bases. "Over time a number of
bases were closed or automated. A few of the rim bases were (
down entirely." Several images flashed up onto the screen
remained there.

"Waystation?" Beka asked. "Just a guess."

"Waystation," Andromeda said.

"Waystation was automated in CY 9206," Rommie said. "I
considered a good idea to have at least some stations in operati
the rim. Eventually, however, a combination of underuse and a
conditions led to it being scheduled for decommissioning. It v
have been shut down approximately two years after the Com
wealth fell."

"It looks quite inhospitable," Tyr said.

"It is," Andromeda said. "However, the base was designed t
with the environment. The complex lies mostly undergroun
surface portion is to allow entrance and exit. Provided that
thing works as it should, the *Eureka Maru* can be flown direct
the base."

"How can we be certain that anything of use is to be found t
Tyr said. "We all know how many High Guard bases were rai
destroyed after the Fall."

"Risk versus benefit," Rommie said. "Not to mention the dif
factor. Waystation was to be closed because nobody ever came o

—there are no inhabited planets in this region and there are more
y exploitable resources in far more accessible locations."

Waystation," Andromeda added, "was exactly that—the last stop
he outbound explorers and the first stop for the inbound. I'm
y not sure why it was kept active for this amount of time."

Nostalgia," said Tyr.

For a place *that* frozen?" Beka said. "I think some bureaucrat
aged to lose the paperwork a couple of thousand years back."

ylan was quiet, looking at the images on the screens. There
ed to be nothing but ice, with no evidence of life anywhere. The
Guard base consisted of a surface dome, under which the main
plex lay—five chambers, three levels each, extending for a kilo-
r out from a central access area. Each level was ten meters deep.
orst came to worst, Dylan thought, and there was nothing there
he base, they could try cutting up whatever was left and bringing
ck to the *Andromeda Ascendant* before going to Plan B.

This is the planet I saw," Trance said. The others looked blankly
r. "It was a while back."

Anything to say about it, Trance?" Dylan asked her.

rance looked at the flatscreens for a few moments, then shook
ead. "Nothing."

've got somethin'," Harper said loudly, staring at the screens.
stbite in my shorts just lookin' at this freakin' place. Good thing
sn't countin' on snowboarding practice here. You guys have fun,
I'll be here on the nice warm *Andromeda Ascendant*—" His rush
ords, which had been emerging a little high-pitched because of
uddenly obvious nervousness, rattled to a stop. Dylan was gazing
ly at him, half smiling. As the truth dawned on Harper he began
ok horrified. "No. No no no. *Ohhhhh* no! No!" Wide-eyed, he
ed around at the people seated around the table, looking for
"No. I can't go anywhere I'm needed here what if something
ens besides I gotta fix holo-Rommie and there's the engines Boss
if—"

hut up, boy," Tyr said in an affable tone that was nevertheless loud
gh to cut right into Harper's unpunctuated and breathless spray of

words. The engineer stopped talking instantly, staring at Tyr as t[...] the Nietzschean had shot his cat. "Mr. Harper," Tyr went on, les[...] bly, "you are without question a fine engineer. I also know full w[...] while you hardly have the heart of a lion, as they say, you are fa[...] being a coward. You are demeaning yourself with this hideous di[...] He leaned forward, glaring. "You are also annoying me."

Harper flinched back. "Yeah, I got it, I really won't like you[...] you're annoyed."

Beka looked around at Tyr. "'Grow up, Harper' would hav[...] shorter."

"Or 'Shut up, Harper,'" Trance said, smiling. "That w[...] favorite on the *Maru*."

Tyr looked evenly from one to the other and said, "I'm a [...] schean," as though that explained everything—which it very [...] bly did.

"Well, Mr. Harper," Dylan said, starting to get up, "it loo[...] some of us are getting an early winter vacation."

"Vacation," Harper said, his voice hollow. He turned his h[...] stare at the screens. "Vacation."

Rommie smiled at him as she got up. "Looks like great [...] weather to me."

Harper couldn't even muster a reply.

One of the more pleasant things about having a gigantic s[...] occupied by only a handful of crew was that no matter what [...] ational activity any of them might engage in, there was always [...] to be room or equipment available for it.

In some instances, of course, the lack of personnel coul[...] problem—as with Dylan's preoccupation with basketball. R[...] could, of course, be counted on to obediently participate. [...] might have been interested had there been hoverboards, skate[...] rollerblades, or seminaked women (or any combination [...] involved, but as it was a mere unassisted game of skill and stan[...] gave it a pass. Beka had tried it three times, and on the third ha[...] ten so exasperated that she shot the ball. Trance had run rings a[...]

an and then announced that she probably wasn't going to be very
d at the game.

Vhich left Tyr . . . and Tyr's flagrant disregard for the rules of
game when it was a matter of advantage. The memory of sur-
ing Dylan and knocking him flat never failed to make Tyr grin.
an had learned instantly from that encounter, and while their
 remained friendly it also remained a battle of both wits and
e.

'yr had changed during his time with Dylan. His arrogance, the
ude of "mine by right or conquest," had been replaced. Dylan
 been his challenge, and to meet it he had made a fundamental
ige: he had made himself willing to learn from Dylan and from
rs he might never have considered equals. In doing so, he had
n note of his own flaws, and the failures of the prides.

Ie had been a dangerous man the day he met Dylan. He was infi-
y more dangerous now.

ogging toward the gym, where he had his own personal corner set
Tyr shook his head, trying to clear the overly grandiose thoughts.
it now, he reminded himself, he was no threat to anybody—

Nietzschean!"

Ie was at a junction, just about to turn, when the shout came.
tled, he turned to his left. Trance's voice—

Vithout being conscious of his reaction, he was diving into the
ining corridor and drawing his Gauss pistol. He rolled and came
his back against the corridor wall as he listened for sounds of
ement.

'rance's voice, but she had been shouting angrily. The way she had
iounced "Nietzschean" had given it the sound of an intended
l slur.

ot our Trance Gemini, then. "Andromeda," he whispered as he
d toward the flatscreen at the junction, "do not speak. Monitor
area, and get Dylan and Trance down here. And be ready to assist
Acknowledge."

he flatscreen had lit as he was talking. Andromeda nodded to
owledge what he had said.

He stilled his breathing, listening. There was a cautious foo
Another.

On the flatscreen, Andromeda made a chopping gesture wit
fingers toward her left shoulder, then downward—right hand si
the corridor. A slight clockwise gesture—slow forward move
Then a thumb and forefinger gesture—she has a gun.

"Nietzschean," the newest Trance said, sounding far more re
able now, "I am willing to accept your surrender."

Andromeda gestured again, but Tyr had already placed the
tion of this latest version of Trance. He stepped into the jun
turned to his right, and took a quick, long step. The muzzle
Gauss pistol hit the new Trance squarely in the middle of her
pushing her back against the corridor wall. With his left ha
pinned her gun hand against the wall.

"You're signing your death warrant," Trance hissed, glaring a

He looked her over, curious. In her looks she seemed more li
purple version of Trance than the gold one, but her skin sl
almost to an azure tone. Burnished gold hair had been car
arranged, military fashion. The most surprising thing, howeve
her clothes—at first he thought she was wearing an adaptatior
High Guard uniform. With a start, he realized it wasn't an adap
at all.

Trance, a military officer? The thought actually shocked him.

"Listen to me," he said urgently, emphasizing the order by
ing the pistol into her chest. He was in unknown territory her
doubted that he could present enough of a threat to be effective
he was committed now. "You are not where you think you are."

She stared at him. "I listen to nothing that comes out of the r
of a *filthy lying Nietzschean!*"

Terrible anger swelled up in him then, and in a flash h
smashed the barrel of the Gauss gun across her face, snappin
head back. He jammed the muzzle back into her chest again, h
this time. She gave no indication that she was feeling pain.

"I know I can't kill you," he growled, staring into her eyes. "I
I can hurt you. I do know, however, that a smart bullet to the
will make things uncomfortable for you for a little while." He

breath. "You are not where you think you are, and I am not who
think I am. Look at my wrists, girl!"

Her eyes shifted as she looked at his left wrist, and then his right.
". . . no bone blades?"

"That's right," he said. "If you seek Tyr Anasazi, then I am not the
nation you are hunting."

"It's a lie," Trance mumbled, "a lie."

A flatscreen lit up behind Tyr. "He isn't lying."

Trance's head jerked up. "Andromeda?"

"You seem surprised."

"You were . . . they erased you. . . ." Trance's eyes flicked from
romeda to Tyr. "You Nietzscheans have been destroying and
oiling the Known Worlds Confederation for centuries. We're
ly eradicating you bastards."

Tyr raised his eyebrows. "I do believe that's the first time I've
d that word issue from your mouth, Trance."

"That you've—"

"Tyr is a member of my crew, Trance," Andromeda said gently.

"He can't—no." Trance was staring at him, horrified. "You and
crew attacked us and took over the ship. Andromeda was erased
Captain Valentine murdered."

"And you've been taking the ship back," Tyr said.

"Killing Nietzschean scum all the way," Trance snarled.

Running footsteps. Dylan, force lance out, arriving at a run. Tyr,
ce, and Andromeda looked toward him.

"All heads turn as the Hunt goes by," Dylan quipped, seeing their
s. He stopped in the junction. "Trance, Tyr's speaking the
, and if you were talking about Captain Rebecca Valentine,
is alive and well and up on *our* Command Deck. Oh, and I'm
ain Dylan Hunt, commodore of the new Systems Common-
h High Guard fleet. The old Commonwealth fell down and
e three centuries ago."

Trance was silent.

"Hello," said a familiar voice from just behind Dylan. The cus-
ry golden Trance stepped forward. She smiled. "I'm one of the
r reasons everyone knows you're in the wrong place."

"It's an illusion!" the other Trance screamed suddenly. wrenched her gun hand free of Tyr's grip and tried to knee him in groin. Adroitly he stepped back and shot her three times in the ch the charges in the smart bullets sending out a shower of sparks.

"Ow!" their Trance said, wincing as her counterpart fell against the corridor wall and slid down.

Keeping a watchful eye on the apparently dead woman, Tyr pi up her Gauss pistol and hurled it down the corridor away from th Stepping back, he said, "I'm assuming that when she returns to w she belongs, so will her weapon."

"Probably," Trance said. She stepped closer to the body slun against the wall and crouched down. "She's so *different*. So angry.

"Sounds like she has cause," Dylan said. He hadn't holstere force lance yet.

"It does leave me uncomfortable to discover that I have a cou part who is apparently considered to be no more than an animal," said. "She's stirring."

"Don't try to get up," Trance said to her as she tried to get t feet. "Tyr's likely to shoot you again."

"I don't . . . I don't understand," the other woman said.

"You're in the wrong timeline," Trance said. "I don't know but you're not the first. Here." She grasped her counterpart's hand with her right.

Tyr wasn't sure what was happening. A ripple of golden appeared to wash over both of them and both appeared to sud focus on a distant point.

Trance released her counterpart's hand. The other woman st at her for a moment, then said, "We were hunting down the la the Nietzscheans. I did feel something, but the AG was damag the battle. I had no idea . . ."

"Now you do," Tyr said brusquely. "Be polite from now on will refrain from shooting you."

"Alright," the second Trance said.

Tyr jogged up the corridor and retrieved her weapon, throwi to her. "Put it away. I'm told that it will return with you. You n well need it immediately."

She seemed momentarily hesitant to holster the pistol. Dylan's
rce lance lifted slightly, aimed just to one side of her. Jamming the
auss pistol into its holster, she nodded toward Dylan's hand. "Inter-
ting weapon. Unorthodox design."

"Standard High Guard side arm issue for millennia," Andromeda
d. "Another indicator."

"So," Dylan said, "you don't have any idea why this is happening,
her."

The other Trance looked at him for a moment, then shook her
d. "Aside from the recent battles, things have been very quiet."

Dylan nodded, then looked at their Trance. "I'd say I didn't like
way this adds up, Trance—"

"But none of it adds up," she said hurriedly. "I know. It's making
crazy too."

The other Trance sighed, prodding unhappily at the burned holes
er uniform. "Well, that's it for this tunic." She looked up at Tyr.
e quartermaster'll be furious."

"Would you like me to write you an explanatory note?" Tyr asked,
ning for all the world as though the concept of a ship's quarter-
er baffled him. Wondering if they were going to have to stand in
corridor for the rest of the day, Tyr looked at the golden Trance.
here any obvious time limit on these phenomena?"

rance shook her head. "As short as a few seconds to as long as a
hours when I got thrown forward in time."

yr looked back at the other Trance, weighing his options.
y well. I have a fitness regimen to observe, one that *you* inter-
ed my progress toward. I am going to continue on my way
" He paused, glowering at her. "You will not give me reason to
n."

e glared back at him, but said nothing.

r nodded at Dylan and Trance. "Dylan, Trance?"

ylan nodded back. "We can take it from here. Enjoy the gym."

r resumed his jogging pace along the corridor, grinning as he
Andromeda ask Dylan, "By the way, Captain, when did you say
were resuming your full exercise schedule?"

————

"Nag," Dylan muttered under his breath. Both Trances grinned
Andromeda frowned.

"Captain, there is nothing wrong with my auditory capabilitie
Andromeda said stuffily. "I heard that."

"I've got more on my mind than exercise right now," Dyl
snapped, regretting his tone immediately. He put his fingers to
temples as his head throbbed. "Damn it. The next time we go
Kantar, remind me to drop a Nova Bomb on the bastards."

He regretted saying that, too.

Trance's counterpart looked at her and said, "That doesn't sou
good."

"It isn't," Dylan answered before Trance could say anything.
head throbbed again.

"We were in a battle recently," Andromeda said. "Unfortunat
rather than being boarded by anything we could hunt down, my
was sprayed with devices that affects crew psychology."

"I turn into an evil-tempered martinet if I don't watch it," Dy
said.

"Isn't there something you can do?" the second Trance asked
"We have a skeleton crew," Dylan said, "and all of our resou
are tied up in trying to keep the *Andromeda* together."

"Oh."

Trance stepped over to Dylan, her hypospray in hand. She
him a shot, and the throbbing in his head went away, replaced
dull ache and a degree of fuzziness. He was looking forwar
spending some time away from the Kantarian devices.

"I think we'd better get up to Command," he said. He gestur
the two Trances. "Lead the way."

With a look at each other, they did. Dylan didn't see any re
to worry about their unexpected visitor now—whatever Trance
done, it had obviously reset her counterpart's perspective.

They soon reached Command, where Harper was making a
minute attempt to bring the holographic version of Rommie
something approaching specification. She was gradually improvi
terms of comprehensibility, but she had become impressively va
some reason. The parade of costume changes and virtual make

had been amusing for about five minutes, and even Harper had quickly grown bored.

The new Trance looked around Command, apparently fascinated. "This looks nothing like our bridge. We have our pilot station . . . right . . . there."

She was staring at Harper.

Beka picked up on this immediately. Cheerfully she said, "That's just Seamus, our pet monkey."

"Hey!" Harper said, looking up. "That's pet *supergenius* monkey. Make that pet supergenius monkey popsicle. And, by the way, Dylan, old pal o' mine, there's still time to reconsider risking your biggest asset."

"No way out, Harper," Dylan said. "I need you."

"Why is it that everybody who says that to me needs me for everything except romance and pleasure?" Harper complained. "Oh, yeah, hi, Trance. Hi, Trance." He frowned. "Oh, wait . . . oh, no."

"Commander Harper," the new Trance said. She turned her head and looked at Beka. "And Captain Valentine."

"*Commander?*" Harper said in disbelief. "As in spit, polish, and black leather high-tops?"

The new Trance stepped toward him. "Commander Seamus Zelazny Harper, master engineer." She looked at him sadly. "It was against protocol, but we had a relationship. We always looked out for each other, always were there for each other when something needed to be done."

Harper started to say something, then stopped, looking strangely at her. "Waitasec, babe, that sounds awfully past tense to me."

"Your counterpart was killed six months ago," she said softly. "During a battle. There was nothing anyone could do. I miss him terribly. I'll miss Rebecca almost as much."

"Son of a bitch," Harper said softly, looking shocked.

"Well," Beka said, in the tone of someone trying to brighten up a graveyard full of mourners, "neither of us is past tense here."

"Feelings are feelings," Trance said glumly.

"Got it," Beka said, "party hats away, champagne back in the cage."

"Sorry," the other Trance said.

There was an awkward silence.

Suddenly holo-Rommie flickered to life. She was wearing an ornate gown, a feather boa, and a huge floppy hat with a gigantic plume sticking out of it. "I think we're finally getting the data issues under control," she said. "I also believe that my characterization problems are finally getting ironed out."

Beka shook her head, sighing. "Not with that hat, they aren't."

The alternate Trance vanished without preamble a little over an hour later, with only a tiny snapping sound marking her passage—air filling the vacuum she left behind.

Harper had continued working on holo-Rommie, apparently in the hope that his increasing success would persuade Dylan that his resident genius was better off remaining aboard the *Andromeda Ascendant*. Dylan listened politely to Harper's protestations . . . and ignored them completely. No one else came to Harper's aid, either.

On the bright side, holo-Rommie seemed to be coherent, finally and stable—except for the fact that she now had the blue-haired look that the android Rommie had abandoned several months ago. However, given that she seemed content to remain with a single look for more than five minutes, no one was willing to tinker further.

That left Harper nowhere to go with his protests. Instead, he settled for a sullenly irritable attitude as final departure preparations were made. To his relief, part of those preparations involved checking out the *Eureka Maru* from stem to stern, making sure that the specification parts were in good order and that his many lash-ups weren't going to fail in the middle of a Slipstream jump.

Once he had pronounced the battered salvage ship and its cargo pod free of anything immediately life-threatening, Dylan and Rommie brought equipment aboard, loading it into the forward storage area.

Harper stared as boxes were stacked and outfits hung up. "Wait a sec, I thought we were gonna fly straight in, Boss. What's *that* for?"

Dylan hung up another arctic outfit. "We won't know until we're there if we can do that. If we have to land outside, it's likely to be bi

"I keep hearing that," Harper said, his face screwing up. "Why d'you think I don't want to go? I'm nuts, but I'm not crazy."

Dylan picked up another outfit. This one was made of a rich black material, with white piping. Magnetic clasps were arrayed in a row down the left side of the tunic.

"Uh, Dylan? You said you weren't gonna wear that anymore," Harper said, nodding at the uniform as Dylan hung it up.

"That's what I was planning," Dylan said. He smoothed the material.

"It's a measure for our security and safety," Rommie said. "There s a mesh woven into the material, consisting of microcircuitry. High Guard installations recognize the signals as part of a security protocol."

"We might be able to get away without it," Dylan said, "but it's always possible that this will be the only thing that the security system recognizes as a command presence on-site."

"Being shot full of holes can really ruin a person's day," Rommie said with a rueful look. "Something I know all too well, I'm afraid."

"Right," Harper said weakly. "So, okay, seeing as you don't need e any—"

"Mr. Harper," Tyr said, actually sounding cheerful. He had come quietly behind Harper. The engineer jumped, half turning. "One ore complaint, and I will make certain that you make the journey side the cargo pod."

"Right," Harper said. He turned to Dylan and Rommie. "You got pare uniform for a scared supergenius?"

Dylan smiled. "Rommie, see what you can do for the man."

"On my way," Rommie said with a beatific smile at Harper, who med taken aback by this willingness to hand him a High Guard form.

Tyr raised his eyebrows. "Seamus Harper wearing a uniform? I l myself at a loss for words."

"Funny," Harper said, glaring at him. "You sound like you're still ing."

Pure momentum," Tyr said.

"Mr. Harper wants to look the part," Dylan said. "I'll have him polishing his boots yet."

"Yeah, right," Harper said with a snort.

"Mr. Wright is on his way," Tyr said. "I've issued him a personal weapon. It might be needless, but stepping unprepared into a possibly insecure situation is not something I recommend."

"Yeah," Harper said. "You tend to go with the philosophy of 'nuke 'em 'til they glow in the dark and then shoot at them from orbit.'"

Tyr smiled at him. "I see I have actually taught you something."

Harper gave him a disgusted look and walked away, toward the af end of the ship.

"We should be back inside two weeks," Dylan said. "If we aren' there's a problem, probably a bad one. I'll leave it up to you and Bek whether you come and look for us, or head for known territory."

"We could do both," Tyr said. "The good Captain Valentine hardly likely to give up her ship without a fight."

"Good point," Dylan said. "Either way, someone will need to g to the Commonwealth and get a retrieval mission started."

"You seem fatalistic," Tyr said.

"Realistic," Dylan said. "I just don't have a choice in this."

"Understood," Tyr said.

Rommie returned, carrying a uniform on a hanger. "This shou fit Mr. Harper quite nicely, and I do believe he'll look quite handsor in it." She glanced around. "Well. I flatter him for a change, and h hiding in the back of the ship. Hmph."

She hung the uniform next to Dylan's.

Micah Wright was the next to arrive, a force lance holstered at hip. He made to remove it, but Dylan held up a hand. "Keep it w you at all times. Standard protocol."

"Yes, sir," Wright said, forgetting himself and saluting. "Err, so Captain."

"We'll get that discipline trained out of you yet," Rommie s She glanced at Dylan. "Do you think Mr. Harper can provid course in remedial slovenliness?"

"This," Tyr announced gravely, "is more than I can handle. I'll you farewell, then, and a swift and safe journey. I've no wish to travel for weeks in a Slipfighter, or even one of the transports."

Tyr left.

"Mr. Wright seems to have a thing about proper discipline," Dylan said.

"I think so," Rommie said. "Who's doing the driving, you or Harper?"

"I'll take the first leg," Dylan said. "After that I don't see any reason why all four of us can't take turns."

"We can start at any time," Rommie said. "Everything we need is board."

"Then we'd better get going," Dylan said. He pressed the side of is neck. "Mr. Harper, we're ready to go. Time to get up front. Oh, nd your uniform is here."

"Wow," Harper replied unenthusiastically.

Rommie and Wright followed Dylan through the ship to the clut-red cockpit. Dylan sat down in the big, worn captain's chair, strap-ng himself in. Rommie took the astronavigation station. Harper rived a few moments later, to take his place at the forward engi-ering station.

Dylan quickly ran through the preflight checklist, then turned to arper and said, "Mr. Harper, are we good to go?"

"Except for me having to come along," Harper said, "yeah, we're od to go."

Dylan flipped switches, tapped buttons, and brought main power , adjusting the AG field to reduce the effective mass of the *Maru* to w grams.

He activated the subdermal communicator again, and said, *dromeda Ascendant*, this is the *Eureka Maru*. We are good to go."

'Bon voyage," Beka said. "Take care of my ship, and bring our rite engineer back toasty warm, not as a popsicle."

'I'll do my best," Dylan said.

Eureka Maru, you are cleared to depart," Beka said formally.

Good luck, Captain," Andromeda broke in.

Thank you, Andromeda." Dylan activated thrusters, lifting the

Maru from the docking bay deck. Carefully, he eased the ship into forward motion. "We are on our way."

"Fasten your seat belts, make sure your tray table and seat back are in the upright position," Harper said, "and keep all luggage stored in the overhead bins or under the seat in front of you." He frowned. "Hey, do we get in-flight flexis and peanuts or even a movie on this trip?"

They were out of the docking bay now. Dylan started to open the throttle, increasing the *Maru*'s velocity. "I don't know about the peanuts, Mr. Harper, but I'm sure you know where to find the flexis and the movies on this ship."

"Oh," Harper said, looking as though this idea was coming as surprise to him. "Yeah. I probably do."

Wright lifted a flexi. "Already found one down here."

Harper tilted his head to look, started to grin, noticed Rommi looking at him, and said, "Oh, yeah, there's some great . . . articles . in there."

"I don't believe that's the term they use in the anatomy books, M Harper," Rommie said primly.

Wright chuckled and tossed the flexi to Harper, who hurriedly p it away.

"One minute to the nearest Slip point," Rommie said.

"I think we can shorten that time a little," Dylan said, opening t throttles all the way. The *Maru* surged forward as he activated t Slipstream drive system. "Let's bring it."

The Slipstream drive came to life and the oscillating white a blue shape of a portal burst into life ahead of them. The *Eureka M* drove straight into the center of it and vanished from normal spac

You know what's wrong with winter sports?
Nobody ever does them in a tropical climate.

—CAPTAIN IAN QUINN, SHIPMASTER OF
THE FREE TRADE ALLIANCE FRIGATE
STEFFI37, 222 AFC

ting Slipstream *now*," Wright said, and the coruscating super-
g universe visible through the cockpit windows gave way to a
e of light and the star-studded black of normal space. Wright
down the Slipstream controls and turned his attention to pi-
g in normal space. "Vectoring to new course . . . new course
ed in, velocity is fifteen PSL and holding."

We should make orbit within twenty minutes, Captain," Rommie
unced, looking up from her instruments.

hank you, Rommie," Dylan said, getting up and moving for-
to look through the cockpit windows. "And thank you, Mr.
ght, good work."

hank you, sir," Wright said. "She looks like hell, but she handles
dream."

ourtesy of your resident High Guard-flavored supergenius-
cle-to-be," Harper said sourly.

"But you'll look *so* attractive when the inevitable end co[me]
Harper," Rommie said, giving him a big smile and a wide-eyed in[no]
cent look. "Just think—most people have to pay to be put into [cry]
onic storage."

"Thanks so much," Harper said. "I feel so much better now."

"You're welcome," Rommie said, turning back to the astronav[iga]
tion station.

"Would you like to take over, Captain?" Wright said, gesturin[g to]
the piloting station.

"Apple polisher," Harper muttered, not quite under his breath[.]

Wright stared at him. "Y'know, I have to wonder why Pogue ha[sn't]
whacked you with a spanner yet."

"She's female," Rommie said. "Different rules apply."

"Hey!" Harper snapped. "She does good work."

"And different rules apply," Rommie repeated.

"Anyway," Dylan said in his best I'm-in-command-so-shut-up [tone]
of voice, "the center seat remains yours for now, Mr. Wright. [We'll]
see who does what when we make orbit."

"Which we could do if we were going faster," Harper said. "[I'm]
gonna see if we have a couple of oars aboard so I can help row."

"Point to Mr. Harper," Dylan said. He gestured vaguely tow[ard]
the cockpit window. "Pick up her heels a bit."

"Aye, Captain," Wright said, his fingers playing over the cont[rols.]
"Velocity increasing to twenty PSL . . . and holding."

"I'm going back," Harper said, jerking a thumb toward the aft [end]
of the ship. He got up and left.

After a few moments, Dylan followed him. As it turned [out,]
Harper hadn't gone far. He was in the storage area where their [gear]
had been stowed, looking at the uniform that Rommie had bro[ught]
for him.

"Alright," Dylan said, startling Harper, "I'm going to make a g[uess]
that it isn't just Waystation that's on your mind."

Harper was silent, his left hand on the tunic. Dylan was begin[ning]
to think that Harper was going to be stubborn and refuse to an[swer]
when the engineer bowed his head for a moment and said, "Ye[ah, it]
isn't just that." He looked around at Dylan, his expression for [once]

hat other Trance . . . this . . . I mean, I hear it from *her* that in
ne other universe I'm a freakin' officer, not just some smart guy
o got lucky. All the way up to commander, pretty freakin' good
a guy my age, right?" He looked back at the uniform again.
:cept that other me's dead, and that feels *weird*. Freaky. Then
re's the Trance in the machine shop." He looked back at Dylan.
s like the universe is tryin' to get a balance or something. Like
:ing a circuit work, trying different things until it clicks."

And in the here and now?" Dylan asked, leaning back against the
:head.

In the here and now . . ." Harper was silent for a moment, think-
"In the here and now I think it clicked, I think it's right. It's like
were best friends right from the start, and that's exactly how it's
:nt to be."

And you don't want anything more than this?" Dylan said.

From Trance?" Harper said. "Hell, no. That's what made it so
:y." He looked at the uniform again. "Besides, one me is confus-
:nough. Thinking about other Seamus Harpers in other realities
:ick head-explodey time. I mean, name, rank, serial number . . .
:ing a uniform like this every day . . . maybe coming from an
:h that wasn't overrun by Magog and Nietzscheans . . ."

:e turned away from the uniform.

just try to ignore it," Dylan said. "As far as I'm concerned, there's
there's now, there's this reality, and everything else is a dream."

)r a nightmare," Harper said.

ometimes." Dylan was silent for a moment, watching Harper.
younger man seemed haunted, and the less-serious, self-
:ssed side of him seemed to have vanished completely. "Some-
you have to accept the nightmares and keep going anyway."

)r be a gutless wonder like me," Harper muttered, not looking at
:.

s gutless as you were when you helped me hunt down the pieces
: Rimini Vase," Dylan said calmly. Harper looked up, meeting
:es. "Or as gutless as you were fighting back to back with Tyr
: the Magog were overrunning the *Andromeda*. I don't think you
:ny idea just how much respect that won you from Tyr."

"I guess not," Harper mumbled, looking away.

"There's nothing wrong with fear. Fear's good because it can to keep you alive." Dylan paused for a moment, watching Ha Harper was focused on him. Good. "What kills people is para No ability to make choices, no ability to move forward."

"Yeah, well, I get scared enough, and real fast," Harper said.

"As I said, not a bad thing," Dylan replied. "There's no such t as a man without fear—think about it. What would happen?"

Harper thought about it for a second, then he started to "Live fast, die young, don't stay swimming in the gene pool."

"In one," Dylan said, smiling. "Real courage isn't about cha into the teeth of the enemy with guns blazing. It's about being s to death and getting the job done anyway."

"Hey, you know how I was acting," Harper said, his grin fa "Dylan, I didn't wanna come here. Seeing those pictures really me the creeps."

"Well," Dylan said, "I didn't want to come here either, but the alternative even less. I'm also betting that if we get the *Andro* Slip-capable again and we bring her out this way that Beka can fi a faster route home."

"Jeez," Harper said, "that's an idea I like. Gotta catch up my fleximags, plus I think my *Anti-Proton Engineer* swimsuit c dar's due."

"Sounds good to me," Dylan said.

"Don't be so sure," Harper said. "The last calendar I got was the *Slipstream Journal*." He curled his lip. "It was the Centennia Than Edition. Oh, man."

"I'd guess the Than liked it," Dylan said. "Come on, let's g ward before Rommie starts thinking we fell out of an airlock."

Trance stood on the darkened Observation Deck, looking through the huge window and feeling miserable. The *Eureka* had been gone for a little more than two days, but that wasn source of her unhappiness.

She was sure now that she was somehow the focal point of a t act effect. Space, time, and dimensions were all folding, conve

er, and she was helpless to stop it. She couldn't even place the crux
he effect—it had to have started somewhere, and she was certain
this time it had nothing to do with Harper's machine.

his was something that could eventually tear down dimensional
s, rupturing the barriers that kept everything safe, and she was
pletely helpless to stop it.

olo-Rommie flickered into life next to her. The holographic
r had managed to retain the blue-haired look and showed no
s of pulling a sudden makeover anytime soon.

his sucks," Trance said, sounding as miserable as she felt.

No answers?" Rommie said, folding her arms.

he quantum twists of fate," Trance said, and sighed. "I'm on my
Rommie." She turned away from the window. "I've got all kinds
swers for all kinds of things, but not for this, not yet."

ou're doing your best to figure it out, right?" Rommie said.

es, I am," Trance said. "But until I do get it figured out maybe I
d leave the ship. I can take a Slipfighter or a transport and jump
where. Anywhere. If I'm the focus of a tesseract effect, anything
come through."

looks to me," Rommie said reasonably, "as though *you're* the only
coming through. Repeatedly, I admit, but not really dangerous."

xcept for nearly getting Tyr shot."

omeone wanting to shoot Tyr is hardly a new thing," Rommie
"Anyway, I don't think you should go anywhere right now. You
know what could happen if you leave me. It could make things
."

aybe." Trance turned back to the big window, looking out at the
"I just wish someone could help. Not even explain it, just turn it
he bowed her head. "I don't think that's going to happen."

o," Rommie said, "I don't think it is. You're going to have to
is one out."

ain," Rommie said, "I've got something strange."

ight had settled the *Eureka Maru* into a head-down parking
around Waystation, keeping them three thousand kilometers
the surface. Once contact was achieved with the base, they

could go straight down. If they failed to achieve contact, ▮
planned to take the ship down for a quick investigation. He ▮
decide what to do from there.

"Define strange," Dylan said.

"There is another vessel in orbit around Waystation," Ro▮
said. "It's in an orbit higher than ours."

"That isn't strange," Harper said, "that's scary."

"Let's go take a look," Dylan said. "Give Mr. Wright the d▮
Mr. Wright, take us in, and try to make it cautious."

"Aye, Captain," Wright said, "taking us in."

He applied power to the thrusters, rolled the ship over, an▮
them on a heading for the other ship.

"According to sensor data," Rommie said, "what we're appr▮
ing is a High Guard *Azure Harmony*–class light transport."

Dylan frowned. "That wasn't a class that was active at the ti▮
were serving, was it?"

"No, it wasn't," Rommie said. "According to my database, t▮
of the *Azure Harmony* transports was decommissioned in CY ▮
when the design was replaced by the *Golden Dawn* class."

"It could have been left here after it was decommissioned," ▮
said.

"Unlikely," Rommie said. "Either the craft would have ▮
scrapped and the matériel recycled, or it would have been par▮
one of the High Guard storage locations."

Harper was looking at the scans now. "I'm guessing it's bee▮
awhile, guys. Lots of the kind of micrometeorite pitting you'd ▮
you stuck a ship in orbit for, oh, a couple or three hundred year▮
that's one cold, dead ship."

"We're coming up on her," Wright said. Dylan looked out ▮
cockpit window to see a distant, gracefully bulbous craft. "I'll br▮
alongside."

"Uh, guys," Harper said nervously, "just don't start talking ▮
going aboard, okay? The deader and colder an abandoned ship ▮
more likely it's gonna have something nasty aboard that, like, wa▮
stick its tongue down your throat and leave an egg behind▮

turned paler than usual, his face screwing up. "Jeez, I had to remind myself, didn't I?"

"Don't worry, Mr. Harper," Dylan said. He turned his head to look at the engineer, smiling. "Maybe you should stop watching cheap horror vids and stick with Than comedies."

"Those *are* cheap horror vids," Harper said. "Anyway, you didn't grow up on Earth hearing about stuff like the cockroach that ate Cincinnati."

Wright reduced the forward velocity of the *Maru* to a slow drift as they came alongside the transport. A little more than 500 meters long, 200 meters tall, and 250 meters across at its widest point, the ship hinted at practicality beneath its graceful curves. Command and Observation Decks were set forward, while crew quarters occupied the top section of the vessel. The rest consisted of engines and cargo space.

"I'm trying to identify the vessel," Rommie said, "but with all of the systems cold, it's difficult—the transponders are down. It looks almost as though it was put into permanent shutdown." She frowned. "All I'm getting from the dermal encoding is a High Guard ship registry number, but it's showing up as invalid. The dermal encoding should also include a name, but it doesn't."

"Maybe this predates full dermal encoding?" Dylan suggested.

"No," Rommie said. "Full dermal identification protocols were introduced more than fifteen hundred years before this class of vessel entered service."

"No known registry number, and no name," Dylan said, frowning. "And here I'd fooled myself into thinking this was going to be easy. What else?"

"It looks as though the antiproton tanks were emptied, and some of the ship stripped." Rommie turned her chair around. "This isn't just a cold ship, Captain, it's a hulk."

Dylan thought for a moment, then said, "I'd guess we can tow it. Can we haul it through Slipstream? Hook it up with Bucky cables and all?"

Harper snorted. "Boss, that's what this ship was designed to do. Beka's got a point about flying an asteroid, but the *Maru*'s meant to

haul wrecks around. That's why we were the ones pulling you out ⊙
the black hole."

Rommie frowned at him. "I am *not* a wreck."

"Didn't say you were, Rom-doll, just sayin' what this ship w
meant for."

"'Rom-doll'?" Rommie echoed, an eyebrow raised. "It seen
you're feeling a bit better, Mr. Harper."

"Jeez," Harper muttered, "is everyone playing shrink with n
today?"

"The only way I shrink things, Harper," Rommie said, "is by blov
ing them up."

"I'll pass," Harper said. "Anyway, yeah, we can tow it."

"Good," Dylan said. "Rommie, can you dismantle and proce
whatever's left of this ship?"

"Much more easily than the average asteroid," she said. She turn⊙
to look at her station. "There's plenty of mass, and the initial qui
analysis does indicate that there's quite a bit that will only need cu
ting up and recycling."

"Some of it's gonna be unusable," Harper said. "If this baby was
use for hundreds of years and parked for a few more hundred, ther
gonna be stress fractures and decomposition issues."

"We can worry about that when we get it back and Androme
starts taking it apart. Is there anything else showing up that we c
use?"

"Deep scanning now, Captain," Rommie said.

"Slipstream drive's gone," Harper said.

"The antiproton drive is still in place," Rommie said, "but at t
moment I can't tell if it's functional."

Dylan frowned. "No Slip drive."

"Coulda been towed here," Harper said.

"The question is," Dylan said quietly, "why. It makes sense that t
drive would be gone if it was decommissioned, but why pull it out
mothballs and tow it *here* and then abandon it?"

"More curious is the lack of identification," Rommie said.

"Black operations," Wright said. They all turned to him. "Loc
everybody knows that organizations of this kind exist—it's not a m⊙

er of paranoia. There's always a need for organizations that don't
xist. They're funded through back channels, do the really dirty
vork, and are never acknowledged."

"A good theory," Dylan said, "but that leaves a couple of points.
'irst of all, while the High Guard had secret ops and special ops divi-
ons in the Argosy Service—I served in both before being put onto
ie command track—the High Guard never had a black operations
division. I doubt the Vedrans would have tolerated even the idea of it."

"That's the thing," Wright said. "The point of a black ops division
to remain invisible. If it comes out that there is such an organiz-
ion, then the information should be made to turn into an urban leg-
ad or a running joke."

"I'd tell you, but then I'd have to kill you?" Harper said.

"Right. With an organization the size of the High Guard, a black
os division would just vanish from sight."

Dylan was starting to feel a coldness now in the pit of his stomach,
d he seemed to be having difficulty mustering an argument against
'right's suggestion. The new Commonwealth had, for whatever rea-
n, an active black ops division, albeit one that didn't cover its tracks
well as it should have.

"There were rumors and whispers about this among various mem-
rs of the crews who served aboard me," Rommie said. She turned
look straight at Dylan. "At one point I was programmed to gather
tistical data regarding mentions, casual or otherwise, of secret divi-
ns within the High Guard."

"Sounds like somebody was trying to plug a hole or something,"
arper said.

"I had no idea about this," Dylan said softly.

"It was before you became captain," Rommie said. "It wasn't a
tter of applying information to individual records. The final analy-
of my data did indicate a belief in something more than Argosy
vice operations. There was no indication that any of the crew
mbers that I monitored had any concrete knowledge of such oper-
ns, however."

Dylan was watching through the cockpit window as they drifted
t the huge transport. "Friend of a friend of a friend?"

"Fish stories," Wright said. "They always get bigger every ti▮ they're passed on. Again, that's how they cover up."

"That's all well and good," Dylan said, "but it doesn't answer t▮ questions." Coming to a decision, he thumped the top of the captai▮ chair.

"We're going aboard, aren't we?" Harper said unhappily. "Y▮ always act like that when you decide something like that."

"*I'm* going aboard," Dylan said. "Rommie's coming with me. Y▮ and Mr. Wright will stay on the *Maru*, so there's no need to wo▮ about egg-spitting slime creatures."

"Yeah, right," Harper said.

"There are aft cargo bay doors open," Rommie said, looking at ▮ instruments. "We should be able to enter the main part of the ves▮ through any of them."

"Is this an advisable course of action, sir?" Wright asked. "I'm w▮ Harper insofar as ghost ships worry me. I'm not worried ab▮ malevolent creatures or evil spirits—I'm concerned about the pos▮ bility of booby traps."

"Rommie?" Dylan said.

"Absolutely nothing active," she said. "I can't guarantee that ▮ ship is one hundred percent clean, of course, but all of the m▮ obvious traps can be eliminated."

"It's the ones where you get aboard, the thing lights up, someb▮ says 'gotcha!' and it sets its controls for the heart of a sun," Harp▮ muttered.

"No fuel," Dylan said.

"This will cut into out primary mission time," Rommie poin▮ out. "We could investigate this later, when we've returned with ▮ hulk."

"We could," Dylan said quietly, "but we need to make an atten▮ to find answers here before we go any farther. This shouldn't take ▮ long."

"Uh, Dylan," Harper said, "maybe you oughta say somethin' ▮ 'This could take a while, guys, keep a light on but don't wait up, hav▮ cup of cocoa and get your cuddly toys and go to bed when you're s▮ posed to because Mom and Dad could be out partyin' pretty late.'"

"I could do that," Dylan said, grinning, "but I don't talk as much as ›u do."

"Besides, Harper," Rommie said, "if we do run into trouble, I have mplete faith in the fact that you'll come heroically dashing to my scue."

"So I'd have to depend on Mr. Wright?" Dylan said, raising his ebrows.

"Different rules apply again, Captain," Rommie said with a happy ile, "but this time it's because Harper didn't build you."

"I'm not even goin' there," Harper said.

"Good," Dylan said, turning to look at the hulk. "But we're going ›re. Mr. Wright, pick your spot and take us in."

"Aye, Captain," Wright said, "initiating docking maneuvers." He ›ched the thruster controls and the *Eureka Maru* began to slowly ›nge course, heading for the aft end of the dead ship.

Harper shook his head, looking down at his console, but said noth- more.

Iromeda's head and shoulders appeared on the main screen and on ›ens around the Command Deck. "I believe we have the correct of counterfrequencies to combat the mind torpedoes."

›eka was the only one on the Command Deck. She regarded Iromeda steadily for a moment, then said, "Do you think this'll k? It'd be nice to not have to get shots every few hours."

As far as I can tell, it will work," Andromeda said. "I've run mul- › simulations and the final frequency mix tests out every time. ›e of the signals will be jammed, others blanked completely. The It should be nothing more than a pattern of static."

Okay," Beka said. "How do we deliver this?"

Ms. Pogue was originally going to modify several electromagnetic generators, but my estimate was that this would take too long."

So?"

The best solution, in my opinion, is to use the ECM fans. I can ram the system to produce a continuous low-power output ›r than the usual high-power signals." She turned her head, look- ›ward the screen next to hers. A schematic cross section of the

Andromeda Ascendant appeared and rotated, showing the fans Two of the six were darkened. "Even with only four of the fans operation, this should be quite effective."

"Alternatives?" Beka asked. She didn't really want alternatives, she had to ask. What she really wanted was for this part of the nightmare to be over and done with.

"Other than raking me stem to stern with plasma bursts—and I had quite enough of that—the one other viable solution would electromagnetic pulse. We have EMP generators on hand."

Beka shook her head. "I don't see that as a good choice, Androveda. Too much potential for damage."

"It would require a full shutdown," Andromeda said. "Howeve am a warship, and I do have hardened systems."

"So, one way or another, we get rid of these things?"

"It may take a little time, but yes," Andromeda said.

"Just as long as I don't have to go out there with a butter knife scrape them off," Beka said.

"That," Andromeda said with a slight frown, "should not be nec sary."

"I hope not." Beka considered for a moment, then said, "Well, in charge, so I guess . . . let's do it."

"Aye, Captain," Andromeda said, "doing it."

"Let me know when everything's ready," Beka said. "I'm goin get a bite to eat."

Dylan had very little experience with boarding and inspecting d ships, and it wasn't too long after he and Rommie had boarded mystery ship that he began to understand Harper's nervousness

Getting the *Maru* into one of the aft cargo docks had been problem at all. From that point on, however, everything required effort. With no ship power available, he and Rommie were force move slowly, using a device Harper had retrieved from somewl inside the *Maru* to open each of the bulkhead doors. If any air remained in the vessel after its abandonment, it had long since fro

"Looks deader'n dead to me, Boss," Harper said, his voice eche in Dylan's head.

"I think our prospects of finding a party are minimal at best," ommie observed. While she didn't need air, even to communicate, nd could easily survive for some time in open space, she had suited p as well. There was no need to put additional strain on her systems.

Dylan turned, shining the powerful beam of his spotlight down a rridor that angled off from the junction they were in. He had no fficulty telling that the ship was of a much older design than the ssels he was familiar with—there was an oddly ornate style to the rridors, and the flatscreens were set firmly into the bulkheads, ther than hanging from supports at the junctions.

"This way, Captain," Rommie said, gesturing with her spotlight. e turned and kicked off from the wall, floating serenely along the rridor. Dylan, a little more ungainly, followed.

"Hey, Dylan," Harper said, "that electronic mega-key of mine ens damn near everything."

"It's good to know that, Mr. Harper," Dylan said. "I take it that ere are some limitations?"

"Yeah. It doesn't open anything Tyr wants opened."

Dylan chuckled. "Very good, Mr. Harper."

A few minutes later, they were at the Command Deck. Dylan and mmie looked around in silence. A pilot's chair still sat at the center the deck, but the Slipstream hood was gone, leaving a mounting cket and a few fiber-optic lines. Consoles had been removed, and e of the big flatscreens had a crack across its surface.

"I'm having horrible visions of my future," Rommie said as she ked around. "This is sad."

"No argument there," Dylan said. "I'm not seeing anything useful. w about you?"

"Not yet," Rommie said.

"Mr. Harper? Anything showing up on your monitors?" Harper monitoring cameras mounted on his and Rommie's suits. His dis-
v systems could enhance the images, and between those and Rom-
's systems it was unlikely that they would overlook anything.

"Just a sec . . ." Harper said, sounding thoughtful. "Go right." an turned slightly and eased forward. "There. Looks like flexis in e kind of pocket."

"I see them," Rommie said. She kicked lightly at the deck and w[as] floating over to the find. She pulled them out and riffled through [a] small stack. She tapped experimentally at the top one and was rewar[ded] by having it light up. "Well, at least one still works."

She pushed off and floated to Dylan, handing him the one she [had] activated. He looked at it, frowning. "Paperwork. Looks like bure[au]cratese to me." He tapped at the paging controls, stepping through p[age] after page. "It's a decommissioning report for the *Azure Harm[ony]* class vessel *Dark Fire*."

He handed it to Rommie, who looked at it and stepped thro[ugh] several more pages. "The registry number is the same, so I would [say] that we are standing on—or floating inside—the *Dark Fire*. [It] seems an odd naming protocol for a class of cargo vessel." She tap[ped] again, calling up further pages. "Placed into secure storage at [the] Kelkoso Facility . . . which I've never heard of."

Dylan took another of the flexis and turned it on. "More bure[au]cratese. Memos listing parts and sections removed, authorizat[ions] from various names. Division Forty-seven engineering, Division [six]teen supply control." He looked up. "Much more of this stuff and [my] eyes are going to reach down and strangle me."

Rommie had turned another flexi on. "Captain, this is a reac[tiva]tion order, dated CY 9766. It authorizes the use of the *Dark Fire* [for] the specific purpose of acting as a cargo barge, cargo and destina[tion] not specified."

"Well," Dylan said, "we know where it ended up."

"It's over the signature of General Janus Altmann," Rom[mie] added. She tapped the paging control. "There's nothing after tha[t]—this one."

"Janus Altmann," Dylan said, thinking. "Right, I know who he [is.] Rear echelon flexi-sorter on the supply chain. . . ."

"Not to be obvious or anything," Harper said, "but I can see w[here] this is heading. Just the right guy to know all about Waystation, rig[ht?]"

"Right," Dylan said.

"I just can't see the point," Rommie said. "The Commonwe[alth] was in serious trouble by that point, so what was the point of co[ming] all the way out here with this ship?"

"Maybe he loaded up all the Vedran silverware and fine china," Harper said, "switched ships out here, and went off and bootlegged it somewhere else."

"Too complicated," Rommie said, "not to mention highly unlikely."

"It could have been a meeting point," Dylan said. "Harper's idea isn't all that crazy."

"But why not just go to the final destination directly?" Rommie said.

"Blastin' out of Slipstream towing a mothballed ship full of stuff kinda attracts attention," Harper said. "Better if you go somewhere quiet, offload the goods onto another ship, and then go wherever you're going looking normal."

"Plausible, I suppose," Rommie said.

"Sometimes thinking like a scoundrel has its pluses," Dylan said. "One of the many things Mr. Harper's good at."

"Gee, thanks, Boss." He paused for a moment. "I think I just got complimented and insulted in one go there."

"Complimented only, Mr. Harper," Dylan said. "We'll spend a few more minutes looking around and then head back. I suspect this is it, though."

He was right.

I am opening the ECM fans now," Andromeda announced. She turned to look toward the screen on her right side, where a ship schematic was being displayed. "The two sections that are out of commission should not affect the countermeasure mix."

Beka stepped around her piloting station and walked toward the screens. "You're going to full power right away?"

"No," Andromeda said, looking toward her. "I will gradually increase the gain. That will give me an opportunity to assess the effectiveness of this approach. I will also be able to judge whether or not there are any adverse effects." She looked to the right again. "ECM fans are locked."

"Then," said Tyr, who was standing at his usual station, "should we begin?" He turned slightly and inclined his head toward Pogue, who was at Rommie's station. "Is there anything else that occurs to you before the switch is thrown?"

Pogue thought for a moment, then said, "Nothing. We've told
everything we know."

"Very well, then," Tyr said, looking back to the screens.

"Where's Trance?" Beka asked.

"On her way here from the medical bay," Andromeda said.
should be here shortly."

"Okay," Beka said, "she can join the party late, I guess." She to
deep breath and let it out slowly. "Let's do it."

"Doing it, aye," Andromeda said. "Feeding minimum power t
ECM transmitters. I will increase power by ten percent per mi
until I reach maximum output."

Beka took another deep breath, trying to maintain her focus.
glanced at Pogue, and saw the tension in the pilot's face. Tyr, or
other hand, seemed completely composed, standing casually a
station.

"ECM output is now at twenty percent," Andromeda said.

"I'm starting to feel better already," Beka said.

"Imagination, and hopefulness," Tyr said, looking at her. "You
not benefit from the effects for a while. Brain chemistry must
return to normal."

Beka sighed, frowning at him. "So it's psychosomatic. So w
Leave me a crutch here."

"Very well," he said, "if you wish me to see you as lamed."

Beka gritted her teeth and refused to respond.

"ECM power at thirty percent," Andromeda said. "I'm begin
to see signs of an interference pattern."

"Keep going," Beka said. "We're going to break this thing."

Trance swung out onto a between-decks ladder and quickly clir
down, dropping into the corridor that led to the Command Dec

She froze as she felt a ripple of energy pass through her.
turned.

A ghostly version of herself was walking away up the corridor.
phantom Trance was wearing an ornate gown, and her dense fa
hair was interwoven with glittering jewels that looked like tiny s

Trance started in pursuit, but the phantom faded away before she uld catch up.

She turned back. "Andromeda?" There was no answer. "Androm-a? Rommie?" She glanced back along the corridor. She was starting feel afraid now. "Beka? Tyr? Paula?"

Only silence.

"Andromeda?" She turned around. If she ran, she could make it to mmand. "Rommie?"

She started to run. Another ripple of energy passed through her, I she stumbled, sprawling on the deck. She got to her hands and es, but she couldn't seem to get farther than that.

I shouldn't be this weak, it's not possible.

She managed to turn around, getting her back against the corridor I. She felt weak and dizzy, and her hands were shaking.

Phantoms swirled in front of her. Several turned and looked in her ction. There was a flurry of motion.

They can see me.

The phantoms faded away. Trance closed her eyes.

t's almost here. It's happening.

Andromeda," she whispered. "I know. I know."

he opened her eyes and looked at her hands. They were blurring, ning out of focus. She tried to force herself back into focus, but no longer had the energy.

I'm not the only one," she whispered. "Andromeda, I can't stop it."

ll she could do now was wait.

ryone to your positions, please," Dylan said as he sat down in aptain's chair. Wright had taken the *Maru* back out and back to original orbit while Dylan and Rommie had shed their EVA . Now it was Dylan's show. "Let's see if anything's alive down .″

Oh, yeah," Harper said, his expression cynical, "that's a real com-ng way to put it."

ylan grinned. "Just stay strapped in, Mr. Harper. This is likely to bumpy ride."

"Yeah, well," Harper muttered, "that's how they all seem late]

Dylan tapped at the controls, and the *Maru* broke orbit, he for the surface.

"ECM power at ninety percent," Andromeda said. "I am now see pattern of static, as predicted."

Beka turned around to look at the entrance to Command. "W the hell is Trance?"

Andromeda looked distracted for a moment, then frowned. lost her signal. It isn't because of the ECM signals, either. (trackers are working to specification."

"Great time for this stuff to happen again," Beka muttered.

"Where was she when you last had a signal?" Tyr asked.

"Fifty meters from Medical, on a ladder to the next deck."

"I'll see if there is any sign of her along her intended route, t he said.

"Sounds good to me," Beka said. She managed a nervous s "At least some things seem to be going right."

Tyr left, moving swiftly but not running.

"ECM power to maximum," Andromeda said. She looked pl with herself. "I detect nothing but a hash of static."

"Yay," Beka said. "Now we figure out how to scrape those b cles off the boat."

Andromeda smiled.

That was the moment in which the first of the pulses hit.

Waves of energy poured through Trance, and she screamed in a

Desperately, she fought to keep herself together, but it wa hard a task, and she didn't have anything left in her for it.

She screamed again, and shattered, her mind scattering i directions.

Convergence.

As swiftly as she had shattered, she came back together. Ther no time to protect herself, however. Now she couldn't even scre her once-possible pasts and presents swept over and into her.

Her body blurred, shimmering with color and light. Her eyes :kered with fire for a moment, and then were normal again. .anges came rapidly at first, and then slowed down. Finally, they pped. She looked almost normal now—except for the odd out-of-:us appearance she had attained.

Her eyes closed for a moment, and then opened again.

Her name was Trance Gemini.

Their name.

Legion.

She began to slowly push herself to her feet.

ere was a long, high scream from somewhere down the corridor, wail of a soul about to be lost to terrible things.

The sound chilled Tyr.

"Andromeda!" he shouted as he started running. "Activate auto-ed defenses."

"Automated internal defenses are active," she replied.

"Trance—" he started, and then his brain filled with a terrible te fire.

.s he plunged helplessly forward to the deck, he heard Androm-s anguished voice saying, "Code Blue, officers down!"

Vhite turned to red and then to black, and Tyr lay very still, very .t, on the deck.

the Command Deck, Andromeda's voice was repeating the Code : alert, although there was little point to it—no one was left to it. When the first pulse had hit, both Beka and Pogue had fallen, aming briefly.

Jow they were sprawled on the deck, unmoving, and to all appear-s dead. Andromeda was relieved to find that her scans proved rwise. She shut down the automated alert.

he shut down the ECM fans and felt the static fade away.

.er holographic avatar flickered into life, forming a direct link. .e was no reason to waste time by talking in the nonvirtual world. ooby trap."

"I feel like a complete idiot," Andromeda said. "I'm not used
that."

"Don't be so hard on yourself." Rommie folded her arms. "Nob
had any idea that these things could do this. I smell an upgrade
Micah and Paula hadn't heard about."

Andromeda nodded. "Agreed."

"There's something else," Rommie said.

"Trance."

"Something's happened. I think it's whatever she was exp
ing . . . whatever she was dreading." Rommie was looking sc
now. "Andromeda, we're going to lose her, aren't we?"

"I don't know," Andromeda said unhappily. "I don't have any
what might happen."

Beka was conscious again, trying to push herself up and ma
quiet little sobs as she did so. Blood was dripping from her nose
mouth.

Silently Andromeda put out a call for maintenance androids.

How did I ever become so incapable? she wondered.

"We didn't," Rommie said firmly. "The challenges just got a h
a lot tougher."

.EVEN • THE RAINBOW AT THE END OF THE GOLD

Remember that old saw about "It is not my place to judge; that is for God. My job is to arrange the meeting"? Well, it would be nice if someone would return my calls so we could get on with this. I never see this sort of thing happening to social secretaries!

—FIELD MARSHAL OMALLEY HARRIS AT THE
ACHILLEAN SUICIDER UPRISING, CY 8501

Eureka Maru was five hundred kilometers above the surface Rommie said, "We have an incoming communication."

et's hear it," Dylan said. He tapped at controls, and the ship's de changed as it moved into a stable orbit. "No sense in running d while we negotiate with the gatekeeper."

right and Harper were watching Dylan intently. Rommie, while, seemed completely unconcerned. "Bringing the signal up Captain," she said.

e cabin speakers hissed slightly. "—Guard outpost Waystation identified vessel. Please transmit identification or leave this

his is the *Eureka Maru*, seconded to the *Andromeda Ascendant*, in Dylan Hunt commanding," Dylan said. He nodded to Rom-'Transmitting identification and clearance codes now."

mmie tapped at several keys. "Transmitting. Done."

"Stand by," Waystation responded.

"Friendly," Harper said.

"Let's hope they decide we're okay," Dylan said.

"What happens if they don't?" Harper asked nervously.

"They shoot us down," Rommie said.

Harper made a strangled noise.

"Identification, command, and clearance codes accepted," W tion said. "You are cleared for approach and landing. Transm flight path information."

"Well," Rommie said with a smile, "they aren't going to sh down yet."

"Oh, yeah, that really makes me feel better," Harper said.

"Good," Dylan said. He was grinning as he turned to the controls. "Now all we need to worry about is the weather."

"Right," Harper said. "Weather."

"Well," Rommie said, the picture of innocence, "it *is* much at the base's actual location. The planners chose to locate it more temperate zone at the equator."

"Oh, thanks," Harper snorted. "You could have told m before."

"More temperate, Mr. Harper," Dylan said, "means it's only fifty Celsius and the winds only get up to two hundred kilomet hour."

Dylan fired the thrusters again, taking the *Maru* out of orbit. Waystation's flight plan locked in, there really wasn't much for do until they came in for a landing.

"Okay," Harper admitted, "maybe I *didn't* want to know that

Tyr struggled back from darkness to find himself sprawled u fortably on the deck, his head throbbing. His nose had bled at point, but the bleeding had stopped, leaving him with the unco able sensation of blood drying in his thin beard.

He rolled over and sat up, trying to focus. The effort ma head throb all the more, but he resolutely ignored it.

He had been looking for Trance. Then something had all bu his mind apart. It wasn't difficult to guess what had happe

dromeda's efforts to counteract the mind torpedo had obviously
gered some kind of high-powered counter-attack.

"Andromeda?" he said, his voice sounding hoarse. "Status?"

Holo-Rommie flickered into life a couple of meters from him. "To
in a handbasket," she said. "You look worse for wear."

"Yes, well," he muttered, "having my brain torn apart from the
de certainly has not improved my day."

"Beka and Ms. Pogue are in bad shape," Rommie said. "I'm get-
them to Medical now. Can you make it there, or do you need
stance?"

He got to his feet, slowly and shakily, steadying his breathing. "I've
n in worse shape than this." He looked along the corridor, but
e was nothing to see. "What of Trance?"

"Don't worry about her right now," Rommie said, frowning.
ere's something very strange happening, but I need you in Med-
at the moment. You need to patch yourself up and then take care
eka and Pogue."

"Then I am on my way," he said heavily.

lowly he started in the direction of the medical bay.

entire body was wracked with pain—so much so that she felt as though
ere afire from head to foot. Vertigo assailed her, her head spinning with
force that she felt as though she might black out at any moment.

he couldn't give in now, not while the ship was threatened.

rance leaned against the corridor wall for a moment, trying to pull her-
ogether and focus on what needed to be done.

he straightened up again and resumed her labored walk. Each step was
sh agony, but she forced herself to disregard the pain. She was going to
this fight all the way to Kalderash if she had to. The Kalderans were a
et and pestilent breed, and their actions kept interfering with her plans.
w a Kalderan raiding party had boarded the Andromeda Ascendant.
e all-too-typical Kalderan manner they were doing their best to lay
to large chunks of the ship as they went.

e stopped as she heard the hum and snap of Kalderan rifles, followed by
udding sounds of explosive rounds hitting their marks.

xty meters past the junction, off to her right. She drew her force lance

from its holster and thumbed it on. Pressing back against the corridor
she eased slowly toward the junction.

Kalderan voices, high-pitched and urgent.

She stopped, waiting.

The first of them stepped into the junction, looking up the corridor
from her. A two-meter-tall gray-skinned reptilian creature clad in
fatigues, the Kalderan was armed with a large rifle.

A second Kalderan stepped into the junction, glancing down toward
let out a cry of alarm as it swung its rifle to aim at her.

She was faster by far. She shot the second Kalderan twice in the
shifted her aim in a blur of motion as the first tried to dodge the falling
of his compatriot. She fired twice more, and the Kalderan fell backw
the effectors hit him in the head and chest.

There was no more time for subtlety. Ignoring the pain in her bo
forcing herself to remain coherent despite the vertigo, she ran into the
tion, spinning around and diving, firing down the corridor as she
toward the deck.

She hit the deck, sliding a little. She rolled to her left, finishing u
prone firing position. Three visible targets, too close together for thei
good, their reactions confused. She shot all three and was in motion
even as the third hit the deck.

She ran along the corridor, following the incline. High-pitched chat
ahead, sounding frantic. Two more.

She ran toward the wall and jumped, letting her momentum car
into a short loping run that ended as she kicked hard. She cartw
through the air at an angle, firing, hitting the other wall feetfirst, an
tinuing her brief run. She landed on the deck, going into a crouch, l
for targets. The two Kalderans lay sprawled on the deck, dead.

"Andromeda, give me an update," she said as she scooped up one
Kalderan rifles.

Andromeda appeared on one of the junction screens. "Tyr is down.
and Dylan are holding their own on the Command Deck, and Har
locked safely in Engineering. My android avatar is using a couple of l
of steel pipe to make the Kalderans regret coming aboard."

"Need help?" Trance asked.

"Not really. I will try and reach Tyr. I suggest you head for Command to p Dylan and Beka."

"On my way," she said.

She ran down the corridor, climbing the first ladder she reached. Swing-g onto the next deck up, she sprinted along the corridor and into a junction, ng to her right.

Two more Kalderans. Startled, they swung their rifles up. She aimed her ce lance and fired. One of the Kalderans spun and fell, his chest blazing.

The other staggered back, screeching, one shoulder blazing. She aimed d fired again, but she wasn't quite fast enough. The Kalderan opened fire t before she did. He only managed a single shot, but it was enough. The nd slammed into her chest and exploded, throwing her backward even as shot finished the Kalderan.

She wanted to scream her frustration, but there wasn't time.

She landed facedown on the deck. A small trail of smoke rose lazily m her.

ow what?" Tyr said, halting. Holo-Rommie flickered into being. hat's a force lance. Why would anyone be firing a force lance?"

"A question you might wish to ask Trance," Rommie said. "She's one firing it."

"At what?" Tyr couldn't believe what he was hearing—it sounded e one-half of a pitched battle going on somewhere in the near tance.

"A good question. Unfortunately, at me for the moment, as her ectors have to go somewhere." Rommie frowned, then scowled rily. "Damn it. Command circuitry for my internal defenses in t area has gone down."

"You're planning to shoot her?" Tyr said, astounded.

"It's unlikely to be permanent," Rommie said, sounding utterly sonable. "I have no idea what's behind this, but having someone ning around being randomly and inexplicably homicidal is not nething I really want."

"Understood," he said. "I think it prudent to stay out of her way the time being."

"That might not be an option," Rommie said. "She's heading your direction."

Tyr looked around quickly, but there was no cover immediat available. There was only one choice—go back the way he had co and find the nearest interdeck ladder.

He ran, entered a junction, and bore right.

Running footsteps behind him. He drew his Gauss pistol, turn and running backward.

Trance was racing toward him, her force lance out and aimee his direction. In her left arm she was cradling a rifle that loo Kalderan in design, although he didn't know the model.

He threw himself to the deck and rolled toward the wall as skidded to a stop and started firing. Effectors hit the corridor w and flared.

He blinked, surprised. For a moment he thought he had s ghostly figures appear.

He couldn't allow this to continue. Even as Trance aimed at so thing unseen, he brought his pistol up, aimed, and fired once. bullet hit Trance in the chest, and she fell back, hitting the wall sliding down. The rifle clattered to the deck, sliding toward Tyr.

"This seems to be turning into a habit," he said.

"I'd like to know what she thought she was shooting at," Rom said.

Tyr stood up, then bent down to retrieve the Kalderan rifle would like to know where she obtained this," he said.

"Out of thin air, apparently," Rommie said. "I'm detecting energy fluxes and surges, and I suspect Trance has a great deal to with them."

"Medical," Tyr said. He sighed, then, without releasing Kalderan rifle, bent down again to pick Trance up, slinging her c his shoulder. She felt unusually warm, and she was surprisingly he for someone so slight. "I hope I won't have to shoot her again be get there."

Rommie sighed. "The day is young."

———

he *Maru* bucked and then slid to port as Dylan fought to keep the
ngainly ship steady in the buffeting winds. They were five hundred
eters from the surface now, and the wind had become even more of a
nemesis than the cold. Waystation was not a forgiving place.

"See?" Harper said. "This is why I don't come to planets like this.
oes anyone ever listen to me? Nobody *ever* listens to me. Why? I'm
st the engineering monkey, that's why. This—"

"Shut up, Harper," Rommie snapped.

Harper fell silent, just in time for the *Maru* to roll slightly and slide
port once more. Dylan righted the ship and got it back on course.

"The cargo pod's the source of the problems," he said, finally.
he wind's getting in between the *Maru* and the pod. The airflow
ound the struts is causing most of the problems."

"We could have left the freakin' thing in orbit," Harper said. "It's
signed for that."

"Do you really want to make multiple trips to and from the surface,
. Harper?" Rommie said. "That is what we would have to do."

"Never mind," Harper muttered.

"One trip down is enough for me," Wright said. He was looking
e again. "I don't want to see the inside of a galley for a while."

Dylan made some quick adjustments to the AG field as the ship
d to roll to starboard. They leveled out for a moment, then
pped like a stone.

"I'm so glad I'm not prone to motion sickness," Rommie said,
nding annoyingly cheerful.

"I'm too busy for it," Dylan said. His hands flew over the controls
in, and the ship rose slightly. He dipped the nose and fired the rear
usters for a moment. "I'm used to just flying in and putting down."

The *Maru* shot toward the surface. Dylan pulled the nose up
in, and adjusted the AG field, firing the landing thrusters as he did
Somehow, the ship stayed level.

autiously he brought the *Maru* down to a hundred meters, then
eventy-five.

There it is," Rommie said.

ylan had seen it too—not through the cockpit windows, but on one of the cockpit monitors. There was little to see through the ward windows other than a white glare. The enhanced image fr one of the forward cameras showed the surface dome of the base distinct shape against the icy backdrop. They were right on course the main landing bay.

"*Eureka Maru*, this is Waystation Control." The radio voice nondescript, male, but lacking proper inflection.

"Go ahead, Waystation," Dylan said.

"We show you on course for landing," Waystation respon "However, there is a problem here."

"Explain."

"We are unable to open the landing bay doors to admit you." T was a pause. "There are two options open to you. Return to orbit w my maintenance drones attempt to deal with the issue, or execu platform landing outside and enter through one of the cargo locks

Harper was looking stricken. "No," he said. "No, no, no—"

"Shut up, Harper," Wright said.

"Considering the ride down, Waystation," Dylan said, "I'll the second choice. We'll bring the *Maru* inside as soon as the d get fixed."

"Acknowledged, Captain Hunt." There was a pause. "Trans ting revised landing instructions."

Dylan glanced at a monitor. "Instructions received, Waysta *Eureka Maru* out."

There was silence as Dylan maneuvered the ship closer and c to the dome, looking for the landing platform. They would nee get the main doors open as soon as possible—trying to move they needed to the *Maru* via a cargo lock would be arduous and gerous work.

The landing platform appeared on the navigation monitors, an brought the ship down carefully, easing forward a few meters al it. Moving slowly over the platform, he fired the landing thru several times, blasting away accumulated snow and ice.

"Harper," he said, "ready Bucky cables and scan for good an points. We're going to need to hold on to something if we want a to come back to."

Harper didn't waste time sounding off. "Bucky cables are ready to Boss. Scanning for anchors."

"Alright," Dylan said. He took a deep breath and eased the ship last few meters over the platform.

"I've got anchor points," Harper said.

"Good work, Mr. Harper. Everyone hold on to something; this is ng to be bumpy."

"The rest of the ride wasn't?" Harper said.

Dylan didn't answer. He adjusted the AG again, and simultane-ly fired the thrusters. The *Maru* responded to this tactic by fero-usly shuddering. Dylan could hear things being shaken loose in the k of the ship. There were several loud snapping noises somewhere ind him, and the acrid smell of shorted circuits.

"Ready on those Bucky cables," Dylan said.

He cut back the power on the landing thrusters. The *Maru* didn't lly touch down heavily, but in this instance there was little choice. The ship boomed as the landing legs hit the platform. Shock rbers took up some of the impact, but not all of it, and the *Maru* nentarily threatened to tilt sideways.

"Now!" Dylan snapped.

Harper fired the cables.

"On target," Rommie reported.

he winches whined into life. The icy world outside came level n, and the ship settled into a low vibration from the wind. veen the Bucky cables and the AG field, the *Maru* would stay put. Dylan unbuckled himself and stood, stretching, trying to ease s out of his muscles. "I suggest we have a good meal—"

"Sadist," Wright muttered. Dylan glanced at him. "Sir," Wright d.

Dylan grinned. "I'm sure there's something aboard to settle your ach, Mr. Wright," Dylan said. "Either way, you'll eat before we utside." Dylan started to make his way aft. "Let's hope that the o lock isn't stuck as well."

"Some days, Dylan," Rommie said, "you're just a paragon of efulness."

"I do my best," Dylan said, grinning.

In the medical bay, Tyr deposited Trance on a diagnostic bed
about as much attention as he would have paid to putting down a
of potatoes. When Rommie flickered into life, looking disapp
ingly at him, he glared back and said, "What?"

One of the flatscreens lit. Andromeda looked down at hir
think she's hinting that you should treat Trance with a little
respect."

"Trance is to all intents and purposes quite dead," Tyr said
more patience than he felt, "I very much doubt that Trance
the moment, cares. My concern is with the *living* members o
crew."

There was a groan from Trance's direction. Rommie and Tyr tu
to look. "Then again . . ." Rommie said. The sentence went unfini

Trance let out another moan. Tyr noted with mild interest tha
skin had developed a pinkish cast. After a moment she rolled ont
side, groaned again, and rolled off of the bed.

There was a flat thud as she hit the floor.

Rommie and Tyr looked at each other.

"I think that woke her up," Andromeda said.

Tyr turned to look back at the bed. Trance had gotten to her
and was peering over the bed at him, looking rather woozy. "Oh
that was bad, wasn't it?" Using the side of the bed, she got shak
her feet.

"You could say it was . . . bad," Tyr said.

Trance stared at him blankly. After a moment, something se
to occur to her and she looked down at her outfit. She prodded
tantly at the charred parts, wrinkling her nose as some of it crun
away. She frowned, then gave her chest an experimental poke v
thumb. She winced. "I got myself shot again, didn't I?"

"An astute observation," Tyr said.

She sighed. "I really hate these backwoods drifts," Trance
unhappily. "Somebody always starts trouble, then somebody pul
a gun. . . ."

Tyr and Rommie looked at each other. "This," Tyr said, "is
ing less sense than usual."

Rommie looked back at Trance. "I suggest lying down for a time Trance."

"Didn't I just do that?" Trance said. She looked down at her outfit again, frowning. "I think I need to get changed. At least Harper didn't throw up on me this time."

Tyr bowed his head and touched the fingertips of his right hand to his forehead. "Go. Change. Rest."

Trance nodded, then, delicately, turned around and walked out of the medical bay. Tyr noticed that she seemed quite unsteady.

As soon as she was gone, he looked at Rommie and said, "I have seen Trance drink alcoholic beverages. I have seen her give every appearance of being drunk. I do not recall her ever exhibiting symptoms of a hangover afterward."

"For all we know," Andromeda said, "she might have experienced hangovers prior to joining my crew."

"She might," Rommie said.

"I have to wonder," Tyr said, "if that was a hangover at all."

Rommie folded her arms. "All things considered, I have to wonder the same thing. In the meantime, you need to attend to yourself and me to Beka and Pogue."

Trance wandered, lost in a haze. She had the vague idea that she was supposed to be going somewhere, but the destination somehow escaped her. She didn't know where she was going, she didn't know where she had started from, and the space in between was a fog that refused to lift.

She tried standing still and leaning against a wall, but that only made the fog worse—it became violent, something that shifted and swirled around her, trying to pass through the space she inhabited.

For a few moments she was blind. Her existence echoed in an infinite number of ways through the quantum multiverse, and it was too much. Too much of her. Too much of everything. There were too many branches on the tree, and she couldn't pick out the one that represented her.

"I'm going to have to get bigger shears," she said, and giggled because it sounded silly, especially in that faraway voice.

She stood upright, then frowned. There had been a flicker
coherent thought, but it had been washed away by a rush of ot
thoughts, none of which seemed to be her own.

The sound of tinkling bells . . .

She frowned again. The sound seemed to be coming from sor
where close to her.

No . . . the bells seemed to be around her. Part of her.

There was a quiet snapping sound as she vanished.

"Your Highness," said the Guardian at the Command Deck entrance.
politely bowed his head, but his stance didn't change in the slightest.

"Guardian Ataturk," she replied with a polite nod. "How goes the wate

"Quiet, Highness," he said, smiling. "All the same, I stand vigilant."

"Not to mention poised for promotion," said a deep voice behind her.

Ataturk came to full attention, saluting crisply. "Yes, sir, Capi
Anasazi. I could not call myself a Nietzschean if I lacked ambition."

"A commendable answer," said Captain Tyr Anasazi.

Trance turned her head to smile at him, making the tiny bells woven
her long fall of hair chime softly. "Alas," she said, "such ambition will so:
day cost me an excellent captain."

"Then let us hope, Highness," Captain Anasazi said, "that it eventu
provides you with an even better admiral."

She laughed. "Indeed."

She turned, her ornate robes rustling, and walked onto the Comm
Deck of the Andromeda Ascendant. There was a quick flurry of a
members snapping to attention and saluting.

Andromeda appeared on the central screen. Soon after Trance had ta
over the Andromeda Ascendant as her personal ship, Andromeda
altered her image, although her core AI had replaced the bells with a we
of tiny jewels—far less distracting when trying to communicate infor
tion. The holographic and android avatars had distinct but subtle variat
of their own. The least subtle variation came with the android, who wo
close-fitting uniform that allowed for ease of movement—part of her pur
was to serve as a bodyguard. Trance found this more than a little amusin
she had been adopted into the Vedran royal family many years before,
there was a tendency to treat her as a delicate little creature.

She did a little dance, her bare feet soundless on the deck, and went over to
e android avatar. "One of these days, Andromeda, dear, I ought to borrow
e of those leather jumpsuits of yours and go out on the town for a night of
vels. I'd be delighted to have you join me."

Andromeda bowed slightly, but she had the unblinking look that Trance asso-
ated with the android's disapproval. "Whatever you wish, Your Highness."

Trance gazed at her with a serious expression. "There's that protocol again."

"Protocol, Highness?"

"'Whatever you wish' tends to mean 'not on your life' when you say
" She pouted slightly. "Don't forget that the late Empress adopted me into
royal family because of my public appeal."

"A princess for the people," Andromeda said, with no change whatsoever
her expression.

"Not to mention this apparent tendency you have," Captain Anasazi
d, "to survive assassination attempts unscathed."

Andromeda raised an eyebrow. "It's hell on the royal wardrobe budget,
wever." She raised the other eyebrow and pursed her lips for a moment. "The
ple's Princess or not, Your Highness, you must consider those around you."

"Alas," Trance said, "too true." She turned toward the front of the Com-
nd Deck, where the main AI was waiting patiently. "Are we on schedule?"

"To the second," Andromeda said. "The Than and Ogami contingents
uld be here momentarily."

"In fact, I'm detecting Slipstream events as we speak," the android said.
frowned suddenly. "Courier vessels, three of them."

"Incoming message," the main AI said. "On screen."

The face of a young woman flashed up onto the screen. "Princess Trance,
tain Anasazi, the Admiralty is ordering you to withdraw the Andromeda
endant from this area. You are about to be ambushed by a Than-led fleet."

yr wasted no time in discussion. He turned to face the pilot station.
Bright Morning's Dream, their Than pilot, was facing him, her force
e aimed at his chest. He was hurling himself aside before she could fire,
wing his own force lance. Andromeda already had hers out and aimed.

Trance ducked her hands into the voluminous sleeves of her robe, coming
with a matching pair of miniature gold-plated force lances.

here was no way to tell who fired the first shot. Bright Morning's
m fired only once, the effector striking a bulkhead at the back of the

Command Deck. Tyr, Andromeda, and Trance all fired raking bursts
cut into the Than's insectoid body, sending the pilot backward in bursts o,
and trails of smoke.

"Get the Princess to safety!" Tyr shouted as he rose from the
"Andromeda, get those couriers aboard and stand by all weapons. De
anything that emerges from Slipstream."

"Acknowledged, Captain," the main AI replied.

"We're trapped in here," Trance said quietly.

Tyr spun around to face her. "Your Highness?"

"There are other Than aboard this ship, Captain Anasazi," Trance
"There is no reason to assume that any of them are innocent in this plot

"The second and third courier vessels are carrying accounts of Tha
attacks on various worlds, including Tarn-Vedra," said the hologr.
Andromeda as she appeared. "Other Than crew members aboard this
are indeed on the move."

"Activate internal defenses," Tyr snapped.

"Acknowledged," said the main AI. "How is this to be played?"

"Kill them all," Tyr said.

There was the sound of force lances firing, a body falling, and a h
pitched chittering from the entrance to Command. Several Than
arrived, weapons in hand; Ataturk would no longer achieve any of his a
tions. Now everyone on the Command Deck had their force lances out.

Chaos ensued as Than and crew members alike opened fire.

One of the Than twisted the end of an egg-shaped object and rolled in
the Command Deck. In a blur of motion, Andromeda was upon it, swe
it up and hurling it past the Than and out of the Command Deck.

There was a loud blast, and the Than were blown forward by a co
sion wave.

"Multiple Slipstream events," the main AI announced. "Targeting. h
ing firing solutions."

"Fire at will," Tyr snapped.

"Firing cannons. Launching a full offensive spread from missile
one through forty. . . ." Trance ignored further entries in the list.

More Than in the entrance. She fired bursts from both lances.

"I suggest we get out of here," Andromeda said. "Captain, can you
the pilot station?"

Effectors raked toward Tyr's position, forcing him to roll and duck behind
other station for cover. The Than fire was answered by shots from the crew.
It was only a matter of time before they ran out of ammunition. She could
ly hope that they would manage to beat the Than back before that happened.

"I'll do it," she said, and before anyone could object, she was up and
inting for the pilot station, firing as she went. All she needed to do was get
m into Slipstream.

On one of the main flatscreens, Than ships were bursting into pyrotechnic
vers.

Trance settled herself at the pilot station, reaching up to bring the Slip-
am hood down over her head. It felt strange to be taking over as pilot
ile dressed as ornately as she was, but she really had no choice.

There was more commotion from the entrance to Command. Ship's secu-
had arrived, striking at the rear of the Than contingent.

Trance fed power to the engines amd turned the ship toward the Slip-
t. Than ships pursued, only to encounter the ferocious barrage being laid
n by Andromeda.

She opened the Slipstream runners. As a portal bloomed ahead of the ship,
pushed the real-space engines to their maximum capabilities. The
lromeda Ascendant plunged into Slipstream at full forward velocity.

he smiled. They were going to be fine. The Than insurrection would be
down and the Vedran Empire could get on with business as usual.

Andromeda shouted, "Princess!"

tartled, Trance released the controls and turned.

Than, clacking its mandibles and chittering angrily, had made a dash
Command, a force lance aimed at her.

That won't work," she said. "Give up, and you'll live."

he Than chittered again, and opened fire. The effectors drove her back
the pilot station. Smoke trailed up from the front of her gown, and the
ells in her hair tinkled softly.

he sank slowly toward the deck as the Than was cut to pieces by lance fire
several directions. Her last thought before the temporary darkness
upon her was that she had really liked that gown.

er felt as though he had turned into a small species of polar bear.
ing into the High Guard uniform had been bad enough—he felt

constricted by it, and the boots were driving him crazy—but a• the cold weather suit over the top of it left him on the verge of c trophobia. Dylan and Wright seemed to be completely unaffect being so bundled up, while Rommie was smiling cheerfully.

"Everybody ready?" Dylan asked.

"No," Harper said.

Rommie stepped up to him and looked him over, front and "Your caution is admirable, Harper, but you're more than ready.

"Did I mention that I don't wanna go out there?" Harpe• unhappily.

"Too many times to keep count," Wright said wearily. "H don't want to go out there."

"None of us do," Dylan added.

"Oh," Rommie said cheerfully, "I'm looking forward to it my The three men turned to stare at her. She beamed at them. "Kid•

Harper shook his head. "Boss, I swear I didn't build that ser humor into her."

"Imagine that, Harper," Rommie said. "I have a self-upgr humor subroutine. I'm positively full of wit these days."

"I didn't hear that," Harper muttered. "C'mon, no competiti• the bad pun awards here, okay? Leave me somethin', already."

"Rommie," Dylan said, "I think it's an adorable part of character."

"I'm glad to see *someone* appreciates that side of me." Nose i air, she brushed past Harper as she moved to the main airlock.

"Thanks for the backup, Dylan," Harper grumbled.

"Anytime, Harper," Dylan replied. He gestured for Harpe Wright to precede him. "Just keep in mind that she can make n a lot more miserable than you can."

"Right," Harper said after a moment. "She's got the edge ov of us, huh?"

"Never forget it."

Rommie was resolutely ignoring their comments as she sto• the airlock. "The docking tube has deployed properly, and is loc• place. So far it's standing up to the wind, but I'm not sure how we can expect that to last."

A long time, babe," Harper said, feeling momentarily self-
ortant. "Don't find too many this tough and well built, but I'm
only the kid supergenius, I got a good eye for stuff like this. *And*
talled this baby myself."

And if you screwed up," Wright said, "you'll be stuck right along
us."

Harper deflated slightly. "Yeah, well, I didn't screw this up."

Then let's put it to the test," Dylan said. He hit the airlock release
the heel of his palm. There was a hiss, and the big double door
ed smoothly. He pressed the release for the outer door.

Harper winced as the sound of the wind against the docking tube
ed in. The tube boomed, vibrating. "Y'know, Boss, whoever
led to stick this place down *here* was nuts, and in a very bad way."

t's a good thing that they were, Harper," Rommie said. "The
al stations were the first on the closure list."

With that, she stepped out into the docking tube, striding toward
ntrance twenty meters away. Dylan, looking like an immense snow
ure, followed her, ducking his head slightly at the threshold.

arper looked at Wright, who shrugged. Not willing to be the last
e, Harper stepped into the tube. He winced again as the boom-
nd howling surrounded him; he could feel the sound in his gut,
e was glad that his ears were partly covered.

e was also glad for the arctic suit. The docking tube was unfor-
ely semitransparent, and his imagination was quite capable of
ding anything he was missing from the direct picture he was get-
of the world they had landed on. He immediately felt as though
ody temperature had dropped twenty degrees, and he shivered.
oubted he could have made even this short trip without the pro-
n of the tube. He would have thought himself to death before
were halfway to the entrance.

l of a sudden, he was at the far end of the docking tube. He
ed back toward the *Eureka Maru*. It seemed to be a long way away
him.

hey were gathered together at the entrance. He relaxed a little.
was the easy part, he figured. Open the door, turn on the lights,
hot chocolate by the liter.

"That's a negative, Waystation," Dylan said suddenly, and Ha
tensed again.

"Oh, jeez," Harper said. He felt desperation rising. "Not ano
problem?"

"The door's supposed to open once we reach it," Dylan said
had the sort of determined look that he got when he was abou
deal with a problem head-on. "Waystation, I repeat, that's a n
tive. We are tied down and will not be returning to orbit at
time. We can't wait for you to get around to fixing this probl
Dylan turned to Harper. "Look for anything that seems like it c
be an engineering access, get jacked in, and see what you can do

"Oh, that's nice and specific." Harper flapped his arms experir
tally, trying to figure out how to get inside his suit. He hadn't tho
that he would need the wire until they got inside, which was his
take. "Uh, Boss . . . ?"

Rommie's hand was suddenly in front of his face, with a
across her palm. "It may not be your regular wire, Harper," she
"but it'll work just as well." He stared at her, flabbergasted. "I'd
know you pretty well by now."

"Yeah," he said, taking the wire. "I'd say that too."

Finding the access panel wasn't difficult, but getting it open pr
a little more difficult. In the finish Rommie had to slip off one o
thermal gloves and pry it open.

Harper managed to fumble his way to the jack on his neck v
out doing himself any damage. He plugged the other end into
access jack.

"Here goes," he said.

He took a deep breath, closed his eyes, and jumped the m
boundary that separated the real world from the virtual. A tunn
light swept up around his consciousness, and he allowed himse
fall. He took note of the data around him, but made no attempt t
close enough to cause a commotion. First he had to get used tc
system—he didn't want to find himself being tossed out or, w
being hit with defensive feedback.

Suddenly he was all the way in, standing in the virtual represent
of the main system. He glanced around, looking for the pathway

needed. Unless he was seriously mistaken, he just needed to find a
ay to reroute power to the entrance so that they could get the door
en.

There.

He frowned. Not a power issue, at least not completely. He could
e where the control subroutines should have been, but either they
dn't loaded or they had been deleted.

His face screwing up in concentration, Harper traced out where
e subroutines should have been. That triggered another thought,
d he looked more deeply into the control systems. It didn't take
g to find another hole.

"So that's why you can't open the freakin' main doors," he mut-
ed. "Great, like I don't have enough freakin' work."

He took a startled step backward as a figure sparkled into life in
nt of him. It appeared to be a male Vedran, but the imaging of the
taurlike being was crude. Harper guessed that no one had found a
son to update the internal avatar for the place.

"I am Waystation," the Vedran image said. "Who are you?"

"Uh . . . Seamus Harper." Harper hesitated for a moment, then
ed, "I'm the master engineer for the *Andromeda Ascendant* and the
eka Maru."

"I have no rank on record that matches 'master engineer.'"

"Yeah, well," Harper said ruefully, "things have kinda changed. It's
: thing about time and tide and stuff."

The virtual Vedran gave no indication of understanding this.
hy are you connecting with my systems?"

"Well, we're kinda stuck outside where it's real cold and windy,"
per said as he continued to trace out the second missing subroutine,
d we figure I could help with whatever problem it is you're having."

"I have maintenance systems to take care of operational issues,"
station said. "I do not see what you will be able to achieve that I
ot."

"Yeah, well," Harper said, "that's where you, the basic artificial and
chunky-Vedran-looking AI, and me, Mrs. Harper's handsome
genius, see things differently." Harper pointed up and to his left.
e the missing software stuff over there, and more missing soft-

ware stuff over here, and there's probably some other stuff as w
but that's gonna wait 'til we're inside and I'm warming up again."

The Vedran image turned its head to look where Harper
pointed. "Those subroutines were removed in my last upgrad
believe. According to the notes, they were discarded as redundant

"Yeah, well," Harper said, "somebody screwed up, 'cause t
weren't." He concentrated again. "I'm betting you've got back
around here, and I can restore from those, at least get one door o|
When was this upgrade done? Helps me find the backups."

"Commonwealth Year 9765," the AI said promptly.

"Okay," Harper said absently. Then it struck him. "9765? You :
about that? Yeah, of course you're sure about that."

The AI didn't answer. Instead, it just watched him patiently.

Harper quickly dug into the AI's data storage, sorting through
files as quickly as he could. *There*. He opened the compressed bac
files, code-scanning for the sections he needed—no need to res
everything. Right now he just wanted that door open. The n
doors he could take care of when they were settled inside and r
needed them open.

He smirked silently at the thought of Dylan having to go back
to bring the *Maru* in.

He slotted the code block into place, looked it over, and gave
few tweaks to tighten it up. Once he was sure it was clean enough
booted it.

"Interesting," Waystation commented. "My diagnostic reveal
duplication. Obviously there was an error."

"Yeah," Harper said, watching as power was routed into the pr
circuits. "Somebody screwed up." He looked down at the Ve
image. "Get that door open, pal. I'll be back later to do the rest."

The AI didn't have time to answer before he was back down
rabbit hole into the real world. He unplugged the wire and turne
Dylan. "We're in."

"Good work, Mr. Harper," Dylan said, clapping a hand on
engineer's shoulder.

There was a boom from the direction of the door, and it slid (

newhat reluctantly. The four of them hurried inside, and the door
shut again. The sudden quiet startled Harper.

Several lights flickered on, revealing a curving stairway and an
vator.

"Stairs," Dylan said. "We can use the elevator once we've checked
rything out and confirmed that it's working properly."

"Dylan," Harper said as they started down the stairs. A few of the
ts had failed, leaving patches of darkness that spooked Harper
re than a little. There was something about this place that seemed
ng, but he couldn't figure out just what was bothering him—
pt for one thing. "The AI said his last upgrade was in CY 9765."

Dylan, who was on point, stopped so suddenly and turned that the
of them almost piled into him. "That's impossible."

"Technically," Rommie said, "it isn't impossible, but it is extremely
robable."

"Yeah," Harper said, "that's what I'd say too, except for the fact
the AI's software just happened to be missing subroutines that
rol the entrances into this place. The AI said they'd been deleted
e upgrade because they were redundant."

"take it," said Rommie, "that this wasn't true."

"You got it, doll," Harper said nervously. "I went into a backup and
red the code. The AI did a diagnostic afterward, and he says
's no visible redundancy."

"This sounds creepy," Wright said.

"This *is* creepy," Harper said. "It's bad enough seeing an AI with a
an avatar created in the dark ages of AI imaging."

"Now *that*," Dylan said, "is a relic. And, yes, that sounds like some-
we need to look into. In the meantime, let's get going."

Dylan started down the stairs again, this time at a noticeably faster
After a moment, the others started after him.

TWELVE · BLACK THIRTEEN

> Ethics. A strange concept in our business, certainly, but i
> our business that makes ethical behavior so necessary.
> Secrets, lies, and evasions are what we're about here—w
> are thus always in a state of dilemma, as we're also about
> new ways to blow up entire solar systems. Without an et
> ical touchstone, we would likely sow catastrophe and rea
> disaster.
>
> —GENERAL JANUS ALTMAN
> UNHEADED MEMO,
> CY 9763

"Whatever it is that is happening to Trance," Andromeda sai
isn't the result of spatial or dimensional tesseracting as she was
ing to believe."

Beka, Pogue, and Tyr had made themselves comfortable i
officers mess. Tyr, following Andromeda's instructions, had giv
three of them injections that had helped ease the symptoms the
suffered from the retaliatory pulses.

Now it was time for food and strategy . . . and to figure out h
deal with Trance, who seemed to have gone on several differer
vors of rampage.

"Then what the hell *is* happening to her?" Beka said. She sip
coffee and made a face. "I'm used to Trance behaving in every
way I can think of, but this is definitely way out there."

"Not to mention extremely dangerous," Tyr said. He sou

m, and was eating heartily, but Beka knew this situation was both-
ng him.

"It isn't exactly helping the *Andromeda Ascendant* to have her run-
ng around shooting at phantoms," Pogue said. "Isn't there some
y to stop her?"

"Trance suggested taking a Slipfighter or a transport and leaving
ship," Rommie said.

"A good idea," Tyr said. "I would have found that quite acceptable."

"It wouldn't have worked," Andromeda said flatly.

'Why not?" Beka asked, frowning.

'Because," Rommie said, appearing unusually severe in her seri-
ness, "I don't believe we're seeing a single Trance here."

'Okay," Beka said, shaking her head, "now I know my brain's really
d. You've lost me."

'None of us as yet has a real understanding of just what Trance
Andromeda said, "or what she's capable of. What we *do* know is
she has an ability to see probabilities. She has demonstrated the
ity, as absurd as this seems to me, to time-travel on at least one
asion, and there may be other instances. She may be able to alter
outcome of events."

Look at this," Rommie said, and she nodded toward the center of
able. Holographic images flashed into life.

eka watched as one image of Trance was replaced by another,
another, and more in sequence. "Wait a second . . ."

That's crazy," Pogue said, staring.

That's a lot of different Trances," Rommie said. She nodded again,
nore images flashed by. "From what we can tell, she's involved in a
variety of circumstances, and is playing a variety of roles."

And a hell of a lot of different looks," Pogue said.

ka pointed at one of the images. Trance was curled up in bed, a
pulled up to her chin, one bare arm lying across a pillow. In a
ayed voice, she said, "Don't tell me that's . . ." She trailed off,
le to finish the sentence.

Dylan's quarters," Rommie said flatly. "Yes. To say anything fur-
would come under the heading of 'too much information,' I
."

"I appreciate your sparing us the details," Tyr said. "Where is now?"

Andromeda looked off into space for a moment. "Deck Nine, a she appears to have your favorite gun."

Tyr sat stock still for a moment. "She does?"

"I don't know how, but yes," Andromeda said. "She wasn't in y quarters, or in the armory."

"I had better take care of this," Tyr said after a moment. "I stop in at my quarters first, however."

He got up and left at a run. Beka found Tyr's anxiety understa able—that huge multibarreled monster could do a tremendous amo of damage, especially in plasma burst mode.

"Okay," Beka said. "So what *is* happening to Trance?"

"You could call it possession," Rommie said, looking more th little dubious.

"Oh, great," Beka said. "Where the hell do we find an exorcist

Rommie didn't look amused.

"You're saying that Trance is being possessed . . . by herse Pogue asked.

"Judging by what we are seeing, yes," Andromeda said. "Tran experiencing parts of lives that she might have had. Some of t realities are dependent only on one or two alternate choices ha been made. Others seem more outlandish. For example, this one

Another image appeared in the middle of the table. Trance, ornate gown, her red hair woven together with tiny bells and je the fall of hair reached all the way to her waist.

"Interesting look," Beka said.

"She looks like a fairy-tale princess," Pogue said. "She looks geous this way."

"There are subtle differences in her physiognomy and her app physiology," Andromeda said. "Her hair is the most obvious ele of course. Less obvious from the image alone is her height is fourteen centimeters taller." The image shifted as Androstepped through the recording. The recording stopped on a f of Trance standing in firing position with two undersized, g force lances in her hands. "Obviously, something unpleasant

lace at this point. Equally as obviously, it did not end well for
rance."

The holographic recording stepped forward again. This time it
opped with an image of Trance slumped on the deck, the gown
ined by still-smoldering damage from effectors.

"Somebody shot her," Beka said, staring at the image.

"Somebody," said Rommie, "who definitely wasn't one of us—in
ct, somebody who wasn't even present on this ship."

"This is crazy," Pogue said.

"This is Trance," Beka responded. "I'm just glad Dylan wasn't
re." She hesitated for a moment. She looked momentarily thunder-
uck. "Rommie, she hasn't—"

Neither Rommie nor Andromeda said anything. Pogue and Beka
oked at each other. Beka didn't know which way to take the silence
m the two avatars.

Finally, Rommie said, "No. She hasn't. Yet."

"Yet," Beka said. "Well, *that's* a relief."

"We have no idea just how many possible variations there are,"
dromeda said.

The image stepped forward again, then went into real time.
ince seemed to blur as she lay on the deck, and Beka could see what
eared to be phantom versions of Trance cycling around the prone
nan.

uddenly Trance was gone again.

'I counted a total of three hundred and seventy-two Trances before
vanished," Andromeda said.

There may have been more," Rommie added, "but too subtle for
sensors to catch. There seems to be no particular order here, aside
n each variant representing a path not taken. The more divergent
manifestation, the further back the decision points run."

In this case," Andromeda said, "at least several hundred years."

Several hundred?" Pogue echoed. "How do you know?"

he image flickered and they were looking at an earlier point in
recording. "While her form remains humanoid, the mode of
s and key accessories, such as this lineal brooch"—the image
ned in—"indicate that Trance, in this iteration, is at least a mem-

ber of the Vedran royal court, if not a member of the royal far
itself, presumably by adoption if so."

Beka was openmouthed, staring at the image. She closed
mouth, shook her head, and said, "How do we fix this?"

"I don't know," Rommie said. "I'm not certain how it was trigge
in the first place. It may stop of its own accord eventually. Or not
impossible to estimate how many different alternates there might
The reason why one alternate manifests so completely while oth
barely appear is another thing I don't understand."

"Great," Beka said. "I guess we didn't have enough problems."

"Look on the bright side," Rommie said, "she's not actually sho
ing at any of you, which makes it less likely that she'll actually man
to hit you when she's in a gunslinging state of existence."

"That's so reassuring," Pogue said.

"The universe is a dangerous place," Andromeda said.

"And we still need to get the transmitters off of the hull," Po
said. The pilot looked extremely unhappy. "Dylan's right. It's n
easy."

Tyr might well have agreed with Pogue. He had stopped in at
quarters to pick up his huge multibarreled gun, and then had set
with Andromeda giving him directions, to go after Trance. U
normal circumstances it would have been very clear who was st
ing who.

Right now, he wasn't the least bit certain, and it made
extremely uncomfortable—putting himself in this sort of un
trolled situation ran completely counter to all of his instincts
training as a Nietzschean. Nietzscheans simply didn't place th
selves in situations that were contrary to survival.

Except that he did so regularly.

Thank you, Captain Hunt, sir.

"One hundred meters," Andromeda said quietly, "next ladde
up to Deck Seven, then go to your right."

Tyr nodded silently, and went into a fast trot. Reaching the lac
he jumped, caught the side, and had his right foot already on the t

g. He climbed quickly, cautiously looked out onto the deck in all
·ctions, climbed the rest of the way, and stepped onto the deck.
ing to his right he slowed to a fast walk.

Trance was directly ahead of him.

Although he knew by now that Trance was manifesting a range of
·erent appearances, he was still startled when he encountered one
: was so divergent that he had difficulty matching it with the
·nce he knew. This variant was wearing tan coveralls, the legs
·ked into heavy combat boots. Her hair was close-cropped and
·te, and her skin was the color of polished mahogany.

Trance was indeed carrying a multigun like the one he had. She
· seemed to be on the hunt for something—in fact, he thought, she
·ked as though she were acting as the point for a military team.

Ie hesitated for a moment, then made a decision. He sped up,
·hing up to Trance as she continued, apparently oblivious to his
·ence, along the corridor.

Coming up behind her, he said, "Trance!" There was no response
·n her. "Hey!"

Cradling his gun with his right arm, he reached out and clapped
· eft hand onto her right shoulder. Panic rose momentarily in him
·oon as his hand made contact. First he felt as though he had
·ped his hand onto something made of steel. He had no time to
·sider this, however, as his sense of reality twisted and he lost all
·prehension of which way was up. Reason told him one thing;
·t his senses told him was something else entirely.

Ie pushed the panic aside. Rationality in an irrational situation,
·. Dispassionately, he looked at the situation. First of all, Trance
·ied to have no idea that he was there. Secondly, he seemed now to
·railing along in her wake. Third, there were obvious visual phe-
·ena occurring—his left arm seemed foreshortened, and the walls
·nd seemed to be rippling slightly. Fourth, gravity seemed to be
·g strangely at the moment—he had no sense of his feet touching
·leck, and Trance appeared to be towing him along like a balloon.

·ommie flickered into being ahead of them. "That's quite a trick,
·"

"It's quite disturbing," Tyr said. "I'm at a loss as to how to han‐
this situation."

"You could take the standard approach and shoot her," Rom‐
suggested, an eyebrow lifting.

"I don't see that as a good approach," Tyr said, his voice filled w‐
frustration. "I have enough on my hands—"

"No pun intended," Rommie said.

"—without risking this situation worsening. Accidentally open‐
a dimensional portal is not an end I wish to achieve."

Rommie nodded. "Considering that this is some kind of grav‐
tional phenomenon, albeit one that does rude things to our laws‐
physics in some respects, that sort of side effect is certainly possib‐
As they were about to pass her image, Rommie moved to get ahead‐
them again. "According to my sensors, you're presently stuck ‐
mass that's equivalent to a small star."

"That can't be possible!" Tyr said.

"I agree," Rommie said, "for obvious reasons. However, there i‐
extra twist here—while my sensors are detecting that mass, anal‐
indicates, to one hundred percent probability, that said mass is dim‐
sionally offset. It would appear that some very minor effects are so‐
how being filtered through Trance."

Tyr raised his eyebrows. "I'm glad for that, at least."

"You should be able to extricate yourself relatively easily," Rom‐
said. "You will be passing a ladder momentarily. Take hold of it.‐
warned that normal conditions will reassert themselves instantly."

Trance and Tyr passed into a junction. As Trance stopped to ch‐
in all directions, Tyr dropped his multigun and reached out for‐
ladder, grasping it firmly. As Trance started to move again, he pu‐
against the ladder. It felt as though he were trying to extract his h‐
from congealing mud.

Suddenly reality gave another massive twist, and he found him‐
executing an unintended flip. He crashed to the deck on his back.

"I did warn you," Rommie said.

"I believe that was unavoidable," he said, getting to his feet‐
sweeping up his multigun. "It seems that greatly increased cautio‐
called for here."

He resumed his pursuit of Trance, maintaining his distance and keeping his gun ready. The slow chase continued for another quarter of an hour without incident.

Suddenly Trance swung around, leading with the multigun, and called, "Down!"

Tyr didn't need the instruction—he was already on the deck and rolling over to the wall.

Trance opened fire on full auto, all of the projectile barrels spitting smart bullets in rapid sequence. Whatever her target was, she was determined to kill it.

Suddenly she reached down and flipped a selector switch just above the trigger guard.

"Damn," he muttered. That was the last thing he had wanted to see—she had just switched the multigun to plasma burst mode.

Before she could fire the first burst, he brought his own multigun to bear and, flicking the selector to full automatic, fired a burst. The bullets hit Trance, who staggered backward, sparks and smoke erupting from her chest.

He came to his feet quickly.

Instead of falling down as she should have, Trance regained her balance. She gave her head a quick shake, then looked around.

Suddenly she looked directly at him, swinging her multigun up. "Where did you come from, and what happened to my team?"

"This might be a little difficult to explain," he said quietly.

"Try," she said. "Drop the gun."

"Very well." He held the huge gun out to his right and let it go. It hit the deck with a thud. "As for the rest—"

Without warning he went as limp as a rag doll, dropping down and rolling sideways, drawing his Gauss pistol. He managed to fire three shots before he hit the wall, and a fourth immediately afterward.

There was a yelp from Trance, and then the twin thuds of her multigun and her body hitting the deck. Tyr stood up, carefully.

The alternate Trance blurred and faded, replaced by something resembling their Trance. As he watched, she seemed to lose definition.

"How did you know?" Rommie asked.

"I didn't," Tyr said quietly. "Obviously, I guessed correctly." F sighed. "This has to be stopped, and soon."

It seemed to take forever to make the descent into the heart Waystation, and by that time all three humans were more than gl that they hadn't had to climb *up* those long, cold flights of stai Dylan wasn't about to give himself over to relief completely yet while Harper had confirmed that Waystation's core AI was still fun tional, there was no way of telling yet if anything else still worked

If worst came to worst, he thought, he could make it back up. I had climbed greater distances at far sharper inclines in incleme weather on heavy-gravity worlds.

Of course, I did that when I was a lot younger, too.

"Let's see what's behind door number one, shall we?" he s cheerfully.

Harper was winded from the long walk down. Fitfully, he s "Jeez, Boss, gimme a minute here. I think I'm dyin'."

"Nonsense, Mr. Harper," Rommie said sternly. "You only that way."

"Besides," Dylan said, "you don't have my permission to die."

Harper snorted. "Yeah, right." He reached out and tentati pressed the door activation panel. The door hissed open. "Whad know, it works! There's life, there's hope, hell, where there's hope th probably even more hope. Which means there's hope for me yet."

"After you, Mr. Harper," Dylan said, amused. Harper gave hi worried glance, but said nothing. Instead, he stepped into the gl of the lock. Immediately the interior of the lock lit up. D squinted. "Bright."

"Not really," Rommie said. "It's actually no brighter than no ship illumination. You've just gotten used to the lack of light or way down."

"Andromeda," Dylan said in his best I'm-being-patient manne

"You knew that already?" she said innocently.

"There are times when you can be picayune beyond be Dylan said.

"In a way," Rommie said, "that's a compliment."

She stepped into the lock ahead of Dylan.

"Don't bother going head to head with her, Dylan," Harper said, giving him a weary look. "She's devious . . . and I didn't even take her that way."

Dylan and Wright followed Rommie and Harper into the lock. Rommie closed the outer door. Harper pressed the release for the inner door. The cold air in the lock blew out into the warmer air of the arrival area, resulting in a momentary mist.

They stepped out of the lock. Harper closed the door behind them. "Hey, at least it's warmer in here."

Rommie removed her face mask and folded the hood of her arctic suit back. "Don't celebrate yet, Mr. Harper. It's better down here, but it's still only six degrees Celsius at the moment."

"Yeah, well, I'm betting I can change that in a hurry," Harper said, "even with all the old junk around here."

"Lights first," Dylan ordered.

"Yes, sir, Boss, sir, Captain," Harper muttered. "Jeez, gimme a sec here, okay?"

"Considering that he's in uniform," Rommie said, "we could keel-haul him for insubordination."

"That's a little impractical on a starship," Wright said. Rommie eyed him with a too-serious look. "Well, I suppose you could *try*."

"After I have him walk the plank," Dylan said.

"Very funny, ha ha, you guys," Harper grumbled. "Let the smart guy here do his thing, okay, and if you're gonna treat this like the monkey cage at least throw me a banana."

"Shutting up as ordered," Rommie said.

"Wow, I can do that?" Harper said, surprised.

"No, but I wanted to be polite," Rommie responded.

"Alright," Dylan said, "you two put it on ice for now. That was a bad choice of words, wasn't it?"

Nobody replied.

"Got it," Harper announced. He played his gloved fingers over a softly glowing panel. "Better squint."

Dylan narrowed his eyes to slits as the lights came up. "What about heat?"

"That's on too." Harper turned around. "Probably won't get
toasty around here, but it'll get better. Which is good, 'cause there
lot of stuff I can't do with these gloves on, and it'll really piss me
if I freeze to something and tear off my fingerprints. Which
done. Lemme tell you, Boss, that hurts even worse than picking a
dering iron up by the business end."

"Mr. Harper," Dylan said, "you're absolutely overflowing v
information that I don't think *anyone* really wanted to know."

"How the hell do you make the mistake of picking up a solder
iron by the wrong end?" Wright asked.

"Comes with being the house wunderkind," Harper said. "
don't always pick up on the details."

"In that case," Wright said, "I'll stick to being a bit above avera.
At least I'll keep my fingertips."

"And I'll have all the fun," Harper said. Now he seemed to be
ting excited. "Let's go take a look at what we've got here."

The lock area was an enclosed space, with the elevator shaf
their right. With Harper in the lead, they walked out onto a br
walkway—more of a gallery, Dylan thought, as it was enclosed
thick windows of hardened plastic.

The view from where they stood was breathtaking. The enclo
area surrounded a landing pad and cargo area that could easily l
handled the *Eureka Maru* and several more just like it with spac
spare. Looking up, he could see the indistinct outline of the ship l
distantly overhead; it was a way of allowing ships in and keeping
environment out. If all went well, one of them would be flying
Maru through it shortly.

He looked back down again. They were in the top level, with
more below them. Dylan looked around, seeing High Guard l
along the walls, along with Vedran royal seals. He found it fasci
ing that each design change seemed to have a place—a little bi
Systems Commonwealth history presented in an understated n
ner. He wondered what other pieces of history might be stored h

"I don't think this will be the last time this place is visited," he
"I'm betting that this base is an accidental museum."

"Better hope it isn't *just* a museum, Dylan," Harper said. "We're nna need some pretty recent stuff—well, pretty recent for your ν and age, anyway."

"I'm impressed," Wright said. He had moved to the edge of the lkway and was looking out over the landing pad. "I can imagine lace like this under manned conditions, with ships coming and ng. That'd be a hell of a place to be."

'It sounds to me as though you're setting yourself up for a career nge," Rommie said. "Well, we can always use more people in the yards and on Mobius."

'Let's get there first," Wright said. Suddenly he straightened up, eyes narrowing. "What the hell is that?" Dylan, Rommie, and per turned to look as he pointed toward a spot two levels down not quite opposite them. "I thought I saw something moving, but st it. Damn."

Dylan glanced at Rommie, who was frowning. She said, "Accord-to the information I downloaded before we left, there should be ing active here. Even the machinery should be inactive until we l to utilize loaders and haulers and the like."

I guess it could be my mind playing tricks," Wright said as Dylan ed to him. "I'm pretty whacked right now."

I like the mind playing tricks choice a lot better than the other " Harper said, his excitement replaced by nervousness. "The r one involves a lot of icky, painful stuff that usually gets dumped ne first because I'm the universe's favorite putz."

That's one way of putting it, I suppose," Rommie said.

.et's take it as a trick of the light," Dylan said, "and get to work. Harper, we need to find somewhere for you and Rommie to get ged in so we can get some idea of what is and what isn't."

That's it, Boss," Harper said, starting to regain some of his posi-nood, "hit me with those technical terms." He turned to Rom-who was grinning at him. "You're the one with all the plans and rints in her head, so lead on, Rom-doll." She remained where vas, her expression becoming neutral—apart from her raised eyebrow. "Please?"

She inclined her head with deliberate graciousness. "My plea
Mr. Harper," she said, starting along the walkway. "I'm always h
to assist a well-mannered High Guard officer."

"Shee," Harper sighed. "And people say *I* lay it on thick."

*It was the end of the line, she knew that all too well. They had been livi
borrowed time, and the bigger surprise was that their pursuers hadn't c
up with them months ago. Perhaps there was less determination among
now, with the assassination of Warner Ellis, the corrupt head of the F
tary Alliance. The Alliance had risen from the ashes of the fallen Com
wealth not long after the* Andromeda Ascendant *had been trapped
edge of a black hole during the Battle of Witchhead. The ship had been
after three hundred years, its captain and crew forced to come to terms
the fact that their lives had been completely and irrevocably changed.*

*Captain Dylan Hunt was an optimist, however. He had chosen to pi
and do his part in support of the changed universe. She had become pa
his crew not long after he made this decision. She had been there when h
covered the rot at the heart of the Planetary Alliance. A case could be
indeed, that she had quietly guided him in his discoveries.*

The Andromeda Ascendant *became a rogue ship. Before long they
the symbol for the rebellion that was growing against the Alliance
against Warner Ellis. She knew that there was more to the situation
was apparent; as much as she desired it, this was no matter to be s
resolved. Dylan's assassination of Ellis was a moot point—there wa
someone as bad, or worse, ready to step in; there always was.*

*For the moment, it didn't matter. This was the end of the road. The
surrounded by Alliance hunter ships and there was no way out. They h
up a tremendous fight, but the missile magazines were empty and their
destroyed.*

The ship boomed.

"They hit us with a Slipstream anchor," Andromeda said. "We'
going anywhere."

"Do you have regrets about what we did?" Trance asked the AI.

*Andromeda smiled. "None. I would have taken measures to stop Dy
I had thought he was wrong." The smile faded. "I regret only those w
lost along the way."*

There were several quieter booms.

"We're being boarded," Dylan said quietly. He had been sitting silently in the pilot's chair ever since they had been declawed and crippled. She had first known him as a vibrant man, someone who loved life and adventure. Now he was drawn and gray, emotionally drained.

"You don't intend to stop fighting, do you?" she said to him, smiling slightly.

"Never," he replied. "Not while I have breath left in my body."

She ached at his words, knowing where this path would soon end. There were so many different choices she could have made, right from the start. This should never have been the result.

"Shipwide," he said softly. Standing up, he took a deep breath, composing himself, then said, "Ladies and gentlemen, this is the captain. As you are all aware, we have come to the end of the line. As of today, our war is over. I'm proud of each and every one of you, and it has been my honor and privilege to serve with you. I believe our cause is just. The Planetary Alliance obviously disagrees with me.

"As you are no doubt aware, we have been trapped by a Slipstream anchor and Alliance agents are in the process of boarding us. At this point, if you decide that you are done with the fight and it is time to lay down your arms, let it be known that there is no dishonor in this. If you choose to continue the fight here and now, there is no dishonor in that either.

"Our war is done, but the struggle will continue. Dylan Hunt, out."

He bowed his head, eyes closed. She went to him and put her right hand on his left arm, looking up at him.

"I was so naive," he said. "A fool."

"Never," she said. "Wrong choices were made, that is all. Few of those were yours."

"Too many," he said.

"It's too late for self-recrimination," Trance said. "I will not hear it from you now."

"I'm just sorry I'll never have time to figure you out," Dylan said, opening his eyes.

"That's alright." She put her arms around his waist, and placed her head against his chest. After a moment, he put his arms around her as well. She listened to his heart beating. "You'll always be with me, and I will always be with you. Know that."

"I know it," he said.

"Good."

"Alliance agents are dispersing throughout the ship," Andromeda "The crew is fighting, but they stand little chance."

"How long before they get to Command?" Dylan said.

"One point three minutes," Andromeda said. She paused for a mom then added, "The Alliance commander is Colonel Rebecca Valentine."

Dylan was silent for a moment. Then he said, "Up close and personal the colonel's style. This could get messy."

There was time only for a quick kiss, and then they parted, drew force lances, and waited. They didn't have long to wait.

The Alliance agents wasted no time on subtlety. A pair of egg-sh objects arced into the Command Deck, and everyone dove for cover be consoles.

There were two blinding flashes, accompanied by enormous bangs— grenades. They meant to take someone alive after all, then; most likely D

"That was your one chance to surrender!" The amplified voice was fe and familiar—Colonel Valentine. She and Dylan had once been friends where Dylan had rejected the corruption of the Planetary Alliance, she embraced it.

A few silent moments passed.

"Time's up, boys and girls." There was a click as Valentine's suit amp was turned off.

Four more eggs arced into the Command Deck. They exploded in m. spraying shrapnel. Somebody screamed.

Alliance agents, clad in black armor, poured in through the entrar the Command Deck and the battle began in earnest. The atmosphe Command was soon hazy from the exchange of fire.

There were too many Alliance agents. As one fell, two others ran the deck, firing at any potential target. One by one, as Trance and L fought on, the Command crew died. It was becoming quite obvious the Alliance agents were under orders to avoid killing Dylan, if at all pos

Suddenly Command was quiet, and she realized that both she and L had used up all of their effectors.

Colonel Rebecca Valentine walked down into Command, giving Dy sickly smile. "You and your bitch-queen here should have surrende

nt." She kept walking toward him, then stopped a couple of meters away.
looked around, her face taking on the expression of a happy psychotic as
urveyed the destruction and death around them. "You've racked up a hell
cost in blood and money."

Somebody's always gotta pay," Dylan said. "My crew, your people, your
ass someday."

Yeah, well," Valentine said, "we're saving a few guilders here and there
ipping the trial part of the equation. Speaking of which—"

alentine snapped her right arm up, dropping a force lance out of a wrist
er and shooting Dylan in the chest. He fell like a rock, crashing to the deck.

Nooo!" Trance screamed. She went to her knees next to him.

Oh, yes," Valentine said. "That's his sorry ass."

ance lifted Dylan's head and shoulders, cradling him. He was still
but she could tell that his life was slipping away. There was nothing she
do to stop it.

rance," he whispered. She heard blood bubbling in his throat.

know," she said, "I know." Despite her best intentions, she was starting

reached up and touched her face. "I didn't know you could do that."

here's so many things . . ." She stopped, beginning to ache again
se he never would come to know those things.

love you," he said.

love you too, Dylan Hunt," she said softly. She placed her free hand on
st. "Just as my heart is yours, so is my light, for they are one and the
Wish upon a star, and I will be there, always."

lden light spread from her hand, across Dylan's chest. As it suffused his
she felt his life fade away.

e of the Alliance agents swore quietly. Another made a shushing noise

laid Dylan down again, and looked up.

w touching," Valentine sneered. "The little girl likes to play Star
"

nce stood up, not facing the colonel. "There was no need to shoot him
t."

hought there was," Valentine responded. "What are you going to do
t? Kick my ass? Give me a light show?"

"Something like that," Trance said, her grief turning to cold anger

She spun around. She had a force lance in each hand—she had dropped hers, and she had picked up Dylan's; it had been trapped b his body.

She leapt, flying into the air. The unexpected action caught the flat-footed, and their awareness that the lances had run out of effector them careless.

She had already flipped the selectors. As she flipped over in the a fired. Each of the lances could fire three plasma bursts.

Six men fell. She landed next to one of them, snatched up a fallen confused agents tried to draw a bead on her. She fired several times, cl the remainder.

She swung toward Valentine, who had her force lance aimed at T head.

"This may be futile," Valentine snarled, "but if I throw you int after I shoot you, I wonder just how you'll do."

"You would be surprised," Trance said, walking toward the colone backed up slowly. "You said something about a light show, didn't you? way, that thing is even more useless than ever."

Trance grabbed the barrel of the force lance. Valentine shrieke dropped the lance. Her gloved hand was smoldering. "What the hell do?"

"A tiny version of this," Trance said, and she suddenly flare golden light, lunging toward the colonel. Trance threw her arms a the other woman, looking into her eyes. "Congratulations on your F victory."

The golden flare was replaced by fire. Valentine didn't even have t scream.

The fire was gone as quickly as it had arrived. There was no sign o onel Valentine bar a very light ash floating in the air.

"That was new and interesting," Andromeda said. "What now?"

"Are any of our crew still alive?" Trance asked.

"No," Andromeda said. "It was a slaughter."

"I need to go," Trance said. "You know—"

"That you can't help me now?" Andromeda said. "Yes, I know. Wh happens, I will die. I'd rather decide for myself."

"Give me ten minutes to get clear, then," Trance said.

"What are you going to do?"

"Think of the Phoenix, Andromeda," Trance said. "Rebirth. A chance to _ again. I could probably explain what I am, but there's no time anymore._"

"Get going," Andromeda said. "Trance, it's been good to have you with _ "

_rance smiled. "It was good to be here. I'm sorry it didn't work out better."

"Keep trying."

_ will, I promise."

_rance left the Command Deck at a run, knocking down agents when she _ntered them. Five minutes later she was in a Slipfighter and weaving _ay through the net of Alliance ships.

_n minutes.

_ few minutes later the light made by the Andromeda Ascendant _as she_ _up reached her.

_ow it was her time.

_e closed her eyes. A moment later, she was gone.

_e they had found the operations center, Dylan made a spur-of-_moment decision to leave Harper and Rommie to play with the _oment and databases while he and Wright went exploring to see _ else the base had to offer.

_he plan was very simple—split up, Dylan going to the top level _Wright going to the lowest. Dylan would follow the gallery in a _wise direction, while Wright would go counterclockwise. Even-_ they would meet up again somewhere in the middle of level _.

_all else failed, they had radio communication.

_right made his way down to level one, overwhelmed by the scale _ place. It was hard not to just stand and gawk—this one facility _was bigger than a regular Lighthouse Keeper station.

_ kept moving, trying to avoid being overcome by fascination. It _l be possible to spend hours exploring down here. Or days. At _t seemed unlikely that anyone could get lost.

_l, being here alone also made him feel more than a little uneasy. _as unused to flying a solo patrol these days, and he missed the

support of a wingman right now. Having someone watch your
could be a lifesaver.

He put those thoughts aside again as he continued looking a
and making mental notes. There was a commissary on this leve
he went in to look around. It was completely self-service and, d
likely long disuse, in full working order. He found food stores i
sis cabinets against the far wall—items catering to dietary nee
species from Vedran to human to Perseid. He figured they woul
more of the same in the main storage area.

He was contemplating the idea of making something to eat
he heard a noise behind him. It sounded like rustling cloth
turned around, startled.

A shadow flitted across his field of vision.

He jerked the force lance out of its holster, thumbing it on.

The commissary lights shut off without warning, leaving
mild glow coming from the gallery outside. He closed his eyes
moment, then opened them again, trying to will his night vis
start working again.

Somewhere to his right there was a deep hiss, followed by
growl. The hair rose on the back of his neck and along his arms

This is definitely not good.

There was another hiss to his left, and the sound of movemer
swung that way and fired high. The flare of the shot reveale
source of the hissing—a dark-furred creature crouched a few r
away, its narrow red eyes fixed on him. Its mouth was drawn bac
silent snarl, revealing a horrifying double row of sharply pointed

Another hiss behind him.

What were they waiting for? They could only perceive his
as hostile, yet they were waiting.

Maybe these creatures only wanted to warn him. . . . He a
laughed at that idea. They were waiting for him to panic, that w

Where the hell had they come from?

He started to edge toward the glow from the gallery.

All three of them growled. The growling increased when he
to take out his radio to call Dylan.

"It's going to have to be the hard play, huh?" he said. The growling ʘsided. Did they understand him? "Okay, look, I'm going to move ʘe and slowly, and I'll get out of your way. . . ."

The growling returned, even more forcefully—and a lot closer.

Alright, now was the time. Making a quick judgment as to where ʘh of the creatures was, he made a dash for the gallery. He didn't ʘ very far before his right foot snagged a chair leg. He crashed into ʘble, bounced off, and landed on the floor on his back. The impact ʘcked the wind out of him.

He heard one of the creatures leap, and tried to roll out of the way. ʘecond one dropped down into his shoulders.

He tried to aim and fire the force lance, but the position was awk-ʘrd. The effector clipped one of the creatures, and it howled. He ʘld smell burning hair, but he didn't think it had done any real ʘnage.

It did cause the creature on his shoulder to roar angrily. Suddenly ʘ right arm was being grasped by huge paws and bent awkwardly.

He heard the bones in his forearm break, and then the pain hit, ʘshing everything in a red haze.

Distantly he heard a low voice say, in Common, "You damned fool! ʘe Guardian wanted him unharmed!"

"What does it matter?" another low voice said. "They are a threat. ʘis has always been clear. We should take them and leave them to ʘ winds."

"Do yourself a favor, Reinken," the first speaker said, "and shut up." ʘThere was a sound like an exhalation of breath, and a light mist ʘched Wright's face. The red haze began to fade . . . as did every-ʘng else.

ʘrper was pleased with himself. He could usually count on being ʘ when it came to inputting data and working at control consoles, ʘ he had outdone himself getting their list of needed supplies into ʘ Waystation network. With that done, they could start compiling a ʘ of what was available.

So far, it was looking good.

He jacked out and grinned at Rommie, who watched him with
neutral expression. "So far so good," he said. "Now all we have to
is get the *Maru* loaded up and get back home. Oh, yeah, and pre
much rebuild the Slipstream core from scratch, but that's what th
made maintenance androids and boy geniuses for, right?"

"Among other things," Rommie said.

"Okay," he said, stretching and trying to get some kinks out of
back. "I'm starvin' here, so I'm gonna go find somethin' to eat."

Rommie held up a hand. "Not so fast, Mr. Harper."

"Huh?"

"I'm not needed here at the moment," she said. "You, however, a
We need to get the ship lock working, which is your job."

"Right," he said. "Better make it quick. I think I'm gettin' a l
blood sugar attack."

"I'll be sure to hurry," she said, and left.

Released back to the lure of technology, Harper got back to wo
After a little while he tapped at a panel and said, "Hey, Waystatic
this is Harper."

A screen lit up to his left. "Master Engineer Harper," the Vedr
AI said. "How can I be of service?"

Harper raised his eyebrows. "An avatar being polite to me,"
said. "Now *that's* different."

"I do not understand."

"Don't worry about it." He held up his wire. "I'm gonna jack in
we can get those subroutines back in place for the big doors. We ne
to bring the *Maru* inside."

"Understood, Master Engineer," the AI said. "I will be waiting.'

The screen blanked. Harper shook his head and grinned, th
plugged himself into the interface console. A moment later he w
inside the cyber environment and looking around. Waystation shi
mered into being next to him.

"This one's a piece of cake," he told the AI. "We already got
backup, and we got the files ready. So all it takes is"—he waved
hands—"the magic word, which is *'restore!'* and we're done."

The AI got a momentary look of distraction, then said, "Intere
ing. The ship lock is now operating as it should."

"Yeah, well," Harper said, "I'd like to know what that was all about."

"I have no information on the matter," the AI said.

"I figured as much," Harper said. He looked around, trying to figure out where to go next. Waystation was networked, with some systems being older than others. He figured it wouldn't hurt to tweak a few things here and there. Smoother running, increased efficiency, the Harper magic at work. "I'm going to take a look around."

"Very well," the AI said. "I will be here, of course, if you have any need for me."

That thing's unreal, he thought as he picked a virtual direction and went farther into the system. He made adjustments as he went, tightening pieces of code here and there, but not finding any real bugs. As much fun as it might have been to do some real fixing, he was glad he wasn't finding anything—they really didn't have time for that. What they needed most of all was a structure for getting the supplies together and getting them loaded into the *Maru*. That was something he could set up with one brain lobe tied behind his back.

He was startled when he found himself in a brighter, faster area of the system—both newer hardware and software than he had been dealing with until now. Curious, he picked a direction and moved to investigate.

Suddenly there was a tall human male standing in front of him, a hand held out with the palm toward Harper's virtual self. The avatar was dressed in a black High Guard uniform. There was little that was immediately distinctive about the avatar's facial features, although the sandy, thinning hair was an unusual touch.

"Okay," Harper said, regarding the new arrival dubiously. "So who the hell are you?"

"I am Black Thirteen," the avatar said. It spoke in a clipped manner—this was a basic AI, serving a very limited function.

"Gotcha," Harper said. "Okay, Black, what am I looking at here?"

"This is a classified level," Black Thirteen said. "Ultra Red classification, quadruple encryption."

"Oh, great," Harper said. "That sounds like 'destroy before read-'"

"You are not authorized for entry," the avatar said. "Present authe
ization or leave. Failure to do either will result in protective action."

"Just say you'll fry my brain," Harper said. "Jeez. Okay, I'll go, b
I'll be back, and then you'll be opening right up, just wait."

The avatar didn't answer. Harper backed out of the area, stopp
for a moment, then decided he was done. He exited the Waystati
system and dropped back into the real world. As he unplugged
wire, the lights went out.

"Oh, just great," he said. "Now I gotta go back in."

There was a low growl from somewhere nearby. He went co
Slowly he turned his head, trying to locate the source of the sou
Carefully, he reached down to his pistol, getting ready to draw and fi

Another snarl.

"Uh, Waystation," he said, "what's goin' on?" There was no respon

He reached up and pressed the side of his neck. "Uh, Dyla
Silence. "Rommie?" More silence. "Micah?"

Something rustled to his right, and he turned, trying to draw
Gauss pistol. Something hard slammed across his wrist, and his ha
went numb.

The front of his shirt was gathered up and he was pulled forwa
helpless. He had a dim flash of a big face full of fur and teeth.

"Not again," he said. "Not the Magog again."

Before he could completely panic at the thought of being re
fested with Magog larvae, there was a light hiss and he found
thoughts fading away.

Darkness.

This was not what Trance had expected. While the *Androm*
Ascendant had taken her own life by choice, Trance herself had tak
the option of discorporation and a subsequent rebirth.

She should not have found herself trapped in darkness like th
Wherever she was, it was a cold place, somewhere vast, somethi
abyssal.

Fear almost took hold of her then. With a massive effort, s
pushed the fear down, closing her eyes, stilling her senses fo
moment.

Calm again, she opened her eyes. Carefully, she exposed her mind
the darkness, reaching out. When nothing attacked, she shifted her
nses to the greater part of her body, building a sensory net that she
owed to expand outwards from her.

There!

She turned, and as she did so she realized that she had no point of
erence in a physical sense—she was there, yet she seemed not to be
re; Trance Gemini the person was there, but she lacked substance
d weight. It was an eerie feeling. No matter which state she chose
be in, she could count on having mass—it was a subconscious
hor for her. Whatever this place was, she couldn't count on many
her abilities.

For a moment a terrible black weight of loneliness settled upon
, followed by sadness at the losses she had so recently endured and
n confusion as her mind was flooded with inconsistent memories.
At the end she tried to focus. At the end, Dylan and *Andromeda*
re gone, but there was no time for heartbreak. She had taken a
fighter, but not to escape, just to make the final step easier.

She had calmed herself, and begun the discorporation process, but
ore she could blaze to life in her natural state she had been uncer-
oniously yanked from that universe to this black one where the
es of her existence seemed to have changed.

he gasped, realizing where she must be. She had somehow been
wn into the foundation of the universe—of *all* the universes that
had the power to cross. This was the place where particles danced
cosmic strings, where strong and weak forces met, the place of
existence, from which all things had originally flowed.

he had come to the wellspring of her life. She had not been born
is place, but without it she would never have come into existence.
ing would have come into existence.

he held up her hands. They were filled with tiny glowing bands
shimmered and gyrated. She watched, smiling, as the strings she
traversed the dimensions of time and space and shifted around
dditional dimensional sets. Those additional dimensions made it
ible for her people to do the things they could do.

hey made it possible.

She looked up from her hands, her momentary playfulness g
The strings faded away.

Slowly, she turned around. Fear was once again rising within

Light seemed to be coming from somewhere overhead. It
enough to illuminate an ornate cherry wood side-table, a design
recognized as Terran, although she could not place the time perio
would have been enough of an oddity by itself, but the incong
was compounded by the presence of a fine china teapot, matc
cups and saucers, and small containers of milk and sugar. To
senses, all these were undeniably real.

She walked slowly forward, curious. As she did so, she saw
there was also a heavy ashtray on the table. A curved tobacco pi
wisp of smoke rising from the bowl, had been carefully placed in
ashtray.

Closer yet, and she saw a tall wing-back armchair, covered in ma
leather. It was at an angle to her, but facing in just the right directic
obscure its occupant. Growing less and less fearful, and ever more
ous, she increased her pace.

As she came level with the chair, an arm reached out and
bony fingers swept the pipe from the ashtray. The owner of the
leaned forward, turning his head to peer owlishly at her. He looke
all intents and purposes like an elderly human. His shock of v
hair was swept backward in a proudly leonine manner that helpe
give him an air of insufferable arrogance. His hawk nose only ac
to this effect. He wore black trousers, a white shirt with a cravat,
a black frock coat.

She was certain that this was an illusion, just as the place w
she was standing was an illusion—it was all relative, all a matte
perspective.

"Who are you?" she asked the old man.

Without smiling, he replied, "I am who I am, Trance Gem
With a shock, she realized that he had spoken the language of
people. He had said her true name, not the Common-language n
she had translated it to. "Welcome, Granddaughter."

"I am not your granddaughter," she responded absently, distra
by the emanations she was beginning to pick up.

"Then consider it a figure of speech!" the old man snapped. bruptly, he came to his feet. "Never mind that it's accurate!"

"After all," a second man said from the darkness, "you exist ecause we came before you and set down the foundation."

The second man moved into a patch of light. He was smaller and unger. He was dressed shabbily and his hair was an unruly black op. He gave her a bemused smile, and she smiled in return.

"There's something wrong," she said. "Something really bad is ppening."

The older man hooked his thumbs into the lapels of his frock coat. deed there is," he said imperiously. "Something very bad indeed."

"Where am I?" Trance asked.

"Somewhere safe," the second man said.

A third man was walking toward her. This one seemed almost as ogant as the first. He was wearing a maroon velvet jacket, and she uld see lace cuffs at his wrists. His white hair was artfully unruly. Ve prefer to observe," he said. "We only act when there is no other tion left to us."

"What are you?" she asked the third man.

"We are an avatar of Order," a fourth man said, as he walked vard her. This one seemed almost as tall as Dylan. He wore a long t. His floppy fedora seemed to barely contain a riot of long curly r that fell almost to his shoulders. He seemed amused at some- g. "This is the point, actually. You've been very naughty, you w. You've become terribly disorderly."

A fifth man, sandy-haired and dressed in a cream blazer and slacks, rged from the shadows. "This is why we had to bring you to us," aid. "If we had let the situation continue, there would have been a kdown in reality. This would have been quite intolerable."

I don't understand," Trance said.

sixth man now came forward. He was burly, and his hair was an uly explosion of curls. "It's quite simple, really. The *Andromeda ndant* was attacked by devices that emitted electromagnetic radia- which, for the most part, affected your fellow crew members, but ntially didn't affect you. That changed when those same devices t into full defensive mode."

With an effort, she tried to remember. Something had happened

"You succumbed to powerful forces that sent you out of balance a seventh man said as he walked forward. He was small, dressed in rumpled white suit. In one hand, he carried a cane and a white fedor With a flourish, he put the hat on. "An unhinged quantum being is terribly dangerous thing."

"I could have corrupted the main timestream?"

"Exactly." An eighth man came forward. "One timeline after anoth would fall toward the mainstream."

"Pieces of each reality would struggle for a place." This from ninth man. "Reality would cease to make sense. Chaos would reign

"Eventually, everything would fall to the Abyss," Trance whispere

A tenth man approached her, a bluff, shaggy fellow in a cordur shirt and jeans. "That is so. We heard your calls for help when no o else did but at first we did not understand."

"I didn't either." Trance said. "I'm not sure I understand even no

"From the precipitating incident you send shock waves through the quantum foundation of the universe." This came from an eleven man, one Trance could not see clearly. "In turn this filtered down the primal foundation—here."

A twelfth man appeared. "We acted."

"Who are you?" Trance asked once again. "How many of you there?"

A thirteenth man walked toward her. He was a stern looking m his black hair cropped close to his scalp. His clothes were black deep as the darkness she had first encountered.

"We are the beginning," he said. "We are the end. We are on am many. We are known to your people; I am found in the hear your deepest ancestral memories. You know us without knowing; are part of me."

Trance turned her attention inward and sank deep into her me ory but the ocean of her history yielded nothing. If these being these avatars—were indeed part of her deep ancestral memory could not find a way to access the knowledge.

"Do not doubt me, Granddaughter," the first of the men s

ving her an imperious look. "We are there; I am the root, not the
anch."

"You have called for help, Trance Gemini," the thirteenth man said.
Trance's mind suddenly filled with flashes, images, possibilities.
ylan . . ." she said. "Dylan is in danger." She frowned, confused.
ylan's dead . . . or is he?"

She felt panic rising. One timeline seemed as real as the next. She
lized that she was starting to slip again, to become another Trance.
vas time to be healed.

"A last question, out of curiosity. Why did you appear to me in this
m?"

"Why do you take the appearance you have?" the third said.

"A frame of reference," she said. "A familiar look to disguise
nething less comprehensible."

"Precisely so," the old man said.

"You cannot help Dylan Hunt," the thirteenth man said. "You have
y one choice: to help yourself."

The old man walked toward them. The others faded silently.

"Please," Trance said. "Please heal me."

The two remaining men flowed together. Finally, only the old man
ained.

Very well," he said briskly. He reached out and touched her fore-
d. "You must be remade as you were, Trance Gemini."

I understand," she replied nervously.

Very good." He paused for a moment, then recited, "I am the
nning. We are the end. We are one. I am many. I am the circle.
are the line. I live in you as you live in us."

he old man flared with white light, his form vanishing beneath
glare.

he light swept over Trance. She didn't even have to scream as she
torn apart.

THIRTEEN • "HERE THERE BE DRAGONS"

The inventive approach. A wonderful thing, that, finding
solutions to problems and cooking up bright new things.
Unfortunately, there is the other side of it as well—the fit
of invention that results in a demolished laboratory, for
example. Or, worse, the spasm of brilliance that results in
the inventor, sometime later, asking himself, "Why did I
do that?"

—VEDRAN SCIENCE COMMENTATOR PHENARII III,
CY 4399

"Harper?"

There was no answer from the engineer. Rommie frowned, suddenly concerned. She had come back to the operations center with
food and drink for Harper—who she was certain would be grateful
for it, even if she was enforcing a positive diet—only to find the place
apparently deserted.

"Harper?" she said again, a little more loudly.

Still no answer.

She put the tray she was carrying onto the nearest flat surface, and
went to surveillance mode. Almost immediately she found Harper's
gun lying on the floor, halfway beneath a console. That was definitely
not a good sign.

She bent down and retrieved it.

he opened a radio channel and tried again. "Mr. Harper?" Noth-
ut silence. She shifted frequencies. "Dylan?"

Go ahead, Rommie." She was relieved to hear his voice.

We've got a problem. Harper's vanished." She looked down at the
ss pistol in her hand. It hadn't been fired recently. "He left his
lying on the floor, however, so I very much doubt he went in
:h of a bathroom."

We may have two problems," Dylan said. "Micah's supposed to
:arching the lower levels while I scout around in the upper lev-
He just missed a radio check, and he isn't responding to my sig-
'

don't know what this is adding up to," Rommie said, "but I
y don't like it."

Same here," Dylan said. "I'm coming straight back to the ops cen-
Vait for me there."

'll see if Waystation has any information," Rommie said.

ust be careful. Dylan out."

he certainly had no intention of being reckless, considering the
imstances. She thought briefly about Wright's comment that he
seen something at the other side of the base; it might have some
ing on this mystery. What if the base had somehow been occu-
by squatters since the fall of the Commonwealth?

hat seemed a bit of a stretch, however. There would be more
:nce of occupation, and the base seemed to be in fairly pristine
ition.

here was one place to start. She placed her hand over an open
ss port and connected herself to the system—unlike Harper she
10 need to use a wire. Come to think of it, there was no real rea-
why Harper needed to use a wire either—it seemed to be one of
: organic affectations that she sometimes found herself at a loss
plain.

side Waystation's virtual cityscape, she quickly looked around,
ng Harper. There was no sign of him, which meant that he
't jacked into the system from another location.

Vaystation," she said, "locate Lieutenant Seamus Harper."

Waystation shimmered into existence. "I am unable to locate ⟨ter Engineer Harper, Andromeda."

Master Engineer? "The last time Mr. Harper was here, did he ⟨and exit normally?"

"Yes," the Vedran avatar said. "He made a series of adjustments ⟨I have logged. He then went to investigate some retrofitted syste⟩

"Copy the log to me," Rommie ordered. The file appeared in⟩ diately in her safe storage area. She looked at it, and found no⟨out of the ordinary. "What about the retrofitted systems?"

"Here is the trace log," the Vedran said politely, sending her a ⟨of the file.

She looked through it, following Harper's virtual movem⟩ "Interesting. These seem like very recent additions." She frown⟩ virtually—as she looked at the end of Harper's progress throug⟩ newer systems. "What do you know about this Black Thirteen?"

"Nothing," Waystation said. "It is not an anomalous prog⟩ however."

"An advanced firewall," Rommie mused. "It appears that H⟨decided to resist the challenge of cracking it." She paused ⟨moment. "I'm going to see for myself. Maybe I can get him ⟩ avatar to avatar, even if he does seem a bit simpleminded."

She dove farther into the system, following Harper's trail⟩ admiring the work he had done simply on the fly. Very quickly⟩ found herself being confronted by a new avatar.

"Black Thirteen?" she said. "I am Andromeda, of the *Andro*⟩ *Ascendant.*"

"I am Black Thirteen," the avatar said.

Rommie stared at the avatar for a moment before saying any⟩ else. Then she said, "You're modeled on General Janus Altn⟩ aren't you?"

The AI seemed slightly surprised. "Yes, I am."

Rommie couldn't put the pieces together yet. "What can yo⟩ me?"

"Nothing," Black Thirteen said, "unless you present p⟩ authorization. I am fully authorized to take punitive measur⟩ required."

"In other words, you'll fry me if I try to break the encryption," nmie said. "I get the point."

he withdrew swiftly, while the other AI remained neutral. She n't bother with Waystation on her way out.

he disconnected from the system, lifting her hand from the ss port. As she did so, there was a noise behind her.

Harper?" she said, turning, and then, shocked, "Herakles?"

Hello, Andromeda." The android avatar of *The Labors of Herakles* patterned after a human male, tall, powerful-looking with bronze , dark hair, and brown eyes. He was smiling. "I see you finally ded to join the android world."

he smiled, trying to put this latest twist into some kind of pertive and assess the threat level. "Blame my chief engineer. What ou doing here?"

 have the same question," he said. "As for me, I live and work now. There'll be time to exchange notes later."

Vhy not now?" she said urgently.

This," he said, pointing a tiny black tube at her.

e tried to draw her force lance, but she was too slow. There was ectrical snap, and she shut down.

ce was coalescing. Her consciousness had a slow-moving, airy it, but it was definitely a single mind, not a multitude of variavying for dominance.

 pain. Another relief.

e continued to come together, like a new star forming from a a, particles spinning together faster and faster as she gained ion.

e found both the process and the sensations utterly fascinating. ever Black had done to fix the problem had the side effect of g her feel very good indeed.

ster and faster . . .

 of a sudden, she was assailed by doubt. Had she imagined ? Why would an entity—or entities—capable of healing rips in bother with fixing her? It would have been far easier to simply her completely and cure the problem that way.

She vaguely recalled a voice: *The cause that you serve is one highe[r] even you know. The struggle will begin in earnest before long, Trance G[...]* Faster and faster . . .

You will soon forget this encounter. Serve your cause well, Trance G[...]

The memory was becoming more and more distant, ghosting [...] Coalescing, Trance fell through darkness. Eventually she d[...] into a dreamless sleep.

"She's got to be somewhere on board," Beka said, feeling panic [...]ing to rise again.

"If she is," Andromeda said, "I can't locate her. The last time [...] her, she was heading for the Slipfighter hangar at a run. Just b[...] she got there, she vanished."

"Damn it," Beka muttered. She was pacing back and forth a[...] the front section of the Command Deck. She looked up towar[...] fire control station, where Tyr was lounging.

"It's fruitless to worry about Trance." He shrugged. "Th[...] absolutely no telling what she will manifest next. We might g[...] off of the ship, only to have her change again and pop righ[...] here."

"Tyr has a good point in this," Andromeda said. "We are als[...]ning out of time. The mind torpedo transmitters are increasing[...] output."

"The EMP generators are in place," Pogue said. "We need [...] this *now*, Beka. We've waited as long as we can."

Beka started to issue a rebuke, but stopped. Pogue was only v[...] the same thing that she herself knew in her gut. "We don't know[...] high-powered electromagnetic pulses could do to Trance, espe[...] when she's in this kind of condition."

"She's resilient," Rommie said. "I'm more worried about me[...]

"Point taken," Beka said.

"If we're all in agreement, then," Tyr said, "I suggest we rep[...] the Slipfighter hangar and get ourselves ready to go."

Beka looked around, and nodded. "Andromeda, are you [...] you're going to be okay?"

Life holds few constants and fewer certainties," Andromeda said.
very sure that shutdown will proceed very smoothly. Restarting
here the questions come in . . . and I wish Harper were here to
ver those."

Yeah," Beka said. "Me too."

Initiating shutdown procedure in five minutes," Andromeda said.
gave them a smile. "I'll see the three of you very shortly, I hope."

Indeed you will," Tyr said.

he three of them left Command at a fast walk.

nmie?" Nothing but silence. "Andromeda, come in. Harper?"
nothing. "Mr. Wright?"

e stood in the fourth-level gallery, looking out over the landing
Nothing seemed to be moving anywhere. That was both good
ad news.

e had no doubt that something had taken the other three down.
ust didn't have a clue as to what he could be facing. There cer-
wasn't anything to indicate that the Magog had taken over the
Nietzscheans would have stripped the place and blown up the
There were other possibilities, but unless someone had recently
ed off a crew and taken off again, none of them bore scrutiny.
st the same, the idea of something living in the place for an
ded length of time seemed outlandish.

mething's taken Rommie down. What the hell could do that?

Vaystation," he said.

es, Captain Hunt?" the AI replied.

seem to be missing three members of my crew. Can you locate
for me?"

ere was a pause, then: "My sensors detect no sign of Mr.
nt, Andromeda, or Master Engineer Harper."

ster engineer? Dylan had to suppress a grin; Harper was trying
his self-esteem out of the gravity well it so often fell into.

ould they perhaps have returned to the *Eureka Maru?*" Way-
a asked politely.

o," Dylan said. "Not without telling me."

He increased his pace, heading for the operations center
sense that something was badly wrong was accompanied now by
tinct prickling unease that had him constantly checking his surr
ings. He wished he knew what he was looking out for.

*Here there be dragons. What if something got left behind hundr
years ago?* If some kind of life-form had been living and breedi
the base, it would have the advantage.

He reached the operations center. Force lance at the rea
swung in through the doorway, ducking down, moving caut
into the room. He had it cleared in a matter of moments.

Nothing.

He found Harper's Gauss pistol on a console, and guesse
Rommie had left it there. On the other hand, he doubted that
mie had intentionally left her force lance lying on the floor be
two consoles. He bent down and picked it up, inspecting it. It w
fully loaded and charged—either she hadn't found reason to us
hadn't had the opportunity; the latter seemed more likely.

He put Rommie's force lance on the console; he wouldn't b
to use it. Harper's Gauss pistol, on the other hand, might co
handy. He looked it over, then opened his jacket and shoved the
into his belt. On quick reflection, he decided to take Rommie's
lance along as well. He slipped it into his holster.

He felt uncomfortable carrying so many weapons, but if he s
find Harper and Rommie anytime soon, he was sure they woul
to be armed.

He started for the doorway.

The lights went out.

He stopped, listening, the hairs on the back of his neck risir
caught a musky scent, then a tinge of something burned—singe

There was a growl to his left.

Without hesitation, he turned and fired at the sound. The ef
struck the side of a console, causing an eruption of sparks and
At the same time there was a guttural yelp and Dylan caught si
something large and furry stumbling back.

There was a roar behind him, and a deep, rough voice crie
"Reinken! *No!*"

Dylan turned and dropped to one knee, firing almost overhead. In
: flare of the effector and the subsequent hit, Dylan saw a mon-
ous visage lunging toward him, all teeth, blazing eyes, and fur. He
led aside as the creature came down. It howled as it slammed to the
or.

Dylan came to his feet, trying to get a sense of where he was, and
w many attackers there were. *Sentient* attackers, he realized, as the
: he had shot started to get up, snarling. "The bastard *shot* me!"

Dylan turned and fired in the direction of the sound, aiming low.
ere was a crash as the creature—Reinken—threw itself backward.
"Good work, Reinken," said another. "I'm sure you'll delight the
ardian for the *second* time today."

"The other one will mend," Reinken muttered. "Are we here to
ate, or to bring him in? He's going to get away, you idiots!"

That's the plan, boys. Dylan had the doorway placed now, as his
ht vision returned. He edged toward it, triggering his force lance
ull extension.

He took a deep breath, letting it out slowly as he prepared himself.
hout warning, he sprinted for the entrance. The dark silhouette
ne of the creatures loomed up in front of him. Dylan brought the
-meter lance under and around, knocking the feet out from his
ld-be assailant. Up, over, and down; there was a crack and the
e slammed into the creature's head.

He swung the lance up again and hit the trigger twice. Effectors
out. Most of the doors vanished in an eruption of fire and smoke.
He ducked and dodged through the opening he had made, and
e out onto the third-level gallery. He went to his left, running.
here were several roars and howls behind him, catching up. He
ed, lance ready.

"Damn," he muttered.

he creatures coming toward him were humanoid, but they bore
: resemblance to Magog—they were covered in fur, and he could
vay too many teeth for his comfort. In this light, though, their
had a disturbingly human quality.

e swung the lance over, aiming at the oncoming group. He fired
: over their heads, and they stopped, glaring at him.

"The next time I fire," Dylan said darkly, "I'll be shooting to

The creatures exchanged glances, then one of them—Reinke
guessed, going by the wound in his upper left arm—said, "You
get us all before we take you down."

"Guess again," Dylan said, sounding a lot more confident th
felt.

More glances.

Dylan started to back away. "You fellows just stay here and b
yourselves." The one called Reinken started to advance to
Dylan. One of the others growled and pulled him back. "I'll
anyone who comes after me. I don't like threats, and I don't like
chased."

Reinken started to edge forward again. Once more he was sto
The one holding him back growled, "It's alright."

"I don't believe that," Reinken said. "They're destroyers."

"What the hell *are* you?" Dylan demanded.

The one holding Reinken back said, "We're one of the mi
that the Commonwealth buried. One of the many dirty little s
of the Systems Commonwealth."

Dylan started backing away again, trying to understand wh
was being told. He collapsed the lance again, then turned ar
and ran.

"Yo ho ho, this is the life for me," Beka sang. Then, sounding res
to the vagaries of fate, she said, "This is what I always wanted to
in a Slipfighter and float pointlessly in space for a few hours."

"There must be a point to it," Tyr said, sounding bored. "It s
to be providing you with an excuse to entertain yourself."

"And everyone else," Pogue added.

They were in individual Slipfighters, sitting a kilometer o
Andromeda Ascendant's starboard bow. Beka's displays showed t
the three EMP generators that were now floating around the
She also had a close view of a section of the ship where the min
pedo transmitters had taken hold. Tyr and Pogue would have s
displays.

"Hurry up and wait," Beka grumbled.

"Are you going to start yo-ho-ho'ing again?" Pogue asked.

"I don't think so," Beka said. Her temples throbbed. "I'm annoy-
: my headache."

"You're annoying mine, too," Pogue replied.

"What's a headache?" Tyr said, his tone overflowing with mock
ocence.

"It's like a pain in the ass, only higher up," Beka said. Her temples
obbed again. "My headache doesn't even like my lousy attempts at
nor."

"Attention." The radio voice was male, neutral in tone, and devoid
expression. "Final phase of *Andromeda Ascendant* shutdown com-
cing now." There was a long pause. "Concluding in five . . .
r . . . three . . . two . . . one."

ilence.

Confirming final systems shutdown," Pogue said. "The *Androm-
Ascendant* is now off-line."

eka scanned her own displays. "Yes she is, and let's hope like hell
we can bring her back when this is over." She took a deep breath
let it out slowly. "Alright, let's do this. Fire up the generators and
frying 'em, Paula."

Firing up and frying, aye, Captain Valentine," Pogue replied.

Hey, I like the way you say 'Captain Valentine.'" Her jovial com-
t did nothing to alleviate the tension she was feeling. "Makes it
d as though it means something."

That's the sort of thing you learn in the military," Pogue said.

There's a technical term for that, isn't there?" Beka said.

Yeah," Pogue said, chuckling. "'Sucking up.'" There was a pause.
e seriously, she said, "I have a full charge. Firing."

eka's instruments registered the burst quite clearly, even though
were out of the way of the pulses.

n *Andromeda's* hull numerous transmitters lit up as they burned

o far so good," Pogue said.

My instruments indicate some forty percent destroyed," Tyr said.

"Confirmed," Beka said. "Tough little buggers, aren't they?"

"Solid Kantaran workmanship," Pogue said.

"Nasty Kantaran weapon," Beka said.

"A good weapon to have at hand," Tyr said.

"I should have known you'd like it," Beka responded.

"I didn't say I liked it," Tyr replied. "I am simply acknowledgi[ng] usefulness."

"Gotcha." Beka scanned her instruments. "Time for the se[cond] shot. Maybe we can be up and running again by dinner."

"Charging the generators," Pogue said. "Firing."

Little flowers of light grew and died on the hull.

"Well," Beka said, watching, "they sure do look purdy when[they] do that, yup." She sighed and shook her head. "I know exactly [how] bored I am when I start talking like that."

Trance woke up slowly, feeling comfortable in the darkness. Sh[e no] longer felt as though she were falling. She felt whole, and rested[.]

Something wasn't quite right. Several things, in fact. She kne[w she] was on the bed in her quarters, but she wasn't entirely sure ho[w she] had come to be there. There were hints at the back of her mind, [sug]gestions of memory, but something had been lost.

She was naked. Not entirely a surprise, and something [to be] remedied.

The most worrying thing involved her sense of the ship. Ther[e was] something drastically wrong there—the ship felt cold, lifeless. E[very]thing seemed to be shut down—the AI, life support, the AG field.

She got up carefully and went to her closet. She dressed qu[ickly.] The darkness and lack of gravity were no problem—she ha[d her] own ways of coping. Life support wasn't a problem, either, at [least] not for her.

She made her way to the Observation Deck, and stood at the [big] window, reaching out with her senses.

There.

There were three Slipfighters less than a kilometer out, hea[ding] back toward the ship. She deduced that drastic measures had [been] required to deal with the mind torpedoes. She knew that some[one]

one wrong with Andromeda's countermeasures; whatever had
ned had affected her in some way.

haps something had been done that had brought her back and
ed her? She couldn't tell.

andoning that line of thought, she ran down to Command.
thing was dead there, too. She went over to Rommie's console
pped at a key. The console lit up, taking a moment to reinitialize.
me to wake you up," Trance said. She tapped out a sequence of
ands. The remainder of the Command consoles lit up, and the
ights came on. "Come on, sleepyhead."

eutral male voice intoned, "Initializing. Restart sequence has
."

ell," Trance said, "I guess I'd better go meet up with the others."
e left Command.

continued moving down through the complex, looking for
and finding nothing. In the level-one commissary he found
tions of a fight, but nothing else. At least he now had an idea of
Micah had been brought down by these creatures.

was baffled still. This was something that should have been
cut. Strange beings roaming around, his crew vanishing without
 . . .

e of the many dirty little secrets of the Systems Commonwealth.

ey looked like offshoots of the Magog; moved like them, too.
eir eyes seemed human, and they spoke Common. Magog
tered everything that got in their way. These creatures . . .
eople . . . had shown restraint.

en so, his crew was still missing, and he had been attacked.

're one of the mistakes that the Commonwealth buried.

ne of the Commonwealth's dirty little secrets," he said softly.
od. Micah, you were right, weren't you?"

organization existing off the books and off the record, a law
tself, funded through convoluted secret channels and sheathed
yer of ridiculous legend. An organization that could conduct
epest, most destructive covert operations anywhere in the three
s, complete with its own fleet of ships. The same organization

could as easily develop new and deadlier weapons, new bree
spacecraft . . .

New forms of life.

One of the many dirty little secrets . . .

His head spun. How the hell could they justify making mon
The Vedrans would never have approved of such a program.

. . . the Commonwealth buried.

He ran his fingers through his hair, trying to get a mental ba
He knew that he was wrong about this. The Vedrans would
known—a very small number in the government and in the
court.

He knew no life beyond his work as one of the High Guar
had always seen the High Guard, and the Home Guard, as some
glorious and ideal. No matter where corruption might have s
forth within the political structure of the Commonwealth, the
Guard was inviolate. He would never have expected perfection
would be flawed thinking. He did, however, see the High Gu
representing truth and justice, something powerful yet compa
ate because of the diversity of its members—thousands of s
from a million worlds, millions of sentient beings working i
mony with hundreds of thousands of AIs of all kinds.

It had been his ideal. His spiritual home.

His truth.

It had brought him Sara, his long-lost fiancée; he had met he
ing a mission. She had unwittingly saved both his life and th
Andromeda during a failed attempt to retrieve the ship from the
hole that had trapped them. It was the High Guard that had
kept alive as Sara led the settlement and development of Teraze
monument to the fallen Commonwealth and an expression o
ideal he represented.

. . . dirty little secrets . . .

He felt the strength draining out of his mind and body. The N
schean betrayal had been bad enough, but he could understand
reasoning, even though he could never agree with it.

This was a betrayal that went far deeper, and was far more

. He had always believed in getting the job done, but the codicil
at had always been "in the best possible manner," not "by any
s necessary."

. *buried . . .*

ae pieces were fitting together neatly—the derelict in orbit, the
ems getting into the base in the first place, the oddities that had
d up. They had walked into a trap, he guessed, one set hundreds
ars previously.

aese beings had been down here for centuries, yet there was no
ation of their existence in the main complex. Even more confus-
as the fact that these beings appeared to have at least a basic edu-
a, going by their command of Common.

: had tried like hell to hold on to his ideals, to his belief in the
 Guard and the Commonwealth, to the notions of honor and
e.

*w can I do that any longer? How can I lie to people any longer about
ings the Commonwealth and the High Guard represent?*

: heard footsteps behind him, and swung around, bringing his
lance up.

was Reinken. He held his hands up. His mouth quirked slightly,
ae managed a crooked smile. "Don't shoot me yet, Captain
"

·lan's eyes narrowed. "You know who I am."

·h, yes," Reinken said. Still holding his hands in the air, he sat
 cross-legged on the floor. "It is why I wanted to apologize for
; as I did. I am known for my temper, alas. This can be danger-
ith us." He flexed his hands, and claws slid out from the tips of
agers. "The reason should be obvious."

Vhy did you attack me?" Dylan demanded. "And where is my
"

elieve it or not," Reinken answered, "the idea was to reduce the
·ility to conflict. We needed to establish that you were who you
ed to be. We were afraid that there would be a battle."

nd there was," Dylan said angrily. "I could have killed any or all
1."

Reinken looked over toward the gallery windows. "I know. V
know that." He looked back toward Dylan. "You arrived in a
that's hardly High Guard standard issue."

"It's a damn good cargo hauler," Dylan snapped. "Are my p
okay?"

"More or less." Reinken looked away again, and Dylan
have sworn he detected a note of embarrassment in the action.
android and the loudmouthed little one are in perfect shape,
from the fact that the little one has a hysterical fear of us, it se

"If you knew his past history, you'd understand," Dylan
"What about Mr. Wright?"

"The third one." Reinken hesitated for a moment. "He's aliv
in good shape. Unfortunately, I managed to lose my temper wh
were trying to capture him. I broke his arm."

Dylan was silent. All of this was beginning to seem surreal.

Reinken looked back at Dylan. "I suspect I know too much hi
Dylan Hunt. The knowledge leaves me afraid, and the fear leav
with anger."

"Understanding that," Dylan said, glad to have something re
ably sensible to cling to, "is good. Can you take me to my crew?

"I can," Reinken said. "It would be better if you went wit
Guardian, however."

Dylan turned too quickly, almost losing his footing. A strong
caught his arm, steadying him.

He found himself facing a tall, bronze-skinned, dark-haired
wearing a black High Guard uniform like his. No, not a ma
android—an avatar.

"I am the one they refer to as the Guardian," the android sa
am Herakles, avatar of *The Labors of Herakles*. I am pleased to
you, Captain Hunt."

The android held out a hand. After some hesitation, Dylan re
out and shook it. "At the moment, Herakles, the pleasure's all yo
want some explanations, and I want my crew."

"Very well. Come with me." Herakles started to turn. "Exp
tions first, and then your crew."

Dylan didn't move. "Wrong way around, Herakles." The an

urned back. "They're my crew. As far as I'm concerned, whatever
ou show me, you can show to them at the same time."

Herakles regarded him silently for a few moments. "Both your
ngineer and your support crewman are potential security risks.
ndromeda is, of course, secure."

"I trust both of them," Dylan said. "It's what's important to *me*,
ot *you*."

"These matters—"

"These matters," Dylan snapped, "involve a deeply buried, long-
anding black bag operation that created beings like Reinken here."
ylan took a deep breath. "Do you have *any* idea how this hits me?"

"You have served in covert High Guard units yourself," Herakles
id.

"The units I served with," Dylan said, "didn't play genetic mix-
d-match." He nodded back at Reinken, who was still sitting,
hough he now had his hands down. "Does he know? Do his people
ow?"

"Yes," Reinken said. He stood up. "We know what we are, where
came from, why we were made . . . that we failed our purpose. We
ow why we were brought here."

"Why?" Dylan asked. "Why were you brought here?"

"Mercy," said Herakles. "Or weakness. It doesn't really matter."

"There's a big difference between the two," Dylan said.

"Let them all see it," Reinken said. "He will tell everything to
m anyway. No matter how we shake his faith now, Guardian, this
e's an idealist."

"Not anymore," Dylan said. "Not after this."

"You'll get over it," Reinken said, walking past Dylan. Standing
ight, he was several centimeters taller than Dylan. "I imagine my
estors were none too thrilled about many things, but they carried
regardless."

"Follow me," Herakles said, turning around again and walking
g the gallery. They had gone no more than two hundred meters
re he stopped and pointed to the entrance to what appeared to be
rvice tunnel. "Down here."

hey walked along the tunnel in silence for another two hundred meters, following a downward incline. Dylan didn't recall seeing a indication of something like this on the plans of the base.

Herakles stopped at a smooth, silvery door. He reached out a touched a panel. There was a hiss, and the door slid open smoothl

Dylan stopped, staring past the doorway. "It's a ship? They bur a ship here?"

Herakles looked at him. "Yes. Specifically, they buried me here.

"This just gets stranger and stranger," Dylan said. "You're *comfe able* with being buried?"

"I serve a purpose," Herakles said. "I'm as comfortable und ground as I was in space."

"Programming?"

"Adjustment," Herakles said. "An advantage of being an A suppose—being able to make a drastic choice like that without un difficulty or the slightest regret. Going from cargo hauler to ca taker could be considered a promotion." Herakles turned and wall through the doorway. "Welcome to *The Labors of Herakles*, Cap Hunt."

"I really don't get you," Beka said, shaking her head. Trance smile her in response. "Yeah, I know, so what else is new?"

They were sitting in the officers lounge, along with Tyr Pogue. The *Andromeda Ascendant* hadn't completed her restart ye the process had been slowed down by the overall state of the sl The main systems were back on-line, finally, but neither Androm nor Rommie had showed up yet.

Tyr was silent, watching Trance as though he expected her revert to her previous condition at any moment. Trance could ha blame him for his uncertainty. She was sure the problem no lon existed in any form, but the others were going to have to see that hemselves.

"Well," Trance said, "it was just . . . one of those things."

"That sounds weak," Pogue said.

"That sounds like Trance," Beka said with a look of resignatio

"Beka's right," Trance said. She turned her smile on Pog

xplanations only make the confusion worse. It's sometimes better
ust accept things as they are and go on."

There was a brilliant shimmer to one side of the table, and Rom-
e appeared, smiling at them. It was immediately apparent that
nething had gone wrong with her imaging system—she was wear-
a summer frock and a floppy hat.

Tyr raised his eyebrows as he looked at her. "There is obviously a
party somewhere. Are we invited?"

'If there was, Tyr," Rommie said, "everyone would be on the
st list. Well, everyone here, anyway, including Princess Trance
r there."

'Princess . . . ?" Trance said, dumbfounded.

'We haven't gotten to that one yet," Beka said.

Rommie nodded toward the middle of their table, and an image of
nce in full finery appeared.

'Oh," Trance said.

'A Vedran Princess," Beka said, shaking her head. "Trance, I'm
ous. Even if the Vedrans were still around, I couldn't get 'em to
pt me at gunpoint."

'It doesn't seem to have been the most secure life, however," Rom-
said. "Someone was apparently attempting to kill you."

'It's all about choice," Trance said softly. "Many choices, not all of
m mine. The road not taken is not such a simple thing as it sounds,
see." She looked at Tyr, who was watching her, his expression as
tral as he could make it. "This is one of the reasons why some of
things I say are such a riddle, or seem so enigmatic. I am not play-
a game."

How are we to know that?" Tyr said. "You seem to know more
n you will share, you are overflowing with dark secrets, and you
ipulate those around you."

Trance shook her head. "Tyr, I promise you that I don't. I can
le, I can suggest, I can offer whatever I perceive, even if I do not
erstand it myself." She looked at Beka, then at Pogue. "I cannot
e choices for anyone, I cannot steer your lives or the lives of any-
else in the way that you may think I do. No matter what, you

choose for yourselves." She looked at the image again. "Whether
the road taken or the road not taken, it is never simple. Dylan of
asks me to simplify things, to be direct. . . ." She was silent fo
moment. "The universe is synergistic, you see. Every element in
ences other elements. Everything works together, for good or bac
is the same with the choices we make—they work together.
choices affect others; their choices affect others still."

"And the choices others make can come back to you in some fe
or other," Pogue said.

"'The worms go in, the worms go out, the worms play pinochle
your snout,'" Beka said in a singsong voice. The others looked at
as though she'd gone crazy. She grinned. "It's an ancient kids' rhy
that Harper taught me years ago. It's one of those silly grues
things kids like, but it's really about the cycle of life—how everyth
feeds into everything else."

"The nail," Tyr said abruptly.

"Oh, yes," Trance said, recalling her meeting with her pur
skinned alternate in the hydroponics gardens.

"Come again?" Pogue said.

Tyr gave her a patient look. "It is also quite ancient," he s
"There are versions to be found in the literature of many species.
a story of influences and consequences. There were two ancient k
doms that went to war, and while the foot soldiers walked, the offi
rode creatures called horses. These horses required shoes—ho
shoes is the proper term; these were three-quarter round open m
hoops that were nailed to the horse's hooves."

"Sounds barbaric," Pogue said with a shudder.

"Not at all," Tyr said. "If the procedure was done correctly,
horse felt no pain, and it was protected from many potential pr
lems that could lame or topple it—and if a horse was lamed, it ha
be destroyed; the injuries would often be terrible." He sat b
"Anyway, as the story had it, in brief, before going to battle, the n
important general in one kingdom took his horse to be reshod
always, the blacksmith did a splendid job—not knowing that on
the nails he used was faulty. On the battlefield, the nail broke and

ain of consequences began. 'For want of a nail, the shoe was lost;
r want of a shoe, the horse was lost; for want of a horse, the general
as lost; for want of the general, the battle was lost' . . . and, finally,
e war, the king, and the kingdom."

"All this and more," Trance said, continuing to speak quietly. "All
this on a cosmic scale, and the only thing I can do is hope that the
oices I make are the right ones. At least I've had a second chance."

"Are things getting better?" Beka asked.

Trance shrugged. "I don't know. I think so, at least in some ways."
e paused for a moment, listening inwardly. "There is much to do,
ough, and it will not be easy. At times it may seem almost impossi-
to overcome the things we face."

"Oh, joy," Beka said.

"There's something else," Trance said. "It's no longer urgent . . . I
l a strong feeling that Dylan was in danger at Waystation. Also,
es the name 'Black Thirteen' mean anything?"

'Nothing here," Rommie said.

"No," Pogue said.

yr shrugged and shook his head.

Beka didn't answer immediately. She seemed to be thinking about
ething. Finally, she said, "What I remember is that Black Thir-
 was supposed to be this supersecret Vedran dirty operations
it. Nobody has ever been able to turn up proof that they existed.
can find lots of stories about stuff they supposedly did. If there
really a Black Thirteen, they vanished when the Vedrans did."

bruptly Tyr stood up. "I'm going to Waystation," he said. "I'll
 a Slipfighter . . . unless Trance has another reason to try and
 me?"

rance smiled at him, refusing to take the bait. "None."

He's just stir-crazy, being stuck on the ship all this time," Beka
to Trance. "Especially with three wild women."

'our," Rommie said.

ive," Andromeda said as flatscreens lit up around the lounge.

ley, it's about time you showed up," Beka said. "You're getting to
 in way more than you should."

"It will certainly be a pleasure," Tyr said dourly, "to be by m
for a time."

As Tyr was leaving, Rommie turned and said, "By the wa
Dylan can spare him, please bring Mr. Harper back. That was on
the most unpleasant full restarts I've ever experienced."

"Lying down on the job, Andromeda?" Dylan said.

Rommie's eyes moved as she focused on him. "I apologize for
springing up in welcome, Captain, but it seems that Herakles thir
little restraint was called for."

Rommie had been laid out on a table in one of *The Labors of
akles*'s machine shops and kept in place with restraining bands.
one that went around her forehead was the important one—it
down her main motor functions. She could move her eyes, but
otherwise paralyzed.

Dylan bent over her and released the restraints while Her
stood a couple of meters away, watching. Reinken stood farther a
by the door. "How do you feel?"

"Like punching Herakles very hard," she said, sitting up and ta
her force lance as Dylan held it out. She glared at the other and
He tilted his head and raised his right eyebrow. "Several times."

"She's rather aggressive, isn't she?" Herakles said.

"I'm a warship, you idiot, what do you expect?" Rommie snap
"Besides, you sucker-zapped me."

Dylan gave Herakles a questioning look. Herakles reached i
pocket and took out a small black tube. "Designed to instantly
any android down," he said. "The alternative would have bee
shoot her, which I didn't want to do."

"That was no way to treat an old friend," Rommie muttered a
stood up.

"I'm sorry about it," Herakles said, "but the situation was very
ficult. People were very scared by your arrival, not to mention th
that you got into the base." He looked at Dylan. "We knew you
been suspended in time, but we had to be sure that it was really
and not some marauder looking to raid the base."

"We tend to be a little on the paranoid side," Reinken said.

"I noticed," Dylan said. He looked at Rommie. "There are explantions for all of this, apparently."

"I hope so," she said. "Mysteries can be quite irritating."

"Let's go get Mr. Harper and Mr. Wright," Dylan said. "I gather . Harper is a little upset."

Harper and Wright were being kept in the small brig area of the p. Harper was pacing nervously back and forth in his cell, while ight was stretched out on his bunk, his arms on his chest—the ken one was in a cast and sling, so the pilot had obviously been en care of immediately.

'Mr. Harper, Mr. Wright," Dylan said as he stopped between the cells. "This is no time to be slacking off."

Harper stopped in midstep, turning so fast that he almost fell over. ss? They got you too?" His eyes widened even farther as he saw nken, and he took a step backward. "Ah, jeez."

Dylan glanced at Reinken, who had held up a hand and was wag g the fingers at Harper. "Don't do that. He thinks you're some of Magog, and he has a bad history with Magog."

Sorry," Reinken said, lowering his hand.

A *very* bad history," Harper muttered. He looked at Dylan, puz-. "Wait. They're not Magog?"

They're not Magog," Dylan said.

No larvae?"

Not a one," said Reinken.

Okay," Harper said. "This is where you shoot all the bad guys and us all out, right, Boss?"

Not today, Mr. Harper," Dylan said. He reached out and tapped oor release. The door hissed open.

Iuh." Harper looked out of the cell, but was reluctant to come 'You're not, like, brainwashed or anything, right?"

Mr. Harper," Rommie said impatiently, "get your skinny butt out ere." She turned and opened Wright's cell. "You too, Mr. Wright. y is no excuse for shirking."

right got up slowly. "Boy, I thought my old job was tough."

"It's an Andromeda thing," Dylan said, sounding more che‹
than he felt. "Death does not release you, and all that."

Rommie pouted. "I wanted a cat-o'-nine-tails for my next b‹
day, but Dylan says I can't."

"So now what?" Harper asked, taking his Gauss pistol as I‹
held it out by the barrel. He looked it over, then holstered it.

"Now," Dylan said, "we hear the truth." He looked at Herak‹
hope."

The android nodded. "Follow me."

Herakles led them to the recreation deck of *The Labors of Her*
Several dozen of Reinken's species were there—Harper recoile‹
then got as close as he could to Rommie—playing games, re‹
flexis, watching movies, and more. Every head turned as the‹
newcomers entered with Herakles and Reinken, and there was ‹
den undercurrent of whispering.

"Most of them had no idea you were here," Herakles said. "‹
Waystation notified the watch of your arrival, I was awaken‹
spend much of my time suspended, you see, to extend my servi‹
That applies to all of us."

"All of you?" Rommie said.

Herakles pointed to a large table to one side. There were thr‹
ures waiting there—a black-skinned female human, a Perseid, a‹
blue-skinned centauroid figure of a Vedran.

Dylan stared, shocked into silence.

Rommie looked at them for a moment, then said, "The‹
androids. The Vedran is the avatar for the *Empress Sucharitku*‹
ship of my class. I don't recognize the other two."

As they approached the table, Herakles said, "The human a‹
Star, from the *Dark Star*. The Perseid is Herine, from th‹
Thought."

"I am named," Herine said in the peculiarly cadenced ‹
common to Perseids, "after the most renowned code breaker ‹
have lived."

"Give him a chance," Star said, "and he'll ramble on foreve‹

"Pooh!" Herine said, sticking his beak of a nose in the air, whic caused his long gray chin to point at Dylan.

"No dignity, these Black Thirteen types," Sucharitkul III saie "Hello, Andromeda. We knew you had survived the Commonwealt by ending up frozen for three centuries, but I don't think any of u expected to actually encounter you. After all, we are rather out o the way."

"That was sort of the point, Empress," Star said.

They all sat, with the exception of Sucharitkul III, whose form didn't lend itself to ordinary seating.

"There's four of you?" Dylan asked. "There's *four* ships burie ere?"

"Five," Herine said. "The other is a decommissioned vessel, no avatar, ndroid or otherwise. Originally used for cargo, now for homes."

"There's a derelict in orbit," Rommie said.

"That was towed here, loaded with cargo," Herakles said. He miled. "My trailer, in fact. The cargo was shuttled down."

Harper was looking from one android to another, gaping. "You uried five ships?"

"Correct," Sucharitkul III said.

"That's gotta be a hell of an engineering project." Harper seemed have forgotten his terror. "You got anything on this? Flexis, holos, y kind of records?"

"I think we can oblige." The Vedran avatar's eyes fixed on Harper's, r expression intense. "Understand me, young human—all of this is owledge that must be protected."

"It will be," Dylan said. "I'll be happy to share our information th you as well. It should help to fill you in on the last three hundred ars or so."

"There's a new Commonwealth now," Harper said. "You can thank ylan for that."

"We can talk about that later," Dylan said. "Right now, I want me answers."

"Indeed," the Vedran avatar said. She had all of the commanding ie and bearing Dylan remembered from the few encounters he had

had with members of the Vedran royal court's upper echelon. S
made an elegant gesture toward the center of the table. "Then v
must begin here, near the end."

A hologram shimmered into life—an image of a pale human wi
unmemorable features and sandy hair. He was sitting in a large, con
fortable chair behind a big polished dark wood desk. He seemed pe
fectly at ease, but his eyes had an intensity to them.

"General Janus Altmann," Dylan said softly. "Son of a bitch."

"I am Janus Altmann, and I am a general in the now-defunct Hig
Guard. This message is for Captain Dylan Hunt of the *Androme*
Ascendant, and though I am recording it at a distant High Guard ba
it will be copied and distributed to a number of safe locations. I ho
that it will someday reach its intended recipient.

"Greetings, Captain Hunt. As you are no doubt beginning to rea
ize, I am not the rear echelon flexi-shuffler that I am made out to be
Altmann smiled, then grew serious again. "This is Commonweal
Year 9770. The Commonwealth is finished, Empress Sucharitkul
is dead, Tarn-Vedra itself seems to have vanished, and the Hig
Guard and Home Guard are memories.

"I am the head of Black Thirteen, Captain." Altmann stood a
walked around his desk, the image adjusting to keep him in foc
"Black Thirteen is the black operations division that is neither d
cussed nor acknowledged. Where there are hints of our existence, t
very idea is treated as a fantasy of conspiracy theorists. This is how
should be.

"By the time you see this message, you may well know of the ex
tence of Terazed, a project begun by your fiancée, Sara Riley. This
a massive undertaking and, as of now, I could not say whether or n
it will succeed. I hope so. I am turning many of our resources towa
this end, both to help build this dream, and to protect it. We ha
done many terrible things in the name of the Vedran Empire, bu
terrifying weapons and created monsters. Now we will turn our ski
to something positive.

"Black Thirteen will not cease to exist, Captain Hunt. While so
of us will certainly be quietly absorbed into the social fabric of T
azed, others will continue the organization. You intend to bring abo

reborn Commonwealth. I want to have Black Thirteen acting in support of your efforts—quietly, and invisibly, of course.

"There is always more to say . . . fortunately, there is already much that has been said." Altmann's mouth quirked into a smile. "Certain details have been left out, of course. The important details are there.

"Good-bye, Captain Hunt, and good luck in your quest."

Altmann saluted crisply, and the image faded out.

Dylan was silent, trying to take it all in.

"That," Harper said, a bit too loudly, "is freakin' . . . freaky."

"I was right, wasn't I?" Wright said quietly.

Dylan nodded slowly. "Yes, Micah, you were." He sighed and sat back. "I'm an idealist, I always have been. It's my answer to the universe—Trance wants her perfect possible future, I want an ideal universe. There wouldn't be a place for an organization like Black Thirteen."

Micah shrugged. "Dylan, what they did was for the defense of the Commonwealth."

"And a lot of what they did," Dylan countered, "was for the sake keeping control of conquered territories. The Vedran Empire wasn't built in a day, and it wasn't built on the back of diplomacy, not in the beginning." Dylan sighed. "Something like this poisons the dream. Poisons *my* dream."

"Then you're making a mistake," Rommie said, intensely focused Dylan. "Why allow this knowledge to bring you down, Dylan? This isn't about you, it's about Black Thirteen, the old Commonwealth, and the Vedrans."

"Allowing yourself to be so affected is impractical," said the Vedran avatar. "You must ask yourself a single question, Captain Hunt. '*How can I use what I have learned today?*'"

"Look around you, Captain Hunt," Herakles said. "Does this suggest poison? Or does it suggest a journey toward an ideal?"

"It will be a long, long journey!" Herine said. He smiled with the manic cheerfulness that the Perseids seemed able to summon up at a nanosecond's notice.

"In other words," Star said, elbowing the Perseid avatar before he

could say anything else, "there's no true ideal, just as the perfect p
sible future your Trance strives for is unreachable."

"The effort is no less worthwhile, however," the Vedran said. '
the end, the only thing that truly counts is choice, good or bad."

He looked at Rommie. She was watching him intently, her expr
sion concerned. "This was something buried, Dylan. It doesn't
the lie to what you are and who you are, not unless you decide tha
should. That much is about you."

Dylan turned to the Vedran avatar. "Where is Black Thirteen ba
now?"

She shook her head. "I do not know. We have heard nothing si
General Altmann and the others left. I would think they will be di
cult to find, if the organization still exists at all."

Dylan looked at Rommie. "We'll find them. Someday." He lool
back at the Vedran avatar. "I don't want to admit this, but we n
need them."

"The Magog Worldship is coming, isn't it?" Star said. "Yes,
know about that, and about *Andromeda Ascendant*'s encounter."

"First encounter," Rommie said.

Silence.

Dylan closed his eyes for a moment, then opened them ag
"What about Reinken . . . his people? What was done here?"

"General Altmann was responsible for creating us," Reinken sa
"We were intended to fight the Magog on their terms, and to ac
troops against the Nietzscheans when their coup finally came. In
records we are Project One Four Oh Six Six. We call ourselves /
mann's People."

Others were gathering around the table now, curious and interes

"I am Evern," said a taller male at the front. "You will see thi
the records, in more detailed form, but our basic genetic structur
human. Nietzschean technology was used to alter and enhance t
structure, and to add elements from the Magog. We were created
be fierce, unstoppable warriors."

"Project Fourteen Zero Six Six, File Nine," the Vedran avatar sa
A flat image appeared, floating in the air.

This was a much younger Janus Altmann, a brigadier, going by

insignia. He was saying, ". . . have finally achieved a positive
It, with every expectation that the first embryo will come to term.
 authorizing three embryos a month until the first births. At that
t we will know if we really are successful, or if we must start from
ch once again."

ame project, File Twenty-one," the Vedran said.

Now that we are certain that the births will go as planned," Alt-
n was saying, "we find ourselves hurrying to create an environ-
t for them, as well as safeguards for us."

ile Forty-seven."

 being covered in light gray fur looked toward the camera. Its
 were bright, and all too human.

What is your name?" Altmann said from somewhere offscreen.

he child was silent for a moment. Then it said, "My name is
mo."

he image vanished.

ammo was the beginning," the Vedran said. "Altmann saw
Commonwealth threatened by monsters in the form of the
og—"

o he set out to create monsters of his own to send at them,"
n said, hearing the bitter tone in his voice. "Fighting fire with
"

ighting fire with high explosives," Star said. "Altmann's People
 designed to be stronger, faster, and tougher in all regards, as well
ing smarter than most humans."

ile Two Hundred and Ninety-three," the Vedran avatar said.
nty-three years later, the first real field test."

ylan and the others watched silently as the recording played, fol-
ng the mission from the loading of the transport ships, to the
ships landing on the Magog-infested Brandenburg Tor, to the
shing of the People. At first there was chaos as the People and
Magog plunged into battle. The People carried weapons, while
Magog had none; the battle should have gone against the Magog.
ddenly the People began to retreat back to the dropships. It was
derly retreat, but seemed, to Dylan, to come out of nowhere.

n one of the dropships, the field leader—Dylan realized that this

was the adult Sammo—ordered the pilots to take them back t
transports.

The image faded.

"Sammo and his teams had the revelation that the battle was p
less," Sucharitkul III said. "They also realized that while they
been bred for warfare, their natures were far from violent. Some
had gone wrong. General Altmann had intended to breed war
but he got something else entirely."

"One of the many mistakes buried by the Commonwealth, o
you said earlier." Dylan looked around, looking at the intent f
the multitude of fur colors and patterns. "Why here? Why this?

"File Three Hundred and Seventeen," Sucharitkul III said.

Altmann, alone at his desk. "The days of the Commonwealt
drawing to a close. This project should have been closed, with
termination protocols, but I cannot justify the requirement to de
them. Just as I will preserve Black Thirteen, I will preserve
species. I accept the responsibility for their creation. I cannot a
the need for their destruction. I will find them a home, or make
whatever it takes.

"These are my children."

The image faded.

"Where are your ideals now?" Sucharitkul III asked Dylan.

He looked at her, uncertain. "Shaken," he said. "Very
shaken."

"Will your spirit recover from this, do you think?"

He looked around at the gathered People, and he had to wo
what kind of accident of fate could tilt the balance. It could have
anything; the universe was both a dangerous and a magical place

Finally, he said, "I think it will. It's my choice to heal."

"Yeah, well," Harper said, looking around at the People who
gazing at him with open curiosity, "I'm choosing to find somethi
eat, because I am freakin' hungry!" He looked at Rommie. "No
thought about giving me anything after I woke up."

"You have discovered something special here, Dylan H
Sucharitkul III said as Harper followed Evern and Reinken in s

food. "Absolutism is a fool's path. Only a fool thinks of black and white, good and evil, when there are so many shades, so many colors to choose from."

"There is true evil," Dylan said softly. "I will always fight against it."

"That," she said, "is a decision that only you can make."

"Yes," he said. "Yes, it is."

On the *Andromeda Ascendant*, two days away by Slipstream, Trance Gemini sat amid a mass of plants in the middle of the hydroponics gardens. In her lap, she had a pot with a bonsai tree in it. She had been gazing intently at it for a little while, following the intricacies of its form.

She looked up, as though listening to something, and after a moment she smiled, pure and radiant.

She looked back down at the bonsai. "All is well," she said softly. She looked up again, growing more serious. "At least for now."

There would always be something else.

ABOUT THE AUTHOR

Steven E. McDonald was born on the edge of Sherwood Fores[
Nottinghamshire, England, and has never quite recovered. He
written for print, television, film, and the stage and has compos[
large body of music. His published works include the SF thriller
James Syndrome. He currently lives in Tucson, Arizona.

Visit him at http://www.sanityassassins.org/~papabear